Siege Ta[le]

Spells, Swords, and Ste[a...]
By Drew Hayes

Copyright © 2018 by Andrew Hayes
All Rights Reserved.
Edited by Erin Cooley (cooley.edit@gmail.com)
Edited by Kisa Whipkey (http://kisawhipkey.com)
Edited by Celestian Rince (https://celestianrince.com)
Cover by A.M. Ruggs

No part of this publication may be reproduced, stored in a retrieval system, or transmitted in any form or by any means electronic, mechanical, photocopying, recording or otherwise without the prior permission of the author.

This is a work of fiction. Names, characters, places, and incidents either are products of the author's imagination or are used fictitiously. Any resemblance to actual events, locales, or persons, living or dead, is entirely coincidental.

Acknowledgements

This book goes out to every Dungeon Master putting in the hours to make a great game. It's not always the most glamorous gig, but we truly couldn't play without you.

As always, I want to say how much I appreciate my beta-readers for helping with their feedback. Thanks Bill Hammond, E Ramos E, TheSFReader, and Priscilla Yuen for all their wonderful assistance.

Prologue

The last guard fell, head caved in by a hand covered in leaves and grass. With him dead, the room was silent, save for the gentle rustle of plants and her own determined footsteps. The priestess had no name; it had been lost long ago, so she'd issued no challenge as she mowed down the fodder. Normally, these might have been an obstacle for her, but as this was her final errand, she was well-equipped for such mundane dangers.

Here, she was to pick up the final item – the last one for good reason. Should she die and lose the others, it would slow Kalzidar's plans, at most. But this, this was something special. Even her god considered it a rare find, a treasure the location of which had only ever been detailed in a single missive. The guards had no idea what they were protecting; this was just another treasure room to them.

Near the rear of the chamber, behind piles of gold and a few flickering gems, she swept the glittering refuse aside. Carefully, following the instructions just so, she pressed her hand against the bricks in a precise sequence. Dimly, almost inaudibly, sounded a *click*. The corner of the room parted, revealing a hidden seam that opened to a small chamber, too tiny even for a gnome to slip through. No, this existed only to house a single item. Concealed without magic, using mundane trickery, it might well have stayed hidden until the whole building aged into dilapidation.

As soon as her eyes fell upon the soft emanating glow, she knew her task had been a success. She'd found the final piece of her glorious god's plan. Reaching forward, fingers trembling slightly, the priestess laid her hand against a smooth face of the surface. Immediately, the world warped, shifted. New magic and information came pouring through her head. For a moment, the priestess feared she would lose herself entirely in the flow.

Then, mad as it had started, the feeling came to an end. She dropped her prize into a bag at her hip. The priestess was warned the retrieval might be intense and had mentally prepared herself. There would be time to learn how to use the item as Kalzidar needed, although not as much as she might have liked.

From what she'd been told, many of the pawns were nearing their positions. Soon the conquest would begin, and Kalzidar's glory would flow from one end of the seas to the other. With his faithful at hand, watching as the world fell and kingdoms burned, they would see their wrongs avenged in a blaze that wiped the land clean.

All of that would come with time and dedication. For today, the priestess had more tasks to handle. Yes, she had completed the gathering of supplies, but that was only the first step. Now, it was time to start on her real preparations, just as the others already had.

1.

If there was one benefit to the extraordinary circumstances Russell had found himself in, one silver lining to the bizarre madness engulfing his game, it was that the events he'd endured had definitely raised his threshold for weirdness. Once, receiving a strange summons from a company he'd spent the last few months scouring the internet for more information on—to no avail—would have seemed insanely coincidental, but that was before Russell had been possessed by a magical item *inside* the *Spells, Swords, and Stealth* module he'd been playing with his friends. After glowing dice and having his body used like a puppet, there were few things on Earth capable of rattling his nerves, and a simple invitation was not among them.

Much as he'd grown, however, Russell still wished he could have brought someone else to this meeting. The instructions he'd gotten were very clear: this special "VIP" meeting was for Game Masters only. No players or friends could tag along for the ride. It was news that hadn't gone over especially well with Cheri, Russell's sister and the party's blast-happy mage, Chalara. Getting her to agree to drive him and then wait in the car had been a near week-long fight; if their parents didn't insist on her driving anywhere outside of town, Russell might have risked trying to ditch her. He still wasn't completely certain she wouldn't come bursting in the front door after five minutes of being left alone outside. In fact, he could definitively say that the only thing keeping her in the car was the same element that had pulled Russell into the drab depths of an unfamiliar office building near the outskirts of town: magic.

Magic was real – either that, or everyone in his gaming group had come down with the exact same type of crazy. The latter was possible, mass hysteria and group food-poisonings did happen, but they all knew that no matter how much easier it might have been to say otherwise, they were all sane. Which meant that what happened during that game had been actual, tangible, magic. Here, in their world, not imagined or animated or drawn with computers onto a large screen. It had flowed through Russell's actual body; he could still recall his mouth moving without the permission of his brain. After a revelation like the existence of true magic, there were really only two options: run as fast as one could away from the source, or race after it with every ounce of strength they had.

He and his group had gone with the second option, and ever since, Russell had been working nonstop to discover anything he could about the mysterious creator of the modules producing these effects. Unfortunately, his efforts had yielded one dead-end after another, until the day the letter came.

It wasn't especially complex, this letter. An invitation, some rules, a time and a place. Bare bones, by any measurement. The sort of dispatch most would presume to be trash, or some kind of scam, and toss away. Only the people looking for Broken Bridge Publishing, the ones who knew there was more going on than should be the case with a normal game, would care enough to show up at the appointment. And that, presumably, was the point. With every release, there were supposedly fewer and fewer modules up for grabs. Even the rumors about Broken Bridge had dried up around the third release; the limited number of players who'd gotten the module were smart enough to not talk too much about what the experience entailed. Not that Russell blamed them. He hadn't exactly raced off to the forums to recount his own incident. Even the ones who wanted to believe him wouldn't, not deep down in the core of their beings. Some stories were just too big to choke down unless one saw it with their own eyes, and even then, that often wasn't enough.

Smoothing out the wrinkles on his button-down shirt, originally bought for a school dance the duration of which he and Tim had hung around the back of the gym, Russell arrived at the office specified in his letter. The door was boring, like the others in the building, though with one key difference. Drab as the rest were, they at least had some manner of signage indicating which business lay inside. Not Russell's door, though. It was perfectly bare, not so much as a logo or initials to be seen. That lined up with Russell's experience; Broken Bridge never seemed too keen on others finding them. Their marketing and brand management were pure shit from a fiscal perspective, but Russell was reasonably certain those weren't aspects of their business that particularly concerned them. Knowing what Broken Bridge *did* care about was another matter, one where Russell kept coming up empty. Hopefully, today would change that. Russell hadn't just come here hoping for another module; he also wanted some damn answers.

With one last glance over his shoulder to make sure Cheri hadn't stormed in after him, Russell grabbed the doorknob and pushed, revealing a plain room on the other side. In it were three chairs, all facing a door on the opposite wall. Above the door were two lights, one red, one green, the red one currently illuminated. A piece of paper was taped to the wooden door itself, its digitally printed words offering a single, simple instruction: "Wait for the green light."

Maybe it was a crowd management system; maybe it was a test to see if he could follow directions. If someone thought Russell was going to goof it up on a task like this after the Herculean effort of convincing Cheri to not do whatever she wanted today, they had another thing coming.

He took a chair on the end and settled in, ready to wait however long was required. If they kept him out here for an hour, or three, or even the whole night, Russell would wait. There were cabs to call if Cheri bailed on him, and he hadn't drunk anything on the drive over, so his bladder was empty. His whole party was counting on him. Russell would hold the line however long he had to in order to see what came next.

As it turned out, he may have been a tad overprepared. In fewer than five minutes, the light switched to green, turning with so little fanfare that Russell almost didn't notice. Not wasting time, he rose from the chair and pushed open the next door, half-expecting to find an identical room where he'd have to wait more. Once again, Russell discovered that the owners had gone another way. There was no dual-light system in this room. Rather, he found himself staring at a large table, several portable safes stacked up along the edges of the room, a few chairs, and one semi-familiar face.

It was the hair that triggered his memory more than anything—multi-colored, bright, and garish—though the facial piercings accompanying the coiffure stole the remainder of Russell's focus. Their last interaction had been brief, but between her looks and the context, it was one that was stuck firmly in the center of Russell's memory.

"I know you. You were at Double Con, the place where I got my last module."

She looked up from the table, as if she'd only just realized he was here, and met his confused recognition with a barely mustered shrug. "Yeah, apparently I didn't fuck up that last temp job, so I got to do another. Any idea who the hell these people are, by the way? They pay great, but the actual work they ask me to do gets weirder and weirder."

Part of Russell wanted to doubt that someone would continue taking odd jobs from a company with no idea of what they were really part of, but living with Cheri had shown him that not everyone put extensive critical thought into their actions. Especially when there was a sound motivator, like high pay, in the equation. Still, Russell was taking everything she said with a grain of salt. So far as he'd seen, she was the closest thing to a face Broken Bridge had. For a company that seemed to do nothing by accident, the idea of them using the same random temp twice felt slightly tenuous.

"As far as I can tell, they make *Spells, Swords, and Stealth* modules like nobody else. And I'm guessing they know it, too, since those of us who want to keep playing them have to keep jumping through all these hoops." This could be a test, to see if he'd give away the secret of the modules to an apparent stranger. Sometimes, Russell missed the days when he could just buy a module for his favorite hobby without putting everything through three mental layers of conspiracy screening.

"Must be some fun as hell games." The mystery woman flipped through several pages of the binder in front of her. "I think I remember you, but I'm going to need a name and some identification anyway. The directions I got made it clear they want these going to the right people only. No exceptions."

"Russell Novak." He'd already put his driver's license at the front of his wallet, prepared for such a demand. In another life, he'd have been consumed with the idea of getting a car; in fact, it had been one of his major ambitions as little as a year ago. Now, the idea was barely a blip on the radar. The deeper Russell and the others dove into this mystery, the less he found himself concerned with the normal, mundane world. It probably wasn't healthy—much worse, and his grades would start to slip—but he already knew he couldn't turn back. Russell had found a loose thread in the fabric of what he'd thought to be reality. He'd never be able to stop pulling on it, to cease unraveling the mystery, no matter how hard he tried.

She skimmed the binder before tapping once near the bottom of a page. "There you are. Let's see here… hmm, interesting. You have some of the most varied choices I've seen so far."

A shiver prickled the hairs on Russell's neck. "Choices?"

"Yeah, choices. That last module I gave out was some kind of hub-town type deal, from what I've gleaned talking to the others who came in. Not every group made the same choices, so some of them have opened and closed different paths. I assume you all sent in box-tops and reports or that kind of shit, so the company knew how your game went. If you didn't, don't tell me. I'm just here to cash a check."

Maybe Broken Bridge really had hired the same temp twice. She struck an interesting balance of caring enough to be sure the job was done right while not actually giving a shit about anything that was happening around her. In this way, she might just be the perfect employee.

"Anyway, since not every group took the same journey, they can't all choose from the same options. Nobody on here has access to the whole list, not even you. Based on what I've been given, it looks like you can decide to head toward Baltmur, Lumal, Solium, or Keelport. Those names seem to have meaning to everyone else, so I presume, and hope, you don't need any further explanation."

No, of course none of the others would need more. Any Game Master worth their salt would be intimately familiar with each of those names by this point. They were major geographic markers in the module-world Broken Bridge had constructed.

Baltmur was a civilization built by supposedly-evil creatures, populated with races like ogres and trolls that usually served as the cannon-fodder of evil antagonists. Reading deeper, Russell had learned that it was a city originally dedicated to Grumble, god of the minions, which left him uncertain as to whether or not Baltmur was truly an evil place, or had merely been branded as one. His interactions with those who served Grumble had been unsettling at times, but Russell certainly hadn't gotten the impression he was an evil god.

Lumal was a single city kingdom founded on knowledge. Supposedly, those who gained access via one of its hidden entrances had access to wisdom, information, spells, and lore that existed nowhere else in the world. Of course, the caveat was that getting into Lumal was legendarily difficult. Even if one could find an entrance, which was often a quest in itself, the residents of Lumal hated most outsiders and would often refuse them entry without some manner of task or quest being passed first. Proving one's worthiness to be in Lumal was part of getting in the door. Normally, as the GM, Russell could weaken the hurdle if needed; however, with these modules, he dared not meddle. Either they played the game as intended, or it would be the last module they received.

Solium was an interesting option. For his party, and presumably most of the others, if they were following the same module progression, it would be essentially doubling back. There surely would be new content—time had passed in-game—but Russell didn't bother entertaining the idea for long. His party wanted to progress, to move forward. Going back wasn't an option, not as things stood now.

That left only Keelport. As the name implied, it was a port city on the Western coast. Getting there would be a hell of a trek from where they were, but maybe the module offered a magical means of travel to help them cross so much land. Regardless, if they made it, they would have access to items and information from different lands. Keelport was a major hub through which countless ships and people passed. Plus, unlike Lumal, there were no barriers to entry. If they could make it, they could waltz right in.

It was a hard decision, even more so because he didn't have his party with him. They should have a say in this; it was their game as much as his. But life wasn't fair, and the burden of choice sat squarely on Russell's shoulders. He could either make it or walk away—which was still making a choice in itself. At the end of the day, it was a question of what he thought the group would care about most, and when Russell drilled the issue down like that, his choice was a shockingly easy one.

"I'd like the module for Lumal, please. My party has a lot of questions they want answered, and that is probably the best adventure to accommodate that kind of goal."

"Popular choice," the woman noted. Reaching down, she hauled up one of the portable safes which was small enough to carry, but hefty enough to cause her a slight strain. By the time Russell noticed and felt inclined to help, the deed was already done, the safe resting on the table before him. On a sticky note, the woman jotted down a few quick numbers, then slapped the note on top of the safe. "Apparently, we've had issues with people trying to get their hands on these without going through the proper channels, so you'll have to deal with the extra security. Inside here is the module you've chosen, and whatever other documents the company decided to include. Follow the rules, play the game well, and above all else, have fun. I'm required to say that last part. Any questions?"

"Literally countless ones," Russell admitted, lifting the safe into his arms. It was heavy, but since the contraption was small enough to house only a module, he could manage it with a single hand. The sticky note he tucked into his wallet after staring at the numbers a moment, refusing to risk losing them. "But I'm guessing you can't, or won't, answer most of them. I've got one you might, though. Last time, you said I had to seek them out to continue, only for the company to invite me here and put the next module directly in my hands. So, I guess my question is, change of heart?"

"Funny, I asked that too when they brought me in for this gig. The answer didn't make sense to me, but everyone else I tell it to seems to get the message. All they said by way of explanation was 'this isn't the world where they have to do the seeking' which sounds *completely* insane out of context, by the way."

"It doesn't get much saner, even with the context." Despite his words, Russell did feel a touch more at ease. While it wasn't exactly cut-and-dry, the message seemed to confirm what he'd expected: their continuation was based on what the characters did in the game world. They'd explored Alcatham, played the module to the end, and discovered a small piece of the truth that lay at its core. Presumably—hopefully—that meant they would succeed or fail based on the game itself, not Russell's ability to hunt down a company that almost seemed to not exist.

With a slow, exaggerated motion, the woman dragged her pen across the sheet with the names, scratching off Russell's entry. "I expected as much. Broken Bridge would like me to close this by saying drive safe, play well, and never doubt the truth before your eyes. Like most of this, that sounds like half-gibberish to me, so I guess it means go have fun with your new game."

Hefting the portable safe up into his grip, Russell clutched it tight. "Thanks. Have a nice day yourself. Maybe I'll see you next time there's a module release."

For a second, she looked at him, actually looked at him, no longer staring sullenly off to the side. Her eyes were surprisingly intense, nearly causing Russell to take a half-step backward. That piercing gaze went from him, to the safe, and back to him before a lazy smile stretched across her face.

"I'd say that's up to you and your group, don't you think?"

2.

The *crack* of the branch landing came seconds before Gabrielle hit the ground, several feet away and spinning her axe in a flourish. She'd leapt into the air, sliced cleanly through the thick limb of wood, and hit the ground all in a single motion. There was no doubt about it; she was more graceful than she'd been before. Coupled with her increase in strength, as the perfectly-severed branch demonstrated, there could be no question that whatever kind of undead she'd become, the change came with physical augmentation.

Gabrielle's condition had been their main concern as the party made the trek from Alcatham into the wildlands of Urthos, heading toward one of the secret entrances to Lumal. The only thing they focused on more was general safety, which was the reason Eric and Timuscor (along with Mr. Peppers) were both currently doing sweeps of their camp's perimeter. Training and testing were well and good when opportunity permitted, but they also had to survive the night.

Thistle watched Gabrielle land with the same critical expression he'd worn through the entire demonstration, a neutral gaze he'd perfected in his henchman days that showed he was paying attention without conveying either emotion or judgment. Originally, it had been a tool to keep him safe, lest an evil mastermind think Thistle was ignoring them or pondering above his station. Today, on the other hand, he was merely using it to conceal the utter confusion he was faced with.

As Gabrielle and Grumph moved into light, careful sparring, Thistle analyzed every movement the formerly-blonde barbarian made. Gabrielle's golden locks were now pitch-black—one of the many side effects from her transition to being undead. It was a strange symptom that served as a constant reminder of the conundrum she'd become. Thistle had been racking his brain every day, accounting for each piece of evidence her condition presented, and he was thus forced upon the same, inescapable conclusion: he had no idea what kind of undead she had turned into.

Her symptoms were too unique. None of them aligned entirely with any existing undead creature he knew of. She didn't need to eat flesh or blood and had experienced no cravings for either. In fact, she didn't seem to be hungry at all, though she'd joined them for meals to no ill-effect. Continual direct sunlight mildly burned her now-pale skin, but that typically healed within an hour of sunset. She was stronger, faster, more dexterous, tougher: physically augmented in every way. Still, she wasn't showing the pure raw strength of a high-level undead, like a lich or a vampire. Gabrielle's changes were mere improvements. Her biggest apparent weakness was also the element that made classifying her so difficult, and was the same thing that had likely caused her condition. So far as they'd been able to tell, Gabrielle was now quite literally dependent on the cursed axe clutched between her hands.

"Slow. Careful. Controlled." Grumph was taking Gabrielle through the motions of an attack stance, substituting his own demon-blade staff for her axe. He didn't have the training to guide her through any advanced axe-fighting techniques, but that wasn't really the point of this session. Their goal was to make Gabrielle comfortable with her new body and strength. Despite whatever it was she'd become, she was still a barbarian, first and foremost, which meant that when she lost herself in the rage of battle, she was going to be dangerous. The first time they'd had a wild animal attack—a bear no bigger than Grumph—it had become clear that Gabrielle needed to master her power. Flecks of that poor bear had coated every speck of grass around them, and Thistle was still washing the occasional stain from his boots. That was without her even tapping into her barbarian anger.

The axe had always fueled her rage. Now, however, it seemed to be fueling Gabrielle herself. Through trial and error, they'd discovered she could be parted from it, albeit unhappily, but the longer they were apart, the slower she moved. No one had been willing to risk letting her go completely still; they were all scared she'd never reawaken if they took things that far. Gabrielle was in a tenuous situation. She'd been given this status thanks to using a potent, cursed item in the middle of a literal storm of malfunctioning magic – as best as they could tell. And so until they knew exactly what had happened to her, they had to be exceedingly careful not let her go from undead to normal dead. Otherwise, there was no guarantee they'd ever be able to get her back.

"Ten more minutes, and then Gabby will need to go hunting." Thistle would have liked to let them train longer, but this too was part of their new situation. In Alcatham, Gabrielle had seemed perfectly normal as they rode back onto the road. Unfortunately, after only a few days of uneventful travel, she had grown visibly weaker.

They had tried feeding her, using raw animals to see if that would either restore her or otherwise stoke her undead hunger. It had been the bear that actually offered the solution, though. After obliterating it, Gabrielle was suddenly lively and spry once more. When tested afterward to confirm, the results held the same. Whatever power the axe had once drawn from harming its wielder, Gabrielle in her current condition was no longer able to provide. Killing and wounding other creatures, however, did fill whatever magical pool was inside the weapon. Since that power also seemed to be what kept Gabrielle mobile, the party entrusted her the task of hunting every night. The axe got its kill, and the party received fresh meat, meaning nothing went to waste. It was far from an ideal solution, but until Thistle knew more about the situation, he was at peace with holding steady. Better to make no moves than the wrong ones, when time would permit such consideration.

Sadly, that allotment of time was beginning to run dry. In their weeks crossing through Urthos, they'd been free to train, test, and hunt as needed. They had only a couple more days before reaching the entrance to Lumal, however. Once inside, Gabrielle's situation could be much more difficult to manage. Lumal was hardly the sort of place where one found wandering beasts readily available for the kill. The best idea they'd come up with was to allow Gabrielle to spend their entire final day doing nothing but hunt, hopefully building up enough of a reserve in the axe that she'd be able to last without killing in Lumal.

This added yet another wrinkle to their plan, one more spot where things could go awry. Taking into consideration the fact that Thistle was using outdated information on the entrance, the unlikeliness of him and Grumph being welcomed, and now their murderous-by-necessity barbarian, maintaining an optimistic outlook on their chances of being admitted was becoming difficult. The one ray of hope that Thistle could still cling to was his faith. Whatever lay before them, it certainly seemed as though Grumble, god of the minions, had been leading the way thus far. So long as he was watching over them, Thistle could believe it would all work out somehow, even if "somehow" potentially involved running for their lives or crawling through sewers.

Footsteps announced the return of Eric and Timuscor, with Mr. Peppers trotting along behind. Without the clanking of the knight and his boar, Thistle might have missed their return. Eric, already quiet in his movements, had attained a whole new level of stealth after his intensive month of training with Elora, the rogue in Alcatham they'd paid to teach him. He might have been truly silent, if not for the pack secured firmly to his back. Eric refused to let that out of his reach, and it wasn't an unreasonable precaution. Inside that bag was a piece of the Bridge, a magical artifact that none of them fully understood. What they *did* know, however, was that anyone holding it for too long would be driven mad. Only Eric seemed to be capable of handling a single piece without losing himself, though that control vanished if he tried to wield more than one. Better that the piece they had remain in his care than the others'—or worse, an enemy's.

"Clear, as far as we're concerned, although I spotted a pack of some kind of furless wolf-looking monster some ways off. They didn't look that big. Might make good fodder for Gabby's axe." Eric had adapted his scouting role in accordance with Gabrielle's new condition, using the time to search for potential targets the axe could feed upon. One of the party, usually Eric himself, followed her when she hunted. It wasn't always necessary, but after nearly losing Gabrielle inside the dragon's cave, no one was up for taking needless chances. The party never allowed a single person to undertake any given task; there was always someone to watch the other person's back.

"Were they just wolf-like, or did they have distinguishing characteristics, aside from the lack of fur?" Thistle asked. As the member who'd spent the most time around adventurers before becoming one himself, he was the default font of knowledge in regard to monsters, dungeons, and the strange workings of the adventurers' society.

Eric nodded. "Kind of a blue-green skin, and what looked like small spines along their back."

That was a surprising amount of detail, especially for something described as being "some ways off" from Eric and Timuscor. Thistle was mostly sure that there was no training that could improve one's eyesight, yet he found himself wondering about that prospect near daily, it seemed, with the new and improved Eric.

"Hmmm. They might be a good target. They're called hemlunxes, and while they aren't especially strong from a physical standpoint, they positively *drip* with venom. A bite, a claw, a poke from one of those spines on their back, any one of them will flood your system with a painful, partially paralyzing toxin. As you can imagine, that aspect makes fighting them especially difficult."

"Unless you're undead, and your body no longer responds to poison." Gabrielle sauntered over, axe resting lightly on her shoulder. Several steps behind was a sweating Grumph, leaning on his staff for support. Enhanced constitution just one more boon of being undead. "Sounds like I could take those beasts out easily."

"*If* your body acts like a traditional undead in that regard," Thistle reminded her. "While you fit many of the usual categories, I've never seen an undead that was bound to a weapon, or had to feed by using it. We can't assume that you have any given immunity or ability until we've tested and confirmed it for ourselves."

There was a soft rattling as Eric began digging through a pouch at his side, the slight tinkle of glass fading when his hand emerged with a small vial. Inside was an emerald green liquid that clung to the glass like a heavy wine as it was swirled. "Thistle is right. We can't send you out to fight a bunch of poison monsters until we're sure that you're immune. This is a mild paralyzing poison, best I've been able to make with the tools Elora gave me and the materials we've found so far. If you drink it and there's no effect, we'll know you're at least poison resistant. You'll only be down for an hour, at most, if it works, so there's still enough time to squeeze in some hunting after."

No hesitation, not that any of the party was foolish enough to expect it, as Gabrielle snagged the vial and downed its contents with a single gulp. Carefully, she returned Eric's glass to him—the vials were irreplaceable outside of civilization—as they all waited to see what would happen. After several full minutes had passed, everyone silent and on edge, Eric finally let out a relieved sigh and put the container back into his side-pouch.

"If you're standing after this long, then it means the poison didn't work. We'll still back you up, of course, but it looks like poison is one more thing you don't have to worry about."

Gabrielle let out a whoop of joy, followed by a wide grin. "Damn, being undead kicks ass. Had I known it came with all these perks, I'd have made the change years ago."

And there it was. Thistle almost winced at her words, barely keeping a stoic expression in place. That was the largest problem he'd discovered since the party set out from Alcatham. No one else, save perhaps for the naturally stoic Grumph, seemed to understand the danger Gabrielle was in. She'd been handed a slew of physical increases and immunities, so it was easy to understand why she might be blinded by the positive, but Thistle knew there was another side. Being undead came with limitations, weaknesses, and made one a target for those sects that felt the undead were an abomination against the gods. Sooner or later, one of those aspects would hit home for Gabrielle, and when it did, she was going to crash in a big way. Everything she was pushing aside, everything she wasn't facing yet, would slam into her all at once, and when that happened, there was no telling how she might react.

Sadly, Thistle was unable to think of a way to push that realization on her, and even if he could, he wasn't sure it was his place. Gabrielle had to come to terms with what had happened to her in her own time, her own way. As a friend, he would be there for her when it happened, and as a paladin, he would damn sure help protect her until that time came.

"Eric, you hunt with Gabrielle. If she doesn't completely decimate the bodies, it should be possible to extract some of the hemlunx-poison from their glands. The substance is famously potent, so I can see plenty of occasions where it may become useful. Timuscor, you go as well. With your armor, you can avoid being directly injured or poisoned, and it's good to practice defensive strategies sometimes."

Clanks filled the air as Timuscor rose from the seat he'd taken on a log. He paused, though only to kneel down and speak to Mr. Peppers eye-to-eye. "Since our enemy is poisonous, I can't risk bringing you into battle with your current armor. Stay here, and keep the others safe."

Mr. Peppers let out a snort, the miniature armor protecting his body rattling slightly. It was impossible to say why the boar listened to Timuscor, which he often didn't, or why they'd catch the odd flash of intelligence in the creature's eyes. Originally a summon that refused to vanish, Thistle had later learned that some force cloaked Mr. Peppers from the eyes of the gods, including Grumble. Whatever the boar was, whoever he served, the one thing Thistle felt sure of was that he was loyal to Timuscor. It was a trust that might come back to bite them all down the line, but with so many problems and enemies already on their heels, Thistle wasn't in a position to start casting aside allies. Besides, they'd all grown rather fond of Mr. Peppers, strange origins and all.

The boar trotted over to Thistle and stood proudly, as if daring any beast or monster on the plains of Urthos to challenge the crooked-boned gnome. Satisfied that his boar was safe, Timuscor and the others headed away from camp, toward where Eric had spotted the pack of hemlunxes.

As they left, Grumph made his way over to the log where Thistle was sitting and dropped down next to him. A soft crunching echoed from the log as it tried to support the muscular heft of a full-grown half-orc.

"The closer we get, the more dangerous this is." When not around outsiders, Grumph felt comfortable using full sentences. The broken language he defaulted to in public was merely an affectation meant to conceal his intelligence. In their time together, Grumph and Thistle had each discovered that playing the roles expected of them allowed both to seem unremarkable, which was an essential skill in the game of survival.

"Trust me, old friend, I am keenly aware. The more we discover about Gabrielle's condition, the more I question my choice to lead us toward Lumal. Yet I dare not turn us back. If there's anywhere we might find answers or a cure, it is within that city. Untangling the magical effect active upon her will require a true expert, the likes of which even your guild might not be able to offer. Of course, if Lumal fails, then the Mage Guild will have to be our next recourse, assuming we can make it to an outpost."

Absentmindedly, Thistle reached down and scratched one of the few exposed parts of Mr. Peppers' flank, earning a snort of approval from the boar. "No path before us seems perfect, so I'm doing the best I can with what we have. If anyone out there would like to offer up some manner of divine guidance, I certainly wouldn't object to a little direction."

Nothing happened, which was exactly what Thistle had expected. As far as gods went, Grumble was a reasonable and accommodating one, but not even he was a fan of dropping signposts in the middle of the road telling his paladins where to go next. And that assumed there was no divine protocol in effect—another god having a stake in what came next, most notably—that would bar anything other than cryptic visions from being delivered to a god's followers. It never hurt to ask, though, so Thistle dropped these opportunities every now and then, just in case Grumble had been waiting for a theatrically sound moment to intervene.

"I suppose no direction means we stay on route to Lumal and pray for the best."

"At least Lumal is safe," Grumph pointed out. "Be nice to get a good night's rest."

"Aye. My weary bones wouldn't object to a soft mattress and four solid walls. But I don't think I'll sleep well while we're in Lumal. That city unnerves me, it did even before we had a newly-made undead in tow. That much knowledge and power, in the hands of so few... While it's true that Lumal is in no danger of being sacked by bandits or invaded by ogres, I fear that when something does go wrong in that town, it will be an utter catastrophe."

"Think we'll be there when it happens?" Grumph looked as though he already knew the answer and hoped to be proven wrong. On that account, Thistle was going to have to disappoint his old friend.

"Honest, paladin's truth?" Thistle threw a glance over his shoulder, in the direction the others had wandered off in. "I'd say there's at least a fifty-percent chance we'll end up causing it."

They sat in silence for a moment, the only noise Mr. Peppers' heavy breathing, before Grumph hauled himself to his feet. "Only fifty percent? Didn't expect getting old to turn you into an optimist."

3.

"One last time, because this is important. Is everyone okay with what we're about to do here? Any objections? Anyone want out at the last minute? If so, that's fine, just say so now. Once we start... I don't know the rules. I don't know if you'll be able to quit. Make sure this is really what you want."

Russell had never started a game like this, because, for him, there had never *been* a game like this. With the other modules, he'd only suspected something was up, and at the time the far more likely theory was that he was simply going nuts. Now, things were different. He knew, they all knew, that magic was truly in play. What came next for them was a mystery, which made the idea of a new game terrifying and irresistible all at once. Safety was far from guaranteed, and Russell refused to drag anyone into danger. If they took the plunge with him, it would be of their own volition or not at all.

He looked to the nearest player at the table on his left: Tim. Player of Timanuel the paladin, Tim had been with Russell since the first Broken Bridge module, when his D20 glowed, spun around, and then dissolved into dust. At the time, they'd thought it the most insane outcome possible from a *Spells, Swords, and Stealth* game. Part of Russell wished he could still think that way. It was no surprise to find Tim nodding enthusiastic agreement to his terms. Like the paladin he played, Tim saw things through, especially where his friends were involved. Danger or not, he was going to be at Russell's side.

"I'm in. Timanuel is in. Whatever comes next, we face it together, as a party."

A paladin's response, if ever there had been one.

Russell's gaze moved farther up the left of the table, to where Cheri was sitting. He didn't even manage to squeeze a word out before she piped up.

"Let's just skip the part where you bother asking me. We're family. Your insane magical bullshit is my insane magical bullshit. Chalara has her spells ready to rock. Let's see what this fucking game can throw at her."

Although Russell might have preferred if his sister hadn't issued a challenge to whatever magical entity was acting through these modules, he did appreciate the support. Shifting his gaze to the far right side of the table, he met eyes with Bert. Unlike the others, Bert didn't have an answer locked and ready. His thick, muscular form was hunched over the table, eyes darting among Russell, the new module book resting in the center of the table, and the sheet for his character. Wimberly was a gnome gadgeteer who'd been vital in battle many times over. Losing her would be a true blow to the party, yet Russell wouldn't say so much as a word to stop him if Bert walked out the door.

"I'm an engineering major. I like systems, and rules, and finding out ways to maximize efficiency. But all of that comes from knowing and understanding the fundamental laws of the world I'm working in. Part of me wants to run out that door and never play another tabletop game again. Much as I would love to pretend I never saw what I did, I can't. It's not in me to deny something I know is true. So if I leave, I'm going to spend the rest of my life never sure of anything. Maybe Santa is real. Maybe astrology works. Maybe there *is* something under my bed or hidden in the shadows. I'll never be able to dismiss anything, because I am now keenly aware that I don't actually know the rules of our world. If magic is real, then anything else is fair game. My only way through this is forward. Learning more about what's happening, understanding what we experienced, it's the sole option I see that offers me a chance at some sense of normalcy down the line. I'm in, because I have to be in."

Not quite the upbeat enthusiasm of the first two, but Russell appreciated having at least one player who seemed to be going into this with eyes wide open. They'd come through the last incident all right; however, there was no guarantee that this module would turn out the same. Either way, Bert was set on his choice, so Russell glanced over to the final player, this one seated to his immediate right.

Alexis was the quietest of the lot, except when role-playing her forest warrior, Gelthorn. Instinctively, Russell leaned in, prepared for her usual half-whispered tone. To everyone's surprise, she lifted her head and met his eyes, speaking so clearly she was almost doing Gelthorn's voice. Perhaps she was channeling her character a touch, for courage if not speaking skills.

"This scares me. It really, really does. But a lot of things scare me. The world is so big, and so loud, and most of the time, it doesn't seem as though there's a place for someone like me in it. Role-playing games are the only time I get to feel what it's like to be brave, courageous... fearless. I'm honestly terrified of what comes after you open that book, but I still want to be here. I love these games, and I really like playing with you all. Just once, I want to stand *my* ground, not Gelthorn's. I'm here to the end, with the rest of you. So please get this going already, Russell, because the anticipation is nearly the worst part."

With the entire group opting to continue, Russell could see no reason to delay any longer. He lifted the module book from the table, cradling it carefully, as one would a priceless antique. Taking one last look at the scared, excited faces of his players, Russell pulled open the cover to reveal the first page.

"When last you left off, your party was in Camnarael, having survived the Grand Quest—"

* * *

Urthos was not, strictly speaking, a kingdom. The ruling system of the region was divided among nomadic tribes throughout the plains. This meant that, in a technical sense, Urthos was quite easy to conquer, since it lacked a standing army to oppose another kingdom's forces. However, the simple fact that there were no cities to sack and overtake also meant that any would-be invaders could do little more than set up camp in the wilderness and declare that this was their land now. Several kings had attempted just this, in fact.

It was only after declaring their intentions that some of the logistical hurdles came into play. No cities meant no walls to protect them, and a lack of farms to steal from meant all food had to be brought in via magic or supply line, the former of which was limiting and costly. Still, these means might have been tenable, if not for the Urthos tribes. Unlike the invaders, they knew how to live off this land. Harrying the supply lines usually came first, cutting off the army's food. Then they would strike in the night. Never a full assault that committed the entirety of their forces: just a flaming arrow into the tents here or a guard suddenly dead there. Enough to ensure that no one slept well.

Sometimes, in the face of this uncertainty, the army would add reinforcements, a move that only stretched limited food supplies further. By the time the tribes finally attacked in full, they were facing exhausted, half-starved invaders, many of whom were likely to surrender and desert before the first blood of true war was shed. No one ever tried to invade Urthos twice, especially once they realized there wasn't enough gain to justify the effort. Urthos held no great industry to take over, no mineral deposits that had been discovered, and no ancient magics to pilfer. It was simply the tribes and the plains, both of whom seemed to want little more than simply being left alone.

What this meant for Eric's role as a scout was that there was little chance of being ambushed by bandits. Unlike the roads of other kingdoms, few merchants made this trek, and those who did usually attempted it with the blessings of the local tribes. That meant bandits would have slim pickings, and those they did steal from could bring untold repercussions down upon their heads. There was no jail in Urthos; matters of justice were handled more swiftly and permanently. Of course, that also meant any thieves they *did* encounter would be desperate and willing to fight to the death.

Monsters, on the other hand, were a larger concern than normal. With no kingdom guards to regularly sweep the roads clear of beasts, they could be attacked at any time. Worse, on the plains, there was nowhere to escape. Wherever they ran, they would be in full view until they could clear the horizon. That was why the party had decided to skirt the edges of Urthos, hugging the side of a huge forest that sometimes butted up against its border. While it put them at greater risk of ambush, it also provided a feasible escape route. Given that the King of Solium's bounty was still on their heads, it made the most sense to prioritize keeping a place to hide within reach. It was far from ideal, but then, there really wasn't an ideal way to be pursued across kingdom borders by a vengeful tyrant chasing a similar artifact to that contained in Eric's pack.

The potential for monster attacks had Eric even more vigilant than normal. Every rustle of leaves from the forest, each shivering blade of grass on the nearby plains, all of them instantly drew Eric's attention. His eyes were keen, and mad as it seemed, Eric would swear his vision had gotten better after working with Elora. Eric thought Thistle had noticed, too, though he was polite enough not to say anything. The best theory Eric had was that working in the dark of Elora's training area for so long had simply sharpened his focus. Not the most adept or complete hypothesis out there, but part of being an adventurer was learning to roll with the unexpected as it occurred. On that front, at least, Eric had received ample practice.

And as his eyes swept right, back toward the forest, he realized that he might just be getting a tad more. "Hold." Eric held up his hand, in case anyone had missed the word. Instantly, the others slowed their horses, eventually bringing them to a stop near him. They were close enough to hear, but spread out, so that if they had to flee in a hurry, they wouldn't collide with one another.

"What do you see?" Thistle asked. His hands were already on his belt, inches away from the throwing daggers with which he'd had countless occasion to prove his prowess. These were not a traditional paladin weapon by any means; then again, Thistle was hardly a traditional paladin.

Slowly, Eric pointed up ahead to a small, nearly imperceptible break in the tree line. "A path. Rough, and hidden, but there."

His announcement was met by silence. That was to be expected. It would take the others a moment to search the area and spot the trail. It stretched longer than Eric was expecting, however. Eventually, he turned to face the party, finding squinting eyes and confused expressions looking back at him. "Come on, it's not *that* well-hidden."

"Must be decent, because I can't see a damn thing." Gabrielle was leaning so far forward she threatened to tumble out of her saddle.

At her side, Timuscor nodded agreement. "I too am unable to find your path, although I have full confidence that it is there."

Strange, neither were renowned for their attention to detail, but it was so close. Was the path really that well-concealed? Based on the still-searching gazes of Thistle and Grumph, it sure seemed that way. Or… maybe something else was at work.

Carefully checking the plains once more for potential threats, Eric dismounted his horse and walked up to the path's entrance. He didn't hear or see movement, yet his hand remained on his short sword. A glowing gem on the hilt meant the weapon's daily enchantment hadn't been spent; the power would allow him to deliver a single, incredibly powerful strike. Not enough to win a battle against multiple foes, but a display that would at least buy him enough breathing room to get back to the others. Eric didn't bother to shift his armor's color. While the ability was fantastic for camouflage, his whole point in doing this was so the others could see him. Blending in would be counterproductive.

Eric easily reached the path, and from this angle could confirm it indeed went much deeper into the woods. He took a few steps onto it, then backed out of the forest and waved to the others. "Can you see it now?"

"From our perspective, all we can see is you wandering into a thick grove of trees," Thistle called back. "We must be dealing with some manner of illusion."

That certainly made the most sense; it would explain why, no matter how Eric pointed, the others couldn't spot the trail. What it didn't explain, on the other hand, was how Eric was able to see through the enchantment in the first place. Much as he might not have liked to, Eric *did* have a guess at what might be causing that.

Reaching into his pack, Eric brushed ever so slightly against their piece of the Bridge. The world tried to spin away from him, flooding his mind with visions and knowledge beyond what mere mortals were meant to know, but he'd learned that touching the Bridge lightly kept him from being fully engulfed. More importantly, doing this altered his senses. Not for long, and certainly not to the extent that actually gripping the artifact would, but the effect was definitely tangible.

For a moment, a split-second, Eric could see beyond the world around him. He could see the planes brushing against theirs, the unnatural shadows just past those borders, and the flow of magic coursing through their world. A substantial amount of that mystical energy was knotted together directly in front of him, formed into a spell far more powerful than he'd anticipated. This was no fly-by-night illusion. This was art, masterful craftsmanship to create a ward that fooled all but the most skilled of adventurers. Or, in Eric's case, those who were in possession of an artifact containing a nigh-limitless power that was slightly altering their senses. He'd known that just being near the Bridge had an effect on the others—it was part of why they'd ditched the first piece they'd found. This was an unexpected complication, though.

"As near as I can tell, it's an illusion formed by a master magician. Don't ask me how I know. When I'm not touching the Bridge, I lose the specifics. I just remember being awed by the talent required to make something of this caliber. Whoever constructed this illusion is powerful, definitely not the kind of person we want to cross."

"I guess that means this was a nice detour, but it's time to get back on the road," Gabrielle surmised.

Thistle's horse trotted closer to Eric, obeying its rider's silent commands. Even from a few scant feet away, the gnome squinted, still trying and failing to make out any manner of trail hidden among the trees. "There is a possibility that warrants discussing before we pass this by. Perhaps the Bridge opened Eric's eyes to a hidden path, or maybe the source is a divine one. If it's the former, then we can write it off as random chance. However, if it's the latter, then we must consider the possibility that we are meant to take this fork in the road. Gods lead us where we are needed, not where we expect to go."

"Forgive me, I do not mean disrespect with this question, but if this were truly the work of a god, then wouldn't Grumble send the vision to you, his paladin?" Timuscor looked wildly uncomfortable about proposing the idea that perhaps Grumble was playing favorites with someone else. Thistle, however, merely tilted his head forward in agreement.

"Aye. Were this a boon from Grumble, or at least solely from Grumble, then I would be the most likely recipient. But there are other gods, and we know at least one of them has an interest in Eric."

It was no secret from the others that Tristan, god of the rogues, was currently having a dispute with Grumble about who held claim to Eric's soul. At this point, Eric himself barely mattered: it was more about the pride of the two gods who'd pitted themselves against each other. Both wanted to win, and Tristan hadn't been shy about plying Eric with divine gifts. The ability to sense immediate danger, setting up proper rogue training from Elora, even their influx of treasure from a hidden base, could all be partially laid at Tristan's feet. Did that mean one god, possibly two, could be urging them to take this unexpected detour?

"Thistle, you're our expert on gods. If I can see the trail and you can't, does that mean Tristan wants us to go, but Grumble doesn't?" Eric appreciated the help Tristan had offered thus far; however, he'd actually met and talked with Grumble. Between the two, he was willing to trust the divine kobold who watched over minions more than the god who served sneaks and thieves, even if Eric now belonged to said sneaks and thieves.

"Working with as little information as we have right now, it's impossible to say for certain. Even our assertion that this is the work of the gods is speculative. It could just as easily be a Bridge side effect, as you no doubt suspected." Thistle hesitated, his eyes drifting toward Gabrielle, then jerking away. "However, speaking as an adventurer more than as a paladin, my instinct is to see where the trail leads. Lumal is not going to be an easy hurdle for us to clear. There are many obstacles in our paths, and countless ways the visit could go terribly wrong. If we're stumbling onto something like this only a few days from the entrance, part of me can't help suspecting that it's not by coincidence. Whatever lies down that path might very well help us in our goal of entering Lumal."

"Or it's a trap," Grumph added.

"You're quite right, old friend. That, too, is a possibility. If the party wishes to walk past, I won't object. Whatever we do next, we do it together."

All eyes were on Eric, and the stares were beginning to make him uncomfortable. Usually, Thistle was their default leader, but lately, he'd been throwing some key choices onto Eric's shoulders. This seemed to be another such case. At least in this instance, Eric could understand the reasoning. As the only one who could see the path, he was also the sole person who might be able to help them along it and spot hidden dangers. Sadly, all Eric could make out at that moment were a few squirrels scampering among the nearby branches.

"Let's decide this together. Thistle votes for going down the mystery trail. How does everyone else feel about it?" Eric asked.

Gabrielle was the first to respond, barely waiting until Eric had finished. "Honestly, I know we have to go, but I've been dreading being locked up in a stuffy town with no fighting or monsters. This seems more interesting, so I say we see where it leads."

"Where you all go, I follow. To Lumal, down a hidden road among the trees, or into the Plane of Fire itself. Lead us where you see fit, Eric. My role does not change regardless of where we are." It was about the response they'd expected from Timuscor. The man was stalwart and loyal beyond a shadow of doubt, although his strange origins and core of uncertainty made him hesitant to dictate the course of others.

That left only Grumph, who'd raised the idea of this being a trap in the first place. His expression, like that of most half-orcs, was hard to read. The large wizard sat atop his horse for nearly a half minute of silence before trotting over to Thistle. "Strong magic means a strong mage. Dangerous enemy. Useful ally." Another beat of silence. "We have plenty of enemies, so one more may not matter, but we could use more allies."

Three for going and one abstaining. Even if Eric were inclined to pass this up, which he wasn't, the will of the party was clear. "All right then, let's run some rope between the horses. I'm not sure if you'll see through the illusion once you're in it or if there are more wards ahead, so let's be certain we can follow each other no matter what twists this path might take."

As the others began pulling rope from their packs, Eric looked down the trail one more time. It was impossible to tell precisely where it led, but he had a hunch it would be somewhere interesting. He just hoped it wouldn't be *so* interesting that they didn't make it out alive.

4.

No one looked up as the door creaked open to reveal the diminutive form of Jolia the gnome wandering in from outside. At this time of day, the only people inside the Vengeful Ale were those who regularly stopped by during the day: a small table of older friends downing mead in the back of the room, shifty-eyed characters who were here more out of habit than for any true purpose, the burly bartender himself, and, of course, Kieran. While not much for the drink, Kieran was here almost daily for lunch. Cooking, it was alleged, was one of the few skills he'd failed to master in his time journeying across the lands. That was the excuse, anyway. Most of the townsfolk thought Kieran really came to argue with Brock, the bartender. About what, it mattered not. They seemed to enjoy the act of disagreeing with one another more than making ground on any actual topic.

Today, the gnome could hear them through the door as she approached, and was already aware that they were debating whether or not mages were more dangerous with wands or staffs. Personally, she was on the side of staffs, but that was as a wielder. Considering the danger of an opponent equipped with such an item was an entirely different equation.

"It's a hunk of fucking wood. You get past all the spells, all the wards, all the mumbo-jumbo, and they can still crack you on the head with a length of oak. You're really going to sit there and tell me you think a wand is more dangerous than a legitimate weapon?" Brock sounded precisely the way anyone who looked at him would expect. "Rough" was often the word used to describe their local bartender, and it fit him in virtually every capacity. From his loud, grizzly voice, to his calloused hands, to the way his beard had been choppily trimmed with a dull blade and was always a little dirty.

Kieran, in contrast, was the very picture of composure: clothing clean and pressed, boots polished, sword and scabbard positioned just so on his hip. Not that he would ever draw on Brock—or anyone else in town, for that matter—without just cause. Small scrapes would occasionally happen around town, but fighting seriously, with a weapon drawn, was grounds for expulsion from their village. No one held to that rule more than Kieran, since he was viewed by many as a default leader and took that responsibility seriously.

"You make it sound like you can't handle someone with the physical skills of a mage and a wooden club. The wands are more dangerous because they make all that 'mumbo-jumbo' you dismissed exponentially more accurate. I'm not worried about fighting a caster when I get to them; it's the getting there that's the hard part."

"Speaking as someone who actually wields these tools," Jolia interjected, "it shouldn't matter what the mage is using. If they let you get to them at all, then they've fundamentally lost the battle. A good caster should never get blood on their robes; bit of wisdom my teacher imparted."

Kieran and Brock both nodded. They appreciated the opinion of an expert when it was applicable. "Jolia's got a point there," Kieran agreed. "The worst would be when you finally make it to them, and then they pop some kind of teleportation or transformation spell. I once had to make it through a gauntlet of magic, only to fight a mage turned four-headed hydra at the end."

"Four heads was a challenge? Were you poisoned or something?" Brock sneered back.

"Just young." For the first time, Kieran appeared to realize that Jolia hadn't immediately ordered a drink upon entering. His eyes lingered on her colorful robes for several seconds. "Anyway, what brings you into our daily bickering, Jolia?"

She scanned the room once, though there was no need. This community didn't keep secrets— not from each other, at least. Most things would be found out eventually, and they were all mature enough to handle whatever issues arose head-on. Still, as a former court magician, secrecy and betrayal had been bred into Jolia, and some habits were harder to shake than others.

"Someone's coming. I felt my wards be disturbed a few minutes ago and did some quick scrying. It's a small group, no one we're expecting, and while they're colored by some strange magics, they don't seem strong enough to pose any danger. My larger concern is how they discovered the path in the first place."

"Could be a lot of things," he replied. "Maybe the gods are guiding them, or they have an item that lets them pierce illusions. Perhaps it's simply pure, dumb luck, that rare sudden moment of unexpected competence."

They all knew what Kieran was referring to. Everyone who dealt with adventurers did. Sometimes, seemingly apropos of nothing, an adventurer would have sudden bursts of incredible fortune or failure. A rookie with a bow could accidentally land an arrow in the eye of a dragon, or an experienced combat veteran could completely miss something as slow-moving as a slime. After seeing it happen often enough, they began chalking the whole thing up to natural phenomenon. It wasn't as though they had many other options for how to deal with the curiosity.

Taking one last bite of the too-thick stew Brock was serving, Kieran stepped down from his seat and stood to his full height. It wasn't terribly impressive. He was taller than Jolia, but that was assumed for a human when compared to a gnome. Brock, who was also human, towered over them both. Once, when he was young and brash, Kieran had possessed quite a temper regarding his height. But time had softened even that; nowadays, he considered it more of an interesting quirk than something to get riled up over.

"How they got in doesn't really matter. We've had the occasional wandering adventurer make it through before. The real question is whether we let them make it all the way here or drive them off. If they're weak, then they probably aren't coming here to conquer. So long as they pass our test, I favor turning them around quickly like the rest."

"Do they have anyone interesting with them?" Brock interrupted. "I could go for a new story or two inside these walls. Been a while since anyone made it through."

Jolia hesitated. There were some unusual aspects to this party, but she was reluctant to get Brock too excited about the prospects. If Kieran opted to drive them out, then Brock would pout for a full week, and his cooking often paid the price for his moods. Still, this town operated on openness, so there was little point in keeping secrets.

"You'll have to forgive me if any of this is wrong; I wasn't kidding about the odd magic swirling around them. That said, from what I could tell, they were being led by a human with few distinguishing features. After him was a gnome with a high concentration of divine energy, so most likely a priest, except he was wearing armor. Old armor, at that, with its own divine aura. Near him was a half-orc I nearly mistook for a spear-wielder, until I noticed that he was glowing with enough mana to qualify as a caster. First caster I've seen with a blade on their staff, but then, he's also the first half-orc mage I've seen, so I suppose it makes sense. After that was an undead woman carrying an axe that's practically dripping with power, and behind her was another man in armor, this one human and mostly normal."

Brock leaned his head halfway across the bar, excitement already glowing in his eyes. "Mostly?"

"He had a wild boar rigged up on the side of his saddle so it could ride with him, adorned in what looked like a miniature version of the man's own armor," Jolia explained. "That seemed... not so normal."

"Strange group, unusual equipment and energies, heading directly our way." There was a heaviness to Kieran's words as he more fully considered the situation before them. "That seems a tad too specific for it to be random chance that brought them here. Some god must be damn desperate, if they're sending this party in our direction. I doubt it's even their fault. Nothing inherently malicious about taking a path in the woods. What do you think, shall we test them?"

Jolia and Brock both considered the proposal. They didn't get many visitors, save for those with permission to come here. The few who did find their way onto the path were rarely allowed to continue. Testing was a way they'd come up with to decide whether or not any given party was the kind of people they wanted to permit inside their borders. The methods varied each time, depending on the party makeup, but the core goal remained the same: to see, when pushed to their limits, what sort of people these adventurers turned out to be.

"Testing sounds fair. Shame we drive almost everyone off, sounds like they've got some members that could be fun." Brock paused, growing visibly uncomfortable. When he spoke again, the reason became immediately evident. There was only one person in this town, perhaps in the world, who truly scared Brock down to his bones. "Much as I hate to say this, if they've got an undead with them, the testing should go to Simone."

Jolia and Kieran exchanged a brief look until the former spoke. "Think she's willing?"

"She joined the town council. Part of that means pitching in when these situations arise." Kieran took a step toward the door, visibly steeling himself. Brock wasn't the only one who felt unnerved by Simone. "I'll handle asking her. It will take them a few hours to make it here by that path, so we've got time. Hopefully enough for me to convince Simone."

Without another word, he strode out into the open air, only slightly slowed by the burden of his duty. Jolia hopped up into his bar-chair using the rungs Brock installed for his smaller customers. "Let me get an ale, then, while we're waiting."

Brock cocked an eyebrow, even as he began to pour. "You sure you want one while we've got intruders in the woods?"

"I've got a hunch I'll want a buzz before this day is over. Besides, we're both aware that Kieran will succeed, so Simone should start casting in the next few minutes." Jolia paused to take a long, deep draw from the tankard Brock set down in front of her. "And once Simone gets going… well, there's not much more we'll need to worry about. That woman knows how to handle a job."

* * *

Thistle felt the shift before he saw it. A twist in his gut, not quite like the sensation when evil was around, yet not nearly far enough from it for Thistle's liking. Some force was coming, a power that bristled against his own connection to the divine. Not wasting a moment, he pierced the air with a sharp whistle, high and long—their signal to indicate that trouble was approaching, and fast. There might not be time to coordinate, but he could at least give his friends enough time to draw their weapons. Already daggers were dancing in Thistle's hands, waiting for a target to sink into.

Their first visual confirmation came seconds later, when a streak of black shot across the sky. For an instant, Thistle thought it was an airborne enemy hunting them through the trees. Then he saw the streak widen, faster and faster, until every last ounce of daylight had been blotted from the sky. Visibility shrank rapidly as the forest darkened. Within seconds, they'd be nearly blind.

Quick as his body and armor would allow, Thistle leaned forward and pressed his hand onto Eric's saddle. Gleaming white light rippled out from the item, illuminating their nearby surroundings. Without wasting so much as a word, the others clustered near Thistle so he could imbue their items with the same light-giving magic. He always hesitated to think of it as casting—the act felt more akin to seeing a small prayer granted right before his eyes—but from a practical perspective, he supposed it was the divine equivalent of casting a spell.

Before a full minute had passed, Thistle had managed to use his light enchantment on Grumph's staff, Timuscor's shield, his own daggers, and Eric's saddle. Only Gabrielle declined the magical aid, since her eyes seemed to still be working fine. It made sense—no need to put a glowing target on one's back without reason—but Thistle hoped her vision would hold up in this magically created darkness. They were dealing with an unknown assailant; taking anything for granted was dangerous.

"Intruders."

The word came from all around, above and below, as if whispered by an army hidden perfectly within the trees. Thistle undid the rope on his saddle and rode forward, getting in front of Eric. Leading them through a disguised path was one thing, but when danger reared its head, it was the paladin whose place was at the front of the party, so as to better protect the others.

"Mysterious Voice, I offer my sincere apologies. We found this trail—admittedly concealed, but otherwise unmarked—and chose to explore it. Clearly, that was a mistake, and we have wandered onto property under your possession. I ask only that you permit us to turn around and leave peacefully, as we mean no harm and wish for no bloodshed."

Playing the most likely odds, they'd either walked onto the property of someone evil, or someone who simply treasured their privacy. Despite the strange magic in the air, Thistle wasn't sensing any actual evil, so he'd pinned his hopes on the latter situation. If they could convince this entity they'd come here by mistake and not with ill intentions, then they just might make it out peacefully. Any caster who had the kind of magic to make it appear as though they'd darkened the entire sky was not someone this party was ready to tangle with.

"A mistake? You journeyed past a series of powerful wards and illusions by mistake?" There was laughter in the voice, a kind Thistle didn't care for.

"We were curious to see what had caused such things, but had no way of realizing someone was living here. It was our mistake, clearly, and again, I am sorry for any inconvenience we have caused."

Silence this time, or near silence. There were still some small sounds: scraping, rattling, noises that didn't bring anyone who heard them much comfort. When the reply finally came, the laughter at its edges had grown stronger.

"Very well. A mistake it was. Yet, errors must be atoned for, mustn't they? Most of you may flee. The undead woman, however, stays behind. She seems interesting, quite the subject for study. Cast her aside, and rest of you may depart in peace. Refuse, and you can try to leave together."

A sharp flash of light lanced the darkness. No more than a split-second of phosphorescence, but to the party's dilated eyes, it was enough to illuminate the entire forest. From behind the trees and out of the ground, the monsters came. Skeletons, shambling corpses, flying creatures that looked like normal animals carved apart and stitched back together – a veritable army stepped into view just as the flash came. When the bright spot faded, the party could still see them, lingering at the edges of Thistle's magical light, a mere fraction of the actual force they were facing.

They were surrounded by a swarm of undead, and the only way out was to hand over Gabrielle. Not for the first or last time in his life, Thistle silently cursed the paths his god loved to lead them down.

5.

Abandoning Gabrielle was a laughably stupid proposition. Even if Thistle weren't a paladin and thus forbidden by the gods to perform such cowardly acts, there was no chance the others would leave one of their own behind. From the instant the demand was made, they all knew the only way out of this would be through combat. Still, they held their positions, eyes on Thistle and the monsters, waiting for either to make a move.

For his part, Thistle was scouring his brain for any kind of solution to their current conundrum. Undead enemies were all around them. It would only be a matter of time before they were overwhelmed in battle—and not a very long matter, at that. The rotting army hadn't been here earlier, though. The undead had shown up at the same time as the darkness and the voice. There was a slim chance they were illusions, but Thistle wasn't quite that optimistic. Then again, they almost certainly *were* some kind of magical summons; it was the only way to explain how they'd appeared all at once.

Summons meant a caster, which gave them a weak point. Theoretically, if they could deal with the mage, the undead might vanish. Or, with no one to control them, they could suddenly run wild and overwhelm them even faster. And that was assuming his party was skilled enough to handle a mage who could cast this level of magic, not to mention clever enough to *find* their true opponent in the first place. All Thistle could see in every direction was darkness and more undead.

However, that wasn't all he could feel. The lingering twist in his stomach, not quite the sensation of evil being nearby, but close, had some limited directionality. When Thistle faced different directions, the intensity of his gut pain varied, meaning there was a difference in what he was looking at, even if his eyes couldn't see it. Turning in the direction where the feeling was the strongest, Thistle adjusted his grip on one of the light-enchanted daggers. If this was going to work, he needed every advantage, including surprise.

With all the force his arm could muster, Thistle hurled the blade deep into the shadows, farther than he'd ever managed without the enhanced strength of a paladin. The moment it left his hand, Thistle turned to Eric, meeting his eyes and then jerking his whole body back toward the dagger. It was a split-second communication, but mercifully, Eric got the message. Not sparing a single moment to hesitation, Eric leapt off his horse and raced after the dagger, plunging into the darkness. There was a good chance he'd figured out what they were up against, as well; the man was learning quickly, cataloguing each lesson like a tax collector absorbed gold. Even if he didn't have every detail, he at least knew that his job was to go after the true enemy while the others fought for time.

"I presume that is you declining my offer. Pity. I would have liked her in one piece before taking her apart."

Much like Thistle, the voice gave no direct command to attack. The undead surged forward, seemingly of their own accord, as Thistle's party rushed off their horses. Thankfully, the undead had little interest in the mounts. No sooner had boots hit the ground than skeletons and corpses lumbered forward, teeth gnashing and hands outstretched.

The first wave quickly discovered why Solium and Alcatham both had new rumors about a terrifying woman in blood-red armor, as Gabrielle met them with a mighty swing of her axe. Bones snapped into splinters as she tore into the nearest skeleton and followed up with a clean sweep through the neck of a stumbling corpse. Filthy, half-congealed blood poured from the wound, sending up a smell that might have threatened everyone's stomachs in less dire circumstances.

Behind Gabrielle, Grumph was just finishing up a spell. The instant he was done, his muscles bulged with unnatural power. In terms of overall impressiveness, a spell to temporarily increase one's raw strength didn't hold a candle to summoning tornados of fire or opening holes between planes, but there was something to be said for pure functionality. With the demon blade atop his staff positioned at the fore, Grumph began his own assault, taking at least a limb with each blow he landed.

To the rear, Timuscor and Mr. Peppers had positioned themselves as guards, making sure their friends couldn't be flanked or snuck up on. The knight's shield served as a makeshift wall, slamming into the undead and driving them back so his sword could cut them down. It lacked the brutality of Gabrielle and Grumph's methods, but it also left him far less exposed, ensuring that he'd be able to keep up the task for a while longer.

Of all the party, only Thistle had his eyes trained upward. Setting himself in the center of the group so he had space to focus, the gnome whipped his daggers through the air, taking out every one of the stitched-together abominations that came swooping for his friends' heads. Fighting the ground troops was bad enough; if they had to split their attention, they'd be overrun in seconds. Even with his support and their aggressive opening, it was only a matter of time. For every one enemy they dropped, three more moved into its place. This was not a fight they were going to win.

Impractical and unfair as it was, all of their hope for survival had been laid squarely across Eric's shoulders.

* * *

They were gathered around a giant cauldron behind Jolia's shop. There were other ways to watch—she could have conjured an illusion around them so vivid it would feel as if they were actually in the battle—but such measures took time, whereas she could have the cauldron going in under a minute. Therefore, that was the method she often deferred to. It wasn't as though detail mattered tremendously in this situation, and all of those present had seen enough battles to make sense of the chaos.

"The gnome is the one putting light on the daggers. And, unless I'm wrong, he just sensed their larger threat despite the darkness." Kieran inched closer to the water shimmering with images. "Never seen a priest wear armor like that before. Times are always changing, I suppose."

"There's a boar in armor fighting at a knight's side, and you can't look away from some priest's fashion choices?" Brock sounded disappointed as he took a mighty bite of his roasted lamb. He'd brought more than enough for everyone, catering their impromptu viewing party as usual. "Now that's an odd one."

"I just watched a half-orc perform a spell, then use his staff to handily chop through body after body. Honestly, I'm still trying to figure out if that's blasphemy to the arcane arts, or a genius blending of two different combat styles," Jolia added.

All eyes turned to Grumph, who, at that moment, was ramming his demon-bladed staff directly through the skull of a skeleton that had been trying to claw Thistle. The head collapsed from the force of the blow, sending the rest of its bones tumbling loosely to the ground.

After several seconds, Kieran let out an annoyed grunt. "All right. I suppose I will admit that, in some limited circumstances, a staff might be scarier than a wand."

* * *

Leaving his horse and saddle behind meant Eric possessed no direct source of light as he sprinted after Thistle's dagger. In a way, that was a blessing. A single glowing target was easier to track, and the limited visibility meant Eric couldn't see many of the things he was sprinting past. Given how terrible the few bits he saw were, reduced vision didn't seem like such a bad bargain.

Thistle's aim was true, which was little surprise. Even for a throw in the dark, he'd managed impressively. Eric followed the dagger just to the left of a small gap between two trees, the left of which was now host to Thistle's weapon. The undead were thinner around this area, leaving Eric enough time to pry the dagger out. Just as he yanked it free, his eyes passed across the darkness between the trees, and a jolt ran through his spine. The first time he'd experienced this, Eric had no idea what he was feeling. However, training with Elora had expanded his awareness, and now he knew precisely what that sensation was.

Attention. Rogues could sense when someone nearby was watching them closely. Last time, it had been another rogue on their tail. This occasion felt different, although it was possible the circumstances were tinging his perception. Of course, a sudden sense of awareness around an undead army was scarier than the same feeling on an open road. Yet there was something more to it, like each version had a mental flavor or scent, something intangible and undeniable. Whatever, or whoever, was watching him made the hairs on Eric's neck stand on end.

A normal, reasonable person would have taken that information into account and then run as far and as fast as their legs would take them. Eric, unfortunately, could no longer consider himself a reasonable person. That title had been lost the day he and his friends were forced to become adventurers. While they weren't always perfect at their parts, their journey had taught them many things about the roles they'd adopted. And the first, largest lesson of all was that, when adventurers found something dangerous, they ran in with weapons drawn and smiles on their faces. Especially when their friends were in danger.

Flipping the dagger around so it could be quickly thrown if needed, Eric plunged into the gap between the trees. He was squeezed briefly between the rough bark, and then popped out into an open space on the other side. Immediately, the change in sound stood out. Gone were the noises of battle and combat. Instead, there was near-silence. A scuttle here, a rustle there, otherwise, this small clearing was empty of sound. Empty of anything, actually, so far as Eric could see. Inching his way along, Eric moved in deeper, dagger held in front to illuminate the imposing darkness.

"Let me get that for you."

A snap came on the heels of the voice, and seconds later, a gentle green glow ebbed through the clearing. Insect-sized lights drifted through the air, each acting like a miniature torch. As the world snapped into view, Eric became quickly aware of two key elements: one—the size of this clearing was roughly circular, only about fifty feet across at the widest point, and two (perhaps more importantly), he was not alone.

This wasn't a slight against his senses, at least. One look at the man standing across the clearing made it obvious that Eric wouldn't have heard him breathing or shuffling about. Those were habits of the living, and this fellow was blatantly undead. Pale skin, sunken face, and hands that looked like bone wrapped thinly in skin. He was clad in dark leather armor, with a pair of blades hanging at his hips. The most striking feature was his eyes—blazing green orbs that matched the color of the gnat-like lights in the air.

"Your voice is different than the one we heard before." Eric shifted his footing, deciding if he was going to strike or defend first. Given the situation, planning for any other outcome was optimism to the point of foolishness. "I take it that means you're not the one who caused all this?"

"I could be. Perhaps I use a different voice to disguise my true identity." In spite of the fact that he was dead, there was more life to the undead man's voice than the first one they'd heard. A smile even seemed to tug at the edge of one thin lip.

"It's possible, just unlikely. I've admittedly met only a few mages in my time, but I've yet to see someone with this kind of power who didn't want to get credit for it. If you were the caster, I have a hunch you'd use your own voice."

Those glowing eyes tracked his movement, attention never wavering for so much as a blink. "I suppose it's hard to deny that there's truth in that. Magic and ego often go hand in hand. Very well. You have found me out. I am not the orchestrator of this attack, merely another pawn within it. My master is the one who has engineered your demise. She was kind enough to offer you an exit, and in turn, you attacked her soldiers."

"Leaving you behind to clean up in case we were too strong for the skeletons," Eric surmised.

To his surprise, this drew an actual chuckle from the stranger, as well as a shake of his head. "My, my. And here you did so well at first. You've deeply misread this situation, unfortunately. I am not the one here to 'clean up,' as you stated. My role is that of bait. Due to the specifics of my particular undead condition and some unique aspects of my past, I make an extremely potent target for priests and paladins, most of whom can sense my magical aura. The power of the divine often serves as an excellent counter against the undead, you see. Hence why we lure those with such abilities away from the rest of their party."

Another snap, and this time, Eric heard the shifting of branches. He spun, just in time to see the gap he'd entered through close up as the trees behind him grew closer together.

"The armor is a touch odd, but between the glowing dagger in your hand and the blessing I can smell coming off that short sword, I'm guessing you're a paladin." The undead man drew both his blades, swinging them once before taking an offensive stance. "For your sake, I hope that's accurate. A priest isn't going to last very long against me."

6.

They were losing. They'd been losing since the fight began, really. From the instant they'd looked at the forces they faced, it was obvious the party was outmatched. All the same, it stung as they were pushed back, more and more wounds accruing slowly. Everyone, save for Gabrielle, was starting to get tired. Unlike most engagements, there was no dance to this, no alternation of fighting and analysis, no time to catch one's breath. It was a ceaseless torrent of one enemy after another, and no amount of dropped skeletons or corpses seemed to lessen their numbers.

Grumph was visibly panting, Thistle's face dripped with sweat, and they could all see Timuscor's movements growing slower and heavier. Gabrielle, like the rest of the undead, still seemed to be going strong, but even she could only cover so much for them.

A trio of skeletons surged forward. One managed to slam a sharp claw into Grumph's bicep before being knocked away. The damage was still done, sadly. His heavy staff wavered; Grumph was no longer able to wield it with one of his arms compromised. The others scrambled to get near him, but already, they knew this was the end of the fight. Together, they'd barely been holding the horde at bay. With a break in their circle, a weak link in their chain, collapse was inevitable, especially given their weary states.

Then, without warning, the army stopped. It was still there, every undead face staring at them with arms raised, yet all were utterly unmoving. If they hadn't just been on the verge of defeat from this very army, it would have been easy to mistake them for macabre statues. A subtle crunch of leaves filled the air as a new figure stepped into view.

She was pale, though not quite to the degree of the undead. Her dress and robes were simple—black with silver trim—yet the quality of their material made it plain at a glance that each garment was wildly expensive. In her right hand was a staff unlike anything the others had previously seen. Slender, tall, and pitch black, it seemed like she had shaped the very essence of night into a tool. There was an energy to the weapon as well, a gentle ripple in the nearby air that made one's head ache if they stared at it for too long. Every step was careful and small as she wound her way through the frozen undead. At last, she came to a stop about ten feet away from them, the path between her and the party largely clear of both obstacles and enemies. Perhaps it was an intentional choice, to show them she wasn't afraid. Or maybe she just wanted a clear view of whatever came next.

"A fine effort. Pointless, certainly, yet fine regardless. You didn't want to abandon a friend without trying to save her. I can respect that. What sort of adventurer gives up an ally so easily? But now, having experienced a small fraction of my forces, perhaps you are more willing to see reason. These creatures are like mayflies to me. I can bring forth so many that I could physically drown you in them, or I could call on something mildly stronger and see you all torn to pieces in under a minute. This was my warning, trespassers. Heed it, if you have any desire to live through the hour. Yield your undead to me and—"

"Never." Thistle cut her off, staggering forward despite the exhaustion in his legs and the weight of his armor. As he moved, his eyes met Grumph's briefly; a flash of a look, and nothing more.

To their surprise, Gabrielle also shifted slightly forward. "Look, I obviously am not in love with this idea, but maybe we should consider it. If we can't win, isn't it better if we just lose me?"

"No," Grumph replied.

"Absolutely not," Timuscor agreed. "And even if we did concur, we couldn't very well leave Eric, too."

The woman looked up at the name, tilting her head a hair to the side. "Ah, is that the one you sent deeper into the woods? I wouldn't worry about him. By now, Julian has certainly carved the fellow into pieces."

Part of her had expected that fact to douse their spirits: being down a party member often changed the odds in substantial ways for adventurers. What met her gaze, though, was not surrender. Rather, they glared at her with anger and healthy skepticism. Evidently, they had more faith in this "Eric" than to believe he'd go down easily. Since that avenue hadn't panned out, she quickly shifted gears.

"Am I to take this as you choosing death over leaving just one of your people behind?" While not an overly demonstrative person, she did have to suppress a small smile at seeing them hold together so well. Rarely did an entire party pass the test, demonstrating such loyalty and strength of character; she was glad to be present for this occasion.

"In that case, allow me to show you—"

Once more, Thistle cut her off, although this time it was with nothing so benign as a mere refusal. "Grumph, now!"

*   *   *

Diving to the side, Eric scrambled through the grass, narrowly dodging a blow meant for his head. Without his high-quality armor and dodging skills, the fight would have ended in the first ten seconds. His enemy wasn't quite as graceful or dexterous as Eric, but his skill with those swords more than closed the gap. Counterattacking was as much a hopeless dream as defeating a dragon bare-handed. It took everything Eric had just to keep from receiving a fatal blow. Reflexes kept him out of range from the killing attacks, while his armor absorbed most of the glancing strikes. Unfortunately, those hit so hard that the armor-muted blades created bruises with each contact. If this was what the glancing blows felt like, Eric was reasonably certain he couldn't survive a direct one.

His only hidden card to play was their piece of the Bridge, tucked away in his pack, and Eric wasn't sure how much that would help. Using the Bridge was dangerous for a number of reasons, not the least of which being that he had no idea what might happen. Maybe it would give him enough strength to win, or maybe it would shatter the very magic keeping this man, and potentially Gabrielle, alive. Unless the stakes were truly dire—end-of-the-world or death-of-his-friends dire—it was hard to justify using something so unpredictable.

To his surprise, after coming to his feet from evading the most recent strike, Eric discovered that his enemy had halted the assault. Wary though he was, Eric needed the chance to catch his breath, so he didn't object.

"You've lasted a full three minutes. That's rather impressive, given how clearly weak you are. Nevertheless, it's a feat that warrants some reward. I give you my name, adventurer. You may call me Julian."

"I'm Eric. Does the introduction end our break, or was there something else you wanted to talk about?"

"Me? I have little that warrants discussion. No, I paused because I was ordered to. The one who commands us all is speaking to your friends once more, giving them a path to freedom. What they, and you, choose will decide whether or not this continues."

A waste of time, then. The others wouldn't give up Gabrielle. It went against everything that had gotten them this far. Sticking together was their only hope. "I'll go ahead and give you my answer now, then: hell no. We leave as a party, or we die as a party. That's it."

"About what I expected, yet my orders are still to wait. So unless you do something as idiotic as attack me, your time stretches onward. It matters not. Our commander will be triumphant regardless."

Knowing the others, they'd tell that mystery voice to shove it up her ass—maybe more politely, if Gabrielle was occupied with fighting. As soon as they did, the fight would be back on, and Eric had no delusions it was a battle he could win. There was an idea percolating in his head, obviously a long shot, yet still a huge improvement over his current situation. It was a little underhanded, admittedly, but that was part of being a rogue. He just needed to catch Julian off guard, and there was one fact Eric could toss out that might just do the trick.

"Oh, I wouldn't be quite so confident about that if I were you." Slowly, concealing his movements as best he could, Eric altered his stance so he could close the distance between them in a single bound. "See, you and your boss made one key miscalculation."

"I hope you're not about to say that we failed to account for the bond between allies making you all stronger, because we did, and it is still wildly not enough," Julian replied.

"Good guess, but also way off." Eric lowered his sword hand a few degrees, ensuring he was positioned perfectly for what came next. "Nope, see, you misread the situation and your opponent both. Divine magic hurts the undead? Well, bad news for you then, Julian. Because *I'm* not the party's paladin."

Those sunken, glowing eyes widened in a flicker of surprise, then glanced away from Eric. A perfectly understandable reaction. Maybe he was able to see his commander where Eric was not and was checking up on her, or perhaps he was mentally informing her of the new development. Either way, he wasn't looking right at Eric, and that was exactly what the rogue had been waiting for.

The gem on Eric's sword flashed as he bolted forward, every bit of his remaining strength left pinned on a single swing of the blade.

*   *   *

"*Rouse.*"

The final word of Grumph's spell was also the only one any of his friends could understand. Conversely, they knew the effects of the magic quite well. This was a spell technically above Grumph's capabilities, imparted to him thanks to Eric and the first piece of the Bridge they'd found. While it did burn the remainder of his mana, it also reinvigorated him and nearby allies. Certainly, it was far from perfect; they were still wounded and outnumbered by a healthy margin. But this at least gave them some energy to fight with, and that was especially relevant since their true target had finally appeared.

Thistle was already in motion, a pair of daggers flying straight for the staff-wielding woman's head. Gabrielle and Timuscor were running forward, Mr. Peppers on the latter's heels, ignoring the frozen enemies as they rushed to flank the lone target. As for Grumph himself, his mana was spent. However, his strength-enhancement was still in the mix, so he lowered his staff like a lance and charged. It was a graceless, obvious attack, as were Gabrielle and Timuscor's. In a situation like this one, subtlety was a lost cause. Their only viable hope was to try the same tactic as their enemy: overwhelm through superior numbers. Even if she could see the attacks coming, at least one might land. What came after that was anyone's guess. They were dashing from moment to moment in a frenzied effort to stay alive.

The first of Thistle's daggers crashed against an unseen barrier, creating a flash of light followed by a sharp noise like a taut wire snapping. They had just enough time to register a flicker of confusion on the woman's face before the second dagger flew past the barrier unimpeded. Unfortunately, she effortlessly knocked it away with her staff, although her eyes were now locked on Thistle.

"It seems I misjudged your skill set."

"Get used to that." Gabrielle had arrived, power all but rising off her like steam from a morning lake. She brought down her enchanted axe like she meant to split the world beneath their feet. It was a glorious blow, right on track to land—until it slammed against the pitch-black staff and completely halted.

"You aren't nearly as surprising." The mage didn't seem especially bothered by the effort of stopping such a blow. With a step forward and a single motion, she shoved Gabrielle back, sending her stumbling into a tree. "And while I'm sure the augmented strength in your possession makes you feel invincible, you really have no idea the depths of power that can be plumbed from necromancy."

Timuscor didn't announce himself, but his armor made the charge impossible to miss. As soon as he drew close, she spun around and blocked his sword with her staff, using the same ease she'd demonstrated against Gabrielle. Grumph was nearly there. If he could make it while she was locked up with Timuscor, they might yet score a hit. The damn frozen enemies between them were slowing him down, but he was making progress. Timuscor just had to last for a few seconds.

"More of the usual, I see, save for the boar. He's quite adorable. Where did you—?" As the mage spoke, her eyes swept upward, meeting Timuscor's. Instantly, she froze, gaze locked with his.

Grumph didn't understand, nor did he have the luxury of puzzling it out. For the first time in the entire battle, there was an actual path to progress. Racing ahead with all the strength his muscles could offer, Grumph angled the staff so that the blade would plunge through her torso and come out the other side, away from Timuscor. He expected her to block again, or dodge, or raise a magical barrier, yet still he pressed on. At least this way, there was a chance, however slim, at success.

To the surprise of everyone present, and a few unseen people watching from a cauldron, the mage didn't so much as flinch. Grumph's blade caught her just below the ribs, sliding through her torso and out the other side. They'd done it. They'd managed to land a single blow, one that should be crippling, if not deadly. Unfortunately, she seemed no more nonplussed by the makeshift spear running through her than she had Grumph's charge. Her attention was firmly locked on Timuscor.

"You are... aren't you? I can see it in there. The confusion, the uncertainty, the loss of your place in the world. Forgive the rough greeting. I had no idea this party kept an echo in their company."

*　　*　　*

Eric's gambit had failed. Fast as he was, focused as he was, the gulf between him and Julian was simply too much to overcome. While he had managed to gain a fleeting moment of surprise in the attack, Julian shifted fast enough that the strike merely took one of his arms, rather than his head. In other circumstances, that might have been enough. Sadly, one of the many issues with fighting the undead was their unwillingness to die from dismemberment. Even with that, Eric could have held on to hope if he'd had any more stamina left; perhaps taking out one of the swords would make a difference. His heavy limbs told the truth whether his mind wanted to hear it or not: this match had taken Eric to his limits. Aside from—at most—a few more dodges, he was done until he rested. Whereas Julian, despite being an arm down, looked spry and ready to continue.

"That was pretty decent." Julian evaluated the slice through his arm, clean and even the whole way down. "For someone of your abilities, the fact that you scored a hit is remarkable, let alone that you took off a limb. Of course, using a blessed weapon helped with that, but still, kudos."

"I'd feel more complimented if you seemed even a little bit bothered by the wound," Eric replied. While it was a chatty battle, as the one who needed time to recover, he wasn't going to object. "You don't even seem annoyed."

"How can I phrase this kindly?" Julian was walking again, sizing Eric up and blatantly choosing his next angle of attack. "It would be like if a kitten bopped your nose hard enough to sting. Painful? A little. But certainly not enough reason to feel anger or fear toward the kitten. This was never a fight, Eric. If you were ten times stronger, it still wouldn't be. There is power in this world well beyond your comprehension."

The weight in Eric's pack rested heavy against him, a tactile reminder of what lay within. Was it time? Had things gotten that desperate? Without knowing how the others were faring, it was impossible to say, and Eric didn't feel his own life warranted the risk. Besides, if Julian was really that much stronger, then couldn't he have ended the match whenever he saw fit? Either that was a lie, which seemed unlikely given how the fight was going, or there was more going on than just a simple duel to the death.

"You might be surprised by what I can comprehend."

"On that account, I suspect you could be right." The voice hadn't come from Julian this time. It was softer, the same tones he'd heard when they first entered the forest. Both men spun around to find the trees opened once more, a woman holding a pitch-black staff visible in the space. At a closer inspection, Eric realized she also had a familiar bladed staff impaling her through the torso.

Instantly, Julian hit the ground in a kneel, eyes to the dirt. "My lady Simone. I apologize. Has my performance demanded intervention?"

"Never, Julian. The situation has simply grown more complex than we first suspected. They had an echo with them. I've already transported the others. Knock that one out, and we'll head home."

Eric had just enough time to wonder what the hell they were talking about before he realized an attack was coming. The realization did him no good: Julian was already there, remaining arm raised overhead. Fast as he was, Eric had just enough time to see the pommel of Julian's blade coming down before the entire world faded out in a bolt of pain, followed by darkness.

7.

The first step of getting into Lumal was finding one of the hidden entrances. According to legend, Lumal first began as a settlement by scholars who wished for a safe place to store and conduct their research, paired with mages who sought a place for their more potent experiments. Between the two groups, they were able to construct a new, miniature plane of existence, a pocket of space kept partially separate from the rest of the world through complex spells and enchantments. This was Lumal's greatest protection; it could be neither invaded nor infiltrated. Only those granted permission were allowed to cross the divide between planes.

Myths existed of potent enemies cracking through the wards, forcing their way in, but they were all ancient. The amount of knowledge and skill concentrated in Lumal meant that they were always developing new ways to wield magic. After hundreds of years of focused study, their defenses were considered nigh impregnable by anything short of a god. Breaking in simply wasn't an option. If a party wanted to access the City of Knowledge, they had to go through the proper channels.

"Let's see. The phoenix ashes should be available in a few days, so that's one potion component down. We've got the water from the river of the naga, and an order for the lesser base components, so that just leaves... *five* more minor magical items for the potion? I swear, this list is getting longer every time I look at it." Bert frowned as he stared down at his sheet, as though he could will their required tasks to grow smaller.

"Hey, Chalara wanted to take that deal from the black market where we only had to hunt for a few and could steal the rest. We could have had an actual location by now if we'd gone that route," Cheri reminded them, not for the first time.

Already, Tim was shaking his head. "We can't do that. Stealing is wrong. Same as hurting people if they caught us. At least this way, we only have to fight something that's attacking."

"You do remember we're trying to find answers for what happened to us in real life, don't you? I think maybe fictional stealing from fictional people is forgivable in pursuit of finding out why this game can control a GM." Cheri kept staring at Tim as they debated, even if she might have wanted to look at Russell and make sure he was still himself. Ever since the possession, it was hard not to keep stealing glances just to check.

"If you only do the right thing when it's easy, then it's convenience, not virtue," Tim countered. "I would also argue that the fact that this game can influence our world is all the more reason to treat its people and their possessions with respect. We saw what happened to the party that acted like nothing they did mattered."

A quiet moment filled the previously boisterous space as everyone felt memories bubble up unbidden. Much as they were set on moving forward, that didn't mean parts of this game didn't scare them. It certainly hadn't escaped Russell's notice that despite having multiple ways they could take to gather ingredients, the party was so far defaulting to ones that required the smallest amount of interaction with non-player characters, despite those methods being more difficult. The party was still coming to terms with what they'd learned, and for now that largely meant sticking to themselves.

"Enough bickering! Our party has chosen a course; there is no gain in looking back at the road already traveled. Turn your eyes ahead to what still needs to be accomplished. Put your energies there, and soon we'll be past this challenge and on to the next!" Alexis—or more accurately, Gelthorn the forest warrior—made a good, loud point. Yes, they still had a lot to do, but infighting wasn't going to make their task any easier.

Bert drummed his fingers on the table a few times, looked at his character sheet once more, and then reached for his dice. "Aside from creating the base potion and proving our worth to Lumal, we need some other serious ingredients. Tempting as it is to wait for the phoenix ashes, based on the timetable we received, there's a few in-game days left before the hatching. Why don't we try to go for one of the major items in the meantime? The golden roc feathers make the most sense. There's a mountainous region only a short ride away—the most likely place for them to nest. With a good Historical or Geographic Awareness check, we may be able to get a general idea of where to search."

It wasn't enthusiastic, but Cheri eventually nodded. "Fine. I can deal with that. Just one thing to keep in mind: Chalara doesn't have any flying spells. If we want to search a roc's nest, we go up the hard way. And if any of you fall, you're probably screwed. My only fall-slowly spell requires touch."

"I may have an idea in that regard. Let's see what our checks get us first, before we get too far into planning." Bert waited for the others, who also picked up their dice. "Might as well kick things off with Historical. Roll them well, people. We could really use some more information."

* * *

Timuscor's eyes opened without warning. One minute, he was asleep, the next wide-awake. That was to be expected with magical slumber, he supposed, and given that he'd passed out in a forest surrounded by undead enemies, such could be the only explanation for an unplanned nap. He was resting on a hard surface. After lifting himself carefully, it soon became clear that he'd been laid across the pew of a church. Strangely, in spite of the hard wood on his back, Timuscor felt well-rested. Actually, he felt downright great, as though every ache and pain he'd gathered on the road was washed away. Magical healing, obviously, but an overabundance of it. Thistle, with his limited reserve, could only heal the worst of their injuries each night, perhaps mending a few of the smaller ones on slow days. This was a complete treatment, down to the tiniest cuts and blisters.

On the heels of his surge in health came two more realizations: his armor, weapons, and gear were all missing, and the others were also waking up nearby. Their heads rose one by one. Most appeared confused, save for Gabrielle, who just looked pissed. They were all stripped of their equipment as well, only this time, there were two exceptions. Gabrielle's axe had been sheathed in an unfamiliar holder and strapped to her back, but was otherwise still present. The other piece of equipment still in the room was Thistle's armor, which didn't surprise Timuscor. That armor was powerful. It had belonged to Grumble's first paladin and was gifted to Thistle at his god's discretion. Items like that didn't part easily from their owners.

When Eric's head popped up, a visible surge of relief ran through the room. They hadn't known what happened after he raced off into the woods, and it was hard not to imagine the worst, given the odds they'd been facing.

"Good morning, everyone. I hope you slept well. We allowed you a brief nap to recover from your travels. Plus, if I'm honest, you all looked like you could use the sleep." The speaker was a man standing on the pulpit. He was a shorter fellow, though no one would mistake him for a gnome, dressed in casual clothes and with a single sword on his hip.

"That's great and all, but I wasn't asleep. That robed bitch just froze me and blocked out all my senses." No wonder Gabrielle had come up looking pissed; she'd been trapped in her mind instead of merely unconscious.

"Yes, unfortunately not every solution works for every adventurer. We do the best we can and make up the rest as we go. I'm sure you're familiar with such methods. But look at me, being rude." He paused, bowing deeply to them. "My name is Kieran, and while our town doesn't have a 'ruler,' per se, I'm the one who often ends up dealing with situations such as this."

That earned an uneasy look between party members. The phrase "situations such as this" left a lot open to interpretation. Although they were all grateful to be healed and in one piece, they'd also been stripped of their weaponry—a fact that didn't necessarily bode well.

Kieran *was* making an effort to be cordial, though, so the least they could do was return it. Thistle stood up on a bench, which allowed him to be seen from the pulpit, and returned Kieran's bow. "My name is Thistle, paladin of Grumble. With me are Gabrielle, our fearless barbarian; Grumph, our esteemed wizard; Eric, a silent rogue; as well as Timuscor and Mr. Peppers, the classic pairing of a knight and his boar."

"Gnome paladin, that's an unusual one." The real surprise hit Kieran a moment later, as he processed Thistle's words. "Hold on, Grumble? As in the god of the *minions*? I didn't think he had paladins."

"All gods may have paladins, if they can find those willing to serve," Thistle explained.

Kieran looked Thistle over once more. "I suppose that might explain why your armor refused to come off. Divine will is stronger the fewer servants a god has in their employ. Easier to pay attention, I presume. You are all a mess of curiosities, I must say. At first, we took you for another party of adventurers who'd had the misfortune to stumble onto a trail they were never meant to find. When Simone realized you had an echo with you, we knew something else was afoot. Then we found your artifact, and it all fell into place."

It was the first time they'd all realized that Eric's pack was gone. The serenity of the church and waking up healed was immediately dispelled. Gabrielle went so far as to grab her axe, only to find it unwilling to leave the new sheath around it.

"Don't worry. We aren't keeping it. None of us want any of those damn pieces around. But the fact that you have one indicates that they're active again, which means quite a bit for the world as a whole, and some very specific things for us. It's also why we decided to let you into our town. Feel complimented. Most who pass the test of character are merely allowed to escape. It's been some time since we actually brought outsiders into Notch."

Silence met Kieran's declaration, as the party tried to absorb the rapid-fire words of near nonsense that had been leveled their way. Not only did he know what a piece of the Bridge was, but his people had no desire to use it? Or even have it nearby? That in itself wasn't incomprehensible; those items courted danger. It was part of why the party had buried the first one they found. Intriguing as that was, it was another hook that dragged one of them to speak first.

"You're talking about me, aren't you?" Unsteady with the sudden disappearance of his armor, Timuscor rose from the pew. "An echo. That's what the mage woman said when she looked into my eyes."

"Her name is Simone," Kieran clarified. "And we'll get to that in a moment. This is easier digested in pieces, and choking down the first parts make the later ones more palatable. Also, this analogy is disgusting and clearly got away from me, so I'm going to stop talking about eating for a bit. Instead, let's start with where you are: Notch. Notch is a town you won't find on any map in any kingdom. We built it out here, at the edge of the Urthos plains, where no tax collector or stray merchant could stumble upon its location. This place is a very weighty secret, so before we go on, it's important to me that you understand the situation. If you ever depart, you are not permitted to tell anyone what you have seen. The sole exception is gods, of course, since they already know, and I understand that, as a paladin, it might very well be impossible for you to lie to Grumble."

There was a flicker of surprise in Thistle's eyes at that. Evidently, that was news to him, if it was true. "Forgive me, but you said *if* we depart. I can tell you're trying to be accommodating, but that sort of language does leave an implied threat hanging in the air."

"No one here is planning to hurt you, although injury is possible. I simply meant that most who are permitted to come here choose to stay. Our town is roughly fifty people strong, not counting children, even if the vast majority keeps to themselves. We're a tight-knit community, a safe place in a chaotic world, and for many, that's what they've been searching for, whether they knew it or not."

Everyone save for Timuscor and Mr. Peppers exchanged a glance. Before all this, before the adventuring and the Mad King's bounty and the Bridge, they'd been mostly normal people. True, Thistle and Grumph had each had excitement in his past, yet even that had long since faded into a mundane existence. They knew all too well the simple pleasure of living within a community of good people. And deep down, each of them had been aching for it since the day they stepped out of Maplebark.

"Sounds lovely," Eric spoke up from the back. Despite the fact that no bruise or scar was present, he still rubbed the side of his head where he'd been struck. "And while I can't question your assessment of this being a safe place, given defenses like that, you'll understand if we're curious about a fifty-person town that can employ someone as powerful as Simone as its guard."

That earned a laugh. Not derisive or mocking, but the short chuckle that comes from surprise of the unexpected. "Simone is a civilian here, not a mere guard. She works in a house behind this church, at the edge of the graveyard. The truth is, we only sent her because you had an undead with you, so it made the easiest story to sell. All of us on the town council take turns playing that part, depending on the party and the situation."

"I see." Thistle's brow was knit, his fleeting moment of confusion replaced with intense concentration. "The crux was never whether or not we could defeat the undead army; it was a test to see whether we were the kind of people to trade a friend's life for our own. Presumably, failure would have put our lives at risk, while success earned us the freedom to leave, maybe with a parting word or two of guidance if we were truly impressive. Am I close?"

"You fudged a detail here and there, but you've got the spirit of it," Kieran confirmed.

"There's only one issue I can see with such an arrangement. For you to so easily trade out on who fulfills that role, wouldn't that mean you'd all have to be roughly as powerful as Simone?" Thistle had the look of a man dearly hoping to be proven wrong, which explained why his face lit up as Kieran shook his head.

Tapping his hand on the hilt of his sword, Kieran whispered to himself, counting off some unseen data on his fingers as he mumbled. "Not quite that bad. As I mentioned, only those on the council tend to fill the role. You've got the right idea, though. Simone is definitely one of our more powerful residents. I'm certainly not claiming that everyone is on her level. By my count, we've got about five who are her equal, and only three I would classify as substantially stronger. That said, even those who are weaker than she are still far stronger than any of you, and most of the adventurers who come through here as well."

"You can't seriously expect us to believe—" Gabrielle's words were cut off by the sudden appearance of a blade two inches from her skull. In less than a blink, Kieran had vanished and reappeared with his weapon drawn: an entire church crossed before she'd even gotten out a full sentence.

He stayed like that for only a moment before he smiled and sheathed his weapon. "Forgive the parlor trick. I've been at this long enough to know a moment of demonstration will save me an hour of debate. Yes, the people of Notch are by and large incredibly powerful. No, that's not a coincidence. You see, all of us who live here share a common thread."

Calmly, as though he hadn't just shown he could kill any of them in a heartbeat, Kieran made his way back to the pulpit, speaking as he went. "We were all adventurers, too, once. Most adventurers die; that's hardly a surprise to anyone. Yet, on occasion, they don't. Luck, the gods, perhaps fate itself, something keeps driving them forward until they complete their ultimate goal, usually in a fight so difficult that only a few members of their party survive, if that. Imagine, if you would… finishing your quest. Seeing it through, walking away triumphant. Do you know what comes after?"

Kieran paused, climbing his way onto the pulpit, waiting to see if anyone would answer. They were smarter than that; each realized that no response they could give would be relevant. This was a story, and they didn't know the conclusion. Finally, when he was back at his starting position, Kieran resumed.

"Nothing. Nothing comes after. And I don't just mean there's no looming, dominant objective to rule your life. I mean a sensation of nothingness soon descends. It happens slowly, usually some while after the battle is over and the rewards are reaped. This… emptiness just starts growing inside you. Like something is missing. Something is gone. And then suddenly, everything you've done, everything you've fought for, disappears. When you look back at your life, you're met with only one, inescapable question."

"Was that really me?" Timuscor was crying—not sobbing, nor heaving, nor even seemingly aware of the tears rolling down his cheek. "Why can I remember doing all of these things, but not why I did them, or what I was feeling, or what made it seem so important? Why does the person I was before feel so different from who I am now?"

"And here, at last, I can finally answer your question." Kieran's tone was somber, unexpectedly fitting for their surroundings. "When the quest is done, when the compulsion for adventure fades, we are what is left behind.

Shadows of who we once were, beings with skill and power far beyond that which most could dream of, yet lacking the core of what drove us to acquire them. We are, in essence, echoes of our former selves."

Holding up his hands, Kieran gestured to the large wooden door at the back of the church. "Out there lies Notch. A town whose citizens are almost entirely former adventurers. A city composed of echoes."

8.

As much as Urthos was a land of open plains and wild riders, one did still have to take a few of Alcatham's roads to reach it if they were approaching from the south. On the major avenues, this was a safe prospect, as kingdom guards still regularly patrolled for the sake of safety. Some of the paths were not quite so secure, however. This was a blessing for those wishing to transport goods away from the prying eyes of guards, or attempting to travel without being seen. Of course, this also made such roads a boon for bandits: their targets not only often had wealth, but also wouldn't be able to report the crime if their enterprise was illegal.

Some bandits set up shop and cut off all travel around them, hitting every target they could. It was a valid strategy, yet it came with an immediate disadvantage. The moment word spread, traffic would halt until a squadron of guards were sent to take care of things. Most bandits moved on before the guards arrived, realizing that when the traffic died off, there was no more gold to be made. They'd have to ride until they could set up camp elsewhere, and the cycle repeated.

Tormin was never a fan of that tactic. True, it paid well while it lasted, but the costs of time, travel, and changing locations all quickly mounted up. He'd found, through trial and error, that it was better to let most of the traffic continue unabated. Rumors of bandits on the road should be just that: rumors. For every one account of robbery, let there be nine saying how they crossed without incident. Enough to keep the kingdom hesitant at committing resources and make sure the travelers who used such neglected routes felt it was worth the risk.

In that setup, it was tempting to go for the most tantalizing targets: merchants smuggling forbidden enchantments or outlawed potions. Too few realized what a rookie mistake that was. Merchants had money, which they were more than happy to spend on protection. In his youth, Tormin had seen more than a few older bandits turned to pulp by a formidable knight or wizard paid to protect the cargo. No, merchants were too protected. Tormin liked to liberate his gold from those who thought themselves wily. Too poor to afford protection, so they pretended to have less wealth than they did.

As the sun rose on Tormin's stretch of highway, he saw just such a potential target riding toward their choke point: a small wagon with two priests sitting up front. Disguising one's self as clergy was a common tactic for those hoping to avoid robbery. Aside from having little of value, traveling priests, like all who served the divine, were also closely connected to their gods. It wasn't worth risking divine wrath for a few silver coins and a pair of threadbare robes. Clever an idea as that was, too few who used it paid attention to the details. Today, for instance, Tormin could plainly see that the wagon they were using lacked any church inscriptions or symbols; in fact, it was obviously one of the carts sold near the border of Camnarael. In his line of work, Tormin saw so many carts and horses he could have written a whole tome about them, and the one heading toward him was certainly not the kind of wagon priests would use.

That alone might not have been enough, but there were other factors, too. Lack of identifying symbols, the fact that both were driving and neither had so much as a single holy book out, dozens of tiny indicators that all pointed to a single conclusion: these were not actual priests.

Letting out the call of a sparrow native to the region, with a touch of extra trill so the others knew it was him, Tormin signaled for them to drop the trap. As soon as the wagon passed a predetermined point, a huge log was quickly pulled into their path. Rigging up the pulley system had been a bastard, but it beat trying to block travelers with their horses and bodies. Behind the wagon, a second log was dragged into the narrow road, cutting off any escape.

Normally, this was where Tormin would step out to make demands. Lately, he'd been trying his hand at delegating, so today, Omphel would be giving it a go. Had they been more dangerous enemies, Tormin would have taken over, but the ones who dressed like priests were rarely an issue. Still, Tormin waited near the edge of the trees, blade at the ready in case he needed to step in.

Omphel, a wide man who brandished a sword too heavy for most to wield easily, planted himself in the road, staring down the phony priests. "Well met, travelers. As you can see, there's been an accident in the road today. My friends and I would be more than happy to clear the path, assuming you can afford our services."

On cue, the other bandits crept into view. They stayed spread out; if one of these people was a mage, it wouldn't do to give them a single, clustered target. No, the goal here was to minimize bloodshed on both sides. An unwinnable fight made for more docile victims, which let Tormin finish the job without putting his bandits at risk. Any robbery where everyone walked away alive was a good one in his book.

"Oh my. Such a terrible event. Yet, if it is in our path, then it must be the will of our god." The driver was the one speaking, his gray hood concealing any features beyond the voice. His passenger was dressed identically and would have been impossible to differentiate if they weren't nearly a foot taller than the one holding the reins. "What say you, my fellow clergy? What shall we do?"

From the back of the wagon, two more figures in gray robes slid out onto their feet. Something was off. Tormin could already tell. The voice was all wrong. It wasn't scared, surprised, or even uncertain. They'd either seen this coming, or that man was among the greatest actors alive. Tormin wasn't willing to bet on the latter. Part of him wanted to signal for a full withdrawal. Instead, he waited for a moment longer. Omphel was running the robbery today; he should have noted the curiosities as well. The man deserved a chance to show that he could use discretion when it was demanded.

In spite of his sour expression that always seemed to be spoiling for a fight, Omphel hadn't been given the position of liaison without merit. His forehead creased in distrust; the voice and the way the priests were acting hadn't been lost on him. "My apologies, good men. I took you to be charlatans masquerading as clergy, yet now that I study you more carefully, it becomes clear that you are indeed among the devout. Permit us a moment, and we'll have this road cleared."

"No need for that. What our god has put in our path, we shall see dealt with." The driver held out his hand, and from it came a bolt of dark purple, bordering on black, that struck the tree and left only a handful of ashes and a hole in the road behind.

Omphel swallowed hard, raising his mighty sword while gesturing at the rest of the bandits to run. "That's no priest spell I've ever seen. Who are you people, really?"

"Us? Well, that's something of a hard question to answer." As the driver spoke, the others were circling, taking careful aim at the bandits who'd crept out from the trees. "Much as we all love our god and serve him faithfully, introductions have always seemed to be something of a sticking point."

In that moment, Tormin knew. He was running, trying to get close enough to warn them, but it was already too late. Just before the world erupted into screaming, magic, and death, the driver completed his explanation.

"After all, how is one supposed to handle a formal introduction when they have no name to give?"

*   *   *

"Not every adventurer turns out like us. Most die, as I've stated. But even among the few who finish their quests, not all experience this sensation. Some transition into a role befitting of their skill, or go live on a mountain and train new talents. So far as we've discerned, the key difference seems to be those artifacts. Only those of us who have been exposed to them, or even merely spent time in an area where one was active, ultimately grapple with the sudden absence in our souls."

Kieran paused, looking the group over. They were skeptical, that was to be expected, yet none had hardened their gazes in disbelief. Best to ease them in, anyway. "We can go over why that is a little later; it might be the hardest part of all of this to believe, and I don't want to overwhelm you."

"It's because there's another world out there, influencing ours." Thistle, unlike Kieran, was favoring a more aggressive strategy. Get it all done, put the truth out in the open, and move forward from there. "We don't have all the details by any measure, but we've seen enough to put that much together. Some adventurers are connected to that world. I'm not sure if it's complete control or merely a whisper in the ear. I just know it exists. And I also know that the connection can be severed. It's what happened when we pressed a different piece of the Bridge to Timuscor, and I can only guess that's also what happened to all of you."

On the pulpit, Kieran blinked, the first unplanned reaction he'd shown since they woke up. This was more information than he expected from random trespassers, even ones with a chunk of artifact. Hairs on the back of his neck began to rise as Kieran suspected a whiff of the divine in the air. For the most part, the denizens of Notch and the gods kept out of each other's way. The gods were scary in their own right; however, the collective skill of Notch was high enough that if they had cause, they could easily wreck any given deity's respective plans. Only the most reckless or desperate of gods had ever attempted to play a game with Notch as a component, and Kieran was far from thrilled that another might be trying.

None of that was the fault of these people, of course. They were mere pawns, being led to-and-fro by powers well beyond their comprehension, parts of a system that everyone in town had been a piece of at some point or another. "Well, that takes a load off my mind. Breaking the whole 'our world is inhabited by beings controlled from another plane' speech doesn't ever go over well, and that's if I can even convince them to believe at all."

"If you know more about all of that, we would love to learn," Eric piped up. Not everyone seemed to share his enthusiasm, but none of them vocally shouted down the idea, either.

"One bit at a time. Besides, I doubt we'll be able to offer satisfactory answers. Those artifacts are a mystery that stretches back further than any history we've found. Even if a few people in the world have realized a small extent of what they can do, it's a far cry from knowing where they came from or how they work. Today, let us focus on getting you acclimated to Notch. Eat a meal, have a hot bath, get some non-magical rest. We've all been on the road before; we know how much a body aches for small comforts."

The mere fact that all of them could lay on pews and not think it uncomfortable was a testament to just how numb they'd become in their travels. At even the mention of the word "food," at least two stomachs groaned audibly. Seconds later, Eric shot a panicked look over at Gabrielle.

"Wait. We might still have an issue. Our friend is under a strange curse at the moment, and part of that curse requires her to feed her axe through killing. Last night's hunt was a failure, so depending on how long we were out, she might need sustenance."

"Didn't want to make a fuss, but I do feel a tad sluggish. Guess all those skeletons I bashed in didn't count." Gabrielle didn't appear scared, though that really told them nothing. She'd try to keep a poker face even when staring down a nine-headed hydra; it was just part of who Gabrielle was.

Unlike their knowledge of the Bridge, this revelation wasn't even a hiccup for Kieran. "We didn't know the exact extent of it, but it occurred to us that the undead in your party might have a different way of feeding. Right now, Jolia, a talented wizard who helps out around Notch, is setting up a pen near the edge of town. She can summon up a herd of sheep, living ones, with little effort. If that doesn't work—summons and curses *can* be tricky—then we'll switch to a daily hunting schedule."

He stepped down from the pulpit, the first time they'd actually seen him walk away from it rather than teleporting, and motioned for them to rise. "I think we're about at the end of what talking can convey. From here on, it's better to start showing. Just try to keep in mind one thing: no serious fighting is allowed within Notch. That applies to everyone, you and us, the same. When you're as strong as some of our townsfolk, one real fight could raze the entire village. You don't need to worry about combat, anyway. Outside of a few closely guarded vaults and chambers, this is probably one of the safest places in all of the kingdoms."

Kieran arrived at the back of the church, gripped the handle of each massive wooden door, and flung them open effortlessly. Sunlight poured through, and as the party blinked it away, they were able to make out what lay beyond those doors. Slowly, the shapes came into view, and each member of the party experienced the same procession of curiosity, expectation, and... disappointment.

It was a nice town, just like many others they'd passed through in their travels. Small, compact, apparently hosting a large enough populace to support a tavern with an inn on top and perhaps a couple of general-use shops. If not for the obvious differences in architecture, it could have passed for Maplebark.

"I know it doesn't look like much," Kieran admitted as he waited patiently for the others to join him at the front of the church. "But keep in mind, this is a town founded by people who specialize in fighting, not building. People are what make a village, and I think you'll find ours is quite interesting. Where would you like to start?"

Thistle looked to his friends. While he usually filled the role of leader, that didn't mean he ignored their wishes. It was a brief exchange; every gaze looked back with the same certainty. This didn't need to be talked about or argued over. They were adventurers, in a new town. There was really only one place they could possibly start.

"If you have no objection, Kieran, I think we would like to begin at the tavern."

9.

The tavern was large, with a variety of chairs, tables, and stool sizes they rarely saw outside of Maplebark. Most places defaulted their fixtures to the human/elf size. Anything larger could risk it or stand; anything smaller could climb. Here, there were accommodations for any of the usual races one might see in an adventuring party, as well a few toy-sized ones in a corner with a large sign warning that they were not to be played with.

Standing behind the bar, as somehow always seemed to be the case, was a burly bartender. And yet, common as the sight was, Thistle had to work hard not to reel at the appearance of this man. It was if he was the prototype from which all muscular bartenders had been fashioned. Simple clothes, an earnest smile, and a body so powerful every move seemed as though it should shatter the floor around them. Amazingly, this hulking fellow was as gentle as he was fit, pouring five tankards of ale with smooth grace and setting them down softly in front of his newest customers.

"Please enjoy some of my house special, a way to say, 'Welcome to Notch.'" His voice boomed, as they'd all known it would from the first glance, but the friendly tone made it more tolerable. "I go by Brock these days, and I'll be your landlord, chef, and bartender for the duration of your stay. Probably also boss for at least one of you. Got to do some brewing in the next week or so, and I could use an extra pair of hands."

"We haven't gotten a chance to go over Notch's economy yet," Kieran said, a not-so-concealed thread of annoyance in his voice. With a heavy sigh, he looked over to the group. "Although most of us accrued substantial wealth in our travels, we have limited trading with the outside world, so coins don't have as much value here. We're more work-driven. Doing a few hours of labor each day will be enough to cover your food and lodging, if you opt to stay for a while. On that note, Brock, why don't you get them squared away with their rooms. I'll go check on Jolia's progress with the pen, and we can give them space to talk. I imagine, after everything that's been thrown their way, they'd like some time to discuss and mull it over."

"That would be lovely." Thistle took a cautious drink of the ale. His smaller body meant that potent drinks could hit him harder than the others, but he found this brew to be overall acceptable. Not the best he'd ever had, certainly, but as Kieran had reminded them, everyone here was first and foremost specialized in combat.

The others followed Thistle's lead while Brock rummaged around beneath the counter before coming up with a box of keys. "Been a while since we had to use these. Now, I've got one room that comes with a window pointing directly east, meaning the occupant gets a face-full of sunrise every morning. Who among you is the earliest riser?"

All heads turned to Gabrielle, who no longer needed sleep, thanks to her condition. With some mumbling and a "Thanks, assholes," Gabrielle reached out and took the first key from Brock. It was heavier than it should have been and slightly cool to the touch. When she examined it closely, she saw that there were small runes etched along the length of the key.

"Jolia wanted some fancy whiskey a few years ago, so I had her enchant the keys as a trade. Can't be lost or stolen, plus using it on the inside of the door creates a potent barrier to block out intruders. I know I could never sleep well unless I was somewhere properly fortified, and I expected my guests might feel the same."

Gabrielle turned the key over a few times in her hand, thinking back on the flimsy inns where they'd stayed before, often so poorly secured that they still slept in guard shifts. Maybe there was something to be said for a town built by former adventurers.

*   *   *

The nest of a golden roc was, for very obvious reasons, not near any of the main kingdom roads. Had it been, Alcatham would have placed a bounty on the birds long ago to clear them away, allowing adventurers to hurl themselves at the problem until they either solved it properly or just drove the pests off by sheer force of numbers. No, the golden roc nest was in a section of mountains to the northwest, which meant taking one of the lesser-used roads.

Bandits were a potential risk, so the party traveled in a careful formation. Timanuel the paladin was up front, ready to take on any challengers while also giving careful attention to any potential sensation of approaching evil. Behind him was Chalara the sorceress, in a position where she could be shielded from assault, yet could still hurl spells at anyone who dared try to stop them. Wimberly came next, a few gadgets within easy reach, should they be required. Bringing up the rear was Gelthorn. As the only other melee combatant and easily the member with the best senses, she was tasked with watching their rear and listening for any potential surprises.

Most of their morning's journey had been achingly dull, so boring it was tempting to let their guard down. That lasted exactly until they crested an upward slope and looked out onto a flat section of road. It was a long stretch; their proximity to the plains was starting to show itself in the geography. Farther away, they could make out something in their path. Smoke was rising from it, though it was thin and dissipated quickly in the air. Not a forest fire, then. The majority of it seemed to be on the sides of the road, leaving the middle clear. Still, everyone drew their weapons. This was exactly the sort of potential ambush they'd been keeping an eye out for. Hopefully, any bandits would see a prepared, armed party and decide to go for easier pickings.

As they rode closer, more of the grisly scene came into view. A pair of logs across the road, the middles of which had been turned to cinder. Odd purple flames still smoldered on the remaining edges, slowly burning them away and sending the thin tendrils of smoke into the air. Worse, by far, was what they saw when they drew nearer to the bodies.

A dozen people, at least, were strewn across the area. Some had been burned, others sliced, and a few had chunks that simply appeared to be missing, like they'd been neatly removed. It was a massacre, and once the smell hit, every member of the party had to force themselves not to leave their last meal on the grass. Horrifying as the sight was, it was the rustling of a nearby bush that brought the party to a stop. Weapons were held at the ready, and Chalara had a spell on her lips, ready to cast as soon as a target stepped into view.

What emerged was not the first wave of an ambush, though, unless it was the most bizarre ambush in all of history. A lone man stepped out into the road, dragging a makeshift stretcher behind him. There was a hollowness in his eyes; he barely appeared to see the world as he moved through it. He didn't even react to the party. Instead, he took the nearest body and carefully, lovingly, loaded it onto his stretcher. As they looked closer, a few noted that this man's arms were coated with dirt, the telltale sign of someone who'd been doing extensive digging.

"Hail, traveler." Timanuel kept his words gentle, and made sure his symbol of the god Longinus was prominently displayed. The last thing they wanted was for this poor man to think he was under attack once more. A paladin of Longinus wasn't a threat to those who kept the law, especially a man so clearly grieving a loss.

For the first time, the stranger turned his head toward them. Looking over each in turn, his dead eyes took in the details with no sign of either interest or care. It was only when he saw Timanuel that any reaction came; a dark snarl of a laugh clawed its way out of his chest. "A paladin. Truly, the gods are cruel monsters, aren't they? Putting a paladin in my path mere hours after—" A sob racked his body, short and furious. "Well played, you heartless divine monsters. You've done the impossible. You've made old Tormin glad to see a paladin. Was it worth it, for something that unexpected?"

The man, presumably Tormin, grasped his chest as another sob racked him. He twisted his eyes upward as he hissed through his teeth. *"Was it fucking worth all these lives?"*

"Sir, we can clearly see that you've endured a terrible trauma, and we will do all we can to help. Please, if you can, tell us what happened here. We understand if you need time to compose yourself."

"Compose myself? I don't think I'm ever going to be composed again. I don't think I'm ever going to be anything again, besides this." Tormin shook his head, staring at the corpses littering the road. "Save your compassion, paladin. They were bandits, every last one of them. Me as well, if you'd like to haul me before a court. Good men, faithful and earnest, with dreams. Some even had families. But they're bandits, so there's no justice to be had. Even if there was, you're not the one to give it. What did this is beyond you, beyond all of you. Maybe even beyond the kingdom as a whole. Four men did this. Four men with no names, and no mercy in their souls."

Searching his mind, Timanuel felt a flood of information pouring in as, in another world, a boy named Tim rolled a high number. "No names must mean priests of Kalzidar. Strange. As I knew it, they usually work alone. Not much trust among those, even for each other."

"Apparently this group found a way to work together. They are death incarnate, and woe to whoever crosses their path. They saw me, you know. I got here just as they were finishing up; the whole thing was over in seconds. They saw me, and I saw them, and they just left. Got back in their cart and kept riding north. I think they knew this was worse than killing me. Dying with my men, I was ready for that. Every bandit has to be. Burying them all, being the only one left—it might be the most brilliant torture I can conceive of."

A loud *clang* filled the air as Timanuel dismounted his horse, his armor rattling with every step. It was so distracting that Tormin looked up from the bodies, eyes narrowing at the sight. "Taking me up on that court offer, I see. Suppose I could ask you to wait long enough that I can bury my men? Or..." Tormin's voice thickened, and he stopped to cough. "Or at least to let me drag them from the road?"

"I haven't seen you commit any crimes, and I do not sense true evil here. Whatever wicked deeds you may have done, it seems impossible to me that any punishment could be worse than what you've endured today," Timanuel replied.

"They why did you dismount?"

"Because there are more bodies to bury, and many hands make for lighter work." Timanuel didn't even have to turn toward the others; he could already hear them following his lead as they climbed off their horses.

Tormin, for the first time since they'd met, had something other than pure, unfettered pain in his expression. Uncertainty, leaning toward distrust yet not quite there. "Perhaps you didn't hear me, paladin. These men were bandits, the kind of people you'd raise your sword against."

"I heard you. I also heard you say that they were faithful, with dreams and families of their own. A paladin may judge actions, even lives, in pursuit of our duties, but only the gods can weigh a soul. Whoever these men were, they are in the care of higher hands than ours. Their bodies carry no inherent sin, and I can see no reason why Longinus would object to giving them a proper burial."

"And what if he does?" Tormin prodded.

"Then he's not the god I thought he was. But perhaps theological discussions are better saved for when the task is done." Kneeling, Timanuel gently lifted a burned corpse into his arms, sending a cascade of ashes down his gleaming armor. "Until then, please, show us to the grave."

*   *   *

Some distance farther up the road, a wagon pulled by a pair of horses trundled along. Only the driver and passenger were visible again, features concealed by the low-hanging hoods on their robes. The few other travelers they passed took little note of them. In fact, most forgot they'd passed the wagon within a minute of it fading from their sight. That was no coincidence; one of the members in the back continually refreshed their enchantment to pass unnoticed.

Worshipping Kalzidar opened the doors to many magics. Unlike most priests, their combined repertoire of spells was closer to that of a wizard or sorcerer. To seek Kalzidar was to seek power, and the god upheld his end of the bargain for those who were faithful. Each worshipper unlocked their own kind of magic when they were accepted into his service. For some, it was based in destruction. Others, manipulation. Others still, precision. There were many who shared similar, if not identical, abilities, yet each gift was always a perfect fit for the recipient. This was one of the reasons priests of Kalzidar had no names. Any priest could possess any power, and without names to track, an opponent could never be entirely sure what they were up against. The world tilted in favor of the good, which meant evil had to be all the more cunning to endure.

As the oldest of the group, the driver was ostensibly in charge, although truly their directives came from Kalzidar himself. No other force could convince four of his priests to work in unison. Trust was not strong among Kalzidar's servants, likely because some believed that to kill another priest was to prove their superiority and would therefore gain them more of Kalzidar's favor. In the driver's experience, their god's reaction depended largely on how capable the murdered priest had been at their job. Dispatching incompetence was occasionally rewarded, but killing the useful risked earning his ire. Still, the rumor persisted, so he was often forced to strike first, before another priest could attempt to bring him down.

Yes, only Kalzidar himself could have convinced these individual priests to function as a unit. Even that might not have been enough on its own for some. It was their task that truly drove home the importance that teamwork would play. Priests of Kalzidar had ample power, yet even they were limited. There were some tasks that one priest alone could never accomplish.

Four, on the other hand, might just have a chance. The driver urged the horses on, eager to cover as much ground as possible before night descended. They still had a ways to go before they reached their target.

And once they arrived, there would be no rest for the wicked.

10.

"Our trip has certainly taken quite the detour."

Those were the first words said as they all piled into the room together. Timuscor locked the door behind them, and then sat down with his back against the wood, just in case someone tried to burst through. It was a fine habit to have, albeit not entirely necessary in this particular environment. The room they were in, where Eric would be staying, was spacious and well-cared for, with a door that looked sturdy enough to slow an angry Gabrielle.

Originally, they'd tried to gather in Thistle's room, only to discover an unexpected issue. While Thistle's room was as large as any other, the furniture and design was only accommodating to a gnome-sized person. Even the doorknob was low enough for him to easily reach. This was the first time any of them had seen such a place, save for Thistle, and even he hadn't looked upon a room entirely planned for gnomes since he'd left his hometown. The real question burning in Thistle's mind was whether the room was always structured like this, or if it had magically re-sized when a gnome took hold of its key.

It was a moot point, or one only worthy of consideration after far more pressing issues were dealt with. Thistle's words, obscene level of understatement and all, were spot on. In what felt like barely an hour, thanks to their time spent in unconsciousness, they'd fought an army of undead, thought themselves as good as killed, only to have woken up in a hidden town filled with former adventurers. When they'd last set out from camp, there was no way they could have envisioned such a change to their plans. That didn't mean it was poor fortune that had brought them here, only that it was unanticipated.

"Let's get the biggest issue out of the way first," Eric suggested. "Do we trust these people? At least enough to believe the story they've told us is true? If we don't, then there's not much value in further discussion beyond how we should escape."

Gabrielle snorted under her breath. "I really hope that if they were lying, they'd have come up with something more believable. A town of former adventurers, most of whom are strong enough to kill us all single-handedly? That's too tough a sell, if it's not the truth."

"Aye, my instincts align with Gabrielle's. Even when fighting the undead, I never felt the tinge of true evil around us, only that facsimile. Add in the fact that they not only knew what the Bridge was on sight, but were also smart enough to be wary of it, and the story holds together well. Perhaps, however, we should turn to another for insight." Thistle looked toward Timuscor, who was scratching behind Mr. Peppers' ears as they both blocked the door. "If any of us were to sense a lie in their words, I suspect it would be you."

The ear-scratching continued for several long seconds as Timuscor stared off into the air, peering at a scene in his mind that no one else was privy to. "I can't attest to their honesty about everything; I don't read people as well as most of you. I just know that they were telling the truth about *us*. Me and them, I mean. Echoes. They knew the pain exactly, and when I look into their eyes... I don't think I could identify another of us on sight, but I can almost grasp how they knew it in me. There's an emptiness; maybe the kind you can only see if you've also felt its pain. On that account, at least, they're telling the truth."

"Agreed." Grumph kept his contribution short and simple. There was so much to talk over; he saw little point in dragging this point out.

"More or less lines up with my own impressions, so it seems we're in agreement on at least that point." Eric looked a tad relieved. No doubt he, like most of them, was trying to imagine how in the hells they would escape a town full of people whose power dwarfed their own. "Which brings us to the next issue: what do we want to do? If we're not prisoners, then we can leave, probably with an enchantment or two to keep us silent, though I doubt any of us planned on spreading this rumor, anyway. We could be back on the road to Lumal by the next sunrise."

His words were met with uncertainty, shifting gazes, and half-mumbled words of response. Gabrielle was the one to finally speak up, as she was the most comfortable in trusting her instincts. "Or we could stay. Not for the rest of our lives, but for a couple of days. We do need a rest; it's been a long trip from Camnarael. Besides, we were going to Lumal to look for answers, weren't we? Well, in just the time we've been here, we've met a mage who specializes in the undead and a swordsman who sure acted like he knew an awful lot about the Bridge. If all the people here really are former adventurers, then there's got to be some useful information to uncover."

"If they talk," Grumph reminded her. "Not everyone is eager to share knowledge."

"A valid point, old friend, yet I find myself on Gabrielle's side. The only way to find out what they're willing to share is to stick around long enough to ask." Thistle pulled out a map from his bag, spreading it out across the wooden floor.

His fingers, one of the few un-gnarled parts of his body, traced along the rough routes painted on the parchment. "We were only a short ride from the Lumal entrance when we took this detour. If we stick around for about three days, it would be long enough to fully rest ourselves and the horses, while also getting a general lay of the town. At the end of that time, assuming that we have uncovered nothing useful, we can then take back to the road and finish our journey feeling refreshed. On the other hand, should we discover that we're here for a reason, we can reassess the duration of our stay. It's not as though we have a pressing appointment in Lumal. We could stay here for a full year and the City of Knowledge would still be waiting for us."

"We should also resupply." Grumph wasn't entirely sure he was on board with this town and its curious inhabitants, but he'd been alongside Thistle long enough to see where the gnome's preference lay. While he might have debated the point if Grumph had possessed a solid counterargument, the truth was that he knew his reservations were simply his own natural wariness manifesting. Maybe this place was on the up and up. Maybe it wasn't. But if it turned out to be the latter, he wasn't going to get caught by surprise.

"Given the isolated nature of the town and their unique form of economy, I'm not sure we'll be able to fully restock our reserves, but I bet we can scrounge up something," Eric said.

There was a heavy thud of movement as Gabrielle pulled herself up from the floor. All eyes naturally turned to her, silently awaiting an explanation.

"Whatever else you all decide, we're agreed that we'll spend the next few days here, right?"

"Aye, that appears to be the general consensus."

Gently, Gabrielle reached around and patted the axe currently strapped to her back. "Then I should go figure out whether or not those sheep summons will feed the axe. You can brief me on the rest when I get back, but that's something I'd like to get sorted as soon as possible."

"Not alone." Eric hopped up, his lack of a cumbersome weapon and general spryness making the affair go much faster. He held up a hand before Gabrielle could speak. "I already know you're a better fighter than me. That's not the point. We don't have much information on this place or these people yet, so we should all stick together whenever possible. It's nice that we don't think they'll kill us, but let's not trust that completely just yet."

"I wasn't going to object. I like having company." A mischievous smile burst onto Gabrielle's pale face. "But thanks for admitting I'm better. Going to hold that one over you for a long while to come."

"I meant better for now. Don't think for a second that I'm not planning to catch up," Eric shot back.

Thistle cleared his throat, bringing their attention back to the room as a whole. "Assessing Gabrielle's condition and how we'll treat it is a good first priority. And Eric is correct; we should take minimal risks until we fully understand our situation. We move in units of at least two when not at the tavern. You both go ahead and see how killing the sheep goes; we'll remain behind and try to decide what comes after that."

"If it's okay, I'd like to go with them," Timuscor said. "My contributions to planning are non-essential, and I want to see more of this strange town."

Before Thistle had a chance to respond, Grumph nodded. "Good idea. Take your time; get the lay of the area. We'll meet back for dinner." Given the bond Timuscor shared with the people of this town, there was a chance Thistle might have prioritized caution and kept Timuscor from exploring until they knew the area better. Grumph understood what it was like to feel lost in the world, though. The fact that Timuscor hadn't gone bursting through the door already was a testament to his loyalty and discipline, but the man plainly wanted to go learn more. Besides, if anyone in this town was going to talk openly with a member of the party, it would be Timuscor. They saw him as one of their own, even if Grumph didn't fully grasp the distinction between him and the rest of the party yet.

"Dinner is a sound idea. Enough time for us to ponder and for you all to explore. Just keep to the town proper. We don't want to accidentally trip any more of their wards or security," Thistle cautioned.

"Somehow, I think we'll manage to amuse ourselves in a town full of weirdly powerful people with thrilling pasts." With that, Gabrielle helped Timuscor up, yanking him to his feet and clearing the door. Since this was technically Eric's room, everyone left together, Eric pausing only to lock the door behind them. Thistle and Grumph adjourned to Grumph's room, while the others headed for the stairs.

As the group separated, both halves silently hoped that this town truly was what it seemed. If not, given the power level in play, this might very well be the last time they all saw each other alive.

*   *   *

"What do we think of them?" Kieran asked the question, despite the fact that he'd been the one to spend the most time around the new party. Simone was in second place on that score, although it was hard for her to give measured judgment, given the context of their interactions.

Jolia was looking into a crystal ball hovering just below eye-level. "Now that we've gotten them away from the artifact, it's much easier to check them properly. From what my spells can determine, no enchantments are in place to shield their appearance or natures. The whole church is enchanted with Truth Compulsion, so if they'd lied, you'd have known it. A few among their number have wisps of divine magic coming off them; however, none appears to be evil in nature."

"That many showing evidence of interacting with the divine is troubling in itself. A paladin is one thing. Rogues are another matter. These people have gotten up close and personal with at least one god, and that in itself should worry us." Simone, given her specialty and history, wasn't inclined to trust those who worked for the gods; a suspicion that applied doubly so to the gods themselves.

She had a point, but Kieran wasn't sure if that should count as a strike against the party. The gods treated mortals like assets at best and playthings at worst, so it was something of a stretch to assume these five had any say in whatever path their god was shoving them down. Kieran would have liked Brock's input, rough though it would have been; however, he was stuck at the inn, keeping tabs on their guests.

"Something else worth noting: one of them has got some sort of divine-shielding enchantment in effect. I mean, wow, this is actually amazing craftsmanship. Such a smooth build, like the spell grew into shape naturally. It sort of blends their presence with the flow of mana. I almost wasn't able to catch it, and I'm scrying specifically for things like that. One of them really doesn't want to be seen by any gods." Jolia leaned in closer, eyes narrowing, a small bit of tongue poking through the side of her mouth as she focused. "Oh, slippery little thing, trying to hide the target of your protection, but I'm going to find… hang on, what?"

Leaning back, Jolia's nose pinched as a rare expression of frustration made its way onto her face. As a master wizard and brilliant researcher, it had been a very long time since she had found herself lacking on a task. Yet, from the evidence before her, there was no other reasonable conclusion to be reached.

"Much as I can't believe I'm saying this, it looks like I'll have to wait a minute and take another crack at untangling that enchantment. Some part of it is concealing the target, misdirecting all my efforts so it looks like the boar is the one being hidden from the gods."

"Any chance that's actually the case?" Simone asked.

"I suppose, in the sense that anything is possible, it could be true. But if so, that raises so many more questions than I can even imagine the answers to." Jolia's nose was still pinched as she wearily shook her head. "No, it's got to be one of the others. Give me some time. I'll crack it."

Damning though that seemed, the mere fact that the enchantment was both divine and strong enough to withstand Jolia's scrutiny meant that it likely hadn't come from any of the adventurers. Simone had made them genuinely afraid for their lives; if they'd had that kind of power, they would have used it. Nothing like putting someone in a life-or-death situation to get a firm assessment of their capabilities.

Kieran decided not to waste time dwelling on the detail. "Obviously, none of them have the power to pull that kind of spell off, and even if they had, it's not like some of our own citizens don't appreciate privacy from the prying eyes of the divine. We'll set the matter aside until Jolia can determine more about its true nature. For now, we simply have to decide if we think these people are really who they claim to be. Someone sent them our way. The question is whether they're accomplices or pawns."

"I think pawns," Simone told them. "They weren't expecting a fight when I surprised them. They really seemed to think they were just exploring a hidden trail. And Timuscor didn't even know what he was. If they were in on whatever it is that brought them here, then I presume he'd have gotten some warning."

Though she was still glaring at the crystal ball, Jolia's expression softened slightly. "Agreed. Either they're the greatest deceivers ever assembled, or they really walked into Notch with no idea what to expect."

"Unfortunately, I'm with both of you on that," Kieran admitted.

Simone's brow creased in confusion. "Unfortunately?"

"Very much so. If we thought they had any idea of why they were here, we could extract that information from them. Them not knowing makes it more difficult for us to figure out the reasoning, and I hate that. Because if it turns out they're unwittingly serving an agenda that conflicts with our own, we may have to stop them. I'd rather know that at the outset, so no one gets too attached."

"Even if that happens, they could prove to be reasonable," Jolia said.

To her surprise, that drew a slightly nostalgic gleam to Kieran's eye. "A nice idea, but remember, they're still adventurers. When did an adventurer ever take the reasonable option?"

11.

By the time Gabrielle, Eric, and Timuscor arrived at the pen, Jolia was waiting. To their surprise, Simone was with her, looking just as pale and imposing as she had in the woods. Her appearance hadn't been some affectation to fill them with fear, then. It was just the way Simone liked to present herself. In the bright sunshine of a proper day, however, she looked less outright terrifying and more like aristocracy slumming among the masses. Her expression was neutral as they approached, making it a sharp contrast to the cheerful grin Jolia was sporting.

"Told you so. First thing a party with sense secures is always food and shelter." Jolia nudged Simone in the ribs before turning to the approaching trio. "She didn't think you'd show up until the day was nearly done."

"I presumed they might spend more time fully discussing and considering their situation," Simone said, a shard of defensiveness in her tone.

"We left the thinkers to the thinking. I'm more on Team Doing." Gabrielle reached back and took hold of her axe, giving it a firm tug that failed to so much as budge the weapon from its sheath.

Shuffling forward, Jolia raised her hands and whispered a few words. There was a *click* from Gabrielle's back, and then her arm came forward holding the axe. Spell done, the gnome hopped back quickly. "Aside from our obvious curiosity to see whether or not this works, we came out to unlock the weapon so the test could proceed. When this is done, we're going to re-seal that axe. I realize this is going to make your feedings inconvenient, but I'm afraid we can't let you all walk around Notch while armed. *Especially* not with an implement that hosts such a potent anti-magic property. If you cut the wrong ward or enchantment around here, you could cause serious trouble."

Hardly an ideal situation, and it certainly hadn't slipped Gabrielle's attention that while her group had been largely disarmed, the rest of the town had no qualms walking around with weapons on display. Even Simone was still holding her dark staff as she waited on the sidelines. Bothersome as it was, Gabrielle also couldn't help noticing that they seemed to know quite a bit about her axe's powers—more than Gabrielle had when she first acquired it. If they could uncover all of that in only a day, perhaps with more time she might be able to get some real answers about this weapon, and her condition.

But that meant playing nice, so Gabrielle didn't object to stowing her axe when the testing was done.

She moved forward, hopping over the wooden fence of the pen. Sheep were crammed into the space, ten at a glance, possibly more, if she'd taken the time to count. Steadying her grip, Gabrielle set her sights on the nearest one.

It stood there, bleating, seemingly unaware of the killer that had just stepped into its pen. The kill would be easy, virtually effortless, yet Gabrielle didn't move quite yet. Something about this felt… wrong. She had killed before—demons, monsters, even humans. She'd hunted as well, even more so now that they lived largely on the road. Never like this, though. It was always done out of need, to feed or protect her party from those who sought to do them harm.

"Don't worry. They're just summons. In an hour, they won't be here, anyway," Jolia called from the sidelines, trying to ease her obvious hesitation.

The reminder should have been helpful, but Gabrielle couldn't help glancing at Mr. Peppers. Maybe most summons were nothing more than mana shaped into flesh, but at least one had possessed the potential to be more. Who was she to say one of these sheep couldn't be the same?

Closing her eyes, Gabrielle blocked out the sound of bleating. This wasn't killing for the sake of killing. She had to keep that in mind. This was hunting, gathering food for survival. She'd eaten meat all her life, and when she was with the goblins, Gabrielle had even helped them trap and clean on occasion. What was happening here was simply a hunt for food. Even if the situation had been warped and distorted, that was what lay at its core. This wasn't cruelty, or bloodlust, or any of the other things she'd been waiting to feel creep through her mind since the change.

That had been her greatest fear since the shock of her new situation had worn off. Would she turn? Would being this new thing draw her into darkness? Undead were commonly thought of as inherently evil, and while she'd seen enough at Briarwillow to know that wasn't always true, part of her couldn't help but think that the association had to come from somewhere. In spite of the brave face she put on, Gabrielle was terrified of what she might become, and the kinds of things she could do to her friends if the change came suddenly.

She didn't want to kill these sheep, and so far as Gabrielle could tell, that was probably the best indicator she could get that no secret evil was influencing her thoughts. There was no glory in this. It was like a bowel movement: done out of pure necessity.

Whipping her axe around, Gabrielle took the head of the nearest sheep clean off. The least she could do was keep any of them from suffering. A sliver of warmth ran through the shaft of the axe; Gabrielle knew that feeling well. It had gotten something from the sheep. Not a lot, but something.

"Interesting. Since the creatures are technically flesh, the axe seems to absorb a small part of the damage back into it; however, their shaped-mana nature creates a diminished output." At some point while Gabrielle was making peace with her task, Jolia had donned a pair of oversized spectacles with glowing green runes running down the sides. "Today, we can make it up in volume. I'll tweak my summoning spell tonight and see if there's not a way to alter the summons so they have a more substantial presence."

"I have to kill all these sheep, don't I?" Somehow, Gabrielle had suspected it would end this way the moment she arrived.

"And probably another batch after," Jolia confirmed. "On the bright side, you're halfway competent with that thing, so it shouldn't take you long."

With a tired, resigned sigh, Gabrielle raised her axe once more. A thought struck her, and silly as it was, she couldn't banish the idea from her head. "Timuscor, turn Mr. Peppers around. I'd rather him not see me doing this."

Her request earned some confused glances from Simone and Jolia, but Timuscor complied without question. He, at least, understood where her head was. With Mr. Peppers now staring back into town, Gabrielle began to cut through the sheep.

They vanished as soon as they died, which was a very real mercy. If the bodies had lingered, she wasn't sure she could have finished the job, both because the corpses would haunt her and because the ground would soon be slick with blood. Summons meant never having to deal with cleanup, thankfully, so Gabrielle whirled through the ordeal, killing the final sheep less than a minute after her culling had begun.

No question about it now. The axe was definitely getting something from these attacks. Gabrielle already felt better, livelier than she had stepping into the pen. Unfortunately, Jolia's estimates were right. She wasn't back to full strength yet. In other circumstances, she might have risked working on a half-full metaphysical stomach, but this was not the place to take stupid chances. They were in a place with no confirmed allies and powerful potential enemies around every turn. If she had a chance to feed, Gabrielle was going to use it to the fullest.

Even if she was pretty sure she'd never be able to eat mutton again.

*   *   *

When the others left, there was little actual discussion to have. Thistle and Grumph went over a few worst-case scenarios, laying out possible contingencies and signals for if they felt an attack was imminent, but the truth was that they simply had too little to work with for anything thorough. The town was unknown, and so far, all they'd learned about the population was that it was supposedly small and disproportionately strong. They had been flying blind since the ambush in the forest, and all the talk in the world wouldn't change that.

So, with the others heading back to the same location they'd already seen, Grumph and Thistle decided to explore the rest of Notch. Brock nodded to them as they made their exit, and they returned the greeting casually, both waiting to see if he'd leap across the bar and stop them from leaving. The burly bartender made no such moves, and seconds later they stepped out into the early afternoon sunshine.

Looking around, Notch didn't seem especially different from any other village they'd been to. Even back in his pre-adventuring days, Thistle had ridden through untold towns like this one. He'd always thought them simple and pleasant, a nice place to spend one's remaining days. That was why he'd settled in Maplebark, when the opportunity arose. Well, that, and Madroria had fallen in love with the village on sight. Thistle had accomplished many great tasks in his life and conquered more challenges than most would expect from looking at him, but never had he possessed anything near the strength it would have required to deny his wife's ambitions. Nor would he have wanted to.

Thistle blinked, wiping away the unexpected sheen of tears that had appeared in his eyes. He had no shame about missing his wife, especially in the company of Grumph; however, this afternoon demanded that his vision stay clear. What they saw, the details they noticed, might prove pivotal in the days to come. Duty came first, and his was to keep the party safe. Thistle wasn't the kind of paladin who could storm onto a battlefield and slay every enemy in sight. His best weapons were forethought and research. And it was time to get started on the latter.

Exploring Notch's town center was a relatively brief affair. Whatever else Kieran might have said, his claims about the population were bearing out to be true. Brock's tavern could, if people were willing to stand, comfortably accommodate the entirety of the fifty people who purportedly lived there. That didn't seem to be a coincidence. No structure was larger than the tavern, not that there were even many contenders. Notch was absent a town hall, or any manner of official gathering place, which made sense for a village with no mayor or formal ruling body beyond the town council. The tavern probably worked as a makeshift communal meeting place when the need arose, with the bonus of available refreshments.

Outside of the tavern and the church, Notch boasted shops owned by a blacksmith, an alchemist, and an enchanter, as well as a storefront bearing a staff and a wand, and a vacant trader station with a note saying that the next showing would be in a week's time. None of the establishments they visited were open, however. Each was marked by some manner of sign that either indicated the owner was off fishing, eating, or engaged in another form of amusement.

This much, at least, was familiar to Thistle and Grumph. In a village this small, there was little sense in minding a shop all day. If someone needed to make a purchase, they would simply find the owner and have them open up. When everyone was on a first-name basis, it was the most efficient way to run a business. The only exceptions were when adventurers came through town and, of course, the tavern owner. One never knew when thirsty townsfolk would come wandering in for a drink.

Beyond the shops, they found little else in Notch's core. A few houses were set up along the edge of the area, but most of the residents seemed to prefer more space. Judging purely by the number of roads leading away from town and the large estates visible at a distance, Thistle guessed there were no fewer than five homes he would have called mansions within walking distance. Others, who came from higher up the social ladder, might not have viewed the houses in such grandiose terms, yet it remained undeniable that they were far nicer than what an average peasant could ever dream of inhabiting.

All of which served to back up Kieran's description of the town. Thistle had already begun to experience the difference in gold accumulation between adventurers and everyone else. In his old life, a single gold coin was substantial income, enough to make a real difference in someone's life if budgeted correctly. Back in Camnarael, they'd all traded thousands of those coins for single items, barely giving it more than a passing thought. How much wealth would those like Kieran and Simone have gathered before they retired? It was hard to say, but surely they had saved more than enough to finance these sorts of accommodations.

The sprawling nature of the housing also told them something else of value: Notch, in its entirety, was much larger than just the town center. To accommodate the plot sizes, it would have to go on for a couple of miles, Grumph estimated, at minimum. This wasn't just some small patch of land locked tightly under some makeshift wards. It was a civilization that had been sealed away from the world, hidden so well that seemingly no one knew about it. Thistle prided himself on keeping an ear to the ground for gossip and information, both of which flowed freely between minions, but he'd never gotten so much as a whisper about this place.

By the end of the day, as they headed back to the tavern to meet for dinner, Thistle was feeling slightly better about their situation. It hadn't actually improved—in fact, his research had only served to confirm just how deep in the thick of it they really were—but Thistle always preferred having some knowledge to being completely in the dark. After their examination, they didn't learn much about the people who lived here; however, they were able to come to a very important conclusion.

Either this was the greatest con ever employed on anyone, going to such severe lengths it over-stepped into madness, or Kieran had been telling them the truth about Notch. The former was possible, if not viable, but more and more, with every detail they learned, the latter appeared to be the clear-cut truth. That presented them with some interesting opportunities, as well as some very real dangers. For Thistle, the most relevant point was that, if Notch really was what Kieran claimed, then it raised at least one burning question, a riddle he knew he would have to solve before they could leave.

If Grumble had put them on the path to find this village, then what were they supposed to find here? And if it had been some other deity who had led them down this road, then whose game were they now being used as pawns in?

Until he knew the god that made this happen, Thistle couldn't trust anything about Notch. Fortunately, there was some recourse for that. When dinner was over, Thistle would do one of the things paladins did best.

It was time to pray.

12.

Timuscor couldn't sleep. The bed was soft, the night soundless, his door secured, yet he was unable to drift off. Every time he closed his eyes, the questions came flooding forth. What was he? What had he been before? Was he the same person as the man he'd been prior to touching the Bridge? Before today, when he was the only one, it had been easy to shove those thoughts aside. Getting hit by an incredibly powerful blast from a magical artifact was an idea he could wrap his head around. If his memory was a little blurry, if he didn't feel quite like himself, if something seemed different, well, wasn't that to be expected after such an encounter? He should just be happy to not have ended up a frog or a statue.

Notch killed all such delusions. True, the Bridge was still part of it, but there was so much more. There were others out there like him, people with the same piece missing, people who had faced the same questions. This wasn't something he could write off as a side effect of potent magic any longer. It was a condition, one that others had faced and apparently worked through.

Rising from his bed, Timuscor found Mr. Peppers awake and waiting. Brock hadn't objected to lodging the boar in Timuscor's room; he'd barely even registered the question when it was asked. Evidently, Notch's citizens had enough quirks that keeping an unusual pet didn't raise so much as an eyebrow. Timuscor was grateful for the company; he reached down and scratched his friend's head. It was easier to lean over without his armor, but Timuscor still wished they'd been permitted to keep their gear. Being exposed like this made him feel uneasy. In armor, Timuscor knew who he was: the knight, the tank, the front wall that enemies would have to fight past if they wanted to get at his allies.

Here, with no armor, no weapons, and no enemies to fight, Timuscor found himself adrift. Even in the party's peaceful times, there had always been some looming threat to occupy his concerns: a Grand Quest they knew nothing about, a secret evil and missing citizens, a series of assaults upon minions to hinder. Tonight was different. They had so little information that he had nothing specific to focus on, turning the worry into a general kind of anxiety that let those damned inner questions rise to the forefront of his mind.

Perhaps what was needed was chemical assistance. Since he would still be inside, going back down to the tavern didn't really invalidate their agreement to stick together. Plus, he would have Mr. Peppers at his side. A tall glass of mead might be just the thing to quell those rebellious thoughts and permit him to rest.

After quickly redressing—a process made far faster by the lack of armor—Timuscor took Mr. Peppers down the stairs and into the tavern. The tables sat completely empty. It was, after all, a village. People had things to do in the morning; they weren't adventurers drinking their nights away in frivolity. The sole other person present was Brock, who set a glass of dark liquid down on the bar as soon as Timuscor stepped off the stairs.

"Had a feeling you'd be down eventually. We all had trouble sleeping when we first started to understand that we were changed. Different. Makes it hard to figure out who you were, who you are, and where the lines between them are etched."

Timuscor took a small sip from the glass, surprised at the wonder that awaited him. This was worlds better than the mead Brock had served during the evening meal—a strong, potent liquor with a flavor that lingered on the tongue. He tilted his head, implying the question even as he went back for a second taste.

"Something special I picked up from a trader that comes through every now and then. In fact, she's due fairly soon. Much as we like to stay secret, trusting a couple of people makes it much easier to get things from the outside world. I save that one for moments too weighty to trust to ale." Brock produced the bottle from under the bar, as well as another glass. After pouring himself a serving, he topped off Timuscor. "So, what do you want to ask?"

The shortest, truest answer was "Everything." There was so much he didn't fully understand, so many mysteries surrounding his life. Brock wouldn't be able to give him all of that, sadly. He was just one person, with his own life and uncertainties. At most, he'd be able to offer some insight. Timuscor decided that it was best to start broad, then narrow things down as his understanding grew.

"You've talked about adventurers, and you refer to echoes as former adventurers, but I'm still questing. I haven't given up the old life, only who I spend my days with. My question is, what's the line between normal adventurers and echoes? Can I be both, or I am missing some piece of this puzzle?"

"Brace yourself for a rare bit of good news: you *can* be both," Brock assured him. "Not all adventurers become echoes, but all echoes *were* adventurers at some point. Some quit when they realize what's changed. Some leave the life without knowing why, their passion for it having just vanished. Others keep going. They find a new reason to fight, to quest, to live that perilous lifestyle. An end to adventuring isn't what makes an echo."

Without meaning to, Timuscor leaned forward, nearly crossing the entirety of the bar. "Then what does make an echo?"

Brock waited until Timuscor had eased back to a more relaxed posture, killing time by sipping from his own glass. He held the container in his hand delicately, turning it so it caught the light of the flames burning in the fireplace. "Different people have different theories about that in a grand, metaphysical sense, but if you ask me, there is one key difference that always shows you who's an echo and who isn't: fear."

Timuscor stared blankly, trying to unravel what that could mean. "I'm sorry, fear?"

"Think back, to before. Who you were in the old days. I know the memories are fuzzy, but this should still be something that stands out. Can you find, anywhere in your mind, a memory of being truly afraid you were going to die? Not aware of the possibility, not mildly worried; I'm talking that deep-in-your-gut, absolute boulder of terror that comes when you're fighting with your life on the line. You've gone against Simone, so I know you've experienced that at least once."

That was indeed a feeling Timuscor was quite familiar with. He'd had it in the collapsing cave, fighting the paper monsters, and he'd been at death's door when he got a hole in his stomach saving Elora. That fear was so real it bordered on tangible, the unseen seventh member of their party, billed after Mr. Peppers. Yet, familiar as that sensation was, Timuscor could find no recollection of it before waking up with Eric and the Bridge over him.

"I remember being concerned, once or twice. Like dying would be a serious inconvenience that I didn't want to deal with. No real fear, though. I wasn't afraid to die." He paused, turning that revelation over in his mind. "*Why* wasn't I afraid to die?"

"Because you weren't you. Kieran shared what you said in the church. You've messed around with that artifact enough to know there's more to this world than what we can see. Those outside influences—I'm not sure they control us entirely, but when they've got their hooks in us, we're more them than us. That's why we weren't afraid to die: to the mind peering through our eyes, we were disposable. That changed when they left us. Suddenly, we each discovered the idea of self-preservation."

It was a very intangible distinction, yet nevertheless a valid one. True fear was a new experience, even if it shouldn't have been. That did raise a fresh question, however. "What about the others? They're adventurers now, and I believe they have always been afraid for their lives. Which category does that put them in?"

"The mere fact that they're adventuring means they are, by definition, adventurers," Brock said. "But they aren't like us. They're a third kind: ones who have never been controlled by outside forces, or not as directly as we have. From the start, each has been their own person. It doesn't happen often, only when a piece of artifact is active, but occasionally, ones like them pick up the adventuring mantle. As interesting a story as I'm sure they have, our condition is something different."

Silence fell as both men attended to their drinks, interrupted by the occasional snore of Mr. Peppers, sleeping near Timuscor's feet. Brock was waiting for the next question, patiently giving Timuscor time to put it into words. Only... Timuscor wasn't entirely sure he wanted to ask what came next. The possibility of not getting an answer was scary; the idea of actually getting one was ten times more terrifying. Once some things were learned, they couldn't be forgotten. For a fleeting moment, Timuscor almost shied away, turning the conversation elsewhere.

Except being afraid wasn't such a bad thing, when he thought about it. Fear was a marker, a distinction, a line in the sand between who he was and who he'd been. Every time Timuscor felt his fear rise up, it was a reminder that he was real and different from his prior incarnation. And in a way, that made it comforting, enough for him to push past his hesitations.

"How much of him—who I was before—was me?"

Brock looked Timuscor up and down, eyeing him carefully. "Hard to say. The work is ours, that much is for certain. Even as echoes, we're as strong as we ever were. The desires, maybe part them, part us? If you're used to wanting something for long enough, it's easy to think that the urge is yours. I often find the largest difference between who we are and who we were is the means we'll use to achieve those desires. Obviously, as echoes, we are all far more concerned with our well-being than we were as adventurers. Even beyond that, sometimes, the way we've acted, the way we've treated others, we've almost all got a few things we're ashamed of.

Were you a bad man, before? I don't ask that as judgment, but because we've got some people who can help you sort through that better than I can."

"Not bad, or not evil anyway. Even then, I wanted to be a paladin, yet my moral fortitude was lacking. I allowed my former party to do things, to act in ways I can't imagine tolerating now. And sometimes, in the heat of battle, I could forget myself and become needlessly cruel. There were enemies I could have spared, people who were too injured to keep fighting back, and I still…" Timuscor trailed off, wiping away unexpected tears for the second time that day. Sometimes, he was thankful his memories were blurred. There were plenty of moments he'd rather not recall clearly.

Brock topped them both off, staying silent until Timuscor had composed himself. "That's rough. And I've got no magic words to fix it. Only who you are now can make peace with who you were. Don't expect it to come overnight, either. Getting past those sorts of issues isn't easy; it's not supposed to be. That said, if it ever gets overwhelming, you should talk to Kieran. The guy still hasn't entirely squared himself away with all his own demons, but he's been dealing with it longer than anyone I know. Any insight to be had, he's the one who can offer it."

"Was Kieran a—no, never mind. That's not my place to ask behind his back."

"It's fine," Brock assured him. "Notch is a small town; we've got few secrets to keep outside of our existence. Kieran used to be an assassin. Part of a band of assassins, in fact. His old party. They were incredible, too. For his last job, Kieran's team managed to successfully kill a king. Of course, kings are well-protected, and even once the job was done, they had to get out. He was the only one to make it."

That certainly didn't mesh with the firm yet friendly man they'd met earlier in the church, but then, the Timuscor of old might not have been recognizable to his current friends, either. Evidently, part of being an echo meant accepting that others had pasts which might not accurately reflect who they were now. It did explain Kieran's incredible strike display, if nothing else. That wasn't a move for fighting; it was a technique for killing.

"What about you, Brock? If it's not rude, can I ask who you were in your past life?"

"I like that. Good way to refer to the pre-echo days. Might have to steal it." Setting his glass down, Brock took a few steps back and raised both his fists. Immediately, Timuscor felt his hair stand on end. There was danger in that stance; power, too. Part of Timuscor knew, without question, that a single punch from Brock would tear his body to pieces.

"I was a brawler. You don't have many of those around here, but in my homeland, we were common. Grew up poor—I mean *filthy* poor. Had to fight for every bite of food that went in my mouth, and it turned out I was decent in a scrap. For kids like me, there were only two ways out of that life: enter my kingdom's gladiatorial program, or join the king's army. I don't like orders, so I took the first one. Got in on guts and willpower alone. My testing opponent beat my scrawny, underfed ass up and down the pit, but I refused to give up. I'll never forget what my instructor said that day; it's one of the few clear memories I have from my past life. 'You can teach technique, you can build muscle, and you can train reflexes, but that kind of stubbornness comes from the soul.' Meant a lot to me."

Relaxing his posture, Brock walked back over to the bar. "Anyway, I got my training, bulked up—clearly—and learned how to win real fights instead of street brawls. After a while, I got bored of that life, so when some other skilled warriors I knew wanted to strike out into the world, I jumped at the chance. We had some good years." This time, it was Brock who wiped a rogue tear from his eye, though he made no effort to disguise the gesture. "Sadly, Kieran's story isn't as unique as it should be. Big final job—we pulled it off, but not without casualties. A lot of casualties. I was one of two survivors. The other went home. She was training new gladiators, last I checked."

Timuscor lifted his glass in the air, and Brock soon took the hint. He picked up his own and gently clinked the edges together.

"To those we have lost," Timuscor said.

"Including ourselves," Brock added.

They finished their drinks, and neither man reached for the bottle to add more. Carefully, Timuscor nudged Mr. Peppers awake, eliciting a snort from the boar as he climbed to his hooves. "Thanks for the drinks, and the talk. I think I'm ready to give sleep another try."

"Good idea. You'll want your wits about you tomorrow, as you try to figure out if we're all secretly planning to kill you."

Jerking his head around, Timuscor found Brock with a big grin stretched across his face. "We're all former adventurers; obviously, I know what you're thinking. You really believe we aren't trying to figure out the same thing about you?"

"Given the difference in our skills, I can't imagine how much you'd have to worry about from us," Timuscor said.

Brock shook his head, even as the smile remained in place. "We're not worried about you, specifically. But some power or other put you on that path to Notch. Until we know whose pawn you are, and in what game, you'll understand if the people around here are a little wary. If it helps, I'm hoping we don't end up fighting each other."

Oddly, it did sort of help. Timuscor could see things from their side. It wasn't personal; they had an entire village to protect. Even if no one used the word, it seemed clear from the outside that the denizens of Notch had replaced their old groups with this town's community. In the same way that he would fight someone he had no personal grudge with to protect his friends, Brock would charge head-first into battle for his fellow townsfolk. But only if the situation demanded it.

"If it comes to that, don't expect me to back down just because you're stronger. I'm known for my stubbornness as well."

Brock's smile dimmed a touch, but new respect glowed in his eyes. "I'll remember that."

There was nothing more to say, so Timuscor climbed back up the stairs to his room. Strangely, in spite of the emotional conversation he'd just had—topped off by a half-threat, no less—he found that sleep came almost the moment his head touched the pillow.

13.

Wind tore at his skin, howling as it whipped through the trees. Thistle clung to the locked door of Grumph's bar, positioned near the edge of Maplebark, as the gusts threatened to tear him away and fling him into the sky. Thistle screamed, yelling his questions to the heavens, yet his voice couldn't even reach his own ears. If they were making it to Grumble, or if Grumble was replying, then all of it was lost amidst the damn wind. Thistle refused to give up. He strained harder, lifting himself up slightly and raising his voice. The shift weakened his grip, unfortunately, and he was ripped from the door, hurling through the air as the world spun below.

The impact of hitting the floor woke Thistle from his dream, albeit not in a gentle fashion. With some effort, he extricated himself from the thin sheets, pulling his head free to see morning sunshine pouring through his room's window.

This was a new one. Thistle had seen Grumble unable to convey as much information as he wanted to before, thanks to the divine protocol enacted when two or more gods had conflicting interests, but this was the first time they'd been unable to communicate at all. Some force was interfering, inserting itself into Thistle's dreams so that Grumble couldn't reach him. To be powerful enough to block the connection between a god and their paladin was no small feat; outside of other gods, it was hard to imagine anyone having such skill. Then again, if there was such a candidate, they would be here in Notch.

As Thistle saw it, there were three options to consider. The first was that the interfering force came from outside of Notch, which meant that he had no way to investigate or remedy the situation. Possible, yes, but true or not, it had no impact on his course of action, so he set it aside for now. His second explanation was that Notch's impressive wards were also tuned to disrupt the divine. Given the town's attitude on outsiders—including gods—that seemed like the most plausible answer. It was far preferable than the third option: someone in town was purposely stopping him from talking to Grumble. That was the worst-case scenario, as it implied someone with an agenda they very much didn't want Thistle to get insight on… the sort of insight a god might impart.

Out of these explanations, number two would be the easiest to research. So long as he framed it innocently, like he had experienced mere interference in the conversation instead of intentional blockage, they'd have no reason not to tell him if the village's wards disrupted divine power. Should that turn out to not be the case, then Thistle would have to consider the other options. Until then, it was always best to start with the likeliest choice.

Dressing was a quick affair, since he'd slept in his armor. Not that Thistle could get so much as a single piece off; it was as though the metal had been bonded to his flesh. Grumble was sending at least one clear message, and Thistle intended to heed it. Thankfully, part of the armor's magic allowed him to rest comfortably while wearing it, otherwise he'd never get a good night's sleep so long as he was in Notch.

Thistle went down the stairs into the tavern, only to find with a slight shock that he was the last of his party to arrive. Normally, Thistle slept lightly, although dreams from gods did tend to put him deeply under. Never had one dragged on so long that he'd lazed about this late, however. Perhaps the act of hanging on, trying to communicate, had left him unconscious for an extended period of time. That, or the weeks of travel had finally caught up with him and his body took the rest while it was plentiful.

"Good morning." Thistle looked over to find Jolia sitting at the bar, helping herself to a plate of eggs and a cold ale. It seemed a little early in the morning for a stiff drink, but then again, as far as Thistle knew, she had nowhere else to be. Given everything these people must have seen in their time adventuring, Jolia probably wasn't the only one to start her days with a potent beverage.

"Morning," Thistle called back. He meandered over to the bar, climbing up on one of the gnome-sized stools and motioning for a plate of his own. Brock pointed at the mug next to Jolia, and Thistle shook his head. He had no idea what the day held in store. Best to meet it with a clear head.

Service was quick, as Brock seemed to have a massive pan of eggs on the fire and was simply cracking fresh ones in on the right side as he scooped out cooked ones from the left. The food was good. Not the best Thistle had ever tasted, but worlds better than what they could usually manage on the road. He'd gobbled up an entire plate before he noticed, only to have Brock slide a fresh one onto the counter next to him.

"You're eating more today. Good sign. Your nerves must be easing." It was the first thing Jolia had said to Thistle since he sat down.

Rather than reply immediately, Thistle finished the bite in his mouth. Though not everyone was a stickler for manners, Thistle liked to put his best foot forth in these sorts of situations. "A day to settle in and a night's rest will do wonders," he finally agreed, pausing to wipe his mouth. "I also want to make sure I have enough in my belly for whatever the day holds. As I recall, we owe you a few hours' work in exchange for our food and lodging, correct?"

Jolia sighed, and took a larger than necessary drink of her ale. "As Kieran told you yesterday and I already reminded your friends, you don't need to jump into work right away. The road is hard, everyone here knows that, so ease yourself in. We promised you a place to rest; you should take a few days to do that. However, given the answer they gave, I'm guessing you'll say the same."

"Assuming my friends said they'd rather be active, then yes, I do have the same answer. Whether we like it or not, we've grown used to the lives of adventurers. Inactivity would drive us mad, and we can hardly afford to let our skills turn rusty. A few hours is only part of the day, and it will help us burn off our spare energy so we can truly make the most of these wonderful accommodations each night."

All of that was, in one way or another, true. The idea of spending days with nothing to do sounded torturous, especially with so many questions lingering overhead and Lumal only a few days' ride away. However, that was not the only reason they'd prefer working through their time here. The more time they could spend around these people, especially in casual settings where conversation easily flowed, the greater chance of learning something useful. Since they'd decided to spend a short time recovering in Notch anyway, it only made sense to try to gather as much information as they could. Aside from the wisdom and experience the townsfolk had as adventurers, they knew about the Bridge. How much had yet to be seen, but Thistle was hoping that by the time they rode away from Notch, it would be with a better understanding of the artifact that had so thoroughly changed their lives.

With a mighty thrust of her fork, Jolia polished off the remainder of her eggs and waved Brock off when he tried to bring more. "About what I expected. Since you slept in, we handled most of the assignments already. Gabrielle will be helping Simone tend her garden in the graveyard, since her undead condition won't disturb the others. Grumph volunteered to give Brock a hand getting ready for his next brewing session—and given the experience he listed, I have to say I'm a little excited for what they come up with. Timuscor is going to be making the rounds with Kieran, Eric is pitching in to aid our local blacksmith, Shandor, and you get the honor of doing paperwork with me."

"Because we're both gnomes?" Thistle asked. It wasn't aggressive or accusatory; the smaller races often congregated when they found one another. Strength in numbers was, for many, the only strength they had.

"Aye. And also, no. It *is* because you're a gnome, but specifically because your friends say you're a quite learned, well-read gnome who was raised in a gnomish civilization. I've got some ancient texts I took with me when I left my hometown for the last time. Even 'borrowed' a few from the royal archives. They're enchanted, so they can't be read by using simple magic, meaning that I have to find someone who can understand the archaic script. It's a long shot, I realize, but it's not like I have other gnomes who come through here often. May as well let you take a look."

Thistle didn't miss the inflection of the word 'borrowed,' nor the subtext surrounding it, but he made no issue of the matter. While stealing *was* a crime, for all he knew, the king she'd taken them from was evil, or had plotted to use their information to conquer a defenseless neighbor. As a man on the run from a king, Thistle understood that not all laws were just or righteous. Paladins respected the law; they did not serve it. They served only their gods, and it was hard to imagine Grumble taking much umbrage with the theft. Minions often stole from their employers, even if it was usually only food or water for the sake of survival.

"I'll do my best, although I should warn you that my years with other gnomes were quite long ago."

Jolia hopped down from her stool, her staff loudly clomping as it struck the wooden floor. "As I already said, I know it's a long shot. Still worth taking, unless you've got another job you'd like to do."

It was tempting—they'd made a point of deciding not to split up the day before, albeit only with regard to walking around on their own—but this was different. The more villagers they engaged with, the better their odds of learning something useful. "No, I'm quite at home amidst stacks of parchment. I only wanted to make sure I was setting reasonable expectations."

"Nothing to fret about there," Jolia assured him. "We've got a firm idea of your capabilities already."

Moving more carefully, Thistle climbed down his own stool until he stood next to Jolia. "Be careful about that. This group has a habit of surprising those who think they know what we can do, and I say that knowing they've probably shocked me more than anyone else."

His warning was met with a gentle laugh. "I hope you're right. I really do. Notch could use a few surprises, if you ask me. We're long overdue for an oversized dose of the unexpected."

*　　　*　　　*

A lone horse trotted along the edge of the forest, its rider's face obscured by the hood of her robes. Overstuffed bags rattled and clanked with every one of the horse's steps, and a truly keen-eyed observer might have noticed that the tracks it left were far too numerous for a single horse. The rider scanned the ground ahead of her, waiting for the break in the trees that signaled the hidden trail. When the order first came down, she was sure there had been a misunderstanding. For Kalzidar to coordinate his priests was one thing, but to set upon them such monumental tasks stretched the bounds of credibility. Though the depth of her faith kept her from questioning Kalzidar outright, she knew nonetheless the other gods could be tricksters too. Perhaps this task was the work of one such deity, luring them into the open so that the unseen servants of Kalzidar could be shackled or slain.

Her doubt had only lasted until she fulfilled the first of her tasks. There, in the sealed temple where she'd met the other four, Kalzidar had offered them proof, along with the power needed to fulfill their objectives. The other four were strong, they had great potential, and they were sent out together to play their part. She, according to Kalzidar in his incarnation as a giant shadow, was different. She was special. Within her lay tremendous potential, a rare gift found seldom in their world.

The others were amplified, augmented, made more of who they already were. Such a blessing was given to her as well, along with something more. Only she could withstand a greater gift. Only she had been trusted with one of Kalzidar's greatest treasures. To see him show her such trust was such an honor that she'd wept right there in that cavern. These were not the last of her tears to spill on this journey, as the act of receiving Kalzidar's enhancement had been torturous beyond comprehension.

Even now, after taking time to practice as she waited for Kalzidar's signal to advance, it felt like there was a sun burning in her chest. So much power in his blessing—a small enhancement to help her better guard the treasure. And this was only a fraction of what her great god could command.

For no other god would she undertake such a task. No other god could she trust when he told her that she was strong enough. But Kalzidar had seen her talent and personally handed her the mission. For that, she would follow him across all nine hells if he demanded it. In truth, that would have probably been easier than the task she'd been given.

With a start, she saw the break in the trees. She didn't go in yet, or even approach it, lest one of the villagers notice. Kalzidar had been clear; there was no underestimating these people. The moment to strike would come when he declared it, and not before. Until then, she would practice and make herself ready. First and foremost, however, she needed to set up the second barrier. Kalzidar could only spare his attention to the job for so long. This was one of the numerous tasks set before her, with a narrow window to complete them in.

Taking on a village of former adventurers was a task one couldn't over-prepare for, even if they did have the backing of a god.

14.

From what Timuscor could tell, Kieran seemed to be the person who ran Notch. That wasn't to say he pulled strings or manipulated the desires of others. Rather, he was the one people came to when they needed something, or ran into a problem. Their morning walk had taken them out past the bounds of the town center and onto the estates of other residents. At every door, suspicious eyes fell upon Timuscor, glares that lasted only until they saw him in the company of Kieran. The moment they recognized the swordsman, their expressions softened and both men were invited into the respective home.

At their first stop, Kieran dropped off scrolls explaining a different method of irrigation that appeared to illuminate an issue the farmer was having with a difficult crop. Timuscor had some trouble picturing this fellow working the field: he was lean and pale, with snake tattoos that quite literally slithered across his skin. The farmer, introduced as Tocur, brewed a fine pot of tea, though, and broke into visible excitement when Kieran produced the new scrolls.

Their second stop brought them to a large plot of land where Kieran handed off a bag of seeds to a female half-orc who was tending to her garden with an oversized axe. At the third estate, nothing changed hands, but Kieran was able to assure the elven couple who lived there that the town trader had been reached and would be bringing in the specialty feed for their livestock. The fourth—and final—stop of the day saw Kieran tuning a lute for a man that looked like he'd be more at home with a bloody saber.

All the while, people would smile at Kieran, sometimes stopping for a brief chat, often merely giving a warm wave or calling a kind greeting. Slowly, Timuscor began to understand their world better. Notch was a town unlike any other, in that its citizens had virtually no real concerns. Their wards and respective abilities meant that they had nothing to fear from bandits or monsters, and the hidden nature of their settlement kept the shifting politics of the kingdoms from impacting them. When one added in that money was so ubiquitous it had lost nearly its value, and they had access to enough magic to fulfill all their basic needs for food and shelter, there were precious few problems for the townsfolk to worry over. Their hobbies appeared to be their greatest concern, and Kieran was the man who made sure even that part of their lives continued to run smoothly.

With the last appointment finished, they began their walk back, Kieran whistling when the wind at their backs grew slack. As they moved, Timuscor watched his strange guide, remembering what Brock had told him. Had someone this cheery and carefree truly been an assassin in the life that came before?

"I know what you're thinking." Kieran's words took Timuscor by surprise. Had he been dressed inside his armor, his startled jump would have loudly rattled. "And yes, this place more or less is paradise. Or as close as we're likely to find this side of death. You can see why we assumed you'd all want to stay; Notch is a town unlike any other out there."

"It certainly is unique." In truth, Timuscor wasn't sure that this location would be quite as tempting for him and his friends as everyone assumed, even if they didn't have other matters to attend to. While Notch was indisputably peaceful and serene, part of the reason its residents could enjoy such a setting was because their adventures were behind them. Their goals, their lifelong ambitions, had all been either realized or cast off. This was a town for those at the ends of their journeys, and although Timuscor could see the appeal of winding up somewhere like this eventually, he wasn't sure it would be quite so enjoyable to those whose life's work remained incomplete.

"In truth, I must admit that you were wrong. That's not what I was thinking about."

"Ah, then it's probably my second guess." Kieran slowed his walk slightly, making it easier for the pair to talk. "You're wondering how a man with so much blood on his sword can walk around casually smiling at people without the demons of his past dragging him down."

"Not precisely the way I would phrase it, but I can't deny there is some truth to your words. Brock told you he informed me of your past?"

That drew a short, sharp laugh from Kieran. "He didn't. I just assumed. We all grapple with our past at some point, and as the default figurehead of this place, most newcomers eventually ask about mine. Once people hear the word 'assassin' that tends to be where their minds get locked up. So, I'll make you a deal."

The walk stopped as Kieran pointed up a nearby hill, toward a mighty tree growing at the top. "We're going to walk up there and pick some fruit. You have until we reach the tree's roots to ask me anything you want to know about my past, and then we let it go. I'd be happy to talk with you about coping with the feelings and uncertainties of our shared scattered memories, but I don't want to keep getting bogged down in my life's specifics. Everyone here has a fascinating history; you'll lose sight of what matters if you don't keep your focus inward. So let's sate that curiosity while we get a snack."

Then they were moving again, albeit still at the slower pace. Timuscor took his time deciding which details he cared to know the most about. There was still some distance to the tree. Depending on how long each answer was, he might not have time for many questions.

"Why become an assassin?"

"Same reason as many before me: service and duty. All adventurers are assassins, in a way. We go out to kill the monsters or evil people making life harder for the normal, everyday folks of our world. I was just better at the killing part than any of the other bits, and so, eventually, that was the task most often handed to me. And it was usually the right thing to do. We could put the lives of a dozen others at risk by climbing an evil wizard's tower, fighting past their traps, losing good people along the way until we finally ended up in a massive battle—or I could slip a knife into that wizard's throat when they stopped by their favorite supply shop in another town. Either way, we're killing someone. My method just cost a few less lives."

It was hard to dispute Kieran's point—at least, in that specific scenario. If he was honest with himself, Timuscor knew that adventuring was a killing job. Back in Camnarael, a Grand Quest had been organized specifically for the task of dealing with Rathgan, a dragon who'd become problematic to the kingdom. Adventurers were collected and aimed at the beast like living cannons, and there was no measuring how much blood had been spilled in their assault. Then again, Timuscor was reasonably certain he'd never killed anything that hadn't been trying to kill him back. In the grand scheme of things, that might not make a difference, but it felt as though it should.

"Have you killed anyone who didn't deserve it?"

This time, the reply wasn't quite as fast. "I don't think so. As a fellow echo, you already know how difficult it can be to delve into one's own memories of the time before we were changed. I've done my best, scouring my mind to see if penance or retribution is owed. So far, every kill I can fully recall was warranted to some extent. I can't swear to that any more than you can, though. But then, that's true for almost all of us echoes."

Timuscor nearly missed a step and went tumbling down onto the soft grass of the hill they'd begun climbing. He'd tried to put that thought out of his head; he dearly wanted to believe that something inside of him would halt such actions. But those other three he'd been traveling with had held no such compunctions. Even if Timuscor gave himself the benefit of every doubt, was he truly certain that the targets that trio had chosen warranted killing?

"Try not to dwell on it," Kieran advised. "Not because it doesn't matter, but because you aren't going to find the answers you need inside your own head. Our minds and memories cannot be trusted; spend too long in there trying to pull out a memory that doesn't exist, and you'll end up creating it. Imagination is a powerful thing, especially when combined with uncertainty and self-doubt. I've seen others build their own hells around them with the fears of what they might have done."

"I will try my best." Timuscor wasn't sure how much success he would have. The further he dug into all of this, the more distressing it seemed, yet he couldn't turn away. To back down now would be to let the fear of what he'd been before win. Whatever had come before, Timuscor wouldn't be able to get past it by running away. It wasn't his nature. Forward and through was the only path that had ever made sense to him. "This next question isn't specifically about your assassination role, merely about your past in general."

"It's your walk, ask what you like."

A glance up the hill showed Timuscor that the tree wasn't too far off now. Long as the walk had seemed from further back, it was never as hard in the doing as in the expectation. "How did you come upon Notch? If it's such a secret, I can't help but wonder how the number of villagers increases."

"That's actually two questions, so I'm going to take them out of order, since that will make the most sense," Kieran said. "We find new villagers through recruitment, in a way. We're not completely divorced from the world at large; our trader brings us news as well as supplies. Add in the many mages we have for scrying, and it becomes easy to spot incredibly famous, powerful adventurers whose careers are winding down. Many of them slip into new roles without issue, and those we leave be. The ones who have trouble adjusting, however, we keep an eye on. After this long, we've learned to spot a new echo with exceptional precision. Once we're sure they *can* adapt to this new life, we offer it to them. Some say yes, others no; we never get specific enough with the ones who turn us down for them to fully understand what this place is. That's how the town grows."

Shade fell across Timuscor's brow as they reached the top of the hill, the tree's massive branches blocking out the sun. Golden fruit unlike anything Timuscor had ever seen swung gently in the wind, each looking as though it was a mere moment from falling, yet with not so much as a single one losing its grip. Scanning the ground, Timuscor noted that there were none in the grass. Those fruits were more tenacious than their appearance let on.

"As for your first question, that's actually why I was taking you up here. See, I didn't find Notch, so I can't properly answer that part. There was no Notch for me to find back then, but I still wanted all this. A place where people like us could be together, safe, split apart from the world that would try to drag us back to bloodshed. If you couldn't tell by walking around today, I'm something of a fixer by nature. It was my role as an adventurer between assassinations, and it's the one I still serve here. When I wanted a place like Notch, I did the same thing I always did when hitting a problem: I fixed it. There was no town for us, so I helped make one. I'm one of Notch's founders."

Based on his appearance, Timuscor would have thought Kieran to be no older than his late-thirties, but for him to be one of the town's founders, he'd have to be well beyond that. His features betrayed no elven lineage that might be slowing his aging, either. Obviously, that wasn't the case, but even allowing for a generous amount of leeway, Notch was too sprawling and too well-used to have been built recently. It was several decades old, at minimum.

"You certainly look youthful for your age." It was the least confrontational way Timuscor could think of to raise the issue. His gifts had always been more with the physical than the linguistic. Luckily, Kieran met the words with a smile, taking them well.

"When you gain my level of mastery over channeling mana through your body, controlling your age becomes a handy side effect. Not every member of Notch developed their power through those means, obviously, hence why I brought you up here."

Kieran moved, though Timuscor saw nothing more than a blur in his peripheral vision. By the time he'd fully turned, Kieran was at his side, holding two of the golden fruits. "Another benefit to living with experienced adventurers: we've accrued our own collections of useful goodies through our travels. This is a tree Jolia brought over from another plane as a sapling. Its fruit is filled with the energy of life, and every bite contains that essence. A single bite will stop you from aging for a week. Eat a whole one, you'll gain a full year. When I said that Notch was unlike anywhere else, I meant it.

Our citizens live as long as they wish. And if you stay, that offer will extend to you, as well."

Slowly, Timuscor plucked the fruit from Kieran's left hand. It was firm, yet yielded with only a slight amount of pressure, releasing a trickle of juice that was pure bliss upon the nose. He could only imagine how delicious a bite would be. At the very thought of it, Timuscor's mouth flooded with saliva. For a moment, he nearly leaned in and tore a piece off with his teeth. His neck even inclined itself closer before he stopped, handing the fruit back over to Kieran.

"Thank you. For the answers, as well as the offer. But this is not for me. Not yet. Tempting as it is, I don't think I'm quite done aging or growing. The truth is, I have long dreamed of becoming a paladin, even in my past life. Thus far, I've had no luck in finding a god who will accept someone who doesn't worship them, but I won't give up. And if there is a path toward paladinhood for me, I do not think I will find it in a town as peaceful as this one. While it might be nothing more than a hopeless dream, it's the only thing I have that truly unites my lives, and I'm not ready to set it aside."

"Good answer." Kieran tucked both of the fruits into a pouch at his side, which seemed to lay empty even after the bulky food had been stuffed in. "The offer was sincere, don't get me wrong, but I respect that you aren't ready to take it. Little as I can recall about my time before, I still remember that fire in my gut... driving me forward, making me want to be better. Don't let go of that easily, Timuscor. You've no idea how hard it can be to rekindle."

He took Timuscor in, looking the man over with a fresh gaze. "You know, this world is not static. Things are always changing. There are legends that, long ago, paladins weren't gifted their power from the gods directly. They were mere mortals who learned to channel it themselves. With nothing more than an oath of devotion and a setting of their will, anyone could be a paladin. Now, obviously, that's not been the case for quite a while, but the point is that nothing is set forever. There very well might be new ways to gain that title, and people like you are the ones who will discover it. Just some encouragement to keep in mind, when things get tough."

Together, they headed back down the hill, leaving behind the tree with the immortal fruit, standing unprotected on a hill. The mere fact that the town possessed such flora, let alone that they casually left it out in the open, was a living testament to their collective power. While Timuscor didn't want a bite of that particular fruit just yet, there were other things he was hoping to take away from his time in Notch. Kieran's tidbit about paladin lore made the next step obvious: he should start with any knowledge that might be useful.

"I have another question, one that doesn't pertain to your past," Timuscor ventured once they'd reached the bottom of the hill.

"Not going to make promises that I'll answer, but you're free to ask," Kieran replied.

A fair response, if not as certain as Timuscor might have liked. "A moment ago, you mentioned being able to channel mana through your body. Does that mean you're some kind of mage, or is there an element to melee fighting that involves learning magic?"

For the first time that day, Kieran pulled up short, surprise evident on his face. "You're joking, right? I watched you fight the other day, and while your party has a long way to grow, none of you are complete amateurs. Someone must have taught you about mana by now."

Timuscor nodded. "Grumph had it explained to him when he received training at the Mage's Guild, and he relayed the information to us. Mana is the magic that flows through all things, which mages can hold within themselves and release in the form of spells. Thus, why I assumed you must also have casting abilities when you mentioned mana."

The stare that met Timuscor's explanation was long and pointed, until finally, Kieran let out a long, steady sigh. "And this is what the others know of mana, as well?"

"I'm not sure I understand what you mean, but I would presume so, yes. We tend to share our information equally."

"When we get back to the inn, gather your party," Kieran instructed. "I'm not going to train you—none of us have the desire to see our techniques in the hands of those we don't know or trust—but at the very least, you need a baseline education. What you do with it from there is up to you."

15.

    The band of raiders slowed as their tracker, Pavtu, held up a hand, signaling that it was time to be patient. Living on the plains of Urthos was a hard life for many, especially those who had been cast from their tribes, but there were rewards for such difficulties. There was always a merchant thinking to save some coin and take a gamble, trying to sneak through the lands without proper protection. Even those that hired adventurers often spared too much coin, employing guards who did little more than add their equipment to the haul. Given the number of hoofprints and the depth of the cart tracks, the band appeared to be on the trail of a few riders with substantial cargo.

    Elnif, a half-orc warrior who rode near yet not quite at the front of the band, sniffed the air. Something was off. The scents the wind was bringing back to him were strangely tinged. The others were excited; some were already chatting about how they would spend their share of the take. Such words were pointless. The gold would go into food, drink, and entertainment, as it always did. If they were the kind of people who could put their coin to more productive uses, they wouldn't have ended up as raiders in the first place.

    A sharp whistle came from Pavtu's mouth as he rose from the ground and pointed east. As a half-elf, he was the band's most talented tracker, yet Elnif felt a needle of doubt pierce his mind. They were already far to the east; another half-day's ride would bring them to a forest near the edge of the plains. While it was true that some riders took that route specifically to avoid thieves such as this very crew, going near that forest set Elnif's nerves on edge. He didn't trust the trees. Life on the plains had made him prefer enemies he could see coming from far away. In the forest, a sudden turn could bring one face-to-face with looming death. Beyond that, there was just something about the border that made him uneasy, as though danger loomed behind every blade of grass.

    The others didn't share Elnif's concern. Letting out whoops and hollers, they spurred their horses to follow Pavtu, already back on his own slender mount and heading east. Elnif rode along with the group, his eyes lingering on the tracks that Pavtu had just finished surveying.

    Perhaps it was too easy; that was what made it feel off. They'd stumbled upon this trail without trying and had barely needed to ride for more than an hour to find fresh tracks. Was it possible that merchants with such a large haul were cutting across the plains, hiding their path so poorly? Certainly. But Elnif didn't trust how simply this was all coming together. He was not a rider of the front, however. He had not yet earned that honor, so his voice was one from the middle. Those in front were drunk on visions of fat purses and easy pickings; they would hear of no dissent towards such a tempting target.

The most Elnif could do for now was to keep his eyes open and his ears alert. If this was a trap, then it would have to be sprung soon. No matter how tempting the prey might be, his band wouldn't wander far from the plains: too many tales of kingdoms laying traps along their borders, trying to coax raiders out of their native lands, where they held the advantage. They might, at worst, press slightly into the forest, although Elnif still hoped it wouldn't come to that.

Each time Elnif looked upon those woods at the eastern border, his flesh would prickle, as if it knew there was something deadly between the trees, always lurking just out of sight. Perhaps it was a silly fear, but he had no desire to find out if those instincts were right.

*　　*　　*

There was some shuffling between chairs as everyone crowded into the small room in the rear of Brock's tavern. Technically, it was probably some sort of office—although, from the chaotic appearance, it was hard to imagine much work ever got done inside. Grumph finished hauling in the last seat from the main room, setting it down in the rear, next to Gabrielle's. Everyone sat, mostly in a line, although Thistle was slightly ahead of the others to make sure he had a clear line of sight.

In the front of the office stood Jolia, who had conjured some sort of glowing board of light behind her. Once everyone was settled, she tapped her staff to the ground, eliciting a sonorous *thump*. Nobody was sure whether it was magic or showmanship, but regardless, the gesture succeeded in capturing the room's full attention.

"It has been brought to our attention that all of you, despite being established adventurers, seem to be lacking on the fundamentals of how our abilities work. Kieran wants me to start from the very beginning, so we're going to start with one of the most basic questions I can ask. Let's begin with Gabrielle, for simplicity's sake. Aside from your condition and the magical axe, are you able to tell me how you wield mana?"

The question earned Jolia a confused stare from Gabrielle, who looked around to her friends briefly before answering. "I... don't. Maybe as an undead, sure, but I can't cast, so I don't use mana as a barbarian."

Jolia stared right back at Gabrielle, almost as if she wasn't sure she could believe the answer. "What about you, Eric? Any uses for mana in your role?"

"Not that I'm aware of, though that clearly isn't the answer you're looking for."

"Smart man. Grumph and Timuscor we can skip—I already know their answers—so how about you, Thistle? As the most learned member of this party, I'm hoping you'll be able to tell me something different."

Thistle squirmed slightly in his seat; this wasn't the first time he'd found himself up against a question and in lack of a reply, but he'd never enjoyed the sensation. "My power comes from Grumble, yet there are limits to what I can do with it. Perhaps that is because mana plays some role in turning his will into the paladin gifts I wield?"

"I didn't ask what you could conjecture from the context. I asked what you knew." Jolia tapped her staff again, this time as a nervous habit rather than as a move to demand their attention. "And, as it turns out, Kieran was correct. We do have to start at nearly the beginning. So let's begin with the one part of this you all seem to understand: mages."

Behind Jolia, a roughly human-shaped figure appeared on the board of light. Next, came a rudimentary stream that flowed through the figure, then out again, a small circle inside the form filling up bit by bit. "Magic is the energy that flows throughout our world, through everything, living and inanimate. When it's collected within a body, we refer to it as mana. Magic is infinite, but one can only wield so much mana, hence the distinction. Now, mages collect that mana into a pool within themselves; the more they practice, the deeper their pool grows. That mana is what they use to cast spells, shaping it with words and gestures to create tangible effects in the world. Everyone with me so far?"

At last, she received nods instead of uncertain eyes staring back. That was more or less the same explanation Grumph had gotten from Dejy, his teacher, which he'd later shared with the party.

"Good. Now, let's take Gabrielle, who fights using barbarian techniques. You don't seem to think she uses mana, so I'll ask it a different way. When a barbarian's fury takes over, why are they stronger? Why is it harder to put them down?"

"People hit harder when they're mad," Gabrielle tossed out, even if she didn't sound especially certain. It was a question she'd clearly never asked herself. As much as they'd learned about their world since leaving Maplebark, there were still parts they hadn't thought to question.

"*That* much harder? And even if it was pure anger, why would barbarians be the only ones to see such a significant difference? Everyone gets angry, yet they don't become substantially more powerful in the process."

Another wave of the staff, and the drawing on Jolia's board changed. Now, instead of the stream flowing into the figure and filling up a circle, the energy spread across the whole body like an invading species.

"The correct answer is that you, Gabrielle, have also been using mana when you fight. Unlike Grumph, you don't collect it. Instead, you tap right into the source, flooding your body with mana to augment your physical abilities. Doing this produces a more immediate and tangible effect than pooling it the way mages do, but it's also much harder on the body. That's why barbarians have to be fit, to withstand that kind of energy flow, as well as why you find yourself significantly drained once the fury fades."

The room sat in silence for several seconds, absorbing this new information, before Timuscor's curiosity shattered it. "There's more than one way to use mana?"

"There are countless ways to use mana," Jolia corrected. "On top of that, there are different kinds of magic within the mana that can be drawn out. What we think of as roles in a party—barbarian, mage, paladin, rogue—these are all just the most commonly known methods for wielding mana. Barbarians like Gabrielle flood themselves with it in a large burst, whereas knights and rogues, like yourself and Eric, learn to constantly channel small amounts. Paladins and priests are more unique, in that the gods give them the power to filter out the divine magic from the flow and store it in their bodies, similar to what a mage does. Priests wield that magic purely, while paladins use a style that mixes casting with physical power. Using mana is why you can grow so much stronger than what your simple, pure muscles would permit, move more silently than should ever be possible, see farther than normal eyes are capable of, and do things beyond the abilities of most beings. Channeling mana is a skill you rely on as much as swordsmanship, if not more."

Thistle was no longer squirming. In fact, he looked rather enthralled by the lesson, even as he raised his voice and spoke up. "What you're saying makes sense, but it's strange that, if this is such a universal concept, I've never heard of it before. I've traveled with adventurers, and we all just spent time around hundreds of them in Alcatham, yet never once has this subject matter been discussed."

"It's something only echoes tend to talk about," Jolia explained. "Adventurers still living the life think no more about it than you would contemplate the impulses going from your brain to your leg. As for everyone else... they can use mana as well, often instinctually, but I've never been certain if they understood their relationship to it. To be clear, my surprise comes from the fact that Timuscor didn't know any of this. I never expected the rest of you to have an inkling. Perhaps being freed so early in his adventuring career means he hadn't yet learned about the uses of mana."

"And where did *you* learn them?" Thistle was pressing now; everyone who knew him recognized the slight lean in his hunched form. "I have read and studied as much as I could at every opportunity, yet this is still the first I've ever heard of such theories. Surely a teacher would have written them down at some point."

Rather than sputter out a quick reply, Jolia paused. She contemplated the question for nearly a full minute, drumming her fingers on her staff as she pondered. Finally, her hand grew still as she met Thistle's eyes once more. "I don't know. The knowledge feels inherent, as if it's always been there, much like my talent with magic. Perhaps the reason only echoes talk about it is that we're the only ones who can. Assuming the knowledge came from whatever force compelled us during our adventures, and since we largely only converse with one another, we never noticed that the information hadn't spread. Again, to me, this all seems rudimentary. I would no more think to talk with someone about it than I would about whether or not they understood how to turn their head. Part of being an echo means recognizing the blind spots that linger when we find them. This appears to be one such example."

"I think I get it," Eric ventured. "Adventurers know this stuff, after a certain point, but they don't talk about it for the same reason I don't ask Grumph how he walks on two legs without falling over. It's what we all do, so the question makes no sense. Even former adventurers, like the people here, think of it as common, default knowledge. Here's my big question, though: how have we four, who weren't originally adventurers at all, been able to use it like we have been?"

"How does a toddler figure out the trick to standing?" Jolia shot back. "Instinct. Probably born from a high-stakes situation in which you were all in danger, if I were to make a guess. Instinct is how many non-adventurers manage to accrue power and skills of their own. But there's a difference between a standing toddler and a person who can sprint for miles at a time, and that's the gap between instinct and understanding."

There was a rough noise from Grumph's throat as he cleared it, not as clean or authoritative as Jolia's slam of her staff, yet equally demanding of attention. "Then we need to learn. Anything you are willing to teach. Please."

His friends soon nodded their agreement. Grumph was right. While it was interesting to wonder about where this information originated, that was less important than the information itself. This might very well be vital to their training; especially if this was something most adventurers knew by default. They needed every scrap of it they could handle.

"Fear not. I promised Kieran I would give you all a basic understanding of the concepts, and I intend to keep my word." Jolia paused, licking her lips and glancing toward the door. "You'll want to have Brock bring in some drinks. This might be a more ambitious project than I expected."

* * *

Past the borders of Notch, just outside the forest, the priestess worked tirelessly. The first strike was important. It would show her how they reacted to invasion. Of course, she could hardly risk herself to garner such information. That was the role of minions, those meant to be sacrificed for those of more value. Had she possessed a touch more introspection, she might have paused to wonder what that philosophy would mean for her when her task was finished. But Kalzidar had chosen her for more than her peculiar talent, even if she was incapable of seeing that particular truth.

Sadly, minions rarely served those who followed Kalzidar, given the mortality rate of such jobs. That was fine; she had other ideas, anyway. An unwitting minion was better, as it was one who couldn't betray her, even if they wanted to. And soon, she would have an entire band of minions charging in, testing Notch's defenses while leading them down false paths of whatever danger they faced.

The hardest part was hiding Kalzidar's presence. If they knew it was him, then they might dig in the right tomes, check the stars, and realize what was coming. That wouldn't do, not until the time was right. Instead, she was scattering trinkets, some emblazoned with the symbols of other gods, across the fake battlefield. Most were useless tidbits, but a few held actual power. Not Kalzidar's power, obviously, but power still. Though collecting these had felt pointless at times, she could now see the wisdom of her god.

When the nearby band of raiders followed the trail she'd laid out here, they would find what appeared to be the remains of a fight, along with enough gold and goods to make them wonder what the survivors had carried off. With a trail leading into the woods and several new magical tools, they should be able to at least reach Notch. There, they would be slaughtered; mere raiders could offer no fight against the power in that town. But their deaths would show the priestess much, and in dying, they would achieve the highest of honors: being of use to Kalzidar.

The time was drawing near; preparations had to be perfectly in place. Once the great night arrived, there would be limited time to work. Her god had laid a flawless plan. The only potential error might be in whom he'd chosen to carry out the tasks. She would not allow herself to be his sole mistake; she would prove that this was her right, her destiny. When it was over, and the ashes fell upon the world like new snow, she would lie at Kalzidar's feet and know a small part of it was thanks to her.

Getting to that future meant working hard in the present, so she continued to sculpt her fake battlefield. The raiders would be along sometime in the morning, and after that, things were going to get quite interesting in the town of Notch.

16.

Another night, another dream, and still no Grumble. Thistle didn't bother trying to hold on as hard this time; he'd rather get the full night of rest if talking with Grumble was off the table. At first, he was steady on two feet, standing once more next to Grumph's burned-down bar, but with every second, the howling in his ears increased, until even staying upright was a struggle. Not long after that, he was sent flying through the air. It was impossible to tell if he woke up right away, or if he slipped into a dreamless sleep for a time. Regardless, Thistle awoke feeling more refreshed than the day prior.

So far, he'd yet to find a way to raise the issue with Jolia. Yesterday had been consumed with plowing through document after document while she raced around her enormous library, bringing Thistle more to try to read. It wasn't an environment highly conducive to discussion, and Thistle wanted to play this carefully. Forcing it or rushing in would not make getting his answers any easier. Once his daily work had concluded, they'd gone right into the mana lesson, essentially eliminating any opportunity he might have had to speak with Jolia in private.

On that topic, Thistle held no regrets. Even though the discussion had worn into the night, delving deeper into the theory of wielding mana than any of them had been prepared for, the entire group had come out richer for the knowledge. Not even their experienced gnome paladin had been aware of all the different techniques and applications for the magical energy that flowed through them. Understanding those abilities was the first step to increasing them; although, how they would do that part was still uncertain. Jolia had held firm on educating them only in the theories of mana, not in how to train those techniques. Obviously, they were gaining experience in battle, but there had to be more they could do. Just as everyone trained with their weapons in between fights, they needed to begin training their mana use. However, that matter wasn't going away anytime soon, so today, Thistle's focus would be on figuring out why he couldn't talk to Grumble.

That wasn't technically a pressing issue: they were planning to leave tomorrow, after which Thistle and Grumble could theoretically gab to the god's content. But something in his gut kept telling Thistle that he was here for a reason, and leaving without figuring out what it was would lead to problems further down the road. For whatever else he could say of Grumble, the god of the minions never worked without a purpose. If it was truly

Grumble who had called them here, then Thistle believed there was a reason. The only question was whether or not he would find it before their time ran out.

Breakfast was a plain affair, everyone largely lost in thought as they shoveled down some food. Grumph was the least bothered, as last night's revelations had minimal impact on him. While mages did, of course, use mana, Grumph had already known that and was actively training daily to be better at it. He didn't have to contemplate new training methods or techniques to incorporate this fresh information. That was a task left to everyone else. The rest had far-off looks in their eyes; Thistle could all but see the ideas dancing through their minds, considered and dismissed one after the other.

The eating was nearly done when the tavern door swung open to reveal Kieran, Jolia, and Simone. Their arrival was so unexpected that even Brock raised an eyebrow before nodding toward the taps to see if they wanted a drink. Jolia accepted, while Simone and Kieran waved off the temptation.

"In what must be the coincidence to end all coincidences, it seems we've got more visitors who have also stumbled across our hidden path this morning, just a few days after you lot did the same." Kieran wasn't accusing them, not exactly, but the danger in his eyes made the suspicion clear. "For the moment, we've shifted the forest so they're wandering in an endless loop. What comes next depends on you all: do you know any bands of raiders who might have followed you here, or are we expected to believe this is a real coincidence?"

"Neither, in all likelihood," Thistle replied. Without realizing it, some part of him had been waiting for this sort of situation. It was never as simple as relaxing in a town for a few days. There was always more, always trouble. At least with enemies to look toward, he could stop worrying about what direction they'd appear from. "Perhaps it was the power of the Bridge that brought us here, but with each passing day, I suspect the divine more and more. And when a god is in play, there's usually at least one other, often working toward opposite goals. It is entirely possible that Grumble brought us here to be of aid to you, and that these raiders are the work of an enemy."

Kieran's eyes all but drilled into Thistle, searching the gnome for any signs of falsehood before eventually looking away. "I believe you believe that, and I don't think you lot had anything to do with these invaders, but try to keep some perspective. These idiots are no more than a trifle to us;

we'll slay them in the forest before they ever so much as see one of Notch's inner roads."

It was a strong declaration that might have carried a touch more weight if Jolia hadn't chosen right that moment to let out a short yelp. In her defense, the burst of sparks firing out of her staff would have caught anyone off guard, especially when occurring that close to her hand. Whatever the reason, her noise and the subsequent concern that crossed her face stole everyone's attention, including Kieran's.

"What is it?"

"The raiders just broke out of the loop," Jolia explained, closing her eyes and mumbling softly. "I don't understand. None of them appeared especially strong. The only way is maybe... oh, shit." Her eyes snapped back open, now alight with a tad bit of worry, and perhaps some excitement, as well. "They've got powerful magical items with them. Some divine, some arcane. Wow. Did they murder a wizard shop owner or something? Sorry, now that I'm sensing the items, it's a little harder to focus. They brought along quite the arsenal, but the good news is that I think most of the tools they've got are too strong for them to use properly."

Timuscor lifted a hand, and out of instinct or consideration, Kieran pointed at him to speak. "I'm sorry, did you say they can't use the items, because the items are too strong? Unless you mean like how a weapon can be too heavy, I don't understand how that's possible."

"Enchanted items use mana, just like people. The simple ones are self-contained, so anyone from a farmer to an archmage can wield them and get the same results. When you get into more potent items, the magic grows in complexity. In many cases, powerful items will use or draw on the wielder's own mana. Sometimes for fuel, sometimes for direction; regardless, it means that if the owner lacks the necessary level of mana or skill to control it, the effects will usually be lessened. Occasionally, depending on the item and who made it, lack of mana means the effects of whatever they use will run wild." Simone wasn't the most talkative of the bunch, but when she paused to explain things, it was hard not to hang on her every word.

There was a heavy sigh from Kieran as he drew the blade from the sheath on his hip. "What that means is that these idiots are running around our woods with the equivalent of magical powder kegs waiting to go off, at least a few which they can apparently use. We can't assume they won't eventually control more of them. Jolia, route them down the trader road, the one that runs directly into the center of town without passing any of the farms."

"I'm familiar with it, *thank* you." Even as she snipped at Kieran, Jolia was already casting, words tumbling out of her mouth so quickly it was impossible to tell where one ended and the next began, let alone what she was actually saying.

"Sorry. I just don't like this much activity in such a short time. Especially now that we've got people showing up wielding items they're obviously not meant to have. Makes me anxious." Kieran certainly didn't look anxious as he stalked about the tavern. If anything, he was growing more graceful with every step, like he was getting back into the groove of combat.

There was a thud as Timuscor rose from his chair. Even without his armor, he was still a man heavy with muscle from a lifetime of training. "How can we help? I know we can't hold a candle to any of you in combat, but maybe there are some traps to lay, or prep work to do?"

"Timuscor is quite right. Weak or not, you're still our hosts, and we won't stand idly by while you get attacked." Occasionally, when he was deeply honest with himself, Thistle couldn't help but wonder if Timuscor wouldn't be a better fit for the role of paladin. While it was true that Thistle had already been contemplating how to offer aid, Timuscor had still beaten him to it. Because Timuscor didn't bother with wonder or contemplation. He just acted, whether it was jumping out of a chair, or in front of a mini-ballista intended for another party member. If the man was running on pure instinct, they were good instincts indeed. Paladin instincts. The kind Thistle had never felt like he possessed.

Kieran was already shaking his head. "While the offer is appreciated, I can't put our guests in danger."

"Danger, no, but maybe they *can* be useful." It was the first time Brock had spoken since their arrival, and he did so while dropping off an ale with Jolia. "Something is off with this. A band of raiders magically geared to the teeth happens to stumble on our town and bust through one of Jolia's spells? They can't win, we all know that, so let's take a step back and assume someone else knows that, too. If so, then what's the point of this invasion? Not victory, not supplies, certainly not equipment. That leaves information."

All of the adventurers' eyes were on Brock as he returned to his position behind the bar and went back to tending breakfast. It was easy to forget that though he was burly and simple-looking, Brock was a warrior with skills honed enough to let him survive his quests and make it to this town. Dumb brutes didn't often live that long on their own; they needed a measure of battle-minded skill to survive. Some paired with smarter people in their party; Brock had evidently cultivated the talent within himself.

"He's right," Kieran said. "This is probably an opening move, a gambit to see how we'll respond. They want to understand our defenses in order to pierce through them."

"Let them try. They could spend a hundred years trying to invade, and we could repel them a different way each and every time." Simone stood a tad straighter as she spoke, her eyes shining with pride.

Sensing his opportunity, Thistle hopped out of his own chair, albeit with less showmanship than Timuscor. "Forgive me if this is rude. I know I am not nearly as experienced as all of you, but weak as I am, I have learned that there are always stronger enemies out there. There may be impossibly few who could stand against this town, but that still leaves some. The gods, if nothing else. Please, I implore you, allow us to properly thank you for all your information and hospitality. Return our armor and weapons so that we may serve as decoys. Give this enemy no more information about Notch than absolutely necessary."

Kieran's gaze grew skeptical. "You think you five can handle an entire band of raiders on your own?"

"Possibly, depending on their respective strength, although it's unlikely, given the equipment you've described them having." Thistle smiled, a casual thing that only betrayed some of the mischievousness in his mind. "But we don't actually need to defeat them; we merely have to look as though we have. If you can buy us a little time, I think we can put something together."

With one mighty swig, Jolia polished off her ale and motioned to Brock for another. "Let's hear your plan. And don't worry about time. I'll keep our invaders at bay for as long as is needed. Or, if luck is truly against them, they'll run into Agramor. But, for planning purposes, let's assume that won't happen."

"Why not?" Eric asked.

It was Simone who answered, a small ripple of fear in her eyes. "Because if they run into Agramor, there won't be so much as bones left when she's done with them."

*   *   *

Elnif liked his new sword. Despite being larger than his old one, it felt lighter, and with every test swing, Elnif was sure the blade moved faster than it should, leaving extra-deep gouges in the trees he sliced as they rode. This he did partly to get familiar with this weapon, partly to leave a trail for them to find their way back, if needed. As a rider of the middle, Elnif would never have received such a prize from the looting under normal circumstances; weapons like these were usually scooped up by those of the front. Yet this morning, they had stumbled onto such a wondrous bounty of items that after all of the front-riders had chosen, there were still options like this blade available for Elnif. Even those who rode in the rear had scooped up some trinkets, but the best gear by far had gone to the front-riders. Some held weapons that were quite literally glowing or crackling with power. Others had taken rings and amulets of considerable worth. Pavtu, still leading the way, was wearing a silver helm encrusted with jewels.

Earlier, one of those jewels had glowed briefly, just before they found a new route to follow. Tracking their prey in these woods was difficult. There were virtually no tracks to follow, and the cart had been left behind. There was no dissuading the others from pursuit, unfortunately. Seeing what the merchants had been forced to leave behind triggered the greed in almost every raider, their minds filling with visions of items so expensive that one could finance a castle. None of them stopped to wonder why a caravan with such incredible cargo would skimp on security. Even if it were all stolen, the thieves would have had to be strong enough to steal it in the first place. This wasn't right; Elnif could all but smell it in the air. As a middle-rider, the most he could do was keep his wits about him. When danger appeared, they had to be ready for it.

They rode on for almost an hour, the shifting of the sun and Pavtu's confidence the only things assuring them that progress had been made. Then, without warning, the trees suddenly broke to reveal a well-maintained road. For an instant, Elnif panicked, fearing they'd gone too far and entered another kingdom's territory. But that was impossible. Assuming they'd accidentally left the plains, they were still days from the nearest city. Whatever they'd just stumbled onto, it wasn't on any map. Given the condition of the stones in their path, this wasn't some abandoned ruin, either. Had someone hidden a road through the forest? And if so, what else were they capable of concealing?

Sadly, the others didn't share his concern. Once the road came into view, their pace picked up. In other circumstances, there would have been yells of excitement and whoops of anticipation; however, they were not new to this life. Celebration came after victory, not before, and right now, maintaining the element of surprise gave them a better chance at making it to that point.

Keeping a tight grip on his new sword, Elnif spurred his horse onward to keep up with the others. The road before them was flat and simple, with trees lining either side. While not quite as thick as the forest, the foliage was plentiful enough to discourage them from leaving the stone path. As they went on, hills on either side began to rise and fall, giving texture to the topography. After roughly half an hour of quick but careful riding, they began to ascend a hill. When they cleared the apex, a new sight lay before them. There was a village not much farther ahead, albeit not much of one: a few buildings, more roads leading out of town, and what looked like a small number of people milling about. The knot of fear in Elnif's stomach began to loosen.

Maybe this was just a group of sloppy merchants, after all. They'd been ambushed, raced into the woods, and come upon this hidden settlement. The mere fact that such a place existed was in itself concerning, but given the natural defenses of the forest, such a thing was possible. Pavtu let out a short whistle to signal that they should ready themselves. Now that they'd crested the hill, some of the riders were already in view of the town. From this point on, they would be visible, and that meant every second wasted gave their enemy a chance to prepare. They couldn't permit that, not if they wanted to keep the advantage of surprise.

Letting out another whistle, Pavtu pointed toward the town. As experienced raiders, they needed no more than that. Moving as one, they surged forward, barreling toward the town with weapons at the ready.

17.

When the herd of raiders rose over the top of the southern hill, Gabrielle's grip on her axe tightened involuntarily. She'd been expecting a crew roughly the same size as the bandit gang she fought with Grumph back on their way to Cadence Hollow. Instead, she was staring at what had to be thirty enemies, possibly closer to forty. Worse, most of them were holding items that shone with power, weapons that one could tell were enchanted, even from a distance. Some were too large to have been held effectively, yet were somehow still being wielded. Others merely lacked the telltale signs of wear-and-tear that mundane weapons slowly accumulated. A horde of experienced warriors at least thirty strong, armed to the teeth with magical gear, and charging in their direction. Confident as Gabrielle was in her own skill, this was a fight she knew they couldn't have won on their own.

Perhaps someday, with more experience and better equipment, but not today. Today, they would be mowed down right in the street where they stood, barely more than a bump in the road to a force that size. Yet even as they raced down the hill, building momentum and getting ever closer to town, Gabrielle held her position. She had been through so many trials and lessons since leaving Maplebark, but one of the first things she'd learned was that when Thistle had a plan, it was usually their best shot at survival.

At least she was back in her armor. The blood-red hide taken from a demon they'd helped kill in their early days felt almost like a second skin, she'd worn it so frequently. Timuscor shone in the early sun, his gleaming armor back in its proper place. Mr. Peppers was armored once again as well, stamping his hooves on the stone in what appeared to be anticipation. Grumph stood nearby, mighty staff clutched tightly in his grip, ready to give someone either a magical spell or a stab with the demon-bone blade on top. Eric was hiding, because no rogue worth their salt stood out in the open when there were places to spring out of. Thistle looked much the same, since he'd kept his armor all along; only the return of his sheaths and daggers marked the change in their situation.

Four adventurers, with a fifth hiding in the shadows, and an armored boar. Not exactly the force Gabrielle would have picked to go up against a threat like this one. Hopefully, it would lure the raiders into a false sense of security. Her party had to seem like an easily crushable force, which wasn't much of a stretch in this scenario. They wanted the raiders sure of themselves, cocky to the point where they might play with or taunt their food.

As Thistle had put it: "Some secrets an enemy will take to the grave in defeat, but will shout from the mountaintops at the point of victory." It was a sound idea, assuming the raiders stopped long enough to bother with taunts. It was possible they would try to roll right on through Gabrielle and the others. If that happened, her group would abandon the pretense and get clear while Notch's citizens handled the threat. That wouldn't be a victory, though. Winning this fight meant finding out everything these raiders knew, and hopefully uncovering a clue as to what was going on.

Just when Gabrielle was debating whether it was time to get clear lest they be trampled, the raiders slowed their pace. One in the front, a half-elf wearing a silver helm decorated in jewels, trotted out ahead of the group. He rode forward until he was a mere forty feet away, then came to a halt. When he spoke, it was directly to Timuscor, as though there was no question who would be in charge of a group like this.

"Good morning. My name is Pavtu, and these dashing warriors behind me are my friends. You seem like a surly bunch, and while we've got no qualms spilling your blood, we're in a cheerful mood this morning. Finding a stockpile of abandoned goodies has that effect on our spirits. In light of that, I'm going to make you an offer. Wherever you stashed the merchants and their cargo, kindly go fetch them. If they'll turn over their gold and their goods, we'll leave in peace. Otherwise, we'll kill you all and sack the town until the locals turn over what we want. Either way, we're getting the rest of this cargo. How much collateral damage happens in the process is up to you."

It was a nice speech, appealing to their sense of reason rather than just attempting to cow them with fear. The problem was that Gabrielle had seen a little too much to swallow it entirely. Pavtu's gang was nervous. This town wasn't supposed to exist; they realized that, and as such this was unfamiliar terrain. For a group of plains raiders, that had to be uncomfortable, all the more so because they knew nothing about this place or how it had been hidden. They were stepping on someone else's turf, and at least a few of them realized how dangerous that could be. That offer wasn't about being in a good mood. It was about hoping to get clear before this all blew up in their faces. Pity Pavtu didn't realize that had happened the minute they set foot off the plains.

"And if I tell you that no merchants have come through here in weeks, I presume you won't believe me?" Thistle had stepped forward, raising his voice to be sure Pavtu and the others noticed him.

The effort paid off, as most eyes turned to the gnome, although only Pavtu bothered to respond. "Given that we found the remains of their cart and some of their cargo in front of the track leading into the woods, no, I'm afraid we won't." Pavtu tapped his helmet on the word "cargo" just in case they'd missed the implication.

"Aye, that does seem to paint me as a liar," Thistle agreed. "But I'm afraid the truth is far worse. You see, Pavtu, there are no traveling merchants here at the moment. I suspect you were led to this place purposefully, sheep taken to the slaughter. This town is, as you must have deduced by now, magically protected. It was founded centuries ago and has wards the likes of which we can only dream. I won't go into specifics, but I do hope you'll believe me when I say that if you try to make war here, you will find only death—that of you, and your friends. Please, take that as the warning it is, rather than thinking it an empty threat. Flee, while you still have the ability to do so."

Unlikely as it was, part of Gabrielle dared to hope that this time, their opponents might listen to reason. This didn't have to end in fighting, in bloodshed, in more dead bodies laid out on the ground before her. Since leaving Maplebark, Gabrielle had killed more and more often. First, it was only demons, then bandits, then eventually any enemy that stood before her. She felt no guilt over these deeds—everyone she'd ever slain would have killed her instead—yet still, it would be nice to have one conflict end without adding more corpses to the world.

This was, sadly, not that fight.

After stroking his chin for several seconds, a malicious gleam entered Pavtu's eye. "Perhaps you are telling the truth. I can certainly admit that the circumstances bringing us here do seem suspicious. In this same situation yesterday, I might have coached caution and recommended we retreat. Too bad for you, little gnome, this is not yesterday. We have collectively found enough magical equipment to successfully take on a troop of kingdom soldiers. It will take far more than warnings about old wards and four adventurers to scare us off."

Pavtu didn't bother waiting for Thistle to respond; he lifted his hand and let out a sharp whistle. Instantly, the raiders behind him surged forward. Thistle watched them come; Gabrielle was sure she caught a flicker of sadness cross his face before it set in determination. None of them wanted this day to end in killing, but the call wasn't theirs to make. The raiders had decided their fate for themselves.

"Grumph. Now."

At Thistle's words, Grumph pulled a stoppered vial from his robes, shook it exactly three times, and hurled it into the middle of the raiders. One of them, a slim human with twitching eyes, actually managed to catch the vial midflight. "You trying to use some kind of magic po—?"

The man's words were cut off as the vial, having been properly agitated, just like they'd been taught, exploded. The force wasn't just enough to blow off the hand that held the vial, although that was certainly part of it. No, this tore through the center of the formation, turning some of the raiders to pulp, throwing others from their horses, and generally morphing a tight-knit unit into a blundering mass of confusion. In its wake came an oozing bank of fog that quickly spread throughout the area.

Step one was breaking them up and knocking them off guard. Seeing as they had an excellent start on this, Gabrielle leapt forward, axe raised overhead as she felt the power in her pale arms. With a single swing, she tore through two of the nearest riders, sending their respective halves to the ground. Being undead had definitely upped her strength, no question about that, but the raiders were beginning to recover. Her next targets would probably put up something of a fight.

Good. If she had to kill, then at least this way it would feel like a fight, not a murder. And there would be plenty of killing left in their day.

*   *   *

The explosion was Eric's signal. It meant that attempts at peace had failed, and the time for violence had arrived. Slinking out from his hiding place behind the corner of a building, his blade was already drawn. Chaos had invaded the battlefield. Grumph's—or, more accurately, Jolia's—potion broke the raiders' ranks and put them on the defensive. With stretches of fog forming along the battlefield, it would be harder for them to regroup or coordinate, not to mention offering Eric useful places to hide. As they scrambled to get a grasp on what was happening, Eric slipped up to the raiders in the rear of the formation. Unlike those closer to the front, their equipment didn't glow or make the nearby air ripple. Whatever hierarchy this group ran on, it was clear Eric wouldn't be dealing with those at the top.

That worked well for him, since rogues were better at hitting and moving than engaging in long, protracted fights. Before anyone near him could realize he wasn't one of the group, Eric stooped down near a thick man trying to free his large axe from its position under a now dead raider. With a quick slice, the man's neck opened. He tumbled down on top of the other corpse and his axe. This was a fight to the death, but that didn't mean Eric had to be cruel. Where he could manage, he would make the kills as painless as possible.

Sadly, the cluster of confusion didn't last as long as he might have liked. These weren't some new thieves out on their first job; it was a band of experienced raiders too collected to let one explosion completely throw them off. Already, they were reassembling in groups. The horses still standing were slapped on the rear and sent running; they were a liability with so many corpses and newly broken stones in the road. Besides, without knowing how many more vials were left, the raiders were smart enough to get their mounts out of harm's way. That also meant they planned to dig in for a fight, unfortunately, since the horses would have been their escape plan if they wanted to flee.

Close to the front, Eric could see strange lights and energy—most likely some of the enemies deciding to test their new toys. His breath caught in his throat at the sight, slipping out softly through his teeth as he ran another raider through with his sword. This was the riskiest part of the plan. They could account for numbers, even take a guess at combat ability based on the raiders' tactics and strategy, but those weapons were largely unknown elements. It was possible one could summon a thousand demons to fight at the wielder's side, or just glow prettily for five minutes and then crumble to dust.

Since the initial vial had been caught and had failed to hurt the raiders near the front, those that remained were getting a chance to use those items. Eric hurried through his work, killing one more stumbling lackey before hustling to get closer to the front. In a fight this chaotic, his presence could very well be the difference between life and death for the others. Rogues might not be much on the frontline, but one could never underestimate the effectiveness of a sword through the back.

*   *   *

Eric hadn't been the only one hiding in town. Concealed by a door, Kieran stood near the front of the tavern. Above him was Jolia on the rooftop, magically hidden under an array of spells to avoid detection. Simone was a few buildings over, and Brock was guarding the road that led into Notch. Since the lumbering bartender couldn't fight without being seen, he'd been placed on sentry duty to protect the other citizens. As residents of Notch, they didn't really need the help, but everyone slept eventually, and flukes could happen. They were indulging the adventurers, playing along with the plan so long as it worked. If it started to come apart, then Kieran and the others would drop all pretense to fight in earnest. Until then, they were stuck hiding.

From his vantage point, Kieran could see the explosion clearly. It rattled their attackers, but they quickly recovered. Several were already raising their weapons, and magical effects began flashing throughout the area. If the adventurers didn't get moving soon, it would be a bloodbath. As it turned out, Kieran wasn't the only one who caught the warning signs. From his position near the front, Thistle began barking out orders louder than one might have expected possible from a body that small.

"Grumph, conjure us some help! Gabrielle and Timuscor, run the flanks, picking off the stragglers. You've all fought with me enough to know what comes next." A pair of daggers twirled in Thistle's hands, one hurled through the air before the sentence was properly finished.

It slammed right into the chest of a raider wearing lesser gear who'd ended up near the front in the confusion. The target staggered back several steps before tumbling down. The dagger vanished at the sound of a whistle, reappearing in the sheath on Thistle's side. While not an especially spectacular or tactically essential kill, it did have the effect of putting all nearby eyes directly onto Thistle.

With a cheerful grin, Thistle pulled another dagger, met the eyes of his enemies… and then broke into a dead sprint going the opposite direction.

18.

After looking at the situation earnestly, what the party had landed on doing was more subterfuge than strategy. Fortunately for them, Thistle was a paladin who understood that sometimes those two things could be one and the same. It had never really been their task to defeat the raiders—that would be a hard fight on even their best of days. Against enemies wielding powerful, enchanted weapons? This moved it from hard to impossible—or as impossible as anything could be in a world with gods and magic. On the other hand, the locals of Notch supposedly boasted unparalleled strength and should be able to easily win the day. The only issue there was that would likely give whoever had orchestrated this something they wanted, and as a rule, Thistle made it a point to never fulfill his enemies' desires.

They had the means to win, yet doing so openly might cost them later down the line. In light of that, the answer became almost obvious: they had to rely on the guardians of Notch without letting on that Thistle and his party weren't the ones doing the real damage. The exploding potion was first; something to stir up confusion. Confusion was essential for this plan, possibly more than any one member of their group. Landing his dagger-throw was also important, which was why Thistle had chosen the weakest target he could see. The raiders needed to believe him as a threat if they were going to buy what came next.

Without slowing down, Thistle burst through the door to the tavern, the nearest pursuer a mere thirty feet behind. They'd been caught by surprise, but a misshapen gnome in heavy armor wasn't going to outrun many people, even with paladin strength coursing through his muscles. It was why Thistle had purposely positioned himself near the tavern—to ensure he had as short a sprint as possible. It didn't matter if he beat them by a foot or a mile; none of the raiders were ever going to make it through that door.

No sooner had Thistle run inside than Kieran went to work. Hunkering down to roughly the right height, he cracked the tavern door open a fraction then held out his hand. Immediately, Thistle slapped one of his daggers into it. The gnome had made certain to twirl them in the open, ensuring that the raiders—and anyone else who might potentially be watching—got a good look. None of this would matter if they didn't sell the charade properly. With a swift throw, Kieran hurled the knife through the crack in the door. With the former assassin hidden by wood and shadows, no one without would see more than a flash of metal. Then there was a dagger directly in the head of Thistle's closest pursuer, who collapsed in a heap without so much as a final whisper.

Already, another dagger was in Kieran's hand and Thistle was calling for the other to return. Between a magic belt with two sheaths and four other daggers enchanted to return, they had a supply of throwing weapons that could be used indefinitely. Not enough of them to cut through the entire force from this position, but that wasn't their job. Kieran would handle picking off the high-value targets the moment their attention wavered, while also defending his and Thistle's position.

A new crackle of magic filled the air as Grumph finished waving his arms around and muttering random nonsense to "cast" his spell. In truth, the magic was Jolia's, but with a spell like this, there was no way to trace the origin. The ground near Grumph shivered and rumbled as the next step of their plan kicked in. With a suppressed snicker, Kieran leaned back and whispered to Thistle.

"Looks like it's time we brought our backup forces to bear."

*　　*　　*

Grumph had no idea how long he needed to pantomime; he simply stopped when he felt the ground begin to quiver. Jolia had warned him about that telltale sign, along with what came next. Threatening as the raiders were in their own right, this was the actual moment Grumph had been dreading since the fight began. All around him, seeming to sprout from the very road under his feet, a half-dozen enormous bears burst forth with mighty roars. The dire bears were larger than normal bears, hulking monsters of such size and fury that to even be near one activated any sentient creature's flight response. And Grumph was stuffed between six of the things. Remembering his role, Grumph pointed forward with his staff, making sure that all nearby raiders could see it. Obviously, this did nothing. Jolia was the one in control of the creatures, but appearances were essential today.

On cue, his ursine army surged forth in various directions, set on a homicidal crash course for the raiders. A flutter of sympathy filled Grumph's heart as he watched the first bear rampage forward. Part of him wondered if this was brutal overkill. That feeling faded fast as he witnessed the bear suddenly explode in flames. A bald human at the front of the raider group was holding up a gauntlet that glowed red with magical heat, and with a point of his finger, another fiery blast struck the first bear. From his left, a second raider came forward, one that looked so similar to the first, they might have been brothers. This fellow didn't have a gauntlet, however; he was hefting an axe that looked much too big for him, yet with a casual swing, he chopped the head clean off the dire bear, spraying curious shards of ice with the impact.

The bear dissolved into nothing. As a summoned entity, it had never been alive in the first place. That didn't seem to quell the fury of the second bear, though, as it attempted to trample the axe-wielder. He was too quick, darting back despite the cumbersome axe. Already, the bald raider was taking aim for another fiery blast. He shot, searing the second bear's flank and sending it off its chosen course. The two raiders were working in tandem, and it was a potent strategy. The flaw in it quickly became obvious, however. While the dire bears were certainly eye-catching and scary, they weren't the only threats on the battlefield.

Before another blast could exit the gauntlet, a sword came smashing down on top of it. Timuscor had appeared from behind, and while he could have killed the man outright, he'd instead chosen to disrupt the attack. That would make for a harder fight, but Timuscor was the right person for the job. He'd gotten fire-warding on his shield when they geared up in Camnarael, so if anyone could handle this particular threat in a one-on-one match, it was Timuscor. The problem was making sure it stayed a one-on-one match—already the axe-wielder was stepping closer, looking to horn in on the battle.

Lifting his staff, Grumph began to mumble once more. Only this time, it wasn't pageantry. He hurriedly cast one of his own spells, a blast of fire that roared from the tip of his bone blade on a crash course for the axe raider. His attack was blocked by the flat of the axe, flames sizzling to steam as they hit the unnaturally cold surface of the weapon. From his vantage point, Grumph could just make out the grin on his enemy's face. It was a short-lived moment of victory, as the raider turned to see Grumph with a toothy smile all his own. The fire hadn't been about hitting; it had been about distracting.

From behind, a still-smoking and angry dire bear slammed into the axe-wielder. The first blast might have put it off, but these weren't mere wild animals: they were summons being controlled by Jolia. She'd sent it back around, and with his attention on Grumph's magic, the raider was looking in the wrong direction to see it charge.

To his credit, the man fought valiantly, trying to maneuver the oversized axe into a viable striking position, but the bear was relentless.

Grumph didn't actually hear the crunch, but he saw the raider's body go limp. After a quick glance to make sure Timuscor was still up, the half-orc turned his attention to the rest of the battlefield. It wouldn't do to have a pair of object lessons in the importance of paying attention and then make the same error himself.

Things had only gotten crazier. Several raiders perched on top of a stone horse that had appeared from nowhere. One seemed to have turned into a strange tree-creature that was fighting two dire bears at once, and all around, Grumph could see sparks and spells shooting into the air. These items were powerful, that much was clear. Perhaps *too* powerful. The raiders may well have been better served using tools they could properly control, rather than ones stronger than they could handle. Another good lesson to keep in mind for the future: functionality was better than raw power. Then again, raw power certainly did have its uses.

Taking a few steps back, Grumph ducked behind the remaining dire bear near him, one that had stayed behind specifically for this purpose. To seem like he was casting this next spell, it would take some time. With his friends busy, the bear would have to serve as his bodyguard until the task was done. Grumph pressed his back into the beast's furry side, then lifted his staff high enough that it could be seen over the enormous creature and began to chant nonsense once more.

*　　*　　*

Elnif raced out from under the heavy paw of a dire bear, rolling to safety just in time. As a raider of the plains, one who had ascended to middle-rider, he'd seen many battles in his time. None of them were like this. On top of the fact that the few defenders of this town were proving to be far more dangerous than expected, their own weaponry was putting them in peril. Huberf had dissolved into ash when he pressed the topmost rune on a magical wand they'd found, Galzim was impaled on sharp spears he'd accidentally summoned from the ground with an amulet, and Pelsor had turned into some kind of tree-monster. Granted, that last one was coming in handy, thanks to the sudden influx of bears, but it was still an issue they were going to have to deal with.

Having a slightly sharper, lighter sword didn't seem like quite the bad deal it had earlier in the day. At least Elnif's weapon probably wasn't going to be the cause of his death. No, that honor would most likely go to one of the odd people who'd greeted their band when they rode into town. Who would have imagined that a crooked gnome could be so deadly with those daggers, or that a half-orc wizard could conjure such fearsome allies? It was all too much, and not for one moment did Elnif believe this to be a coincidence. Something had led them here. Something had orchestrated this. It had all been too perfect, too easy, until suddenly, everyone he knew was fighting for their lives. If he survived, Elnif would hunt whoever did this to them for the rest of his days. But this was not a situation where he could take survival as a given.

Shoving his way through various magical effects, overwhelmed with light and sound, Elnif found himself suddenly outside the fray, standing in the peaceful morning sunshine that was still beaming down upon them. This was insanity. Surely there had to be a way to put an end to what was happening. True, Pavtu was the one who'd rejected the offer of peace, but that was before suspecting they'd been set up. Maybe if he could get to Pavtu now, they could convince everyone to throw down their arms. Even as he had the thought, Elnif knew it to be pure fantasy. The front-riders would never listen, not with enemies to fight and supposed treasure to claim. That drive was what had earned them those positions in the first place.

Shade fell upon Elnif's brow, and as he looked up, he noticed clouds swirling in the sky, ones that hadn't been there seconds prior. With a quick scan, he saw the half-orc's distinctive staff poking up from behind a dire bear. Their wizard was casting again, and if it was half as bad as the last spell, it might very well put an end to this battle entirely. Elnif couldn't let that happen. Wrong or not, aggressors or not, this band of raiders was all he had. Until the end, he would fight for them.

Bolting forward, Elnif tried to circle around the bear, hoping he might get enough speed for a clean strike before the creature could react. Before he could draw near, something else leapt from the sea of chaos that was the battlefield. A pale woman with black hair, clad in blood-red armor and swinging a dangerous-looking axe, shot forth at exceptional speeds before planting herself directly in Elnif's path to the wizard.

"Sorry. Grumph's a little busy at the moment. You'll have to content yourself with me."

Not ideal. She was fast, and from the way she swung that axe, probably strong as well. But she wasn't exploding with unpredictable magical energy, so that at least made her an enemy that could be properly fought. She was aggressive, the way she'd dashed over made that clear, so his likeliest shot at victory was to put her on the defensive. After what he'd seen so far, Elnif didn't want to fight any of these people at their best.

Without warning, Elnif charged, sword at the ready. He opened with a thrust, which she dodged rather than block, arcing her axe upward in a slice that would have opened Elnif's stomach if he hadn't already been backpedaling. Just as he'd thought, her version of defense was more attacking. If he could last long enough to get a read on her habits, it might be possible to catch her off guard during a counter.

Another rush from Elnif, this time bringing his blade around from the side. She blocked, but when their weapons met, neither was prepared for what happened. A pulse of magic rippled out from the point of impact, shaking first the weapons, then the arms of those who held them. Both retreated momentarily until the quivering slowed.

"Nice sword. Not many weapons come away from touching my axe unscathed." Her arms had already stilled; she'd regained control faster than him. Bad as that was, better he knew upfront. It meant Elnif would be at a disadvantage every time she blocked, so he'd have to try pushing her to dodge instead.

She readied her weapon once more, yet waited for him to recover. Evidently, he'd done well enough to deserve a fight with honor. Or she was toying with her food before going in for the kill. It didn't change anything, regardless. Elnif had to try to stop that wizard, and that meant somehow getting past this woman.

Making sure his arms had steadied, Elnif stepped in for another attack, hoping dearly that she wouldn't try to block this one.

19.

In addition to the glowing gauntlet, Timuscor's opponent pulled out a mace with his left hand. Fire magic and a melee weapon together made things more complicated, but given the general madness engulfing them, it was really only one more thing to keep track of. Much as he didn't care to admit it, to the others or himself, Timuscor often felt the most at peace in the havoc of battle. When the world boiled down like this, consolidating into the fundamental concept of *not dying*, it left no room for the doubts and questions that haunted him endlessly. In these moments, it didn't matter who he was, how he'd come to be, or what place there was for him in the world now. All that counted was his skill with a blade and a shield; that, and that alone, would determine who survived to see another day.

The bald man opened with a shot from the gauntlet. The fireball was big and bright, but it still sizzled uselessly against Timuscor's shield. The wards had withstood a direct fire attack from the mouth of a dragon; it would take more than hastily-cobbled heat spells to break through. As the flames cleared, Timuscor realized his enemy had already reached that conclusion. The bald man came in swinging, whipping his mace through the soft haze of smoke created by the burst of fire. A good move, yet one that was perhaps a tad too predictable. Timuscor was already moving back, shifting his position so he could deflect the second blow. It rang hard against his shield, but by the time his sword was in motion, the bald raider was already pedaling out of range, aware he'd just opened for a counter.

"You fight well." Turning the mace out, the raider slammed the butt of it twice against his chest, thudding against his leather armor. "I am Rulln, a rider of the front and feared combatant."

"Timuscor. A knight, for now." He didn't let the conversation dull his focus, and it was a good thing. No sooner had Rulln nodded did he bolt forward, swinging the mace as though trying to shatter stone. It crashed heavily against Timuscor's shield, like Rulln was simply driving him back. Timuscor almost countered before thinking better of it; Rulln had been fighting too smart to make such a blatant blunder now.

Instead of swinging, Timuscor jumped back and to the side. It turned out to be the best move he could have made, as a sudden burst of fire tore through where he'd been standing. Of course. Shooting first, and then using the mace hadn't worked, so Rulln had switched it up. He'd decided to open with the mace, then used the gauntlet when Timuscor moved his shield to attack. A good tactic, if a limited one. Despite the difference in their power, Timuscor couldn't help noticing that Rulln was fighting with a somewhat constrained skill set for a warrior with his rank. Then, as he watched Rulln flex the fingers of the gauntlet, it clicked. Rulln wasn't using much variety because he'd probably never fought with a magic fire glove before. Instead of depending on his tried and true tactics, Rulln was betting heavily on his shiny new toy to make up the difference. There might be a lesson worth contemplating in that revelation somewhere, but for Timuscor, there was only one salient takeaway at the moment: he needed to press the attack before Rulln could *get* comfortable.

Shield at the ready, Timuscor charged forward. As he'd expected, Rulln reacted by shooting more fire. To his credit, the bald raider was smart enough to aim for Timuscor's legs. Reacting with well-trained speed, Timuscor dropped his shield position and angled it downward, sending the torrent of heat directly into the ground. Rulln was the one charging now, mace already whipping through a powerful swing to capitalize on Timuscor's lowered position. A sound move, one intended to take him by surprise, but a tactic that came with serious drawbacks when it was predicted.

Timuscor's shield was in place overhead as the mace came down; he felt the impact at the same time he thrust his own blade forward. The leather armor favored by the raiders was well-worn, which meant it was sturdy enough to have lasted for some while. That said, such armor was meant for front-facing defense, with the fastening mechanisms in the rear. Rather than try to punch through Rulln's leg armor, Timuscor used the proximity and position to maneuver his sword through the raider's legs, then turn it sideways and pull it as deeply through Rulln's right calf as possible.

A piercing howl of pain split the world around them as Timuscor shoved Rulln back with his shield, sending him tumbling back on the bloodied leg and allowing Timuscor enough room to retreat a few paces. Rulln was injured, but so long as he held that gauntlet, he was still a serious threat. Stepping forward carefully, blade held at the ready, Timuscor addressed his adversary.

"Take off the gauntlet, throw down your weapons, and this need not end in death. You have committed a crime, but I am sure the people of this town will jail you for it rather than see you dead in the streets. We are acting as guardians, not murderers. You have the power to help the killing end."

Rulln sucked a breath through his teeth as he glanced down at the blood gushing from his leg. "To you, I know this must be honor, showing mercy to a downed foe. But on the plains of Urthos, we have our own kind of honor. The only way to live here, to survive on this path we've chosen, is to fight with your life on the line every time. Those who cannot would have broken and run long ago." He sat up, flexing the fingers of his gauntlet once more. "To die wiping a dangerous enemy from the battlefield is the greatest death of all."

With a sudden movement, Rulln grasped the gauntlet into a fist and held it. Timuscor could see the glow intensifying, but what it would lead to was anyone's guess. He did a quick scan of the area to be sure none of his friends were nearby, then backed up quickly with his shield at the ready. Based on what he'd seen so far, the most likely result would be one hell of a fire spell.

In a way, Timuscor was right. The first effect was an explosion, although admittedly a smaller one than he'd been expecting. For a heartbeat, Timuscor felt relieved; something like that might very well have killed Rulln in the process. That hope was short-lived, as Rulln began to rise from the ground. Only.. it wasn't really Rulln anymore. He was burning from head to toe, covered in flames that were slowly charring his skin. Flames that were unnatural, almost forming a face to stare at Timuscor, flames using Rulln's body as a platform.

While not a mage, Timuscor did have basic deductive abilities. Lively flames coming from a gauntlet that were moving a steadily burning body—the best guess was that Rulln had activated some aspect of the gauntlet and was using himself as fuel for whatever it had summoned. The fiery monster that had once been a raider turned toward Timuscor, rearing back and letting loose a torrent of flame from the remains of Rulln's mouth.

This time, it was closer to dealing with dragon fire. The flames had tremendously increased in both number and intensity. Rulln's corpse was more dangerous than the man himself. On the upside, at the rate he was decaying, he probably wouldn't be in the fight very much longer. The downside, however, was that attacks like that could still do real damage in short order. Given his shield and the others' roles, Timuscor was the one best suited to draw this monster's attention. He slammed his sword against his shield to avoid losing once-Rulln's notice.

"I'd expect a spell that uses a life as a component to be more powerful. Rulln clearly made a poor trade." Whether or not insults would work on this kind of creature was pure speculation, but it wasn't as though Timuscor risked anything by trying. He had to do anything he could to keep the attention on him until this was over, or the others had been freed up.

Unfortunately, it worked. The burning corpse dashed forward, slamming its gauntleted hand against his shield and sending Timuscor stumbling back. Whatever else the magic was doing, it had also made Rulln substantially stronger. Already, Timuscor could feel the ache in his arm from absorbing even one blow. Many more like that would drive him to the ground. And since Rulln was already decaying, it was hard to imagine a few simple sword strikes would do much of anything to him.

There was nothing to do but survive. Keep fighting, hold the line, live to protect his friends. So long as he could accomplish that, Timuscor would take a deadly opponent off the field. He just hoped Thistle had some healing magic left over when this was all done. At the rate things were going, Timuscor was definitely going to need it.

* * *

Mr. Peppers stood near the edge of the battlefield, watching three raiders work together to fend off one of the dire bears thundering through their ranks. He'd been cut off from Timuscor in the chaos, but there was little need to feel worry. Timuscor was strong; he could handle himself for a few minutes. What Mr. Peppers couldn't turn from was the bears being sacrificed as fodder for their victory. They were unquestionably essential to winning a fight like this, yet they were also being slowly felled one by one. No backup. No aid to protect them.

The three raiders managed to cripple the bear, tearing a chunk from its back and leaving it limp on the ground, with not even the decency to kill it so it could fade. As they raced off to find another target, Mr. Peppers quietly trotted over. The bear let out a soft roar as he approached, but the noise died away as it spied the boar. Gently, Mr. Peppers pressed his snout to the bear's nose, holding it there for several seconds. A soft, gentle glow rippled across the bear, partially mending its wounds. Mr. Peppers was surprised; he'd only expected to offer some small comfort in the creature's final moments. Timuscor must be nearing revelation to produce an effect like this.

More surprisingly, the light had yet to vanish. It flowed upward from Mr. Peppers' snout, continuing across the entire boar. The glow intensified as he moved, following the direction of the three raiders who had nearly felled this noble creature. With every step, his hoofprints grew wider and deeper, until he disappeared in a cloud of magical smoke drifting across the battlefield.

He did emerge, eventually, but it was a very different Mr. Peppers who came out the other side.

*   *   *

With a flourish, Eric rammed his short sword through the back of a raider that was about to charge one of the bears and had forgotten to check their rear. Trying to figure out where he was needed on the battlefield was turning out to be nearly as tough a job as handling their opponents. A lot of smoke and flames were coming from where Timuscor had gone. That looked to be getting serious, but on the opposite side, Eric caught sight of Gabrielle holding off a raider with a large sword to keep him from getting near Grumph.

The clouds overhead were building, slowly and steadily. Jolia had warned that the effect would have to be slow if they wanted to sell their ruse; a spell like this one would take some while for most mages to cast. She was doing it the slow way to avoid tipping their hand, in the hopes that whoever was watching would buy that the magic was Grumph's handiwork. The idea was all well and good from a subterfuge angle, but it ignored the fact that they had to defend Grumph for however long the "casting" required. Here and there, an occasional dagger would sink into a raider's vital organs, a reminder that Thistle and Kieran were still in the fray. If only Gabrielle could lead her opponent to a better angle, the dagger-throwers could help.

Given the options, Eric felt like Timuscor probably needed his assistance more. Whatever fire was over there, it was growing fast, and Gabrielle could likely handle an enemy of this caliber one-on-one. Even if she couldn't, Grumph was nearby in a pinch. Timuscor was more likely to need backup. Eric even started in that direction, making it several steps before he noticed the hurried thudding noise coming up behind him. Thanks to his rogue's reflexes, Eric leapt aside just before an enormous boar tore out from a veil of mist. No doubt about it—that was Mr. Peppers. The bits of wrecked armor hanging off one of his tusks made it abundantly clear.

There were so, *so* many questions Eric wanted to ask. "How?" was, of course, at the top of the list, followed closely by "Why?" and "When?" because last he'd checked, Mr. Peppers was an average-sized boar. Luckily, the one question Eric no longer had was which direction he should go. Mr. Peppers was on an obvious path for Timuscor, meaning that the knight was about to get plenty of backup. Better Eric used his time to go help Gabrielle wipe out her opponent, freeing them both up for new fights.

It was too bad, though. Eric really would have loved to follow Mr. Peppers and see what the boar could do with his new size.

20.

  This raider wasn't too shabby. Unlike most of the others she'd seen so far, he had opted to keep it simple rather than picking up some shiny new enchanted tool. Just a sword—and a damn strong one at that. Gabrielle hadn't seen many weapons that could stand up to her axe, and the fact that he had a half-orc's frame meant that their strength was more evenly matched than she'd have liked. If not for the undead boost, Gabrielle would have been at a serious disadvantage. Or maybe she wouldn't have, because in that scenario, she'd have another option.

  The truth was, Gabrielle probably could have already won the fight if she had been enraged. But she wasn't. She hadn't allowed her fury to break forth since the change, nor had she tried to use her axe's magic-cutting ability. Not knowing what her condition was, or how it related to the axe, made the idea of either terrifying. What if she activated an ability and used up whatever force was keeping her animated? The fear seemed silly when she considered it, yet as soon as the axe was in her hands, it felt all too real. No one knew exactly what she was, or how she was still alive. Until Gabrielle had some answers, she wasn't sure she wanted to gamble with her life, not unless there was a very real need to do so.

  Sadly, the longer she squared off with the half-orc holding the sword, the more she wondered if this would be the day that put her abilities to the test. Her adversary kept slipping gradually closer to Grumph. He was the real target; she was just standing in the way. With a roar and a charge, he ran forward, only to be met by Gabrielle along the way. She dodged a swing from the sword, bringing her axe around in a slice for his shins that he hopped away from, countering with a thrust of his own. Gabrielle parried, resulting in both their weapons shaking from the contact, forcing them both to retreat for a few minutes.

  It was a fight of attrition, one that she was slowly losing. If she went down, that would only leave a single dire bear as Grumph's protection. A fast or skilled warrior could work around that kind of distraction long enough to get in some lucky shots, which meant she had to keep her opponent at bay. The silver lining was that this fight had a deadline, one the raiders didn't even know existed. Already, the sky was dark with clouds. A little longer, and they should be able to finish this encounter off.

  The axe stopped quivering, and she could see that his sword was still shaking, yet Gabrielle didn't press the advantage. Her goal was time, stalling, and the longer this dragged out, the better it made things for Grumph. Plus, if she were truly honest with herself, this was the first time she'd been in true battle without the fog of rage to cloud her thoughts. The idea of spilling blood wasn't quite as easy to jump on in her proper state of mind. It was still probably necessary—she understood and was at peace with that fact. That didn't mean she wanted to make it her instinctive recourse.

Her half-orc enemy didn't share the desire to burn time; he leapt forward the instant his blade steadied. From behind him, Gabrielle caught sight of a figure slipping out from the general din of madness. Eric was creeping along, coming up behind the half-orc. She couldn't afford to pay her friend much attention; there was still a sword-swinging half-orc trying to stab her. Gabrielle focused on defense, continuing to dodge where possible as the sword-swings grew more and more dangerous. Finally, she swung her axe into a position to block, eyes darting past the half-orc to Eric. He was in the perfect position. As soon as she blocked and both weapons began quaking, the half-orc would be defenseless and Eric could slice his legs to knock him out of the fight.

In hindsight, Gabrielle would realize that it was her fault the half-orc caught on. She'd looked at Eric a tad too frequently and permitted her eyes to linger. Because of this, it shouldn't have been a surprise when, instead of taking her bait, her opponent swung around just as Eric was approaching. As a rogue, Eric had made great strides since they first set out, and was capable of far more than he'd ever been in his guarding days. That said, the half-orc was a trained combatant capable of fighting on Gabrielle's level, and he caught Eric by surprise. It was only natural that the enchanted sword ended up jammed through the side of Eric's gut, sending him staggering to the ground.

All of it happened so quick. Gabrielle was still standing there, holding her axe to block a strike that would never come. She could see Eric, stumbling back before collapsing, doing all he could to keep his sword aloft in the hopes of stopping a follow-up blow. Elnif was lifting his blade, taking aim, ready to finish the fight before she had a chance to intervene. The scene smashed against Gabrielle, flooding over her like an unexpected wave, washing away every ounce of self-preservation from her mind. This kind of rage could no more be contained than a hurricane could be reasoned with.

Maybe it was because of their recent lesson, or due to her newly-altered body, but Gabrielle could feel the changes as anger overtook reason and mana stormed into her muscles, swelling them with newfound power.

The axe had a dark, unnatural sheen on its surface, not that Gabrielle paid it more than a passing thought. Her weapon was already in motion, moving faster than she ever could have, even as a motivated undead. No barbarian was at their strongest unless they were funneling their fury, and the strike that slammed into Elnif's back was more powerful than he could have possibly anticipated.

Gabrielle's hit sank right through the leather armor, piercing the half-orc's spine. He cried out, a reasonable reaction considering the circumstances, dropping the sword as he gasped for air. Something wasn't right, besides the hunk of metal that now occupied space in his back. The half-orc appeared to be almost withering. Like he was being drained of something, yet no blood or body-mass was leaking free. Gabrielle shook the husk from her axe, noting that it landed far more lightly than a corpse of that weight should. She checked the sky, seeing that the clouds now covered almost the entirety of the town square. By the time she made it to Thistle, the fight would be done.

Rather than waste time and jostle her friend, Gabrielle planted herself directly over Eric as he worked to keep pressure on the wound. No one would get to him, not unless they were willing to bet their life against hers to do so. She was finally feeling like her proper self again, and would happily share that sentiment with anyone foolish enough to put her strength to the test.

She almost felt a pang of sadness, looking at Elnif's dead body. He'd fought well, and she would have liked to end things properly. It wouldn't be until later, when the anger had faded and left her at full mental faculties once more, that Gabrielle would pause to ask what should have been an extremely obvious question.

How did she know the half-orc's name?

*   *   *

There was no hurting the flame elemental. Timuscor wasn't entirely sure that was what this creature qualified as, but it seemed close enough to the descriptions he'd heard that any distinction would be arbitrary. Rulln was long dead, little more than a burning skull now, yet his body continued to attack, driving Timuscor into tighter and tighter corners. His shield was still glowing from the last round of attacks and showed some discoloration on the edges. Magic had limits, and that included wards on shields. It could only withstand so much damage at once before it failed, and Timuscor had a worrying suspicion that they were nearing that point.

Worse, Rulln's fiery form was driving him back toward the main battle, where the straggling raiders were dealing with a mix of dire bears and their own equipment. More than a few pieces of gear had already gone out of control, leaving behind smoking craters or half-dissolved bodies in their wake. Had the raiders come in with their customary weapons and armor, Timuscor suspected his party would have been in for a far harder battle. He could see why armies didn't merely load up their members with every magical trinket on hand; it risked causing more problems than it solved.

That gauntlet, however, was proving to be quite an efficient pain-in-the-ass. Another torrent of fire drove Timuscor back. Making things even more complicated, the burst of flame caught some nearby raiders' attention. A harried knight made a far more tempting target than an enormous bear, so several shifted their focus. This was rough; the fire monster was hard enough on its own. If Timuscor had to fight while surrounded, his defense was going to give.

Another step back, and a new sound reached his ears. Something was coming. Something big, with substantial momentum. Either an additional bear was on the way, or one of the items had summoned a new element to the fight. Timuscor hoped it was the former, but they had to be running low on bears by this point.

Tusks broke first through a veil of errant fog, slamming violently into a pair of raiders who'd been moving toward Timuscor. Following the bone-white spears was a familiar snout that Timuscor recognized immediately, though it was much larger than usual.

"Mr. Peppers?"

The enormous boar snorted once, as if in confirmation. He was huge, his back practically level with Timuscor's shoulders. With a loud grunt, Mr. Peppers reared back and crushed another raider, one who'd been trying to line up a strike on the nearby bear's flank. The bear roared, Mr. Peppers snorted, and Timuscor began to wonder why exactly he needed to be there.

A blast of flame served as an excellent reminder. Timuscor hurriedly planted his shield between the fire and Mr. Peppers. Small or large, he wasn't letting any of these bastards hurt his boar. When the torrent faded, a new noise reached Timuscor's ears; soft sizzling drifted up from his shield. It was the sound of raindrops boiling to vapor as soon as they landed. The rain had started, which meant "Grumph's" spell was complete. Any second now, the real effect would kick in.

From his vantage point, Timuscor saw the fire-corpse gradually weaken as the rain intensified. Smoke rose from the fading blaze, yet it still struggled forward, set on attacking one last time. Valiant as that determination was, it proved to be too little. A clap of thunder roared across the land, while a half-dozen bolts of lightning split the sky, each one planting itself directly in a raider's torso. The next round came within seconds, as did the next, and so on. Even the burning corpse took a few shots, the overwhelming electrical energy sundering what little connective tissues remained. When the smoke from the body faded, there was nothing more than ash and the gauntlet, which looked untouched.

The lightning smote the intruders for several seconds longer before finally dissipating, along with the clouds overhead. As the rain came, it washed away the remaining fog, providing a clear view for the first time since the fight began. Timuscor scanned carefully, hunting for any survivors that might still have some fight left in them. There were none. No survivors that he could see. Though a few did twitch occasionally, that was little more than an after-effect of the lightning strikes. Between the bears, the lightning, and the raiders' own equipment, his party had managed to survive the onslaught.

It was a humbling moment, both to see how easily the people of Notch could deal with such a threat, and the realization that, without their help, he and the others would have been butchered. Jolia pretending to cast through Grumph had enabled them to endure and survive, supplemented by Kieran pretending to be Thistle, hurling daggers at every high-danger target that wandered too close to the tavern. Without their help, this would have been a different kind of bloodbath. After surviving the Grand Quest, Timuscor had permitted himself to feel as though they were truly gaining strength, but this fight put things back into perspective. There was so much further to climb, and hard as they were all trying, he and the others hadn't even grasped the core of how their abilities functioned. They needed to learn more, train more, grow stronger. They'd put themselves into conflicts between the very gods of the world, and there was no telling how strong their opponents would be moving forward.

Next to Timuscor, a glow appeared, covering the entirety of Mr. Peppers. It was brief, too quick to even properly worry about what was happening, before there was a bright flash and Mr. Peppers was once more at his normal size, the shattered remains of his armor landing with a clatter nearby. Timuscor examined the fractured metal briefly before shaking his head.

"Looks like we'll need to make you a new set. Maybe one that can change size?"

A grunt, possibly of approval, came as Mr. Peppers' only reply. The others were moving now. He saw Gabrielle wave down Thistle as soon as the gnome emerged. Someone must be injured. Tempting though it was to rush over, Timuscor had no healing to offer, so rather than waste the energy, he began moving from raider to raider, making sure that none were pretending to be felled. He would take them prisoner if they could be saved, and spare them the misery if they couldn't, but ultimately, it wasn't an issue.

There wasn't a single raider left to deal with. Each one was dead, several with smoking wounds where the lightning had pulsed directly into their hearts. Jolia could have cast that spell in seconds if not for the pageantry, and the results would have been no less destructive. So much power in these people, in this town, and yet, at some point, they had all stood in the same place as Timuscor. He could reach those heights; it was doable, if he had the talent to learn and the willpower to follow through.

They had much progress to make indeed, yet Timuscor wasn't put off. Someday, they could attain this level of strength. And this might very well be the perfect place to start.

21.

Infuriating. All of the work, the killing, the stealing, and what had she gotten? Inept pawns killed, half by bumbling adventurers and half by their inability to wield the very tools she'd provided. Well, tools Kalzidar had provided, anyway. And it *was* true she hadn't done all of the stealing or killing herself; there were other priests who'd completed smaller tasks that led to the end result. Nevertheless, this was an insult—to her, to Kalzidar, to the very idea of intruding bandits bursting into a small town. Didn't they know there was a way these things were done?

At least it hadn't been a complete waste. Even if the real players had hidden behind their puppets, she'd still gotten to see how they liked to fight. One was good with daggers, and they had at least a single mage. Given the lightning storm and swarm of bears, the caster seemed to have a focus on nature and the elements. That information would prove useful, when passed on to the others. There had to be more, though. More to uncover, more to assess. She still had a few days before the time was upon them. Perhaps she could put together one more assault. It was risky, and would require prayer before a final decision was made, yet it felt like a worthy use of her energy.

For now, she had to slip away. The trader wasn't scheduled to arrive yet, but her instructions were clear. She was not to give any sign that someone was camping along Notch's borders, which meant allowing the usual traffic to pass unimpeded. Although Kalzidar was shielding her from detection by magical means, she could still tip them off by staying in the open view of travelers. A poor morning was one thing; erring on that front risked unwinding the entire plan, and she would not disappoint Kalzidar in such a way. Both out of devotion, and self-preservation.

* * *

Timanuel hurled himself between the roc's claws and Wimberly, taking a hefty scratch along the back of his armor for the trouble. Better mar his appearance than suffer Wimberly's guts spread out all over the nest, which was where things had been heading.

It had seemed like a simple task. Climb the mountain, find the home of the golden rocs, take a few feathers, and be on their way. At first, things went to plan. They made it along the road with only a minor skirmish, managed to navigate their way up the mountain with minimal injury, and stumbled upon a nest by pure fortune. That luck had lasted only until they'd stepped inside, however. Circling shadows were their first, brief warning before the golden rocs began swooping in and attacking. They were young, far smaller than the enormous creatures they'd eventually become. The birds known as rocs were famous for being huge, but golden rocs were a type of tremendous all to themselves. Legend said a fully grown one could spread its wings and block out the sun.

The one upside was that, given the fighting, the nest, and the dive-bombs, the party had more golden roc feathers than they could possibly need. They might even be able to turn a small profit on the rest, if they made it out of here in one piece. Monster parts always had some kind of market, be they for mages or collectors.

"We have to jump!" Chalara was holding a magical shield in place over herself and Gelthorn, who was firing as fast as she could reload her arrows. The quiver was not endless, unfortunately, and there were too many enemies to wear them down slowly.

"Won't that just kill us faster?" Timanuel asked.

"I can cast Light-Fall on us. It will burn up the rest of my mana for the day, though, so you assholes have to protect me on the way down." Chalara sank to her knees, presenting as small a target as possible while a fresh set of talons raked her wavering shield. "Thing is, I can't cast while holding this, so we have to jump first. I'll have to do it in the air."

Timanuel and Wimberly both glanced over the edge. It was a long way down, easily enough to kill them, but not quite so lengthy a drop that they felt confident Chalara would be able to cast that many spells before impact. As they looked, screeches filled the air and another pair of rocs swooped down. Chalara was right. They had what they needed, and this was too overwhelming a force to defeat.

"On three?" Wimberly called.

"Fuck that. Just jump!" Chalara was already moving, her shield dissolving into light, Gelthorn close at hand. They raced to Timanuel and Wimberly, helping the gnome to her feet before taking surprisingly graceful leaps over the edge of the nest. Timanuel and Wimberly went with them, both keeping careful watch on the circling shadows as they began plummeting toward the ground.

Seconds later, they saw Gelthorn's fall slow considerably while they raced past. Credit to her: the forest warrior had her bow drawn and ready in case any rocs tried to follow them down. Chalara slapped a hand on

Wimberly moments later, mumbling under her breath as she cast the spell again.

It was like someone had tied a rope to Wimberly's body. She suddenly stopped tearing through the air and drifted like one of the very feathers they'd come to collect. Heartening as it was to see, Timanuel couldn't help noticing the sheen on Chalara's face, despite the wind screaming past them. This was taking a lot out of her, and the ground was coming up fast. Still, she hurried on, pressing against him as the arcane words came out so fast they nearly tripped over one another. Timanuel felt the magic take shape at the same time he saw Chalara's head start to dip. On instinct, he wrapped her in a hug, then flipped over, putting his back between her and the ground.

Before he'd finished the rotation, Chalara was out. Maybe she'd overestimated herself. Maybe she'd known from the start that she didn't have enough mana to save everyone. Whatever the case, this was all Timanuel could do to try to help now. He wasn't a mage, he wasn't especially clever, but he was a paladin. Taking hits for his friends was just one part of what that entailed.

Since he was enchanted to fall more slowly and Chalara was under gravity's full control, the end result was that they fell together at a reduced pace, just not to the point where they would land without injury. Timanuel came down hard; he felt more than a few bones fracture on impact. He was still alive, though, and based on the gentle snoring drifting up from Chalara, so was she.

Wimberly and Gelthorn were still drifting down, so Timanuel spared a bit of healing magic for himself—enough so he could move properly as they continued their escape. Things seemed to be looking up. The rocs were staying close to their nest, not bothering to give chase. It made sense; all they'd been doing in the first place was repelling invaders from their home.

From his pouch, Timanuel produced a few of the golden feathers they'd gone through so much trouble to obtain. One major item down, some potion ingredients, and two more items to go. He just hoped they wouldn't be quite so dangerous to obtain.

*   *   *

The adventurers were gathered in Brock's tavern, clustered up around Thistle as he continued healing the wound in Eric's guts. They'd stabilized him in the open before moving indoors to finish. The wound might have been a fatal blow to one with less experience, but bodies that were constantly fueled by mana had a tendency to become more resilient. It was one of the reasons adventurers could keep fighting through blows that would fell a mere farmer. They probably didn't know that, Kieran realized as he took a quick glance through the tavern window. They were just acting on instinct, much as they had throughout the battle itself.

While the newcomers were concerned with taking care of their friend, Kieran and Simone were sorting through the gear the raiders had been wielding. Most of their standard equipment had been melted by the lightning or crushed by the bears; the majority of what remained to be were the newly-acquired enchanted items. Turning a gauntlet over in his hands, Kieran examined it carefully, using the magical glasses Jolia had lent him for the job.

"Looks like this one is pretty strong. Gauntlet of the Flame Warden, a near-artifact that was handed down by a powerful warrior from the Plane of Fire. No wonder a mere thief couldn't handle this; you'd need a lot more mana capacity and some primal connection to fire in order to wield it properly."

"Into the sack, then." Simone held out the canvas bag lined up and down with runes. Magical bags that could hold more than they seemed were almost commonplace in major kingdoms; this was something more secure. It had enough enchantments to be sure that those who shouldn't get in wouldn't, regardless of how hard they tried—a necessary precaution when dealing with this many magical items from various sources.

Kieran tossed the gauntlet in, then removed a ring from a nearby finger unattached to any owner. "This one… just a small bit of protection magic, clearly not enough to help its owner."

"Potential loot?" Simone asked.

It was wrong to let the adventurers fight so hard and walk away with none of the spoils. Kieran felt that in his gut as surely as Simone and the others did. Former adventurers or current, there was an order to these things, one that Kieran wasn't going to risk violating while his town was under assault. Then again, Kieran couldn't very well hand over equipment so powerful it might kill the adventurers, so the best solution they'd come up with was to screen the remaining items. Those that were worth having, but were not so strong as to be dangerous, could be used as potential loot for Notch's guests—after more thorough examination, of course. Everything else went into the bag. They would hand it off to the trader when she came through, probably picking up a tidy profit in the process.

"Potential loot," Kieran agreed, tossing the ring into a more mundane bag slung over his shoulder.

"I'll make a note." Simone jotted a few words in the scroll at her side, eyes darting to the corner of her page. It was rare to see Simone uncomfortable, especially with the winds of victory still blowing through the air. "Kieran, be honest with me, what do you think of these adventurers?"

It was more than just a question, she wasn't even trying to hide that fact, yet without knowing exactly what it was she was fishing for, Kieran had no choice but to offer her the truth. "Good-hearted, and they work together well. That teamwork, along with a bit of divine help, is probably what's seen them through their travels so far. In terms of raw power, they have a few neat tricks, but it's clear they started at a disadvantage. They didn't train for these lives, and it shows. Gabrielle is only now roughly as strong as an average barbarian thanks to being undead, Grumph doesn't have nearly the mana capacity as most mages at his casting proficiency, Thistle's weakened form means that he will never properly take a paladin's place on the front lines, Eric was only obviously just recently trained, and Timuscor…" Kieran trailed off briefly, then shook his head.

"Physically, Timuscor is the only one at the level where he should be. He started off as an adventurer, and the difference is clear. But mentally, he's still so raw, even though it's been some while since he was freed. We all lived our first lives long enough to have a sense of ourselves, to mentally divvy things up between what we'd been doing versus who we truly were. I think he might have broken away from his control before forming that, and lacking a sense of self has slowed his growth. The only part he seems to be carrying with him is his desire to be a paladin."

There was no dissent from Simone; she'd almost certainly reached roughly the same conclusions from her limited time interacting with the party. Assessing someone's potential abilities was part of the adventuring life—it helped avoid mouthing off to someone who could knock you through a wall—and the assessment of Notch's newest visitors said only one thing: they were a nice party, not a strong one.

"I know what we decided when this first started. Just a place to rest; maybe a peaceful life, if they were looking to settle down and seemed like a good fit. Does that still feel right?"

"You want to train them?" Kieran asked, already aware of the direction that kind of talk would lead.

Simone held her hand out in the air, palm flat, and shook it along the wrist. "Sort of? I'm not proposing we teach them all our secrets or techniques or anything like that. I was watching Gabrielle when she used her rage today. It was a curious sight, seeing the mana flow in, weaving its way through the axe. I think it's doing more than just keeping her alive, and I'd like to study their bond. Obviously we shouldn't try teaching them to slay dragons in a single blow or anything ludicrous, but they jumped into danger without hesitation just to help us with a little subterfuge. Maybe we can teach them enough to survive for a week once they leave."

"They lived long enough to make it here," Kieran pointed out.

Simone didn't reply at first. Instead, she reached down and tried to pick up a longsword near a body that looked like it had been sucked dry of some essential nutrients. She let out a sharp curse seconds later, dropping it to the ground with a clatter. "Shit, no wonder that blade gave Gabrielle such trouble. There's a hefty amount of divine magic buried in there."

Walking quickly over, Kieran grabbed the longsword by the handle. It was a fine weapon, keen and balanced. There was more to it, however: old magic, the kind woven by a master of an art long since lost to time. Kieran had encountered a few such items on his journeys. For most, they would be nothing more than sturdy, reliable weapons, yet there were a few who would see different results, wielders who satisfied some unspoken requirements known only to the items themselves. Given the tinge of divine magic that had burned Simone, this was a sword most likely meant for a paladin.

"Assuming this one passes inspection, we'll let Thistle take hold of this and see if it produces any other effect, such as resizing," Kieran decided. "If not, then let's offer it to Timuscor. He's the only one of the group who uses a longsword, and I've got a good hunch about this one. Whatever's inside is powerful enough to hide from Jolia's spell, so maybe it can help keep the kid alive once he's back on the road."

"I take it you're on board with helping them?" Simone finished shaking her fingers, the last of her burns already faded.

"We'll give them enough that they know how to grow from here, and you can untangle any potential issues with the axe or other enchantments they might be hauling around. Don't forget, these people came here with a piece of *that* artifact. Someone is using them as pawns, so I think they're a touch more looked after than you think." Kieran jammed the longsword into the ground so Simone wouldn't grab it again by mistake. He'd pick it up when they were ready to head inside, but there was still a lot of work left to do.

Already the town priest, Olipep, was preparing to hold service. Simone had sent her attendants a message to ready the graves, meaning that was one chore they could thankfully skip. They would see these raiders put properly in the ground before the day was done, each one getting a grave on newly consecrated ground. Killing didn't come as easily as it had before, when they were all adventurers roaming the countryside with nary a second thought for the bloodshed in their wake. It was still necessary, when occasion demanded, but at the very least, they could treat what remained of those they killed with respect.

Even if the others had been pretending to lead the attack, it was really Notch's defenders who were responsible for most of this carnage. The bears, the lightning, the daggers planted in people's vital organs—it all traced back to him and Jolia. Brock and Simone had avoided engagement purely by chance; neither of them had needed to intervene. They would have, though, and in a heartbeat at that. Most of the town could enjoy their new lives of peace solely because the town council was still willing to shed blood. Killing was the nature of their world, and disliking it didn't change that fundamental truth.

It would still be true when the others emerged from Notch and headed back into the kingdoms. Monsters, bandits, corrupt politicians, greedy guild leaders, there was no end to the dangers awaiting those who set to the road and called themselves adventurers. That was a concern to deal with later. For now, Kieran wanted to see his town swept clean. Someone had clearly sent these raiders in, and that person was likely smart enough not to be among them. There was much to sort through, and no indication how long they had to do it.

"After the service, we'll gather together to share information and theories gleaned from this battle," Kieran said. "Once that's done, we can talk to the adventurers about extending their time with us a touch. Until the trader arrives, at soonest. At that point, we can give them a guide, or they can make a home here."

"You think she'll have any trouble making it through with whatever is going on?"

At that, Kieran managed to produce a short laugh. "I think she'll be just fine. It's a regretful fool who underestimates that one. Let's just focus on making sure Notch is still standing by the time she gets here."

22.

By the time the last of the bodies were buried, it was near evening. Together, most of Notch's overseers returned to the tavern, where Brock was still overseeing the adventurers. He'd never been much of one for ceremony, be it for friend or foe. In Brock's culture, to die in battle was a glory, not a tragedy, and such accomplishments were meant to be drunkenly toasted. Enemy or ally, he would raise a mug to any warrior who fought valiantly and accomplished deeds worthy of retelling.

Jolia and Simone were largely silent along the trek, making only occasional small talk about their theories on what might be happening. For Kieran, too, the evening felt heavy, this post-burial walk all too familiar. The cost of living so long as an adventurer, and making it to retirement, was that he'd been forced to go to many funerals such as this. When two sides met in a battle to the death, only one dug the graves. For a time, he'd hoped this part of his life was truly behind him, yet now, a new enemy was at the gates, trying to break inside.

That was part of why Kieran had agreed to Thistle's plan. Stepping onto a new battlefield and drawing his blade again—that was no small act. If he began to fight in earnest once more, Kieran wasn't sure he'd be able to stop. In the old days, before he'd gained a sense of self, the killing had merely been part of the job. This would be different. This time, Kieran had a town he'd be protecting. A lifetime of adventuring had taught him much, and one of the most important lessons was that people were at their most dangerous when they had something to fight for.

Such thoughts left his mind by necessity as they entered the tavern to find a semi-festive vibe. Eric had been patched up good as new thanks to Thistle's healing, and everyone was enjoying mugs of ale that clearly weren't their first. Since it was nearly night, Kieran helped himself to a drink, then motioned for everyone to draw near.

"Evening, all. With our enemies now properly laid to rest, I think it's time we dug into what happened here today. A band of Urthos plains raiders, geared to the teeth with equipment they couldn't control, managed to breach our borders only a few days after you lot wandered in. And before we go down that road—no, I don't think you had anything to do with it. Not knowingly. But this makes the idea that your artifact or god led you here just that much more suspect. Thistle, as a paladin, I assume you've been praying since your arrival. Did Grumble ever confirm that he was the one who brought you to Notch? If we can rule out even one source, it would make our task easier."

As a rule, Thistle didn't generally look uncomfortable. He faced everything head-on, and even when bothered, his years as a minion allowed him to keep a steady expression. On this occasion, however, there was a flicker of worry in his eyes. It tipped off several people in the room seconds before his mouth started moving.

"I was planning on bringing this up today, before everything went awry, but I actually haven't been able to speak with Grumble since I arrived here in Notch. Every time I try, I have a dream where I'm being buffeted by winds so fierce, I can't make out his words. My intent was to politely bring it up and slowly draw out whether or not this was a side effect of your wards, or whether it was something more sinister. Given the question you just asked, I'm guessing it's neither."

Although the candor was momentarily surprising, it quickly became apparent why Thistle had admitted that he hadn't fully trusted them before.

"I see. You were concerned we might be the ones blocking your communication with Grumble, and if that were the case, then you'd have to assume we were doing so for nefarious purposes." Jolia was drumming her left hand on her staff as her right hefted a mug to her lips, bringing it back down half-empty. "And you're telling us now because you no longer think that's the case."

"Close," Thistle corrected. "I'm telling you now because, while there is still a chance that Kieran's question was a fake designed to trick me, that kind of thinking isn't going to get us anywhere. For paladins, faith is an essential part of what we do. I decided that it was time to show you some and trust you, though I can't be entirely sure that it won't backfire. It's clear there's a force out there after one, if not all of us, and if we want to come out the other side, I think it's time we stopped keeping one another at arm's length."

A show of vulnerability, rather than one of force. While not the first time Kieran had seen that move brought out, it wasn't a frequent tactic in most adventuring circles. Then again, if they'd been normal adventurers, he'd never have permitted them to enter Notch in the first place.

"Thank you, Thistle. That does indeed tell us something useful. You are hardly the only one of faith here, so none of the wards protecting this town are designed to interfere with a connection to the divine. In fact, until your arrival, none of our citizens had complained of such an issue. I'll check around tomorrow to be sure, but I have a feeling that if it was affecting more than just you, we'd have heard about it by now."

Nearby, Eric was rubbing his gut where the wound had been. Even with healing, it was hard to convince a mind that all injury had suddenly vanished. "That means someone must be specifically messing with Thistle and Grumble's ability to speak. I wouldn't have even imagined that to be possible, but if it is, then surely that means we're seeing the interference of another god."

"Possibly, but they have protocols for when disputes arise," Simone informed him. "To directly interfere in the connection between god and paladin crosses a line, and it's not something they would do on a whim. There would need to be a greater goal, especially considering how much power would be required. It's also possible they created spells or items suited for the task, tools that could theoretically be used by mortals to achieve the same ends. My point is, god or not, this suggests we're in the middle of someone's plan."

"And a plan derailed is harder to recover from than something as flexible as random attacks," Thistle surmised. "We need to figure out the plan, and begin tearing it down."

"Aye, seems our best recourse," Jolia agreed.

Kieran rose to his feet, making sure that all eyes were on him. This wasn't just an announcement for the adventurers; he needed his own people to take note, as well. "Then our first step forward is to share everything we know about what's going on. Everything, from both sides. After that, the way we keep a step ahead is what Thistle suggested: no more half-trust. We let these people into our home, and when danger appeared, they stepped up to fight for us. Whatever we're in, we're now in it together. Anyone have an objection to that?"

Not a single voice of dissent was raised; in fact, the only sound was Brock pouring a fresh mug of ale for Jolia. After waiting a few seconds, just to be sure, Kieran nodded and sat back down.

"Then let's start comparing notes and see where it leads us."

* * *

Another game session successfully completed without incident. Russell should have felt relieved. If things had suddenly turned real and magical in a game where the situation was that dire, they might have panicked and ended up with talon wounds in their flesh. No one seemed disappointed that the dice had yet to glow, or that Russell's eyes hadn't clouded over. Cheri actually looked worried whenever Russell stared at the book for too long before turning toward them. She tried to hide it, but the frequency of catching that look on her face made it easy to notice.

As much as they'd been willing to take this plunge for the chance to see real magic once more, they were also scared of what might happen if they succeeded. So, to them, any session where all they had to do was play a normal game of *Spells, Swords, and Stealth* was a good one. It should have felt the same to Russell; it wasn't like he was eager to lose control of his body again.

Yet, the more time passed, the easier it was to let doubt in. Had they imagined it? Had they all eaten bad fish that day? Maybe there was a gas leak? All of these were such insane, long-shot explanations, and they still came in miles more plausible than *magic*. It was hard not to wonder if, game after magic-less game, there wasn't some other potential explanation for what they'd experienced.

Thoughts like these were what drove Russell to the internet, despite the late hour. He was combing through postings, forums, social media, anything he could find with even a passing mention of *Spells, Swords, and Stealth*'s mysterious limited edition modules. Per usual, Russell found himself smashing against little more than dead-ends: deleted posts, vague word choices, frustration after frustration. Plenty of people were asking about the modules, but no one was *talking*, himself included. Magic or not, it was easy to tell that they were on the inside of something, and loose lips might see them ejected to the other side of the glass.

Russell kept digging, expanding his parameters more and more in the hopes of finding something to reassure him. Suddenly, near the bottom of a page, a link caught his eye. Russell opened it. The link led to an angry review about a comic book shop a few towns over. No wonder this hadn't been picked up earlier; it barely mentioned the game at all. It did, however, describe being trapped at a table and injured based on what had happened to their characters. The reviewer made it sound like a *Saw*-style trap they'd been led into, but Russell recognized key features. Glowing dice, cloudy eyes—it was all there, only framed as a cruel prank instead of magic.

Fast as his fingers would move, Russell clicked on a link to the shop, only to discover it had gone out of business some time ago. That explained why no one seemed to be paying this review much attention, aside from the fact that it sounded like a crazy person wrote it.

A new idea struck Russell. If he could find the reviewer, they could compare notes. Maybe there had been something different at the game shop than what had happened in Russell's dining room. He clicked back to the review, skimming down to see the username of whoever had posted it. People managed to find out real names from usernames on television all the time; there had to be a process for it.

Unrealistic as Russell's expectations of violating privacy were, they also proved to be unnecessary. No sooner had his eyes fallen upon the name than a low, annoyed groan slipped out of Russell's throat. He knew that name. Not from memory, precisely, but from context. This comic shop was near enough that there was probably only one contender who would post under the horrendous screen name "BitchesLuvMitches" without an iota of self-awareness.

The first lead he'd found on someone outside his group who'd experienced the same events, and it was, of all people, Mitch—head of the trio consisting of some of the worst players Russell had ever gamed with, all-around asshole, and now potentially the holder of useful information for unraveling this mystery.

Russell just had to figure out if he wanted the information *that* badly. Part of him wished they'd just had magic spring up during the roc fight after all.

*   *   *

Gabrielle awoke with a start, largely because she wasn't used to sleeping anymore. The closest she'd come to managing was to close her eyes and rest her mind by clearing it. Normally, the act was difficult, but this evening, it had come naturally. Maybe using her anger left an innate need to be soothed, or had tired her out in ways she didn't notice. Regardless, her mind had cleared naturally after the evening's late discussion, and she'd expected to remain like that for another few hours.

Instead, she was awake. Except, no, she wasn't, because she definitely hadn't gone to sleep in the middle of a grassy expanse with the sun high overhead. Was she dreaming? That would mean she was truly asleep. Well, it was the first time she'd risked using her rage since the change; this might very well be an unanticipated side effect.

"Hello?"

The voice was unfamiliar, and instinctively, Gabrielle reached for her axe. That was the moment she noticed that the axe was missing. She was here in her usual armor, hair still dark and skin pale, yet the axe itself was nowhere to be seen. Curious, but one could hardly go looking for sense in the world of dreams. Rising to her feet, Gabrielle turned toward the voice, only to find a semi-familiar face looking back at her.

"You're the half-orc... the one that I... Elnif, right?"

"How did you know that?" He started forward, wobbly steps that pushed him off the ground harder than they should have. The raider had become light, near insubstantial, and as he moved, Gabrielle could spot the occasional ray of sunshine peeking through his form. Dead, then, even in this dreamscape.

On that note, it was strange that she would dream about a place such as this. "I don't know how your name is on my tongue. Let me ask you this: do our surroundings look familiar to you?"

Almost for the first time, Elnif seemed to realize that there was more around than just Gabrielle. He surveyed the landscape, head bobbing almost immediately. "They do. We are on the plains of Urthos, near where I was born. I learned to ride here. My father taught me the ways of a sword here."

Distantly, Gabrielle could swear she heard the sounds of swords clashing, and saw a shadow that looked like a child on a horse flick by in the corner of her vision. If that didn't confirm it, nothing would. This wasn't her dream at all. It was Elnif's. Only, somehow, it was going on inside her head.

No, not "somehow." When she really thought about it, Gabrielle knew what had happened. Not the specifics of how, true, but the results were obvious. She'd drained him, taken more than just blood when she struck him down in fury. That was why her axe wasn't here; this *was* the axe, metaphorically, maybe even literally. Perhaps it had drawn her mind into itself to make this meeting happen.

The logistics weren't important at the moment; she was here and had to make the most of things. Her first concerns should be finding a way out and learning all she could from Elnif. After a night of comparing notes, her friends came up with a few theories of what was going on, but had found no solid ground. Elnif might know a crucial detail without even realizing it.

First things first. If she wanted to have a conversation with this fellow, there was only one way she could start it. "Sorry I had to kill you, Elnif. I'd have accepted surrender, but you went after my friend."

He stared at her for a few moments, then down at his own hands, before letting out a soft sigh. "I forgive you. It was battle; I'd have done the same. I was *trying* to do the same. You just won."

"Really? I kind of expected you to be madder about it," Gabrielle admitted.

"Me, too. Things are clearer here. I have... peace, I think."

He did look peaceful, more so than when they'd been trading blows. A small part of her was envious at that, Elnif's ability to look so serene. But she knew she wouldn't trade places with him for anything, and if she didn't want to end up in the same situation, then there was definitely work to do.

"I'm glad to hear that, Elnif, because, if you're willing, I'd like to talk with you about what happened today, hear your side of things."

The peace faded as his face momentarily darkened. Just as quickly, the rage slipped away. "We were tricked. Set up, sent in as a sacrifice, weren't we?"

Gabrielle nodded. "That's our working theory."

"Then I will tell you everything. Because if I cannot have vengeance by my hand, then I shall have it through yours. Show the one who tricked my people the same hell you gave us."

"I'll do everything I can." Not a true promise, because Gabrielle was starting to learn that there were some fights she couldn't win, anger and determination be damned. The most she could ever promise was her best.

That was enough for Elnif. He made his way over to her side, and began to tell her everything about the trail that had led the raiders to Notch.

23.

Mornings were different now. Before, Timuscor had merely needed to roll out of bed, take care of necessities, and clad himself in the simple traveling clothes he'd been left with after his armor was seized. Such was no longer the case, as he and the others had been allowed to return to their rooms with all of their equipment following the battle. It might have been something that slipped attention with all the other issues to focus on, but it presented a conundrum for Timuscor. To don that armor was to say that he expected, or was at least prepared for, danger to beset them at some point through the day. However, not donning it left him exposed, and if yesterday had proved nothing else, it had demonstrated that even the powerful people of Notch could be surprised.

Ultimately, Timuscor elected to put on his armor. Not because he expected trouble, although he certainly considered it a possibility, but rather because he didn't want his body getting accustomed to moving without the weight. Their last fight had given him an idea of just how much more powerful he could still become, and maintaining the strength to move unencumbered by his armor was the bare minimum he could do. Especially since their days here were spent on rest and work instead of training.

Timuscor descended to find that he wasn't the only person who had slipped on their armor that morning. Gabrielle was clad in her usual blood-red leathers, Eric wore the stolen color-changing armor taken off another rogue's corpse, and even Grumph was in his moon-spider silk reinforced robes. Thistle, of course, still had his armor on. It refused to so much as budge from his skin, which made quite a bit more sense now that they knew some force was cutting off Thistle and Grumble's communication. The god of the minions had managed to tell his paladin to stay safe, even if the message was more oblique than usual.

As he made his way to the tavern counter, Timuscor noticed Brock watching him intently. Before his order was even out, the muscular bartender was sliding over a plate of eggs with a substantial slice of seared meat on top.

"My thanks, but I fear this much will be too heavy a breakfast for the day we have ahead." Timuscor tried to push the plate back, finding it held firmly in place by Brock's hand on the other side.

"Eat. You're going to need the nutrition for what's coming today." He effortlessly moved the plate a few inches closer to Timuscor, making the firmness of his position on the issue clear.

Somewhat befuddled by the aggressive hospitality, Timuscor accepted his meal and walked over to an open seat by Grumph. The eggs were the same as they'd been having for days, whereas the meat was gamey yet tender, cut from some animal Timuscor had never sampled before. It did have a bit of a kick that spread warmth through his stomach, and within a few bites, he felt more awake and alert.

Approximately halfway through his steak, the tavern door swung open to reveal Jolia. She walked in, pausing by the bar to receive a mug from Brock that he'd begun pouring as soon as the gnome entered. After a deep sip and a satisfied smack, she turned to address the remainder of the room.

"Good morning, everyone. Here I was worried that you'd need to be told to gear up, but I can see you all took the hint when we permitted you to keep your weapons and armor. In light of recent events—namely the surprise attack on our town and the revelation that gods are likely at work—we have decided to repay your bravery with a small amount of education. Not training, mind you. I don't want anyone getting heady ideas about how much you'll be learning. Just some basic education and ways to train yourselves." Jolia paused to climb her way onto a stool, making herself more visible to the room as a whole.

"Mornings will now be dedicated to laying that groundwork and helping you better understand your abilities. Afternoons are still for work; it all has to get done, anyway, and will be a good way to give your minds a rest. Once that's done, you're free to do as you please—train, relax, eat, whatever you wish. In a few days, our trader will swing through town. At that point, we'll employ her as a guide for any who wish to leave, since we can no longer be certain the coast is clear. On that note, one of us will stop by in the evenings to bring you up to speed, and to see if you've had any ideas or revelations about our situation. We've got little to go on, so sharing every scrap of information we can get is essential."

There was the sound of gulping as Gabrielle finished off her cup of water in a steady chug. She set the container down with a heavy *thud*. It was a performance meant to draw attention, and she succeeded. "If you don't mind a suggestion, we should probably have those meetings in the mornings, as well."

"In case Thistle learns more in his dreams?" Jolia asked.

"In case any of us learn something in the night. I, for example, had a very interesting evening. Not sure how trustworthy the information I got is, but I should definitely share it." Gabrielle hesitated, as if unsure of whether or not the next words should be spoken. Her nerve soon asserted itself, as did her knowledge that, right now, every clue was vital. "When I killed someone yesterday, my axe seemed to... steal part of him, is the best way I can think to describe it. Then, last night, I was able to talk to him. I have no idea what that means, or if it was even the same raider I killed, but it felt worth sharing."

She could feel the looks from the others burning into her. They were worried for her, scared of what she'd become, and, in one case, weighed down by the guilt of her condition. Every time some new development popped up, it was always the same. Gabrielle was ready to find answers half out of the desire to avoid future moments like these. The other half, however, was to put her own very real fears to bed. Their delay made sense, but she had to start seriously working toward answers about her condition.

"Definitely glad you told me that," Jolia agreed. "We'll table discussion of what you learned until this evening, though. You were going to spend the morning with Simone, anyway, getting a full analysis done on you, your axe, and the connection between you. This is one more thing to have her look into. Once we've got a better idea of how reliable the knowledge is, we can discuss it tonight."

Further words had been ready to leave Gabrielle's mouth, though she'd be damned if she could remember what they were as her jaw hung open. Just like that, so casually, Jolia had proposed solving the question that had been tunneling around in the back of Gabrielle's mind since she changed. Was that even possible? The axe was a mystery, and they'd been bonded in a storm of wild magic—it was the sort of situation one expected only a specialized brilliance might be able to untangle. Simone could handle the undead aspect, she'd shown that much already, but the axe was another matter. Gabrielle had bought the names of artifact experts back in Camnarael, and Simone's name wasn't on there. Then again, that might very well be because no one knew Simone was still alive, or existed at all. The entire point of Notch was that it was hidden from the greater world; that probably extended to information brokers, as well.

"You really think she can?" Whatever words had been lost, these were the ones to take their place, a touch of hope and far more fear than she'd intended permeating Gabrielle's words.

"Without question." Jolia permitted no quiver or hesitation in her voice, and the reply was instantaneous. "In terms of raw talent, I'm a superior mage to Simone. But when it comes to study, research, thought, and creation, she's on a whole other level. She built half her spell book on her own. If there's anyone who can puzzle together what you are and how the magic works, it's that woman."

"Just the expert we needed, perhaps." Thistle took his time with the next bite, properly chewing over both this knowledge and his eggs. "The more coincidences pile up, the more uncertain I become about what drove us here. There are things we benefit from, information we clearly needed that we have come into. Yet at the same time, we're seeing surprise attacks and visible effort to curtail divine communication. It's like we're supposed to be here and not, all at the same time."

The whole thing was equally strange to Timuscor. He did have one thought on the matter, an idea he nearly silenced until he remembered Jolia's words. They knew so little that every piece mattered, even bits that could easily be wrong. "What if it's both? Maybe we *were* supposed to be here, but then someone else decided to use those plans to their advantage?"

He'd been braced for polite nodding, followed by one of the smarter members of his party pointing out exactly why that couldn't be the case. Instead, Timuscor was met by considered silence. Just when he was about to apologize for wasting everyone's time, Eric let out a long breath and leaned forward.

"Shit. That might be it. We keep thinking of this as one connected plan, instead of two mashing against each other. Grumble points us toward Notch, knowing we have serious gaps in our understanding that need to be filled if we're going to get stronger. Where can we get that knowledge and find people sympathetic to our situation? Here. And, added bonus, they've got enough magical expertise to give us some idea of what's going on with Gabrielle. Makes sense. The problem is, it makes so much sense that another god might see the move coming. Instead of this being our chance to relax and learn, they've pinned us in and cut off communication between Thistle and Grumble. What comes next is anyone's guess, but for right now, Timuscor's theory is the best fit I've heard. Anyone else got something better?"

A round of collective head-shaking rippled through the room, Jolia and Brock included. For his part, Timuscor made a point of looking to his plate to hurriedly put away more eggs. Eyes on him in battle was one thing. He felt less comfortable about such attention without the cloud of combat to hide in. At his feet, Mr. Peppers nuzzled up to his side and Timuscor scratched the boar behind his ears, already feeling better.

"That's something I'll talk over with the others before tonight," Jolia said. "For now, let's focus on assignments. Gabrielle, you're with Simone today; first priority for you is figuring out your condition. Timuscor and Thistle, you're with Kieran to start. Grumph, you get the privilege of studying under the wisest mage in all of Notch—me. And Eric, good news for you, looks like you'll be passing the morning with Brock."

Eric looked up from his meal, poorly hiding the surprise on his face. "I'm sorry, Brock? I didn't realize you were a rogue."

"About as far from one as it's possible to get," Brock chuckled. "But you clearly know about sneaking, stabbing, and all that stuff. What you don't know is how to be aware of your mana intake and output, when you use it, and how to use more or less as needed. While I can't pick a lock for shit, you'll be hard-pressed to find anyone who can match my level of physical and mana control."

With a *clang*, Jolia set her empty mug down on the counter and slid off her stool. "That's a lesson most of this lot will need to learn. Even you've got room to improve, Grumph. Finish up your breakfasts, drink some water, and take care of any bodily necessities. Once you leave here, we're not stopping until after lunch. And although I said we don't plan to teach you much, you should know that even the fraction we're going to impart will take a lot out of you. I'd ask if any of you want to sit it out, but you're adventurers. I already know you won't make the smart choice."

She wove her way across the room, then stopped before drawing near the door. "Truth be told, the willful idiocy is my favorite part of adventurers. It's the thing I miss most. Now, hurry up. Daylight's wasting, and every minute you spend on breakfast is time not being used for training. Just be sure to eat it all. You're going to need the energy."

Final piece said, Jolia exited the tavern seconds before everyone except Gabrielle began wolfing down their food at breakneck speed. Whether it was time management in action or pure excitement was hard to say. All that mattered was that the party saw a path toward getting stronger laid out before them. They all wanted to take that first step as soon as physically possible.

Even if Jolia's warnings had made it clear that said first step was going to be one hell of a doozy.

24.

Borrowing the car was easy. Russell had proven himself responsible at virtually every turn in his mother's eyes, especially when compared to the example set by Cheri, so he had more or less free rein over the vehicle when it wasn't in use. Driving over, on the other hand, turned out to be more difficult than Russell expected. It had been some time since he and Mitch had exchanged words. *Spells, Swords, and Stealth* was the only thing they ever had in common, and after the incident with Tim's dice, the odds of any of them playing again had seemed pretty low. The group had drifted apart, which was such a blessing, Russell almost didn't mind having his body eventually used as a puppet if that was the price for freedom.

Dealing with Mitch and his cronies was a slow death, like a frog being boiled in a pot of water. They started out civil, but kept pushing things bit by bit, until Russell had ended up running a game he barely wanted to play for a group of people he largely didn't like. No wonder he'd picked a module with harsh rules for realism that he knew they'd initially ignore. It had all seemed so natural; of course, he was stuck playing with that group. Only, the truth was that he could have taken Tim and bailed at any time. Mitch had managed to make Russell forget that was a choice: he kept everyone around him constantly pinned in whatever role he wanted them in, just by being louder and pushier than anyone else.

Today, that would have to change. Mitch had something Russell wanted: confirmation at the minimum, perhaps even information that Russell's party lacked. The minute he realized that, Mitch would sleaze into his usual role, demanding favors for the trade, perhaps even trying to weasel his way back into the game. Based on his review of the comic shop, the guy seemed to be in denial about whatever it was he'd experienced, so fear of magic probably wasn't a card Russell could play. Truthfully, Russell didn't really know what tactic he was going to use, and sitting in his car conspicuously wasn't making the ideas flow faster. Turning around was technically still an option, albeit one he would never use. Now that there were real stakes involved, Russell had to do everything he could to learn what was going on. The others were taking risks by playing the actual module; the least Russell owed them was an awkward conversation if it meant learning something useful.

He was moving before he noticed, body acting while the brain hesitated. No new revelations struck him as he walked up the concrete path winding through the front yard, leading up to the front door of Mitch's house. Both his parents would be gone—they worked most of the time, including weekends—so Russell didn't need to worry about explaining himself. Now that he thought about it, Russell wasn't even sure he'd ever met Mitch's parents. Not a relevant realization at the moment, but it seemed his brain was pinging all over the place, except to the one subject Russell really wanted it to dwell on.

A quick ring of the doorbell, followed by the slow steps of someone who didn't care if they made it before their caller departed. Almost a full minute later, the door opened to reveal Mitch, clad in jeans and a shirt that had clearly both been tossed on seconds prior, likely from the floor, hair still mussed from bed. The sleepy look in his eyes vanished as soon as Mitch recognized his guest, an unsavory expression of casual cruelty taking its place.

"The fuck do you want?"

"Good to see you, too, Mitch."

"I didn't say it was good to see shit." Mitch's expression darkened, his tired mind sluggishly cranking into gear. "I asked what the fuck you want, and why you're here at the ass-crack of the day to bother me about it."

Just to be sure, Russell double-checked his watch. "It's past eleven. We've barely got any morning left."

"Oh, I see, you came over to wake me up and then lecture me about my sleeping schedule. In light of that, let me ask, have you considered fucking off?" Mitch began to close the door, but, to his own surprise, Russell stepped forward, jamming his arm against it to stop the movement.

"Look, asshole, you want to be a dick about this, then that's how we'll do it." The words were almost as shocking as his body's movement. It felt like he was poorly trying to channel Cheri. Except, the door had stopped, and Mitch appeared to be listening, so maybe Russell was doing a better impression than he realized. "I'm here to talk about what happened the last time we all played *Spells, Swords, and Stealth*. The dice we saw glow and explode."

There it was. A crack in the armor that was Mitch's douchebag veneer. Fear, real and undeniable, darted through those sleepy, angry eyes at the mention of the dice. An instant later, it was gone, smothered under hurriedly manufactured anger, but Russell knew what he'd seen.

"Fine. We played, Tim had a batch of defective dice, one of them fell apart on the table, and the lighting made it look weird. Woo-fucking-hoo.

What an event to come knocking on someone's door about so early in the fucking day." Mitch started to shove the door closed, making quick progress. Neither young man was especially muscular, but Mitch had more brute strength than Russell.

For a moment, Russell considered letting it end there. If Mitch was still in denial about the dissolving dice, then there was no way he could face whatever had happened to him in that comic book shop. But as Mitch strained, his shirt shifted, a sleeve sliding up to reveal the puckered red of a semi-recent scar. A slice, right across the arm. To anyone else in his group, it would have meant nothing, because they only knew what he'd told them. They hadn't been the ones used by the module, nor had they gotten the strange flashes of scenes from within that very treasure room where their characters were fighting.

"I know that wound."

The pushing stopped, and this time, there was nothing fleeting about the terror in Mitch's face, nor was the anger on its heels in any way manufactured. "The fuck do you think you're talking about? I was mowing the lawn and accidentally sent a rock flying. No big deal."

"Bullshit," Russell shot back, an unusual sensation flowing through him. Was this... confidence? It felt strange to have that without a GM screen in front of him, although he certainly wasn't complaining. "First off, pick a better cover story; everyone knows you don't do chores. Secondly, I *know* you're lying."

"Yeah, and how is that?" Mitch was puffing out his chest, mistakenly thinking this was heading for violence.

"Because I saw that attack land. A barbarian tried to rush some guy holding an artifact, and took a dagger from an armor-covered gnome for his trouble. Only, instead of taking it in stride, he screamed like they'd cut his throat and ran as fast as he could in the opposite direction. Dragged his asshole friends with him."

With every word Russell spoke, Mitch seemed to grow slightly paler. By the end of his accusation, it was virtually impossible to recognize him as the domineering force who'd ruined countless tabletop games. Even still, he tried to thrash against the truth. "Glenn or Terry told you. They must have."

"Oh yeah, after an experience like that, they were so eager to start chatting, they looked me up even though we never talked outside of games and spilled the whole thing. No, Mitch. No one told me. I know because I was there. Our dice started glowing, too, and those threads of energy bonded us to them. If we'd been dumb enough to attack, you might not be the only one with a mysterious scar."

"Except you can't have done that, because none of it was real. It was all just a trick some bitch shop owner played to fuck with us!" Though his voice had risen, Mitch didn't seem angry anymore. He was closer to desperate, determined to believe that there was some—any—explanation for what they'd endured.

In that moment, seeing him fight so hard to deny the truth, Russell realized that whatever dynamic had existed between them before was dead. He and his new players had faced their experience honestly, had been able to move forward from it. Mitch couldn't do that; he was too afraid of what it entailed. When faced with real adventure, and the danger that came with it, Mitch had elected to cower and throw ignorance over himself like a blanket. This was not someone who was going to gain dominance over Russell, or his game, ever again.

"Okay, Mitch, if that's how you want it." Russell pulled his arm away from the door, permitting it to be closed. Knowing now that he'd seen Mitch's party reacting to their experience from within the game, Russell had a hunch they wouldn't have any more clues than he did. Those characters had run away as hard and as fast as they could, which meant their players probably followed suit. Russell was the one with the power right now, and he decided to use mercy instead of force. Not facing the truth was visibly haunting Mitch, probably would for the rest of his life. They'd never been friends, but they had played together. Not tearing away all shred of delusion was a simple act of kindness for someone he'd once adventured with.

Perhaps someday, Mitch would succeed in convincing himself it wasn't real. Russell doubted it, but he wouldn't be the one to take that possibility away, assuming he hadn't already. "Maybe you're right. There was weird lighting that first day, and bad dice get made. I can't say what happened to you in the comic shop, but an elaborate setup does sound more likely than magic being real. Sorry to have bothered you."

With that, Russell turned away and headed back toward his car. It hadn't panned out the way he was hoping, yet the mere knowledge that he'd tried made the disappointment easier to bear. He would keep digging, and maybe the next wild thread he pulled on would actually unravel something.

"Hang on!" Mitch jogged up behind Russell, rushing to reach him before he left. Russell paused, allowing him to catch up.

"I'm not saying that what you think happened actually did—make sure you understand that," Mitch said. "All I'm saying is that, if you had some weird shit happen, then maybe it's related to what we endured. As in, organized by the same person. I don't have much, but I can send you the information we had on Jamie, the woman who ran our game, and her shop. The store has been closed since that day. Her email might still work; I haven't thought to try it."

Yes, he had. That much was plain on his face. But Mitch had shied away for the same reason he'd flat-out denied the truth when Russell confronted him with it: getting more evidence would only make denial harder. That didn't mean it couldn't be useful to Russell, however.

"Thanks, Mitch. That would be a real help."

"Don't thank me, Russell. Find that woman, figure out what she's doing, and put a stop to it." Mitch rubbed his arm, right where the new scar had formed. "I got lucky to escape with a minor injury. There's a lot worse ways to get hurt. And if she keeps pulling this shit, eventually one of them will happen to someone else."

"Plus, you want payback," Russell added.

A touch of the old Mitch manifested in the malicious grin that spread across his tired face. "Well, if that happens to be a side effect of stopping her, I'm certainly not going to object."

* * *

Across the plains of Urthos, the cart tottered on. So far, their wake consisted of three camps of slaughtered bandits, a few chatty travelers who asked too many questions, and one diced-up party of adventurers who'd happened to set up camp just as the cart's travelers were getting ready to rest one evening. Killing them had been easier than doing the work themselves, so that's the path that the driver had decided on.

Not that the others needed much prodding. People who would balk at such an idea didn't become servants of Kalzidar. Bowing to the god of secrets and magic, giving up one's very name—these were the acts of those who craved power at any cost. Kalzidar was many things, nearly all of them horrid, but he made no deception about what he stood for, or the kind of clergy he wanted. The men selected for this mission certainly fit the bill; they were likely standouts for their dedication.

It had been wise of their god to assign one as leader. Without his word being made clear, they would have bickered amongst themselves, and at least some would have died before the dust settled. There was no risk of such incidents now. They could all feel the power bestowed by Kalzidar pumping through their veins, fueling their magic and urging them onward. All they could think about, all their minds would focus on, was their goal. They had made good time so far, perhaps too good.

The timing of it all had to be precise. Lost magics were in play, along with the very forces of the heavens falling into alignment. There was no room for error, no chance for mistakes. Entering ahead of the deadline was fine, if their timing lined up that way. The larger concern was getting everything in position and striking at the right moment.

One step at a time. The cart rolled on, passing a massive tree growing alone on the plains, a marker they'd all been watching for. Not much to look at for the time being, but soon, that would change.

After they made it into Lumal, the scenery would be far more splendid to behold.

25.

"The trouble with instinct is that it has inherent limits. Trusting your instincts is important, but improving what they demonstrate as possible is also essential. Running the first time you see a monster is instinct; training your legs and lungs to be better able to escape the next time is taking control of the reaction and improving upon it. That is why it's imperative that you move beyond instinct when it comes to utilizing the mana that flows through you. Until you control it, you'll never be able to purposely train that aspect of your abilities, and you need to."

Kieran spoke as Timuscor and Thistle remained still, weapons in their hands. Before each was a wooden training dummy, though Thistle's was obviously set some distance farther away from him. Each was ready, listening and tense as Kieran went through the speech. They'd been at it for over an hour and were slowly learning the rhythm. First came small speeches, giving them intellectual insight into what they were trying to achieve. After that, Kieran would tell them to strike the dummies with varying degrees of strength. Just as their muscles were tiring, Kieran would switch back to speaking, allowing them a short while to rest.

"Let's take it from the top again. This time, we'll do an escalating scale. Start off weak; the weakest possible attacks you can make. Go slow if you need to. Thistle, it doesn't matter if you get nowhere near your wooden opponent. In fact, these first attempts should come up quite short. Timuscor, same for you and leaving a mark on the dummy. Don't think about your targets; focus on the act of attacking. Every strike should be a tiny bit more powerful than the one before it. Small steps up in strength. Pay attention to everything about your body. Feel the breath in your lungs, the ground pressing against your feet, the wind on your skin. Eventually, you'll feel the difference in your muscles as mana flows through them. When you have that, your training starts in earnest."

The weariness was part of the exercise; Timuscor understood that from the start. Being tired made everything hurt, that was true, yet in doing so, it also made it easier to feel every motion. When each twitch resulted in small tremors of pain, taking note of the twitches was a far easier task. Timuscor tried to put the words out of his mind, focusing purely on his body as it swung his longsword, achingly slow, at the dummy.

According to Kieran's first speech of the day, every adventurer in the world held on to some mana naturally. Mages kept and accessed the most; however, the act of augmenting bodies with bursts of magic also heightened their natural capacity to hold mana. This was why adventurers grew unnaturally stronger and tougher, some well past natural limitations, until they were capable of surviving otherwise deadly attacks. The more a person used mana, the better trained that aspect became. For casters, that involved heightening their overall mana capacity and efficiency in casting.

Physical combatants like Timuscor actively used mana in very careful, controlled bursts. Unlike barbarians, who flooded their entire bodies with the stuff in a single go, knights used their mana-augmentation chiefly in the moments it was needed: the swing of a sword, the pull of a bow, the hurl of a dagger. The trouble was, that meant Timuscor was only going to be able to sense his mana-usage by finding it in those swings. Thistle at least had divine options; the gnome would learn more when he moved on to casting training. For Timuscor, the sword was all he had. His arms shook from the concentrated effort of moving so deliberately, so slowly. He struck the dummy again, increasing his power by the slightest amount.

Hunting for a sensation he'd never noticed before was like being told to search the sunset for a new shade of red. How did he even know what he was looking for, and how would he be sure when he'd found it? It would be so easy to mistake any sensation as the one he was looking for and waste untold time chasing the wrong feeling. Timuscor put that thought quickly out of his head, as he had been doing with all inner doubts and fears. Worry had no place in this process; there wasn't room for it. If the task could be accomplished, then this was the place to do it—under the guidance of a true expert, watching over their every move with intense scrutiny.

Another swing, landing lightly against the dummy. Seconds later, one of Thistle's daggers thudded uselessly in the grass, less than a quarter of the way to his target.

"Excellent," Kieran called. "Keep it up, slow and steady."

The blade felt heavy, but Timuscor didn't permit so much as a tremble as he brought it in for another strike. He hoped the others were having better luck at their training, though he couldn't imagine they were having much of an easier time.

*   *   *

Eric's legs shook as he took another step, the taut rope shifting the slightest bit beneath his feet with every movement. He was only three feet off the ground, walking between a pair of wooden poles that looked like they'd been roughly shoved into the dirt, which very well might have been what Brock actually did. When he'd heard he'd be walking a rope to train, part of Eric expected it to be over a cavern, or a pit of hungry monsters. Only later did he understand that such a situation would have been too easy. In those cases, failure meant death. This way, failure just meant getting back up to keep trying.

"Everything starts with balance." Brock, for his part, was sitting on top of a rope of his own. In fact, he'd lain on it, jumped on it, and generally lounged as though he were on solid ground since they'd started this training. "When I was being taught how to fight, that was how they started every brawler's training. People think that our power comes from our muscles, but the muscles are a result of training, not a goal. Balance is the goal. Power comes from the stance, which comes from the footing, which comes from balance."

Eric took an uneasy step forward, sure this would lead to yet another sudden drop. His footing stayed secure, thankfully, even as he glanced over and noticed Brock leaning back for a deep stretch, effortlessly holding an angle that should have sent him tumbling to the ground.

"You rogues are closer to my kind than you might think," Brock continued. His commentary had been running throughout most of the session, and the burly bartender had already begun to repeat himself on a few topics. "We aren't just the force of our strikes. Our movements are nearly as important. We don't flood ourselves with mana like barbarians, and while we do use bursts when we attack, our kind also keeps an intentional, controlled flow of mana in our bodies at all times. Not just the normal accumulation, either. I'm talking about creating a new autonomic system. Like breathing, or a heartbeat, only instead, you're channeling mana. It's how we have such mastery of our movements that we go faster than our legs should carry us, or silence even the creaking of our bones as we slip through shadows. Since you're working on instinct, you use only the barest amount of mana necessary to complete any given task."

Another step, and this time, Eric's foot wobbled as it landed. In a split-second, he was down, a fresh cloud of dirt congealing around him as he coughed. It was strange, he could see the next step in his mind's eye, could feel the rope beneath his feet, but the more he walked it, the harder the task became.

"Your body will not keep balance on its own. Balance must be taught, be learned, be willful. As you grow tired, your instincts will falter. You'll use too little mana for a task, or too much. Pay attention, feel the flow ebb and shift. When you can feel it, you can take hold of it. And once you control the flow of mana, you'll be capable of finding the exact right amount to pair with your body for any given task. It will take untold time, mind you, to reach that level of mastery. But if you do, your possibilities will expand in countless directions."

Brock finished his stretch, then nodded to the rope. "All of that comes much further down the road, though. For now..."

It was an obvious hint, even if he hadn't trailed off, and Eric didn't ignore it. He brushed his shirt off—they'd shed the armor for this exercise—then walked to the nearest post and hopped right back onto the rope.

"For now," Eric repeated, "everything starts with balance."

*   *   *

Unlike the others, Gabrielle was having a fairly easy day. That was largely because less interest was being put on training her in lieu of focusing on understanding what she was, how her axe worked, and what the relationship between them had become. Gabrielle hadn't precisely known what to expect; she'd half-assumed it would be a lot of questions with pauses so Simone could ponder the responses.

Instead, she was currently centered in a glowing green circle of runes, with a smaller circle of red runes by her feet containing her axe. They'd walked into what looked like a mausoleum near the edge of the graveyard, only to reveal a set of stairs leading down into a massive space stuffed with magical items and books. Simone had set up the circles, and had largely been keeping to herself ever since. Occasionally, she would ask Gabrielle a question, usually about her past with the axe, but every now and then, Simone checked to see if Gabrielle felt different. Those latter questions worried Gabrielle, much as she tried to hide it. What was Simone tinkering with that would produce new sensations, and would she accidentally turn Gabrielle into a real corpse by mistake?

The thought was less terrifying than it should have been, largely because, if there was ever a place to not fear the permanency of death, it was with Simone. All around her lair, skeletons were puttering about, tending to menial tasks like cleaning or bringing her steaming cups filled with unknown liquids. If Simone did accidentally kill Gabrielle, she'd hopefully have the decency to raise the barbarian once more. Being a different kind of undead might not be so bad; at least Gabrielle would have a clearer idea of the rules she was supposed to be playing by.

"Interesting. Very interesting." Whatever Simone was seeing, Gabrielle couldn't make it out. From the way the pale mage was squinting at thin air, there had to be something visible. That, or Gabrielle had entrusted herself to the clutches of a magical madwoman. Not likely, true, but certainly possible.

"Wait... huh. That doesn't... it shouldn't... Wait... Damnation! Is that for real?"

The curse was a surprise, but it had nothing on what came next. Simone stood, walked into the circle of green runes and hunkered down to take a much closer look at Gabrielle's axe. The tip of her nose was less than an inch from the blade, like Simone was trying to check her reflection in the metal. Whatever she saw there seemed to confirm her suspicions, as Simone stood back up and walked out, motioning for one of the nearby skeletons to come close.

"Go find Julian. Bring him here immediately, no matter how he whines. Tell him I *insist* he hurry."

In response, the skeleton let out a few noises that sounded like unintelligible rasps to Gabrielle, yet drew a nod of confirmation from Simone. It tottered off at a quicker pace than bones should probably manage, turning down a hallway and quickly fading from sight.

"Don't suppose you're going to tell me what that was all about?" Gabrielle asked.

"I hope to, eventually." Simone had retaken her seat; evidently, Julian's presence wasn't so necessary that work couldn't proceed without him. "I'd like to wait until we've got more than speculation and theory, however. What you are—what I *think* you are—is not entirely unique, but it is also far from common. Julian is something of an expert in the condition, so I'd like to have him weigh in before I start sharing ideas that might yet prove to be wrong."

It was hard to argue with Simone wanting to be thorough, even if Gabrielle was itching for answers. Better to be sure than to operate under a wrong idea, especially given how varied the undead could be. Sunshine was deadly to some, yet she'd had only the most minor of skin issues in the light. That didn't mean her kind of undead wouldn't have its own version of sunshine, though. The sooner she knew what she was, the better her chances of surviving. Still, it was hard not to be curious.

"Not to be disrespectful, but aren't you the legendary necromancer? Why is this Julian guy more of an expert on my condition than you?"

"Simple," Simone replied. "Because, if I'm right, Julian is another of your kind."

*　　*　　*

Jolia watched as the barrel burned, flames licking at its sides. With a wave of her hand, she extinguished the flames. A flick of her staff purged the damage, leaving the barrel looking brand new again. "For someone working off a crash course, you're holding together quite well. Nice aim and focus, good pronunciation, careful motions. Whoever taught you did a fine job of drilling in the fundamentals."

With a snort, Grumph agreed. His time with Dejy had been limited, so they'd focused on building a foundation above all else. Deepening Grumph's mana pool, learning a few new spells that might be helpful, and practicing the essentials of casting over and over.

As he panted, Jolia handed over a stoppered bottle. Grumph downed the contents quickly, a surge of warmth filling his stomach, stretching out through his entire body. Moving mana from person to person with Dejy had required an artifact. Jolia either lacked one or preferred not to work that way, because she hadn't even proposed the option. Rather, she'd shown up with a magical bag stuffed full of strangely-colored potions. They didn't refill one's mana, per se, but drinking them temporarily increased Grumph's natural mana recovery. While he wouldn't be able to summon a storm like Jolia had, the potions were permitting him to continue casting minor spells long after his natural reserves would have run dry.

"Again, when you're ready. Don't just say the words and make the motions. Understand that what you're doing has a purpose. You are shaping the spell, guiding the magic. If I were your real teacher, I'd be educating you on what every intonation and gesture adds to the equation, so you could build spells of your own, but with such limited time, let's focus on understanding that the relationship exists. When you completely understand a spell, you can make changes on the fly to suit your needs."

Jolia muttered as she waved her staff, and from it came a blast of fire identical to the ones Grumph had been conjuring. Then, she did the same, seemingly identical motions. This time, a stream of sustained flame shot out, scorching the air around them. It stopped, and she repeated the spell a third time. A small red orb, barely bigger than a marble, shot directly toward the barrel. The instant it hit, an explosion came from within, turning the barrel into burning wreckage.

"Same basic spell, with a few modifications. All of that comes with time and study, mind you. What I want from you is to learn one technique, because I think it will serve you the best in your journey ahead. Pay attention as you cast, feel the moment when mana leaves your body to fuel the spell. In that moment, you have control. You can push more mana in to increase the effectiveness, or keep some back if you want to pull your shot. Learn this, and every spell you have becomes more versatile, as well as more dangerous."

They stood, neither moving, for several moments. Finally, Jolia's patience wore thin. "Well, what are you waiting for?"

In response, Grumph merely raised a finger to point at the smoldering remains of the barrel.

"Aye, right, you need a target. My mistake." With a quick wave of the staff, Jolia caused the barrel to fly back together, reforming the parts that had been turned to cinders. "There you are. Now, get back to it."

26.

A full morning's training had left Thistle sore, weary, and with no shortage of things to mull over. He hadn't yet mastered the lesson, which felt forgivable after only a single day of trying, yet the ideas Kieran had put inside his head refused to lay still. The task had been set before Thistle, and as was his nature, he immediately went to trying to puzzle a way through it. Unfortunately, this problem didn't seem to have a way it could be thought around. No tricks, no tactics, no sudden inspiration would move the obstacle from his path. It wasn't the first time Thistle had faced this sort of challenge, but they were always especially problematic for him.

In many ways, that made his afternoon with Jolia a blessing. The task of sorting through an endless stream of documents, all of which were gibberish, was manual enough to keep him occupied and put his mind on a leash. Tracking all of the scrolls he'd tried—and failed—to read required some mental effort, anyway, so Thistle simply put in far more effort than was required, setting himself to the task and mowing through as many pieces of parchment as possible.

When it happened, he almost didn't notice. Another scroll, looking like all the others, was unfurled before Thistle. He leaned in and carefully peered over. The script was ancient, arcane and seemingly incomprehensible—except Thistle understood it. He'd never seen it before, that much was certain, but every time his eyes moved across the writing, his mind somehow processed it into words Thistle knew.

"Jolia, you said these documents were enchanted, correct? Made specifically so magical spells would not permit one to read them?"

"For the most part," Jolia confirmed. She was seated nearby, slowly making her way through a bottle of wine while reading a sizable tome. "It would be slightly more accurate to say the majority of these have magic functioning as a lock on them, enchantments to keep anyone who wasn't supposed to be able to read them from doing so. Finding people who speak the language has unlocked a few on occasion—the only tactic that's worked at all, in fact—so it's the one I keep trying when we get the occasional visitor."

There was a moment, one Thistle took no pride in, where part of him wanted to keep the revelation to himself. Reading this might provide the first piece of tangible knowledge they had that the people of Notch didn't, a small balance in a drastically different power dynamic. But that would be poor repayment for their hospitality, especially since the residents of Notch had just spent the morning trying to help his friends become stronger. "Then I suspect that somehow, I was meant to read this scroll, because the writing holds no meaning to my eyes, yet my brain understands it perfectly."

He'd yet to see Jolia move with such intensity as she cast her own book aside. In moments, she was next to Thistle, peering down at the scroll. "Interesting. Anything special about you I should know, Thistle? The likeliest explanation is that this would be related to Grumble, but I like to have all of the information before I start forming theories."

"I have lived an interesting life, with an assortment of experiences. Going into all of it might take too long, so let's see what this scroll is about, and then I'll let you know if it connects to anything in my past."

"Good call, because I don't think I could have waited through your entire life's story," Jolia agreed. "Now, read it. Out loud, please."

Thistle did as he was told. For the first part of the scroll, he had no idea of what in the piece might be relevant to him or Grumble. Most of the document was about constellations and the movements of heavenly bodies. As it continued, the story branched off, detailing how such movements could affect the flow and intensity of magic. It was near the end of the document that, at last, Thistle was allowed some insight into why he might be someone who could understand this particular document.

"All magic comes from the source, yet it carries with it the many forms and types magic can take. Elements, schools of magic, all of these have their own characteristics that ebb and flow. Tracking and predicting these fluctuations may very well provide one who masters such knowledge with advantages in crafting, enchanting, research, and war. Continued on next scroll."

At his side, leaned in so close that her hair threatened to tickle his nose, Jolia was scouring the document as though she too could read the words. "Interesting. I've heard this discussed in theory before—there are subtle variations in some spells depending on the stars—but it feels as though this scroll is describing something more extreme than an extra-hot fire-blast incantation."

"I saw something once, a long time ago." Thistle's mind was pressing back through the years, all the way to his first party, when he, Madroria, and Grumph had been the loyal help rather than the actual adventurers. "It was in Lumal, when we—my old friends, I mean—well, when we broke into a restricted area in the Vault of Sealed Magics."

That revelation earned him a shocked look from Jolia—the first time she'd looked away from the scroll since he started reading. "I'm sorry, you attempted a break-in to *the* Vault of Sealed Magics? So many questions, the first of which is how, followed by the reasons why. You know that if they catch you in a restricted area, even if nothing's taken, it will result in a lifetime ban from Lumal, right?"

"I do. It's part of why I expected returning would be an extra difficult proposition," Thistle replied. "Anyway, while we were in the section, I looked in one of the rooms. It was immense and dark, surrounded by stars, like standing in a field on a moonless night. There was more than just lights in the sky, however. I saw tracks, predictions, arcane symbols, a mess of things that made no sense at the time. Now, thinking back, I'm reasonably sure it was a place devoted to the study of this very subject: fluctuations in magic and when to expect them."

"Fascinating as this all is—and I'm diving into research the moment we're done here—I hope you can appreciate why I need to ask you something before we move on. Different party or not, why did you mess around in the Vault of Sealed Magics? If it's something silly but noble, like trying to retrieve a friend from the Hall of Souls, or remove a curse from the Spring of Purity, then I could understand. But there are other, more dangerous things in there too, and I have the right to know if I let someone who'll seek them out into my town."

Jolia didn't appear threatening, which might have been more comforting if Thistle wasn't keenly aware of the power difference between them. She didn't need to act threatening; a wave of that staff could roast Thistle alive and leave no more than a smear of ashes to clean up. Thankfully, Thistle had nothing to hide; at least, not when it came to this particular bit of his past.

"We were looking for a map said to lead one to their heart's desire. Not my idea, but the leader of our group had done much for Grumph, my wife, and me. Helping him was the very least we owed. In a twist of fate that I can only now see as funny, we ended up getting lost while looking for the map. The Vault of Sealed Magics has many paths, and somehow, even more rooms. We saw some strange sights—my personal favorite was a glowing white obelisk that pulsed with my heartbeat when I touched it. No map, though. Our luck eventually ran out and the guards caught us. Since we'd taken nothing, there was no theft to accuse us of, so our entire party was booted out of Lumal with a warning never to come back."

"Yet you want to go knock on one of their front doors?" Jolia asked.

"Gabrielle needed help. Finding out what happened to her was the utmost priority. Of our nearby options, Lumal was the only one that might have been able to offer answers. If needed, I was prepared to wait outside the city with Grumph while they searched for aid, regardless of how long it took."

There was some skepticism on Jolia's face as she studied Thistle carefully, before it mercifully faded into acceptance. "Given how you've acted since arriving, and your status as a paladin, I'll take you at your word. Hunting for that map isn't precisely what I'd call noble, but seeking one's heart's desire is not an inherently evil act, either. And hey, if that experience is what let you read this scroll, then I guess it all worked out."

This time, there was no temptation to lie. He wanted to make sure Jolia, and the rest of Notch, knew what they might be in for. "Actually, I can't think of anything from that experience that would account for why I can read this scroll. That said, I do have a working theory. This scroll relates to knowledge of the workings of magic—specifically, magic of the skies and stars. But the sky also has vast swathes of emptiness. Endless darkness. Magic and darkness—we know exactly one god who presides over that specific domain. One who might go to great lengths to bury this sort of information."

"Kalzidar, of course." Unlike many, she didn't grow nervous at the act of saying his name. "Which would mean those touched by his power might be able to read this scroll, if his was part of the magic that enchanted it. Funny, from your stories so far, I hadn't gotten the impression you were on good terms with him. Quite the opposite, in fact."

"Very much so. I daresay we may be among his most hated mortals at the moment." It felt presumptuous to say a god would care that much about him and his friends, but Thistle had helped destroy some of Kalzidar's power. That was bound to cause a grudge. "There's enmity between him and Grumble going back to Grumble's first paladin, who feigned allegiance to Kalzidar, ultimately stealing a piece of his divinity."

"Which makes it even stranger that you can read this, if your idea is true."

Reaching up, Thistle banged on the chest of his armor, armor that had refused to leave his body since he'd set foot inside this town. "Except that I held the container for Kalzidar's stolen divinity in my hands as it was destroyed. And this armor I've been stuck in isn't just magical—it's the armor of that same first paladin who stole the piece of divinity. Not saying I'm fond of it, but if all that's needed is to be touched by the god's power, then I certainly qualify."

Tapping her staff along the floor, Jolia paced briefly as Thistle spoke, taking in every word. "It's a good theory, lines up in the right places. I wish we had some kind of proof to be sure so we could rule out other options. Unfortunately, without that, we'll have to—"

Jolia was interrupted by the sound of metal striking stone. The arm and shin guards of Thistle's armor had fallen from his limbs, landing with quite a racket. Her eyes looked at the armor, then to Thistle, who appeared as perplexed as she.

"Okay then, suppose we assume you're right. That means my next task is figuring out how to get you back in touch with Grumble. If your god felt knowing about this was so important that he led you here and used what might have been his one signal to confirm we were on to something, then it's going to be relevant, and probably soon."

"A fine idea," Thistle concurred. "Whatever Kalzidar is planning, we're going to want as much forewarning as possible."

*   *   *

The detour had been something of a long shot. That was always true to some extent when hunting a lyranx; they didn't move in herds due to their isolated nature and had no habitats more or less suited to their biology. Adaptability was the lyranx's most noteworthy trait. They could be found in tundra, caverns, even lounging in the middle of a forest fire. Worse, they did more than survive; they took on traits of their environment. Lyranxs were all roughly the same size when full-grown—roughly seven feet in length—yet their fur spanned a gamut of colors and textures depending on where the creature was found or had recently been. Their only other constant was their eyes, famous for the way they glittered when struck by light. It was said to be a sight of breathtaking beauty.

Wimberly certainly wasn't breathing, although it had nothing to do with how lovely the glittering eyes before her were. No, her breath was held for the same reason she was standing stock-still—it was an instinctual effort to avoid being noticed. This lyranx had dark purple fur with a matching liquid dripping off the hairs. Each drop sizzled as it hit the grass, leaving dead plants in its wake. As the lyranx took a step forward, Wimberly noticed that its paw prints had the same effect.

Poisonous, then. Not too surprising given that they were only a half-day's ride from a toxic bog. They'd been heading back to Camnarael when a chance encounter with other travelers and a few surprisingly diplomatic words from Timanuel gave them a lead on this lyranx. All they'd had were rumors of something roughly matching the description tearing apart riders who'd gone off the main roads. Deep down, Wimberly hadn't actually expected them to find one. Perhaps that was why she hadn't objected enough when they opted to spread out and search the area.

Another step closer, and those glittering eyes locked on to Wimberly's comparatively tiny form. Standing still wasn't working; not in a long-term capacity. She had to do something else. Pure retreat wasn't an option—they needed one of those damn glittering eyes to get into Lumal. But Wimberly couldn't win this fight alone. She needed to call for help and also survive long enough for the others to reach her.

Mentally scouring her supplies, Wimberly tried to think of what she still had on hand. A few attack options, although nothing that would bring down a lyranx in a single blow. Using them would be as good as slathering herself in a nice sauce to appear more enticing. There were a couple of defensive deterrents; even a few she could reach in time. Unfortunately, those were calibrated to deal with brute force and a few basic elements. Wimberly hadn't anticipated the poison. That would prove troublesome, especially since she didn't use particularly tough armor that could survive such erosion.

There was one trick up her sleeve that might work. It wasn't quite the purpose she'd envisioned for this; however, in a pinch, improvisation was better than planning. Reaching around, slowly, lest she urge the lyranx to pounce, Wimberly produced a custom glass container. With a flick of her thumb, a small vial near the top was smashed by a miniature hammer, sending the meager amount of red liquid into the clear fluid below. Immediately, the container began to heat up, and Wimberly hurled it as hard as she could. Not at the lyranx. Instead, she aimed directly between them.

The cloud of thick red mist exploded outward—Wimberly had already covered her mouth and eyes—as she backpedaled hurriedly. It was too much to hope that a few irritants would be enough to hurt something as adaptable as a lyranx; this concoction had been made with weaker creatures in mind. Also, ideally, Wimberly wouldn't have been in the cloud as well.

The one upside to using her pain-smoke was that it obscured the creature's view and, hopefully, her scent. It was big enough that the others would see the fog drifting up from the brush, while also giving Wimberly cover to escape.

She bolted, running as fast as she could toward the horses. Behind her, there was audible movement as something big blundered around, yet still managed to stay on her trail. Her lungs were burning—she'd inhaled some of the smoke despite her best efforts—and already her pace was beginning to slow. As her body protested, Wimberly drove it onward. Giving up was the same as death right now, and she wasn't ready to see the end of her adventure.

Finally, she broke out of the cloud, back into the clean air of the countryside. Wimberly took a few rasping gulps as she stumbled forward. Whether it was poor timing or her loud breathing was a mystery she'd never solve, but at that moment, the lyranx came bounding out of the fog as well, sprinting toward her with obvious intent.

Her mind and body were both too sluggish; she couldn't think of another plan in the brief window she had. There was nothing else to do. All she could hope for was that her friends would see the smoke and have more warning.

Just as the lyranx readied itself to leap, three arrows landed in its haunch, interrupting its planned pounce. Wimberly whipped her head over to see Gelthorn and Chalara emerging from a nearby crop of trees. The former was already nocking more arrows, while the latter moved her hands around, crafting a spell.

Wimberly let out a small sigh of relief as the lyranx shifted direction, more concerned with a threat than a meal. Their fight was far from over, but at least she wouldn't be experiencing it from inside the lyranx's stomach. Taking another breath of the clean air, she turned her mind back toward the attack options.

It was time to get this battle properly started.

27.

Gabrielle stood in the cooling winds of the evening, eyes unfazed by the dwindling light as she scanned the horizon. There was little chance that an attacker could make it this far without alerting one of the townsfolk, but Notch had already proven slightly more vulnerable than expected once. No reason to take chances. Besides, the open air helped her relax, something she dearly needed after the last few days. What was meant to have been their downtime had turned into training, research, and worried anticipation at what might come next.

At least they were no longer entirely in the dark now. Thistle's revelation about Kalzidar was hardly shocking; even better, it gave them a starting point. Knowing what they were up against always made things a little easier. It was impossible to plan for a mystery; even gods were more manageable than the unknown. The news might have landed with greater impact if Gabrielle and Simone hadn't already shared their own discovery. Technically, Gabrielle should feel the same about her revelations as she did about Thistle's report: more information was supposed to always be better. Yet Gabrielle wasn't so sure she was happier than when she hadn't known. Understanding what she'd become wasn't the same as knowing how to reverse it, and that path was turning out to be more difficult than she'd anticipated.

"So, a lich, huh?" Eric sidled up next to her; he'd been moving so quietly she hadn't heard the tavern door open. She wasn't sure if the others had noticed yet or not, but he'd been making an effort to mask his movements since they gathered in the tavern that evening. It was something to inquire about, when there were less dire concerns to tackle.

"Pseudo-lich, thank you," Gabrielle corrected. "No evil ceremonies or magic rituals, no carefully enchanted gem to keep my soul protected. Nope, my soul is apparently right here, strapped to my back."

At least she wasn't the first of her kind—that burden might have been unbearable. Simone had walked her carefully through what she suspected had happened—or, at least, she'd done the best she could as a mage explaining complex magic to a barbarian. The working theory was that the storm of magic Gabrielle endured had torn her soul from her body. Maybe she'd truly died in the explosion; maybe it was a mystical effect. Either way, her soul had ultimately been bound into her axe. That was why she grew weak when it wasn't nearby; the connection between soul and body was decaying. And unlike most liches, Simone wasn't sure that the connection could be reestablished when broken.

"Yeah, pseudo-lich is a better name." Eric bumped her shoulder with his, lightly, as he moved to her side. "Now, tell me the truth: how are you holding up?"

"Fine. It doesn't change anything. We already knew I was undead. We knew it was a strange condition, and we figured it was related to the axe. All this does is fill in the details we were missing."

"Very true, and a properly stoic response." He bumped her lightly again, as he had since they were children and he was trying to wheedle out some secret. "Also definitely not how you're really feeling. I get it. We don't know these people very well, and you've never been one to open up easily. But I'm not them, and I hope you'll hear me when I say you need to let some of this out."

They stayed like that for some minutes, the sounds of the nearby woods filling the silence. When Gabrielle spoke again, it was softer, the kind of voice she hadn't found much cause to use since they departed Maplebark.

"Simone figured my condition out in a morning. A few hours was all she needed. But the axe… she's having trouble with it. Apparently, it's an artifact, one with a lot of carefully placed enchantments specifically designed to stop the kind of learning she wants to do. That means it's powerful, Eric. Potentially indestructible. What happens to me when I pass on? I was at peace with dying on a battlefield, going to the realm of the gods to meet my ancestors and patiently await my loved ones. This is something else. What if I can't die? Or worse, what if my *body* can die, but my soul stays stuck inside that axe? Will I just be there, forever, looking through the eyes of whoever picks it up next? Will I fade away with time, like what happened to Elnif?"

"Hey now, don't go down that road," Eric cautioned. "We all heard Simone. What you took from him was a piece, a sliver, nothing more."

Whether the axe was originally meant to function in such a manner or not, its recent status as a soul depository had given it an inclination to embrace the new role. Simone had warned them that this part was more theory than fact at the moment, but her hypothesis was that when Gabrielle raged and began pulling in as much mana as possible, her soul within the axe created a similar effect. Only, instead of drawing in mana, it pulled in more of itself from the sources it struck: slivers of soul, pieces of who a person was.

"This time it was." Gabrielle knew Elnif's soul was intact; Julian had been kind enough to fetch Notch's local priest, who cast a spell to seek out the dead. Elnif's soul was in the realm of Prinkom, goddess of bandits and thieves, riding across the endless plains. What her axe had gotten was little more than the shadow of a ghost, one that had soon faded away. "Next time, maybe I'll leave the axe in too long and end up with a permanent housemate."

"Guess you should stick to swift, killing blows." Eric glanced over to her, her skin even paler under the light of the stars. "For now, I mean. We're going to find a way to fix this, Gabrielle. Even if it's something we're not supposed to be able to do, that doesn't mean it will stop us. We still have a piece of the Bridge. If worse comes to worse—"

"No." Gabrielle whipped her head around, meeting Eric's eyes dead-on. "Look, I'm not saying that thing isn't powerful, and I'm sure not telling you to avoid using it when our friends' lives are on the line, but the Bridge is too unpredictable. Even when it works, there are side effects. Or have you forgotten that frequent use of that first piece was enough to let demons break into our realm? Maybe it would work, but there would be consequences. I want your word that you're not going to try to use that thing to save me. However, if it comes down to it, I do give you permission to use it if you have to free me."

"What does that mean?" Eric asked.

"You know exactly what it means." They both did, and Gabrielle wasn't going to let him get out of this. The stakes were too high. "If this body dies, and you can't find a way to free my soul from the axe, then you have my permission to use the Bridge if it means you can crack this thing open and set me free."

He stared at her, eyes harder than they'd ever been during his guard days. What simpler times those had been, when their greatest fears were drunk adventurers and kidnapping goblins. "So, I can't use the power to save you, I can only use it to kill you? Is that about the sum of it?"

"In that situation, freeing me would be saving me. I hope you can see that, Eric. I want to trust this to you, but if it's too much, I'll talk to the others."

That was it; the stare broke as Eric turned away. The man could handle much, far more than he could have even a year prior, but the idea of failing his friends still haunted him. It was unfair to use that against him... Gabrielle was fully aware of this even as she did it. But this was a matter beyond life and death; this was the fate of her very soul. Entrusting the task to the hands of her oldest, truest friend was the sole way she'd be able to put the fear from her mind.

"I'll do it; only if I'm *sure* you can't be saved. I won't go crossing oceans and chasing wild geese to buy time, but I will explore any real options I find before I give up. That's as good a promise as you're going to get, so don't try to haggle."

"As long as none of those saving options require using the Bridge, I can make peace with that bargain. That artifact has to be our 'break axe in emergency' tool and nothing more, at least so far as I'm concerned."

Eric stuck out his hand, and Gabrielle accepted it. "Deal," he told her, and they shook on it.

"Thank you, Eric." She hesitated. This was going to hurt him, but she couldn't think of any way to get around that, so it was best to face the issue head-on. "I want to warn you, I'm going to make another arrangement in case of my passing. The reason I'm not entrusting you with that task is purely because you can't fulfill it. Otherwise, I'd have left it to you, as well."

A flicker of surprise, then, on its heels, understanding. He was getting quicker by the week, taking careful note of everything Thistle did to try to learn what it meant to think critically and strategically. "You want to be laid to rest in your family graveyard, and since that's located back in Maplebark, I can't be the one to take you."

In the grand scheme of things, making a promise to a god not to return to one's homeland in exchange for a second chance at life was a small price to pay, but it *was* a price still a price. One that had never felt steeper than at that moment, as he visibly struggled with the idea of not being around to lay his best friend to rest.

"I understand. Were the roles reversed, I'd ask the same. Well, we don't have our own graveyard or anything, but Mother picked out a good plot next to where they buried Father, and I assumed one day I'd go to rest somewhere in the same area. Now, I think they should just bury me near where I fall, if it comes to that. Promises with gods are said to go beyond even death."

"Honestly, I don't see myself burying you in some random patch of woods, but I get the point about not trying to take you home," Gabrielle said. "Anyway, I've had enough talk of death. Instead, tell me how your training went. We've only got another day or so before the trader arrives and we need to consider leaving, so I hope you're going to tell me you mastered it."

The laughter from Eric was unbidden and surprising, but just what they needed to break the morose spell they'd woven. "Bad news, I very much did not. Good news, I have ample stories of falling on my ass to amuse you with."

*   *   *

The act of writing an email shouldn't be scary. And it wasn't, not in the same way the glowing dice or magical possession had been. No, this was daunting not because Russell feared for his life; rather, it was due to the fact that he feared there would only be a single chance at this. He had a connection to something right now, another person who had experienced what it was like to be controlled by the game. Except, as Mitch had detailed once he finally agreed to help, Jamie apparently wasn't as surprised by the event. If Mitch's account was accurate, she'd been ready for it: waiting, prepared, and in control even as everyone else's ideas of reality were shattering around them.

So far as Russell could figure, that meant there were only two real options. Either Jamie had experienced it before, or she'd known it was coming. The former could mean that she'd taken a different path in an earlier module, or that this had all been going on for far longer than Russell imagined. The latter, on the other hand, would mean that she had some kind of inkling as to what was going on. Whichever it was, talking to her meant potentially learning more about the situation they were in. Assuming he could convince her to make contact.

The more he mulled it over, the more Russell realized that his approach depended on which situation he thought was more likely to be true. If Jamie were another GM in his predicament, he should send a message of camaraderie, a desire to share more information. On the other hand, if she was in on it, then that kind of email would be ignored at best and replied to with false information at worst. But if she was part of all this and Russell let her know he was on to them, there was a slim possibility he might be able to bluff his way into more intel, keeping the threat of going public in his back pocket for emergencies. That was a risky card to play, because without proof, the world would think he was crazy, and this woman would know that, too. Of course, crazy or not, he still might be able to shine a light on something that was clearly meant to be kept a secret, making whatever the goal of all of this was harder to reach.

Ultimately, his choice came down to how well Russell trusted Mitch's account of the incident. As described, it heavily implied that Jamie was part of all of this, but there was a chance that Mitch's anger colored the memory and painted her as more malicious than she actually was. Russell pondered the issue for some time, before finally leaning forward and typing.

"I know about the modules, and about the artifact that reaches between worlds. I just want to talk. Please." He spoke the words as he punched in the keys. Mitch was many different shades of asshole, and part of that included being deeply self-obsessed. For him to notice another person, for them to leave a lasting wound that had nothing to do with the cut on his arm, that person must have done something truly attention-grabbing. Cooperation fit better than complicity, so Russell chose to assume that Jamie had the inside track on what was happening.

Just to be safe, Russell had chosen words that *could* be interpreted as either a threat or a declaration of secret knowledge, depending on the context. The "Please" was there because even if he was coming in with accusations, a little decorum never hurt. He read it over a few times, but the upside to such a short missive was that there was minimal room for error or improvement.

With one final key-stroke, Russell hit send. Leaning back in his chair, he watched the mail icon cycle a few times before a checkmark appeared. Email sent. Now Russell would have to try to keep from staring incessantly at every electronic device he owned until a reply arrived, assuming one came at all.

To keep himself occupied, Russell picked up the latest module and flipped over to where the party had left off, with the lyranx barely slain. He'd need to prepare some maps and miniatures for their next potential paths, a task that would mercifully eat up at least a couple hours of his time.

28.

The rider approached carefully, vigilant for ambushes or roaming monsters. The hood concealed her face, but it didn't hide the constant turning of her head, always attuned to even the slightest disturbance or irregularity. From a distance, using magic to enhance her vision, the priestess watched as the rider gradually slipped onto the hidden path. This was important; the rider presented real danger to the plan. Kalzidar had been explicit in that regard. Her arrival in Notch was the signal to truly turn loose. Once she was there, the priestess would be able to create a proper barricade. No more hiding on the edges. The real job started soon.

In minutes, the rider had vanished from even enhanced magical view, yet the priestess remained. There were to be no needless risks at this point; her orders were clear. Sit, wait, make *sure* the rider wasn't looping back around. The sun was already at its midday point, so the priestess would stay hidden until night fell. Then, with darkness as her ally, preparations would begin. By the rise of the next sun, everything would be in place. Skirmishes and secrets, feeling an enemy out, all of that was preamble.

Tomorrow morning at sunrise, the true match would begin. A good thing, too. After this sunset, they only had two days left before the stars aligned and Kalzidar's full plan could come to fruition.

*   *   *

Morning training had gone roughly the same as the prior day. Grumph was beginning to notice some of what Jolia kept referencing, the moments where his mana drained away, but he'd yet to take control of the mana flow the way she wanted. Although the work was frustrating, that posed little bother. Grumph was accustomed to hitting walls with learning. Not due to a lack of intelligence, simply because few people, aside from Thistle, had ever bothered to offer him proper education in a subject. His knowledge came from what little scraps of information he could gather, combined with ceaseless trial and error. History had taught Grumph that with enough dedication and practice, things would eventually fall into place. It was the same way he'd learned to build a table, cook a meal, and brew fine ale.

The afternoons, however, soothed Grumph's minor ego wounds, giving him the chance to help Brock refine his brewing process along with punching up some of the ale recipes in use. Supplies here were somewhat limited; there were a variety of farms around Notch that could provide basics, but anything special needed to be acquired by magic or via the trader. That put limits on how much Grumph could add to the recipes, so he instead focused on balancing the ratios of existing ingredients and refining Brock's brewing process.

It was simple, straightforward work that Grumph had forgotten he enjoyed so much. Together, he and Brock toiled in silence, the former crushing dried leaves from various spice plants into a fine powder, while the latter fixed small holes in one of the storage barrels. Sometimes, in the rare moments when things were slow, Grumph imagined starting another tavern once this was all over: adding new flavors he'd found on his journey, living a simple life of brewing, cooking, and serving to the natives of a town where he felt at home.

The idea was a nice one, a pleasant fantasy in which to take occasional refuge, but it would never be anything more. Grumph knew that, had known it since the day they departed Maplebark. Adventurers rarely understood when to stop; things had a tendency to snowball around them, so even the ones who wanted to get out rarely could. Their goal had been to save Maplebark from Mad King Liadon's wrath, and in that regard, they'd succeeded. The king knew and cared nothing about their town; his focus was on the party who'd stolen his desired artifact, rather than turning it over. The price on their heads alone ensured that they would never be able to go back to normal lives.

At least, that was what Grumph thought, until they'd found Notch. The citizens of this place had no interest in the pasts of his friends, or the gold their lives were worth to the King of Solium. Seeing a place like this made Grumph uneasy, because it gave him the urge to hope for the future. That sentiment was dangerous, especially in this line of work. Hope could make one think of what came next and hesitate during a critical moment. Grumph had to keep his eyes on the here and now; it was the best chance he had for actually making it to see another sunrise.

That inherent attentiveness may have been why he noticed the footsteps racing toward the tavern, moving at a speed that was slightly too quick to be just a thirsty customer. Grumph lifted his eyes to look over at Brock, whose head was raised and tilted slightly to the side. "It's Jolia. We'd never hear Kieran coming, and Simone doesn't rush. If you listen closely, you can catch the occasional thump of her cane."

Despite straining his ears, Grumph could make out no such distinction. Brock was nonetheless proven right moments later as Jolia came bursting in the door, stopping with a heavy thud of her staff.

"Thought you'd both want to know that the trader arrived less than an hour ago. Kieran is with her, explaining the situation so she's up to speed. We'll spread the word that she's going to be open for business in the morning, giving us the rest of today before the townsfolk start pouring in. Grumph, she usually hangs around for a couple of days before heading out again. As long as she doesn't mind taking your group along, anyone who wants to should be able to leave safely with her, even if there are more threats hiding out there."

"Sounds like I should've asked you to write more of these recipes down," Brock said. "From the look and smell alone, I think that once Jolia tastes the new batch, she's going to refuse to go back to the old version."

"Time-acceleration spells take a tremendous amount of mana, part of why I do them rarely, but in cases of true need, I can be convinced to make an exception," Jolia replied. "So if speed-fermenting is needed, I'd be happy to lend my talents."

Grumph finished pulverizing his spice leaves and added them to the jar he was storing all the finished batches in. When they were done, Brock would only need to measure out the powder, rather than the leaves, creating a mixture that would be easy to consistently add to future batches. "I hope it goes that easy."

"From what I heard, the trader didn't encounter any trouble on the way in. Maybe whoever was attacking us realized how pointless it was." Jolia didn't look like she believed the words any more than Grumph or Brock did. It was merely a polite nod to the possible, even though they'd all seen enough action to know problems never went away that easily. "And if not, then I'm sure she can get you past any trouble you might encounter. Humble as she looks, that woman easily could have been a citizen of Notch if she'd wanted to."

Now that drew Grumph's attention, turning him away from his leaves for the first time since Jolia had burst through the door. "Wouldn't a being of such power stand out in the world?"

"Most of us would. Some keep a low profile, though, even during their adventuring days, and can move with a touch more impunity. As for our trader, she took a different approach. That's all I can say for now. If you want the rest of the story, you'll have to get it from her."

*   *   *

Kieran and his guest were situated in a room beneath Kieran's own home. His was a sprawling farmhouse close to town, although he'd never had much luck sowing a crop into the surrounding fields. Killing had always been Kieran's gift, and it seemed that skill applied to plants as much as people. Most of the house was designed simply, using architecture that reminded Kieran of his childhood village before it was razed, but this room was an exception. It was a basement, lined with a special type of off-white stone and covered in various runes and wards. Every caster in Notch had been through here, giving it the once-over and checking for weaknesses. True privacy was virtually impossible, between the gods and the magic at play in their world; however, this was probably the closest any mortal could achieve.

"—and since then, we've functionally been in a holding pattern. We're training the adventurers on the basics while we wait for the next move. Leaving on their own is obviously too dangerous, and whoever is doing this has enough magic to shield themselves from all attempts at magical scrying we've tried so far. Jolia wants to start using some of the various items and artifacts we have stashed to punch through their protection, but Simone and I agreed that it was too risky. Someone might be fishing, trying to figure out what this village is, and the less we give them to work off of, the better."

"Especially if your enemy is strong enough to withstand Jolia's spells," the trader added. She'd yet to lower the hood of her cloak, a hood that shouldn't be capable of concealing her face from so many angles, yet managed to do so. Even when she put the glass of whiskey to her lips—a favorite vintage of hers that Kieran kept on hand for any such visits—her features remained hidden. "Adds credence to the idea that a god is involved. Kalzidar makes sense, too. He's smart enough to know that charging into this village won't work, and petty enough that he won't *care* so long as it means annoying, or potentially hurting, someone he wants to get revenge on."

Kieran nodded, leaving his own glass of water untouched. "But why would Kalzidar wait until now to strike at those adventurers? They've brought us up to speed on what's happened. I can see why Kalzidar would want revenge, yet was this truly the best time to reach for it? Surely there was a better opportunity previously, one where they weren't protected by a village of former adventurers."

"You're forgetting, it's not a single player moving the pawns around the board." Reaching over, the trader picked up Kieran's glass of water and set it down next to her whiskey. "From what you've told me, we have two gods in play at the moment. Grumble and Kalzidar." As she said their names, she touched the glasses—the water first, for Grumble, and then the whiskey, for Kalzidar. "We can't see *all* the moves, only the ones that are made around us, but even that's something."

Her hand rested on the whiskey, pushing it slightly forward. "Kalzidar is a bastard who lives for vengeance, which means that the moment a piece of his divinity was destroyed, he launched plans for payback. What those were, we don't yet know, but hiding from other gods is a harder trick than hiding from mortals." On cue, she moved the water forward, so it was once more even with the whiskey. "Grumble sees something coming, so he puts his paladin on a path toward one of the few nearby places where it *might* be possible to survive the wrath of a vengeful god."

She was moving faster now, pushing the glasses forward in rapid alternation. "Kalzidar counters by somehow blocking direct communication, forcing Grumble to make the armor stick on Thistle. Kalzidar responds by sending in a group of raiders, and so on. Here's the important part to remember, though: they are acting and reacting, so it's possible that one doesn't know what the other is thinking. Maybe Kalzidar has no idea what this town is; he only worked off the idea that Grumble thought the adventurers would be safe within its walls. The thing that you should be keeping in mind about all of this is that the odds of Notch being the true target are extremely low. If you send the visitors out, there's a good chance your problems go with them."

"We also have knowledge that's proven quite useful to them, too useful for me to trust it as coincidence," Kieran added. "And they, in turn, have been of some help on a few minor projects. My guess is that Grumble always planned on leading them here, he just didn't expect it to become a siege. Hence why Thistle didn't have the loud, windy dreams until he arrived."

The trader picked up the whiskey once more and moments later set back down an empty glass. "I guess the real question is: what you plan to do with them? Not your fight, after all. You wouldn't be the first town to oust adventurers who brought trouble on their heels."

"Maybe not, but we won't add to that number. They're good folks who've given more than they had to. Besides, I told them it was time to trust one another. I'm not going to dishonor Notch by betraying that sentiment." Kieran paused, looking away from the cloak of the trader. "Even if such weren't the case, we'd probably still help. I don't want a piece of *that* artifact staying in this town, and if they take it with them right now, I might very well be handing it over to Kalzidar."

"You could let me have it," the trader suggested, a splash of eagerness livening up her voice. "I'm prepared to pay them well for the sale."

Kieran looked back to the hood as he shook his head. "No, I think not. Professional courtesy and budding friendship aside, you've been chasing these for a long while, and I know how successful you tend to be. I won't say that putting too many pieces into one set of hands is the same as turning it over to Kalzidar, but it's needlessly dangerous just the same. Anyway, I don't see that lot letting go of their piece. They're unexpectedly stubborn."

"Trust me, I'm well aware," the trader replied. She leaned forward and tapped her glass. "And I'll explain that statement, if you'll top me off."

"Are you staying long enough for another? Since you kept your hood up, I assumed you were just passing through for our visit, eager to get to selling." Kieran hadn't actually thought this, but he was getting tired of looking at a featureless void where a face should be.

With a softly muttered curse, she reached up and yanked down on her hood, revealing the lovely features of an elven woman with short brown hair. "Honestly, I leave the thing up so much during my travels that I forget I'm wearing it. Cost me a hefty purse of gold during my last stop in Camnarael, but it's made traveling incognito much, much easier. No offense meant, Kieran. You know I have nothing to hide in Notch."

Kieran stood, walking over to a shelf by a rune-covered wall, where he picked up the waiting bottle of whiskey. He opened it carefully, filling her empty glass halfway before setting the bottle down on the table. "I know, Fritz. And we're always glad to see you. But I'd appreciate it if you could explain that last comment soon. I'm getting tired of not knowing what's happening around me."

"Happy to do so." Fritz reached forward and scooped up her glass before settling deeper into the luxurious chair where she was resting. "Not a thrilling story, by our standards, but something of a lengthy one, so get comfortable. It started when I was on my way to Cadence Hollow, and a blonde woman holding an axe came bursting into my hideout..."

29.

It was still dark out when the opening of a door stirred Timuscor from his sleep. At the foot of his bed, a telltale snort indicated that Mr. Peppers had heard the intruder as well. Hand moving seemingly on its own, Timuscor's fingers wrapped around the hilt of his sword just before a lumbering shadow cut off the light from the doorway.

"You won't be fast enough to hit me, and you should save your strength, anyway."

Timuscor's grip loosened as he recognized Brock's voice. The behemoth looking down at him wasn't wearing the usual patchwork ensemble of a working bartender. His chest was bare, revealing several tattoos winding around his body, and he'd traded working slacks for pants of a material that appeared thick, yet shifted like silk. The boots on his feet were light, with what looked like metal coverings on the toes and heels. While Timuscor had never seen this precise outfit before, he knew at a glance what it was meant for. This was what Brock wore when he went into battle.

"What's happening?" Timuscor asked.

"Not sure. Something entered our forest boundary less than an hour ago. Slipped right through the wards, but Agramor smelled them and sent us word. She was going to devour the intruders until Kieran told her to let them pass."

"Because this Agramor person is a surprise we can only spring once, right?" Timuscor could respect the desire to keep such an asset secret—it more or less lined up with how they'd been dealing with each new threat, giving away as little information about their resources as possible. "But the same is true for you, Brock, so why are you clad in attire clearly meant for combat?"

There was pain in Brock's smile as he looked down at his garb, yet not *only* pain was there. "Maybe these are my sleeping clothes, ever consider that?"

In reply, Timuscor pulled back his covers and began the process of donning his own armor. Eventually, Brock's gave up on waiting for a laugh.

"Fine, not my best joke. Give me a little leeway, you're not the only sleepy one here. Anyway, I'm wearing this for a few reasons. Firstly, because we've decided it's not right to let you all put your lives on the line while we stay hidden. We're going to keep concealing our more unique cards, but there's not much more to discover about me. I'm pure combat. Someone realizing that I hit hard isn't going to give away much, and it will make sure you've all got some backup on the battlefield."

For a fleeting moment, Timuscor wanted to object, to tell Brock that they could handle this and he should hide. That was pride talking, though, not strategy or caution, and Timuscor recognized the trickster almost immediately. Timuscor's party had barely made it through that last fight, surviving only because of the unseen help Notch's protectors had given. He and his friends were already leaning on them to help. This way just put it out in the open.

"Then your aid is appreciated," Timuscor said. "Yet you said there was more than one reason, so I cannot help wondering what the others might be."

Even in the dim light of the room, Timuscor noticed the severe look that darted across Brock's face. "Word has been coming in from throughout Notch. As of last night, we had two more people get divine dreams where they couldn't hear their god speaking. Magic to look beyond the borders of Notch is failing as well. Whatever is happening, it's gotten more serious."

That was indeed a significant development. No wonder Brock was readied for battle. "Any idea what's approaching?"

"Not yet. Jolia is trying to see how they beat the wards. All we know for now is what Agramor told us: there's a few of them, moving fast, and they stink of undeath."

That meant Simone was well-suited in dealing with the threat, if she could covertly cast from the sidelines. No, even that was assuming too much. Whoever was coming seemed prepared for the challenges that came with breaking into Notch. Best to work from the assumption that they'd be prepared for a necromancer as well.

"How long do we have?" Timuscor didn't slow as he added more pieces of his armor, going as fast as possible while still making sure the job was done properly.

"The winding paths of the forest will buy us enough time for everyone to be awake and ready. Get your armor and weapon, and meet us downstairs."

With that, Brock was out the door, although his footsteps didn't travel far before they entered the next room—Eric's. Timuscor paid them no more mind. His focus was entirely on his armor. On the ground, Mr. Peppers bumped over a small pile of armor with his snout.

"Sorry, with all the training, I haven't had a chance to get you a new set," Timuscor apologized. "Hang back for today, and we'll deal with it whenever this next attack ends."

The promise gained him a snort that seemed to accept the orders, albeit not very happily.

*   *   *

From a distance, they were visible. Once, they had been fearsome creatures, powerful and unyielding. Now, they were mere imitations of what they had been: saldramirs, lizards roughly the size of a horse and a half, native to desert climates and known for their nasty bite. A curious choice for a force of invading undead. Some undead held on to their forms, even their sentience, but not all; these offered brute force, certainly, but little else. Few of those gathered in Notch's town square had ever seen one in person, and none would count this as doing so. What was coming down at them were not real saldramirs, only the remains of what had once been.

Their scales were flaking off with every movement; some had chunks of skin missing, which exposed the half-decayed muscles moving them along the ground. Only one of the three had both eyes, and all were missing toes and teeth. Atop the saldramir in the center was a figure wrapped in heavy clothes, concealing all its features.

Three undead beasts on the verge of falling apart, and a single rider. By Thistle's calculations, that seemed more like an envoy than an attack, but it would depend on just who that rider was. If the people of Notch had demonstrated nothing else, they'd reminded him that one person easily could be powerful enough to present a threat on their own. Diplomacy was a pleasant hope—just not an option Thistle could afford to put too much faith in.

"They're barely holding together. Whoever made them didn't plan on keeping their new pets around for long. Even if we do nothing, they'll fall apart within a day or so. Disposable, each and every one." The words were whispered in everyone's ears, Simone's voice reaching them despite her being hidden.

Communication was being given more importance this time around, with Jolia taking the time to weave a spell of whispering between all those who would be present for the confrontation, both on display and hidden. No more running around haphazardly; this time, they would coordinate properly.

As the saldramirs drew near, everyone tensed. The smell had already begun to reach them, and with every lumbering step of the approaching source, the situation worsened. The stink was bad enough, but their proximity also allowed everyone to pick out more horrifying details about the beasts. Thistle wondered if attacks would even land, or if they'd merely plunge right through the exposed flesh.

Mercifully, roughly a hundred feet from where they stood, the rider held up a hand and stopped the saldramirs. Moving with visible caution, the rider dismounted heavily, landing so hard there were small cracks in the road, before walking the rest of the way over.

"People of Notch, there is no need to hide. I do not come to deliver harm to you. I am here only for the ones gathered before me, and not even all of those."

The voice was off. Humanoid-sounding, yet the speech patterns didn't feel quite right, like it was a thing impersonating the way regular people talked.

It *was* some form of discussion, at least. Thistle took that as a good sign. If they were willing to talk, then they might be willing to listen. It would be nice if, just once, diplomacy could solve the problem better than force.

"I take it that means you have come for us." Thistle stepped forward as he spoke. Experience taught him that staying in a crowd would only make it harder for his audience to notice who was talking. "And something tells me your desire is not to hire us for our services."

Still concealed by the abundant clothes—far too many for weather this pleasant—the rider nodded. "Correct. I have come to slay you. The sins you have committed cannot go unpunished. Meet your fate, here and now. Justice shall be served, all debts paid. Or, if you would prefer time to say goodbye, you may depart Notch before nightfall. Failure to do so will result in a full assault, one that will encompass this town and its surrounding areas. Do not make others die for your sins."

"Aye, that would hardly be the paladin way," Thistle agreed. "But nor would it be right to die purely on someone's request. You talk of sins, so tell us what trespasses we are supposed to have committed. Only then can you make the case that death is warranted."

There was no reply for several seconds. They weren't even sure the rider had heard Thistle speak. Perhaps it was getting orders from elsewhere and had to convey the words back, or simply took a while to process the argument. Eventually, words flowed once more, although they were still stilted.

"You have committed the greatest sin of all, to do harm to a divine being. By your actions, a part of Kalzidar's divinity was destroyed. Death is potentially too light of a sentence."

"Then I'm afraid we are at an impasse. I've done things, too many things, in my life that I feel guilt for, but that act will never be one of them. If you want our lives, then you'll have to claim them the old-fashioned way." To illustrate the point, Thistle drew two of his daggers and gave each a quick spin.

From behind, gentle footsteps betrayed Brock's re-positioning. "That's right, and don't count on us to toss them out. I'm getting pretty sick of you thinking this is a place you can come waltzing in and out of whenever you damn well please. You've disrespected our town, our home, and now you demand the lives of our visitors. We've been going lightly thus far, playing your game half out of prudence and half out of boredom, but if you keep pushing, we're bound to get angry. When that happens, we can shed an ocean of blood."

It was a threat scary enough to give even Thistle pause, and he was on Brock's side. This was mostly due to the fact that Thistle knew every word was true. Playing a situation cautiously wasn't the only tactic. If Notch decided to send a message, they could smite this emissary and virtually anyone who followed.

Scary as the words were, there was no reaction from the rider. Not a shiver, not a step back, not even a nervous fidget. In fact, the rider barely moved at all, Thistle realized. The stillness went beyond calm. It was inhuman.

As it turned out, that was precisely the right word to use. Slowly, the rider began to remove its articles of clothing, replying, "I am sure you could. However, you will be unable to do so in this attack. Bloodshed, by its very nature, requires blood."

The first fleck of metal came into view as a glove fell away. Next emerged metal hands, metal arms, and, with the removal of the hood, they could discern parts of a metal face. Not merely cloaked in armor, these were appendages forged from metal, bound with springs and screws in an art long since lost to history. This one was old, chipped and rusty, but the pictures Thistle had seen in historical tomes had showed what these looked like when fresh and new. Beyond that, Thistle had once caught sight of some in person, an unintended detour in the Vault of Sealed Magics. Those had been shiny, gleaming like polished steel in sunlight.

"Well, that explains how the wards were so easily slipped," Jolia's voice muttered in their ears. "It's an automaton. They were invented centuries ago by a gnome who wanted to make war on a cabal of wizards who'd kicked him out. It worked so well that he decided to go for full conquest and built an army of the things. Because they're highly resistant to magic, they were eventually declared too dangerous, and the bulk of them were sealed away. I'd heard a few units were still lost in the world, but the odds of finding one along with the necessary control gem are pretty slim."

More clothing fell away, giving an almost complete view of the entity before them. It was humanoid, at least in terms of shape, but of a height and frame that seemed more derivative of half-orcs. The eyes were the most interesting part to Thistle; the automatons he'd seen before had been mimicking sleep, so he'd never gotten to see the eyes glowing softly green.

"I have not come to deliver your death; that glory will be entrusted to others. I am here to deliver a message. On the sunset after today's, the stars shall align. Kalzidar's power will be at its zenith, and with it, so shall his servants'. We have found the Helm of Ignosa, the great genius who created my kind. When his priests are at their strongest, they will march into this hamlet with an automaton army bolstering their ranks. Strong though you are, not even this town can endure such an attack. Give your visitors up, and Notch will be spared. Wait, and join them in their punishment."

It was a bluff, had to be. Thistle had seen that army; he knew it was sealed safely away in Lumal. But even as he tried to reassure himself, a nagging thought kept popping up. He'd only gotten that glimpse because his group had successfully made it into a restricted section in the Vault of Sealed Magics. Obviously, if his old party could do it, then it was possible one of Kalzidar's servants had as well. Still, stealing a whole army? That seemed like a stretch, even with divine backing.

"And how, pray tell, did you manage to liberate that army despite all of Lumal's security?"

"I do not know. I was not there when the theft occurred. But a magic-resistant army can make short work of a town built upon magical safeguards."

"Aye, that's fair, but there is one more thing," Thistle continued. "As a gnome myself, one who grew up with an unkind view of casters, I'm familiar with the story of Ignosa. His automatons had many functions, including the ability to follow rudimentary orders in combat without direct control. Speech, however, was never part of their repertoire. They could only be used as conduits for communication by those who held the control gems."

There was no facial response, of course. Such a thing was impossible; even if the controller had wanted to make it react, automatons lacked movable faces. When it spoke again, the sound was the same, slightly grating and uneven, but the tone was no longer so unnatural and stilted.

"Pity. I'd hoped to keep this going a bit longer, maybe even convince you that you had a friend who could play both sides. Can't blame me for having some fun while I wait. Feel free to run for it, Thistle. I'm sure there are other methods of escape available to you. Just know that if you do flee, the hunting will not stop. I'll still roll over this town like the tide across sand. Until then, here's something to liven up your day."

It was barely a second of warning. No sooner had the automaton spoken than all three saldramirs burst open, as though their insides were trying to escape their rotting exteriors. Unfortunately, Thistle wasn't that lucky. As he peered closer, he could see hundreds of rats pouring forth, each with wild eyes and gnashing teeth. It was a very real concern, and one he lacked the spare attention to deal with. Because while most eyes had been on the exploding saldramirs, the chatty automaton had seized the chance to rush forward on a crash course with Thistle.

Worse, there was no way he would be able to dodge in time.

30.

Quick as the automaton was, Brock had already been in position and ready. To anyone watching, it was clear he hadn't moved closer to Thistle just so his words would hit home. No sooner did the automaton try to crush Thistle with its metal might than one of Brock's meaty fists slammed into its torso, knocking the automaton halfway back to the saldramirs. Strong though the punch was, their enemy still landed on its feet, albeit with a sizable dent in its center.

Before it had stopped skidding along the road, fire burst forth, rising from the ground in a flaming circle that wrapped around the saldramirs and fleeing rats, catching the last vestiges of the automaton's clothes on fire.

"Smart gold says those rats are carrying diseases meant to infect and weaken the town," Simone informed them. "Since they're planning to use non-living combatants, they can largely ignore the disease and give their living allies potions to protect themselves with. It's the same strategy used to soften up a town before invading with an army of undead."

"Hence why I threw up a barrier of fire to keep them contained," Jolia agreed. "Take care of any that slipped out, but keep your distance in case Simone is right."

The words were scarcely spoken when a red blur darted across the battlefield, cleaving through a speedy rat outside the circle of fire. Gabrielle dispatched two more before bothering to glance back. "What? If I'm undead anyway, I may as well enjoy the perks."

"Yes. Perks are quite lovely." Agreement was rarely something one wanted to share with an enemy, and this was no exception. From her vantage point near the flames, Gabrielle could watch it all. The automaton leaned forward and lay down across the line of fire. Much as she would have liked to see the thing melt, its magical resistance unfortunately kept it safe. Far worse was when, moments later, she realized what it was doing.

"Everyone, get back!" Gabrielle had just enough time to yell before the first wave of rats came surging forth, using the automaton as a bridge to leave the ring of fire. The section they could cross was thankfully narrow, limiting the swarm to a narrow stream of potential plague carriers. It was a small mercy, especially considering how many of the furry beasts scrambled atop one another to get free.

Stepping in closer, Gabrielle brought her axe down over and over, focusing on hitting as many as she could with every blow and trusting her friends to pick off any stragglers. Nearby, daggers landed in a pile of rats to her right, while a blast of fire roasted several to her left. Occasionally, one of the vermin on either side would go down with a crossbow bolt speared through its center. Thistle, Grumph, and Eric, doing their ranged duty. Gabrielle chanced a look over her shoulder to find Timuscor on the edges of the battle, sword and shield in hand, a look of deep frustration etched in his face. She could feel for him. Gabrielle also lacked ranged options, but her undead status made her immune to disease, which permitted melee work in this particular situation. The most Timuscor could do was run the edges and carefully pick off any beastlings making a run for the town. Even that carried some risk, though.

"Simone, I'll start throwing spells to protect from disease on everyone one by one; in the meantime, I think Gabrielle needs reinforcements. Nothing too big, they are just rats." Jolia was speaking quickly; they could almost hear the frantic gestures of her fingers weaving spells.

"Already on it. Gabrielle, on the count of three, slam the butt of your axe into the ground and yell anything that sounds like it might be magical." Unlike Jolia, Simone was still perfectly calm, even as more rats poured forth.

It was hard to focus on the conversation and the rats, but Gabrielle picked up enough snippets to know her next move. Listening to the numbers tick by, she raised her axe theatrically high, spit out a few goblin curses in lieu of arcane syllables, and dropped the butt as instructed. The moment it struck, a dozen skeletons burst from the ground, clawing their way out of the nearby dirt and scrambling forward to tear the rats apart.

"Nice timing," Jolia said. "Timuscor, you've now been warded against poison and disease, so feel free to jump in."

From the speed at which he came dashing in, it was evident that Timuscor had been waiting on pins and needles for just such permission. His blade sliced through the rats, cleaving them into halves as his heavily armored feet crushed a few more beneath their weight. Fast as the vermin were pouring forth, they were somehow managing to keep the swarm contained. The fight was far from over, but they were winning, and that felt good.

It was a fleeting sensation, unfortunately. No sooner had Timuscor charged into the battlefield than a whirling mass of metal and residual flames rushed him. How the hells could an automaton move so fast? Seconds ago, it was acting as the rat bridge, now in a blink it had shifted to offense. The automaton was quick, but there was no chance something so huge and distracting would sneak up on Timuscor. He got his shield up just in time to block the first punch.

Whether Timuscor had improperly braced himself or the automaton was just *that* strong, the blow sent him flying back through the air and onto his back. The attack was an almost perfect replica of Brock's, save that now, Timuscor was in the automaton's position. He hurried to his feet, shield dented but at the ready, even as the automaton advanced.

Gabrielle started forward to help before catching a blur in the corner of her eye. Right; this was a team fight, and they all had roles to fill. Hers was dealing with the rats, and this was a great chance to clear the field. With the automaton attacking, no new rats could escape, so she and the skeletons could wipe out the remainder.

As the automaton rushed Timuscor, the blur, which turned out to be Brock, struck it in the side, knocking the metallic opponent off course. "I wasn't going to drag you out of the fire, but if you want to fight a real opponent, then it's going to be me."

"A regrettable match-up. Your talents use mana to reinforce your body, meaning that the resistance of an automaton has little impact on how you fight. Defeat for me and my swarm is almost certain. And yet, I do hope your friends will watch the fight. Watch and see how hard it is to take down even this battered old version, and then imagine hundreds of shiny new models marching through the fields. Against a force like that, you cannot protect these outsiders, any more than you can protect Notch's citizens."

The taunt only earned a grin from Brock as he raised his fists. "I'm getting pretty fucking tired of you underestimating my town. Bring all the party favors you want—we'll put on a shindig like you can't believe. This is just an appetizer."

In a blur, Brock was on the metallic foe, throwing punches and kicks in a seamless, constant flood of movement. Gabrielle didn't have time to pause and enjoy the show; her job was still going. They'd thinned out the majority of the rats that had escaped, but the pulsating swarm just beyond the fire was still hundreds strong. No matter how many they brought down, there were more waiting to charge.

"Grumph, you are now protected from disease and poison," Jolia announced. "I'm busy warding everyone in case the rats' blood is a contagion, so maybe you can help clear out the main mass of the rats. I bet a fire blast with some extra mana would do the trick."

Already scanning between the few free rats remaining, the swarm sealed in a flame wall, and Brock's fight with the automaton, Gabrielle added in an occasional glance to Grumph, at the risk of making herself dizzy. He hadn't hesitated, already mumbling under his breath as he gestured in the air. Near the end, for a moment, Grumph did seem to slow down. Face scrunched together in focus, perhaps tinged with frustration, Grumph painstakingly went through the final motions of his spell.

The magical fire that roared from his hand was significantly larger than the blast the spell usually summoned. It surged forth, wild and barely controlled, before slamming down near the flaming circle of rats. When it hit, the detonation was substantial. Sadly, the rat circle was not at the epicenter of the blast. Instead, they caught the edges of the flaming explosion. Grumph might have managed to push more mana into a spell, but he'd done so at the cost of his aim. Worse, from the way he was leaning on his staff, it looked like the half-orc wizard had put too much mana in, potentially taking himself out of the fight.

While it was a poor turn in that regard, they still had the momentum in the battle. Gabrielle could see skeletons wiping out the final freed rats, and Brock's automaton opponent was looking more like a blacksmith's cast-offs than a person formed of metal. However, strong as Brock was, none of the others failed to notice how long it was taking him to completely dismantle the enemy. To his credit, part of that delay was certainly due to him fighting conservatively. He was emphasizing defense and control over pure damage, working to keep his opponent corralled, away from the others. Nevertheless, old and rusted though it might be, the durability and strength this automaton displayed were factors to take note of. Especially when one would soon have to deal with the threat of hundreds more, all in better condition.

That was a concern for later. They still had a swarm of potential plague carriers to wipe out. Casting protection from disease might be a relatively simple spell, but curing someone once they were infected was supposed to be a much harder process. Some illnesses responded to simple healing magic, others required specialized treatment by those with high-level divine spells, and if Kalzidar was going through all this trouble, he'd certainly sprung for something exotic.

"Eric, you're warded now. Not much to do except give Gabrielle a hand if more rats slip past," Jolia announced.

"Thank you, but I actually think I've got a fix for those." From the alley where he'd been hidden, as was his role, Eric emerged. Only, he wasn't holding his short sword or crossbow. Instead, he was carrying three bottles and a torch. Walking over calmly, Eric still cut a brisk pace, trusting Brock to handle the automaton. With only corpses to step over in terms of rats, each step came down with grace and surety. Whether he knew it or not, his movements were improving at a steady rate. Between the training from Elora and the lessons here in Notch, Eric was fast becoming a proper rogue.

"I was watching what happened, so I ducked back into the tavern and grabbed some quick supplies. Grumph had a good idea, but, you know, not *every* problem requires magic to solve." Casually, Eric set his load down, keeping only a single bottle in his left hand. With his right, he took his crossbow and readied to fire a bolt. The first bottle arced up neatly, hanging in the air for several seconds before being shattered by Eric's shot.

As soon as the glass broke, liquid rained down inside the circle of flames. Even from a small distance back, Gabrielle could catch the familiar scent of lamp oil. Immediately, the whole plan fell into place—although, calling it a plan felt a tad too grand. It was, in practice, a very simple idea, yet one nobody else had considered thus far. Instead of using magic, Eric was just dousing the rats in fuel before he lit them on fire. Magic and might were falling short, which was exactly the time when rogues shone best.

Two more bottles; two more easy shots. For the torch, Eric didn't bother with flint or steel. Instead, he merely touched the edge to the already burning circle of flames. It caught instantly, and seconds later, he chucked it over the wall and onto the oil-soaked rats. Whatever aspect of the magical wall that had kept the vermin safe unless they were directly against the flames didn't apply to this new, mundane fire. Squeaks, squeals, and smoke began to rise in roughly commensurate amounts, increasing rapidly as the blaze spread.

Everyone, save for the skeletons, backed away from the thick, dark smoke rising off the rats. Many rats tried to push through the wall, taking their chances on a quicker death. Thanks to the utter crush of bodies, a few even slipped past, albeit all who did were on fire and quickly picked off.

Nearby, Brock rose to his feet. The automaton was little more than scrap now, and even that appeared to be almost… melting? Something was certainly happening to the remains. They were softening on the edges, warping at every angle. For a moment, Gabrielle feared it would reform and cause some more trouble, but after a few seconds, the change halted, and there was nothing more than a pile of half-melted junk on the ground.

All in all, the battle had gone fairly smoothly. Rats were contained, no disease had escaped, and the automaton was defeated before it could seriously injure or kill anyone. None of which changed the fact that if Kalzidar was really summoning an army of those metallic soldiers, they would be in for one hell of a fight. Brock might be capable of defeating an automaton with his bare hands, but how many others in Notch could? Strong though the citizens were said to be, an enemy who was resistant to magic created all manner of potential problems. It was something to consider when the dust settled from this bout, yet Gabrielle also felt a momentary thrill at winning today's fight. As she looked around, she noticed the expression was mirrored on the faces around her, with one notable exception.

Thistle wasn't happy. He didn't look especially angry, either—more annoyed than anything, frustration radiating off him as he surveyed the battlefield. Without drawing attention, Gabrielle made her way over to the gnome. "You don't look like a man whose party just won a skirmish without any loss or injury."

"Because I'm not sure I am." Thistle didn't even look at her; he only had eyes for the slowly settling scene before them. "A warning? Even if Kalzidar didn't want to fight the people of Notch, I can't believe he'd really come in like this with threats and demands. Kalzidar is the type to gather forces in secret, make preparations, and then strike when an enemy is most vulnerable. Direct confrontation is a needless risk, one that he doesn't tend to take. Maybe he's trying to trick us into running, into taking a route we think is safe but will really be an ambush. Even that might have been more likely if we didn't just get confirmation that there was an enemy at our gates."

A long sigh left Thistle's lips as he finally looked away. His fingers pressed against the bridge of his nose, rubbing gently. "I don't see it. I don't know what kind of move Kalzidar is making, and while, on a personal level, I recognize that there's no shame in being outmaneuvered by a god, it still bothers me. Mostly because, if Kalzidar is indeed bluffing about the automaton army, then that means that whatever he's truly sending will be that much worse."

31.

With the finished potion, thanks to the costly ashes from a phoenix rebirth, joining the eye of a lyranx and the feathers of a golden roc safely tucked away in their magical bags, the party of Chalara, Wimberly, Gelthorn, and Timanuel said their final goodbyes to the kingdom of Alcatham. There was only a single component left, one they could hunt for on their way to Lumal. Rather than take the roads, the party had decided to spend some of their hard-won gold on magical transportation. It wasn't an option available in every town—few cities had enough mages or demand to offer it—but Camnarael was a kingdom's capital, and therefore, an exception to the rule.

For a sum of gold that seemed borderline exorbitant until one factored in the time and cost of making the journey on foot, they could be teleported to an outpost town on a far northern border of Alcatham. If the information they'd gathered along their quest was right, an entrance to Lumal would be only a day or two's journey from that spot, hence why some enterprising wizards had bothered offering the magical transport option.

It wouldn't just be a simple trek, however. In those lands, a dangerous type of monster was said to lurk. The potion, ashes, eye, and feathers were pieces of a spell that opened the door to Lumal; however, the final component was more variable. Whispers and rumors all lent themselves to the idea that the last piece of the spell was to demonstrate an act for the sake of Lumal. They had to do something for the kingdom before they would be permitted entrance. Some went the route of finding rare items or magics, offering to strengthen Lumal by direct donation. Others undertook tasks, fulfilling some of the few quests from Lumal that had slipped into the world.

Then there was the more direct option: killing. The strange monsters that stood between Alcatham's outpost and the Lumal entrance had, supposedly, not always been there. They were a recent infestation, and Lumal considered each one killed as a service done for the kingdom. It was the most straightforward way to get into the city, and also among the most dangerous. Plenty of people were willing to trade rumors about these roaming monsters, but there were few tales of success to go around. Whatever these beasts were, they wouldn't go down easily.

Even knowing the risks, the party had agreed that it was their best shot. The other methods were too cumbersome and complex, with ample opportunities for things to go wrong. This was better suited to their straightforward style: kill a dangerous monster and be done with it. Only so many ways for that to go wrong, and in none of them would it be a problem for long. Triumph or death; such was the danger of life as an adventurer.

Together, they gathered at the teleportation point and set out, ready for a brief stop-over before heading off on their hunt. That plan fell apart in moments, as instead of a peaceful countryside hamlet, they found themselves surrounded by people screaming and the unmistakable stink of fresh blood.

The outpost was under attack, and they'd just teleported in without any way of getting out. Exchanging a brief glance, each member of the party drew their weapons and began to scout the area, hunting for an enemy. If they were going to be stuck in a fight, anyway, then they'd damn sure try to win it.

*   *   *

Cleanup was a straightforward matter, although not quite a simple one. Everything rat-related was burned on the spot, until even their blood was nothing more than smoking ash. For those who'd been at the frontlines, their armor and weapons needed to be scrubbed as well. For good measure, baths were drawn and sprinkled with purifying herbs, along with a few spells of cleansing, to eradicate any residual bits and blood that clung still to their bodies. Magical disease protection wasn't permanent, and if even one infected chunk lingered past the spell's duration, it could turn the day's triumph into tragedy.

That was how Timuscor found himself in a large metal tub that magically kept the water contained inside warm, letting the heat soothe his various aches and pains. The scrubbing part was long since done—he'd made sure that not so much as a lone rat hair was left anywhere on him—but it wasn't often he got to relax in such a manner. Since he had time to spare while the street was being decontaminated, Timuscor treated himself to a luxurious soak.

His hand dangled over the side of the tub, idly scratching Mr. Peppers, who was standing patiently at the tub's side. Between the heat, the early wake-up, and the post-battle exhaustion, it was hardly surprising that Timuscor fell into the gentle clutches of sleep.

What *was* surprising, on the other hand, was that he found himself somewhere else. At a glance, it didn't seem familiar, just a landscape punctuated by fog. Except… he *knew* this place. Not well, certainly, but Timuscor had been here before. Once, briefly, when his shield, armor, and internal organs were punctured by a projectile and he was bleeding out as death loomed. He wasn't on the brink of death now, though—he hoped—which made the sudden return all the more confusing.

"Hello?" Timuscor took several steps in a random direction, yet the scenery didn't change. Just emptiness and rolling fog as far as the eye could see. "I know there's someone here. The memory is fuzzy, but that voice still echoes clear as a bell throughout my mind."

No response came to Timuscor, momentarily confusing him until he thought back on his previous time here more carefully. The voice wasn't flippant, it didn't waste words, and Timuscor hadn't actually asked it anything yet. Maybe some mysterious beings deigned to bother with polite greetings, but this probably wasn't one of them. He needed to consider what was happening, why he might be here, and then use his chance wisely.

"Have you brought me here to offer counsel once more? Everyone here who follows a god has been unable to speak to them, yet you've managed to pull me to this place, so I must assume you wish to help."

Many gods rely on divine channels, not all. Some prefer a herald.

If there was any doubt in Timuscor's mind—and really, there hadn't been more than a sliver—that Mr. Peppers was connected to this voice, those words put the final scoop of dirt on the coffin. He'd even fallen asleep with his hand directly pressed against the boar's head, and after seeing Mr. Peppers grow and shrink in a matter of moments, it was plain that he was still no ordinary pet. Much as he wanted to ponder that idea more thoroughly, the voice continued to speak.

I am here for counsel, but not for your friends. The games of gods grow wearying over time; I no longer indulge them. My counsel is for you, Timuscor, the aspiring paladin.

"Your herald has been a dear companion to me on my travels. He represents you well. Any counsel you have, I will gladly hear."

Wiser than when we last spoke. Healthier, too. Despite facing peril, you have not stood at the doorstep of Death since our prior meeting. You heard and understood, yet you've still not told my herald the price of being a paladin.

"I... have been grappling with much lately," Timuscor admitted. It wasn't something he was sure he could say even to the others in his party, but here, speaking only to darkness, the truth flowed forth. "I know now that seeking a meaningful death is not the path of a paladin. It is a consequence they must bear. However, my mind is not like Thistle's. I do not come upon things quickly. I must work my way through the slower paths, and at present, I confess, I have been more lost in wondering who I truly am now that I know more about my kind. About the echoes."

You are not an echo, Timuscor. You are awake in a world of those trapped beneath a spell of slumber. The ones who existed before, they were the echoes, the precursors of what was still to come. And you are wrong about one more thing. It is not two answers you're seeking. It is one. That is how you will know it to be true.

Timuscor had no response for that. His prior words were honest; understanding was slower for him than for the others. He would need to consider the advice carefully to glean its true meaning. Thankfully, the voice didn't force him to respond.

Until then, work with my herald and gain mastery over his new power. Because that gift did not come from me. It manifested because of you, Timuscor. After all, what would an aspiring paladin be without his—

"Timuscor!"

The word shook Timuscor from his sleep. He jerked forward so fast that water came splashing over the sides of the tub. Standing in the doorway was Kieran, staring at him with confusion that was slowly giving way to worry. "Are you all right? I've been calling you for a while now."

That couldn't be, except that Timuscor's skin had grown substantially more wrinkled in what should have been the span of mere minutes. Time, it seemed, did not always flow at the same rate for gods—even lost and buried ones—as it did for mortals. Looking down, Timuscor found that Mr. Peppers was staring at him. Carefully, Timuscor reached over and scratched the boar once more, assuring him he'd gotten the message.

"My apologies. After the battle and the early morning, I must have dozed while in the bath."

"You might want to work on not being such a deep sleeper. That's a liability on the road." Kieran didn't seem entirely sure he bought the excuse, but after a few seconds, he continued. "Anyway, I was coming to let you know that this afternoon we're going to have a meeting with the trader. Given what happened this morning, there's a lot to discuss on top of that."

Timuscor nodded, finally looking away from the boar. "Of course. How long do we have?"

"A few hours. We decided to deal with lunch and daily chores first. Plenty of time to dry off and get a meal."

"I appreciate that, but I fear I'll need to spend my time elsewhere." From a nearby stool, Timuscor plucked a towel and began to dry his torso. "It's high time I see Notch's blacksmith about some replacement equipment. It wouldn't be proper to have Mr. Peppers go into combat unarmored."

Accepting the odd statement, Kieran tried to keep the confusion off his face as he shut the door and gave Timuscor some much-needed privacy.

*   *   *

"Fuck!"

Jolia's curse came moments before the sound of glass smashing to the ground. While not a mage himself, Thistle had served enough of them to know some of their tools. As this was the third smashed piece of the morning, however, it was hard to discern what had newly been broken amidst the pile of twinkling glass. "How are they doing this? How are they blocking off all communication between us and the outside world? I can't get any sending spells through, can't touch people in the realm of dreams. I've tried everything short of animating a letter and telling it to go fly and find someone."

Powerful as Jolia was, it had also become clear that she'd gotten out of practice dealing with true obstacles. Life as a citizen, rather than an adventurer, inherently came with fewer challenges. They were all hoping she'd eventually figure out a solution to the new development, pressure that was only compounding her stress.

For his part, Thistle was making use of Jolia's extensive library to research everything he could about automatons and the Helm of Ignosa. So far, nothing he'd found was good. While there were no official numbers on how large the automaton army had become before their capture, it was said to be capable of wiping out even a kingdom's capital city in a single day. Their greatest weakness was the Helm of Ignosa itself, a magical tool that acted as a universal control gem. Supposedly, the one who wore it could control the entire army with no more than a few careful thoughts. A tremendous amount of power, but if one took down the leader, then the entire army would halt. While that *should* have been encouraging, Thistle had yet to find any limitations on distance for the helm. In theory, one could give the order from half a continent away, meaning that they might be facing down an automaton army with no readily-exploitable weaknesses.

Even for the people of Notch, that was a fight they may not win. Then again, all of that was conditional on the idea that Kalzidar's emissary had been telling the truth, a concept Thistle wasn't quite ready to embrace just yet. The trouble was that with no way to contact the outside world, they didn't know if the army had really marched out of Lumal yet. Keeping them cut off ensured they couldn't warn Lumal of the upcoming potential threat or gain useful information of their own.

"Oh, come on! I can't even take control of small animals and send them through." There was no glass breaking this time, although Jolia did slam her head heavily down on the worktable. "This is ridiculous. Not even gods have infinite power, and unless Kalzidar is always giving us his full attention, he shouldn't be able to block us this well, not against me. It can't be a spell someone else is working, though. It's much too comprehensive. Honestly, whatever this ward is, it's unlike any magic I've ever dealt with."

"What if it isn't magic?" Thistle sat up bolt-straight, the idea slamming through his mind like a runaway carriage. "This blockade, keeping us cut off from the outside world, it's working *too* well, right? Almost as if it doesn't obey the laws and limitations of magic?"

From her desk, Jolia swiveled in place, fresh interest in her eyes. "That's exactly how I would describe it." Credit to the wizard, it took only a few seconds for her to solve the puzzle as well, now that the missing piece was in place. "Which is impossible, unless you have one of the only artifacts in the world that isn't bound by those laws. Still, there aren't many of those out there, and even fewer in circulation. It's more likely that there's another explanation."

"More likely or not, using a magical item to skirt the very rules of our world is exactly the kind of thing Kalzidar would do," Thistle declared. "Even if we end up ultimately being wrong, at this point, I think we have no choice but to assume that one of Kalzidar's minions is using a piece of the Bridge."

Hopping down from her chair, Jolia made a quick motion, summoning her staff to her hand. "In that case, it seems fortune is both with and against us. While the idea of facing down such an artifact is indeed worrying, at least we have a piece of our own."

"I must confess, my friends and I have never wielded the artifact for more than a few minutes at a time, and even in our limited experience, we've had things go wildly wrong. For them to pull off constant magic like this, it would seem undeniable that Kalzidar's pawn has a better grasp on using the Bridge than we do."

To Thistle's surprise, the admittance was greeted by a smile on Jolia's face. She beamed as she hustled him toward the exit. "Aye, you make many a good point, but our luck hasn't run out just yet. Whether it was pride or folly, they let someone slip into Notch. Someone who happens to be an expert on dealing with that artifact and how to use it."

It was Thistle's turn to smile as he followed Jolia at a brisk pace. This felt like their first break in quite some time, and it was nice to feel like the gods were still looking down on them, even if Thistle couldn't actually hear Grumble's voice.

The good mood stayed until roughly the instant he saw who the expert was, but it was still a pleasant thirty minutes while it lasted.

32.

Finding the enemy was easy. No sooner had Timanuel popped his head into the street than he'd spotted five of them, most either attacking or chasing citizens. They were strange creatures, with six arched legs ending in a sharp claws spread out equidistant around the main body, which appeared to be little more than a large head with three beaks. Some sort of dark, oily scales covered most of the head, with the exception of a few skin patches, three sets of beady eyes, and the beaks. Like the legs, the faces were spread out at equal intervals around the body, meaning each creature was looking in nearly all directions at once.

"I suppose that means we don't need to bother worrying about stealth," Timanuel muttered. Reaching back, he waved the others forward to his position. He didn't have much of a plan yet, or even a grasp on the situation at hand, but people were being attacked in front of him. For a paladin, there was only one response to that sort of sight.

Timanuel charged from his position in the alley, slamming a sword into one of the beaked monsters that was trying to tear the flesh off a woman pinned beneath an overturned stall. His blade caught it just below the eyes, but rather than cleaving it in two, the attack sent it sailing backward, much farther than should have been possible, before it floated lightly to the ground and its sharp legs clicked against the stone. There was a wound on it, thankfully, a modest slice across one of its faces.

Knitting his eyes together, Timanuel tried to grasp what had just happened, and failed. It didn't make sense; his mind couldn't align the factors properly. Elsewhere, in another world, someone else managed a substantially higher roll.

"They're naturally light and buoyant!" Wimberly yelled from the rear. "Hit them too hard without bracing them against something, and they'll just get knocked back. That's also how they're managing to move around with those shitty legs." On the heels of her words came a bolt of green light that struck the creature Timanuel had wounded. Instantly, sizzling rose from its flesh as an ooze the same color as the bolt spread across its skin.

"Good news: looks like they're vulnerable to magic. Acid is confirmed. I'll cycle through the other elements as we go." Chalara put her hands together, already preparing to weave a new spell. As she did, the wounded monster stumbled forward, its light nature meaning that every step covered a substantial spread of ground.

The advance lasted all of two steps before a single arrow appeared in the left eye of the acid-burned face. There was a sound like someone in the distance whistling as the head partially collapsed in on itself, then the monster fell over in the street, unmoving.

Nocking another arrow, Gelthorn did a quick sweep around them, barely suppressing a shudder at their surroundings. Much as she hated cities, this didn't quite feel like one at the moment. The chaos and bloodshed made it wilder, more tolerable. "Seems arrows work, too."

It had been a lot to take in at once, but Timanuel finally felt like he was starting to get a sense of things. "Okay, new formation. I'll focus on shielding and knocking them back if they get too close. Chalara and Gelthorn, you pick them off as we move. Wimberly, I presume you've got some useful tools to cover our rear?"

"We'll start with this and see how things go." From her magical bag, the gnome had produced what looked like a crossbow, only one that had been tweaked and added onto to the point of near-uselessness. Hefting it up to her shoulder, Wimberly took aim at one of the other beaked beasts on the street before them. "Calibrating shot number one."

She fired, a crossbow bolt slamming into one of her target's legs, sending it spinning backward through the air. As it groped at the ground for control, Wimberly calmly adjusted a few knobs and dials, while also hitting a lever that dropped a new bolt in place. "Calibrating shot number two."

This time, her bolt nailed one of the target's faces. Unfortunately, she hit a scale-armored section, sending the creature spinning backward before it landed against a wall. The attack had left a substantial wound, and from the way it was eyeing Wimberly, she'd definitely succeeded in drawing its attention.

"Calibrating shot number three." More twists of dials and knobs, although fewer than the last time. On her third shot, the bolt sailed true, slamming into an unarmored section of the face and bursting out the other side of the monster's head. It slumped over, more sounds like whistling as its skull was pierced. "I think the sights are as aligned as they'll get."

"About time," Chalara grumbled. While Wimberly had been dealing with her own target, the rest of the team was picking off the others, getting the street cleared out and the people in it safely away. There were no more enemies for now, but how long that would hold true was up to the gods.

Timanuel was moving, now that the direct threat was neutralized. He crouched, taking a good grip on the overturned stall and hefting it off the pinned woman underneath by means of his substantial paladin's strength. She was pale and sweating, yet overall appeared unharmed. No sooner was she free than her arms were around Timanuel, hugging him close as small tears fell down her face.

"Thank you so much. When they came, there was no warning. One minute, everything was normal, and then the balyons came surging through the streets. I don't know how they breached the defenses or slipped inside; it's meant to be impossible. Something's wrong. Our guards were supposed to have found the helsk and killed it by now. This is madness. None of it should be happening."

"But it is." Gently, Timanuel took the woman by the shoulders and pulled her back, looking directly into her eyes. "And much as my friends and I would like to help, we are unfamiliar with these monsters. We came here via teleportation and have not yet acclimated to this land. You seem familiar with these things, so I beg you, tell us what you know so that we might be of aid."

Her eyes went wide, but only briefly. Whether it was his straightforward nature or the odd specificity of such a situation, she didn't bother to question the validity of his statement. Instead, she began to offer up that sweet, treasured resource: information.

"Balyons are what you just fought. They're little more than moving mouths, mostly hollow heads that devour until they're holding as much as possible, when they then return to the helsk to feed it. A helsk is a far larger creature that births the balyons. Helsks appeared within the last few weeks; they've become a problem for the people trying to cross between here and Lumal. The one upside is that balyons are really just a part of the helsk, so if you can find and kill the helsk, then the balyons will lose their agency. You can kill them, or just leave them. They'll eventually die standing there."

Useful information. It seemed that, bizarre as these creatures were, they functioned much like common bees, where a queen birthed and sent out drones to do her bidding and bring back food. For a fleeting second, Timanuel almost reflected on how strange it was that this woman knew so much and was willing to provide such information so readily. That thought died before it fully manifested, crushed down by the powerful force flowing in from an unseen world. Instead, Timanuel focused purely on the information, not on the manner in which he'd received it.

"Sounds like our only real option here is to hunt the helsk. We kill that, and the battle is won. Anyone else see another way?" He paused, looking over at the others. Just because he was looked toward as the leader didn't mean Timanuel would always have the best plan. He'd long ago accepted such an obvious truth. On this occasion, however, there was no dissent as the others shook their collective heads. "Then let's move forward. Any balyons attacking us or nearby citizens, we deal with. Any that look like they're heading somewhere specific, especially ones who move a little slower, as though laden down with food, we follow. Eventually, one has to lead us to the helsk. Then, all we have to do is kill it."

From behind him, the townswoman stepped slightly forward. "I should mention, a helsk is taller than a cottage, often as big around, and always keeps a personal guard of especially vicious balyons nearby."

How did she kn—another thought that died before it was fully formed. Timanuel felt what seemed like a half-headache, something he attributed to the new information they'd just received.

With a shrug, Timanuel glanced over to the others. "New plan. It's exactly the same as the old plan, except we try very hard not to die when we finally find the helsk."

"You should flee," the townswoman insisted. "You are all strong; you may escape before our home is nothing more than ashes."

Wordlessly, Timanuel stepped past her, sword and shield raised once more as he moved toward a turn in the street, their first step toward new territory. The rest of his party followed, save only for Gelthorn, who paused next to the woman they'd saved.

"Do not feel responsible. None may deter a paladin when there are innocents to protect and evil to foil. It is their greatest liability and truest strength." With that, Gelthorn advanced, easily catching up to the rest of her party.

They moved through the streets carefully, methodically, all too aware they were on unfamiliar terrain, facing off against new enemies. Keeping in tight formation, they were able to fend off the clusters of balyons they ran across, Timanuel swatting them back while Chalara and Gelthorn whittled them down. Occasionally, a balyon would leave itself open and he could manage a thrust through their heads, but it was rare that Timanuel was presented with such opportunities. Nevertheless, he made a point never to waste them; the weight of their limited resources heavy on his mind. Eventually, Chalara would run dry on mana, and the other two only had so much ammunition. Every arrow and bolt they used was one less in their arsenal—a situation made more dangerous by their having no idea how many enemies they would face. It was impossible to ration the resources; they simply had to fight as smartly as possible at every turn.

Finally, after a half-hour of making their way achingly slowly through the settlement, Gelthorn's eyes caught a balyon moving sluggishly through the shadows, working to avoid detection. They tracked it, relying heavily on Gelthorn and keeping a fair distance back to avoid spooking it off course. If it noticed them, there was no telling when they might get another shot at finding the helsk. Thankfully, Gelthorn was functioning well in the battlefield, far better than she would if it were a normal city, and she managed to keep on its trail even with the winding route it took.

To the party's surprise, the balyon didn't lead them out of the city, or to a building large enough to house something of a helsk's supposed size. It instead descended a set of stairs near a set of normal-looking, if rundown, shops. They watched and waited, scouting the area to see if there were other entrances and exits it might flee through. What they found was that were indeed other sets of stairs, all of them spaced out around this section of the city, and a few upon which balyons were coming and going.

"I guess I'll be the asshole who says it: the helsk is underground, isn't it?" Chalara asked. "Probably why no one has found it yet. I'm sure more people are looking for big, unoccupied chunks of city or searching from the sky. I mean, how did it even get down there if it's as big as that woman said?"

"Could be magic," Gelthorn suggested.

"Always in the mix," Wimberly agreed. "But there is another possibility. Presumably, these helsks are born like any other creature, smaller than in their fully grown form. If someone brought a helsk into that basement as a baby, it would eventually turn into a powerful weapon of destruction and chaos. Keep it bound in there using magic or restraints, alive but hungry, and then turn it loose at the hour of your choosing."

Chalara gave Wimberly a long stare. "That seems like a fairly involved plan."

"Maybe, but unless these helsks can use magic, *someone* must have helped it get in there," Timanuel pointed out. "Look around. Doesn't this whole thing feel like a surprise attack?"

His words rang true; the speed and ferocity of the strike certainly lent an air of forethought to the endeavor. A truly random monster attack was unlikely to have been so prepared, or to have kept the source so hidden and fortified. Gelthorn was the one who gave voice to the question in all their heads.

"Does that change anything for us?"

Slowly, Timanuel shook his head. "No. It doesn't matter how this happened. People are being hurt, and we have the opportunity to put an end to it. When it's over, maybe we can look into how it all happened and be of assistance to those who hunt the mastermind. For right now, there's a monster in the city, preying on innocent people. You know what I have to do."

"We do. And we'll be right there with you. Well, maybe a few steps back, in my case," Chalara added. "You know, for safety."

It took some doing, but Timanuel suppressed a laugh. It wouldn't do to give away their positions over a bit of mirth. "Of course. Everyone, chug a potion if you need one and make any preparations you can. When we're ready, we find one of the entrances not being used and head in. We'll try to sneak around for as long as possible, then switch to offense once that fails. If the gods are with us, we might get a little ways in before the fighting starts."

Although he didn't say it out loud, Timanuel doubted that such would be the case. Whatever else could be said about today, it certainly seemed the gods were anywhere but with him and his party.

33.

It was nice to see Fritz again. When she'd walked in the front door of the tavern, moments after the rest of the party had gathered along with Brock, Jolia, and Kieran, the elf trader was nearly bowled over by an embrace from Gabrielle, with more subdued ones following from Eric, Grumph, and finally, Thistle. The gnome was the most reserved in their greeting, as he was the only one who'd been warned she wasn't simply here in her capacity as a traveling merchant. Since their last parting, Thistle had known there was more to Fritz than reached the eye. He hadn't suspected her secrets to be centered around the Bridge, though.

As greetings concluded, Kieran stepped in, before the warm sentiment could turn to earnest conversation. "Glad as I am to see that we can skip the introductions, there's a lot to discuss tonight, and I think it will go faster if we give Fritz the floor to start."

That earned him a few uncertain glances, but everyone complied, taking seats around a table while Fritz ordered a mug of ale from the bar. She took a long sip before setting the mug back on the counter. "There's something to be said for the purity of ale made with love. I've got magical devices that produce all manner of food and drink, and yet they always feel hollow when compared to something crafted by hand. Perhaps that's my personal bias, but I don't think so."

One more drink from the mug, and Fritz turned to address the room as a whole. Aside from Brock, who was at his usual station behind the bar, everyone was in the dining area, staring at her with assorted expressions of hope, confusion, worry, and distrust. This was a tricky situation; the people of Notch knew most of her story, while the adventurers were still used to seeing her as a simple trader. Lying risked severe consequences down the line, and as this was the second time she'd stumbled upon the group, Fritz was starting to have a hunch that might be a bad idea. When one had been around for as long as she—especially in her old job, which had prized forethought and wisdom—one got used to seeing the patterns in things. Small group, oddly stumbling into artifact after artifact… maybe it was chance, maybe it was fate, but whatever it might be, Fritz was too smart to assume it was done with them.

"To begin, most of what you know about me is true. My name is Fritz, and I make my living as a traveling merchant. However, that is not the job I have always done, nor the role I have always played in this world. I'm going to keep telling you truth; I just may omit details about how I came upon said truth. Who I was before is irrelevant to this discussion, and I prefer to keep my past where it is, behind me. Can any of you not accept that, or do you *need* to know who I was before?"

It was a risky move. They might very well make such a demand, and she'd implied that it was at least on the table. On the other hand, she'd framed the discussion in such a way where she was already going to give over all the necessary information; digging into her past would be seen purely as prying. She waited, ready for someone to object. No, not *someone*. Thistle. He was staring at her, and there was much going on behind those eyes. He'd known she was more than she presented to the world already; this might push his curiosity past the limits of his self-control.

They locked stares for several seconds before Thistle gave a small nod of his head, motioning for her to continue.

"I appreciate your willingness to let the past be the past."

"It's something we're all dealing with, in one form or another." To Fritz's surprise, this came from the usually stoic Timuscor. He'd grown up a bit since she last saw him. Physically, much the same, but there was a sense of self that hadn't been as pronounced before. His travels were doing him well.

"The longer you live, the truer you'll find that to be," Fritz replied. "But such musings can wait. Tonight, we're here to talk about the collective artifacts you lot have been calling the Bridge." She paused, hesitating for a sliver of a moment. "May I ask you where you heard that name?"

The room filled with hushed discussion as Thistle, Gabrielle, Grumph, and Eric pieced together their recollections. It had been a good while since that first dungeon where they snuck through the minion passageways, with travel and adventure in between, so they were careful to double-check each detail with one another. When dealing with the Bridge, any detail might be crucial.

At last, Eric looked back to Fritz. "We know we heard it from Aldron, back when we found him with that first piece. None of us can remember him telling us where he got the name, but we do recall he mentioned communing with his chunk of the Bridge. Maybe he made up the term; it's also possible he got it from the artifact. We really can't say with certainty."

"He didn't make it up." The usual cheer on Fritz's face was absent, an intensely focused expression stealing in to replace it. "That's an old term for these artifacts, one we try not to circulate around too much. While it is possible this Aldron fellow heard it elsewhere, if he was truly communing with his piece, then the most likely explanation is that he heard it from the Bridge itself. That's impressive. Not many can establish such a connection without their minds breaking first. You four may very well have neutralized a substantial threat to our world before it ever started to gain any real traction."

The compliment was sincere, yet it was also a lure for them to focus on, something to keep the party from getting too hung up on just how Fritz knew all this. They *would* wonder, of course, there was no avoiding that; Fritz's main goal was to keep that curiosity tamped down until the meeting was done. Time was not their ally, and they needed a plan.

"Right then, let's back up," Fritz continued. "The Bridge is a series of artifacts—I think everyone in the room knows that much. Despite looking like misshapen hunks of crystal, the lore I've found says that they are meant to fit together; they were originally one artifact that was shattered and spread across the kingdoms. Supposedly, the power of the individual pieces is nothing compared to the power of the true Bridge. With that said, even a single chunk of the Bridge can warp our world in ways that not even magic seems capable of. The only saving grace is that very few people can actually handle interacting with the Bridge for very long. Most go mad and eventually forget to eat or self-destruct in a more spectacular fashion. We're all set on the basics, right?"

From the back, Gabrielle raised her voice. "I didn't know they fit together. Makes sense when you consider the shapes, though. What makes some people able to use the Bridge while most can't? Eric's the only one of us who can manage to wield it, and even he started to fray when he held two of them at once."

It was one of the few times any of them had seen genuine shock on Fritz's face. "Eric, is that true? Did you hold a piece of the Bridge in each hand?"

For his part, Eric squirmed, visibly uncomfortable with his past actions. "Sort of. I mostly lost it once I had the second one in my grip. Thankfully, Gabby brought me back around so I could set one down. I don't think I'd have lasted much longer if I'd tried to keep hanging on."

"The mere fact that you aren't in the corner making dolls out of feces right now borders on miraculous," Fritz informed him. "In my travels, I've only ever known of two other people who could withstand direct contact with multiple pieces of the Bridge at once, and one of those people is me."

That revelation stunned the room. Even some of the Notch citizens seemed mildly taken aback. Before this fact could knock the meeting off course, Fritz barreled ahead with the next point. "However, there are more ways to interact with the Bridge than just the direct method of grabbing it. Despite not being bound by the laws of magic, the pieces are still connected to the mana that flows through the world. In fact… never mind, that part is mere speculation. My point is, direct handling is probably the least efficient way to use a piece of the Bridge. It's sloppy and imprecise, which is why you'll often find strange, lingering effects whenever a piece of the Bridge is used in that manner: weakened barriers that allow extra-planar creatures to slip through, awakened minds in those meant to sleep, even unexpected magical conditions."

Fritz paused, her gaze lingering on Gabrielle. There was no way to be sure whether it was the storm of chaotic magic that had caused her condition, or Eric's use of the Bridge. She hadn't gotten up until after he was wielding both pieces, and the reason he'd grabbed them was to bring her back. If so, he clearly didn't regret it. Undead Gabrielle beat no Gabrielle, but it was a thought that probably weighed him down, nevertheless.

"Thankfully, we don't have to solely use the direct method." Fritz had resumed her usual cheer, even taking another sip from the mug. "With the right equipment, knowledge, and skill, it's possible to interact with a piece of the Bridge through the flow of mana we all share. It does still require a physical touch to become active, but after that, everything is done via magic and ritual."

A wave of relief swept through the room. Even the uncertain gaze of Thistle softened. It almost hurt that she had to break the bad news to them; however, there was no sense in holding things back.

"I should warn you, I had no idea I was walking into this situation, so I didn't actually bring the aforementioned equipment," Fritz added, successfully deflating the room's joy like a forgotten air bladder. "Don't worry. I talked with Kieran and did a full run-through of Notch's supplies. We can put something together; I just don't want to overpromise. It won't be as precise or as controlled as a true version, but in life, we make do with what we can."

For a moment, Fritz wavered. Her original idea was merely to have the adventurers pitch in with helping to gather the materials and maybe some light assembly. She could still do that, without raising so much as a single eyebrow. Yet...

Eric had held two pieces of the Bridge and come out the other side with his faculties intact. Very few people ever got that opportunity, and only a fraction survived. His connection was strong; it might even be on the same level as hers. This was a prime opportunity to witness Eric interacting with the Bridge firsthand, to see how well he could really handle it. The risk was that it meant giving over far more information than she'd planned and potentially creating a powerful enemy down the road. If he turned to evil with that kind of knowledge in his mind, it could be truly devastating for untold kingdoms.

Her eyes left Eric, tracing over Grumph, Gabrielle, Timuscor, and Thistle. They were a good party and good for each other. So long as they adventured together, Eric's friends would never let him wander too far from the path of decency. If they died, on the other hand—well, that was another issue. Still, it seemed unlikely that Eric would go suddenly evil overnight, and it wasn't as though he'd be the first upstart she'd had to crush. Given that they were doing a simplified version of the ritual anyway, this was probably a risk worth taking.

"There is one way to increase our odds of success," Fritz said. "If I have someone else to help me commune with the Bridge, to shape our desires, we have a better chance of pulling it off. Many hands make light work, and all that. Most people can't handle the sustained interaction, even without direct contact. But then, you're not most people, are you, Eric?"

To his credit, he didn't hesitate; the man was already moving his head in agreement before the first words made it out. "Assuming I can help, I will try my best. If you don't mind, I'd like to hear the answer to Gabby's question before we move on. Why is it that some of us can handle holding the Bridge when most can't?"

There had been any number of probing, problematic questions that Fritz was prepared to rebuff, yet thankfully, his request turned out to be one she was happy to answer. Both because it was relatively harmless information in the grand scheme of things, and thanks to the fact that it would take at least some of their attention off of her.

"My apologies, I didn't mean to avoid it. I can tell you what the prevailing theory among the few of us who know about the Bridge is. We don't have full confirmation, but so far, all tests have proven this to be true." Fritz took one last sip from her mug, finishing it and waving off another.

There was too much work to be done for her to be cloudy-minded. "By this point, we all know that the Bridge connects us to another world, one whose influence permeates our own in countless untraceable ways. The Bridge, in turn, allows us some influence in their world, along with a tremendous amount in ours. The reason we think so many people who touch the Bridge go insane is that their minds aren't equipped to handle straddling two entirely different dimensions of existence. We aren't talking about another plane; this is a place with completely different systems of reality, and that puts strain on a mind. It breaks them, fractures their ability to tell real from false, erodes their sanity."

Moving forward, Fritz stepped away from the bar. This next part needed to be gentle, just in case. She didn't know Eric's family history, so there was no way to tell how he was going to react. Fritz settled down at the same table as Eric, carefully putting one of her slender elven hands on top of his.

"The only ones who can bear it the way we do are those who are also touched by both worlds. Those whose blood, whose creation, is tinged with the very essence of that other place. Eric, were either of your parents adventurers, by chance?"

"My father. He was a paladin." Absentmindedly, Eric put a hand on his short sword, the sword he'd inherited from a father that barely existed in his memories. "But it can't just be that. I mean, adventurers lay with people constantly. Some towns have entire brothels solely supported by their patronage."

Smart. Fritz hadn't expected him to catch that. "It's not just the making of a child that does it. There's more involved. The parent has to care, has to love you, has to truly give over a piece of themselves. I warned you, this is all theory at the moment, so you'll have to forgive the vagueness. Truthfully, we don't entirely know all the factors that contribute to our ability. The one thing I do know for sure is that when your father made you, he was still a true adventurer, connected to the other world. Which means, in a small way, you are as well. Enough to handle brief uses of the Bridge."

Eric was staring at the table now, absorbing everything she'd laid on him. That was fine; they needed to do prep work for now. It would be midmorning, at the soonest, before the ritual could start. She squeezed his hand, forcing him to look up at her.

"I think that's enough for tonight. Why don't you rest? Come morning, you'll need your focus." She started to rise—that was enough compassion to keep things moving along—yet stopped before she walked away entirely.

"And, for what it's worth, as someone who's already had to grapple with the same questions you have, remember that how you got here doesn't really matter. Parents, magic, divine creation, none of it means a damn once you exist. We're not defined by where we come from; we're defined by what we make of the lives we have."

With that, Fritz walked back over to the bar and motioned for Brock to bring her another mug. One more wouldn't be the end of the world, and after the memories that last bit had dredged up, Fritz could damn sure go for a drink.

34.

Common sense dictated that a paladin, clad in heavy armor, would never be capable of sneaking in silence for more than a few careful steps, and even that assumed a lot of good fortune or deaf opponents. However, those who adhered to this kind of sense didn't have someone like Chalara in the group. For as much as she might seem the type to learn spells of unchecked destruction—which she very much was—Chalara also had a curious amount of insight into the perils of adventuring, almost like she'd done it before in a previous life. She was incredibly easy to underestimate, a fact that she counted on and used to her advantage frequently.

On this occasion, her expertise paid off in the form of a spell named Muffle, which cloaked the target in magic that made them significantly harder to hear and slightly harder to notice. Much as Chalara might have liked to cast it on everyone, the spell consumed a fair chunk of mana, and this wasn't the kind of fight where she could risk starting off drained. Only Timanuel got the magical aid. The rest of them would have to manage to sneak in on their own.

Gelthorn led the way. There was no discussion or question regarding it; even outside the forest, she was the most adept at hiding and tracking. Following her, the others stayed close, but not so close they risked stepping on one another. Getting noticed was one thing; drawing attention to themselves by tripping on an ally was more shameful. Plus, they really couldn't risk it. Not until they knew how strong this helsk creature was.

For what felt like the first time since they'd arrived, luck was with them. The staircase they chose to descend turned out to be empty, with no balyons clattering about. Although everyone kept their eyes peeled for traps, it turned out to be unnecessary. There were none, absent along with something as seemingly indispensable as a door.

Wimberly puzzled that over as they made their descent, going from the first narrow passage after the stairs to a wide hall leading them elsewhere underground. Why go to the trouble of bringing in a giant monster and setting it loose on the city without adding so much as a locked door for protection? Was the helsk that powerful? No, it couldn't be raw strength; even dragons laid traps in their lairs. Looking down, Wimberly noticed a few claw marks on the ground. In another world, dice landed roughly across the table, and suddenly, it all clicked into place.

It was about efficiency. The balyons fed the helsk. They were equipped to fight and eat, but nothing more. They didn't even have hands to pick a lock or turn a knob. Open tunnels meant that they could leave, eat, and return with as little hindrance as possible. Someone with allies might have been able to post sentries to open doors for the balyons, or at least to help defend this place. Since there were neither, the perpetrator was probably working alone, although even that was speculation. Alone or not, the main goal seemed to be feeding the helsk as fast as possible. Did it do something when it got full? Wimberly tried to scour her mind for all of the odd tales and strange rumors she'd heard, but this time, she came up empty. Before she could whisper to her friends to share her concern and possible realization, Gelthorn took them around three sharp turns, navigating the increasing numbers of routes and hallways with unnatural surety.

All these halls couldn't be necessary; they'd counted the number of staircases, and this was far too many. But it if was designed to be a labyrinth... Now the situation made more sense. The defenses were set up in a labyrinth style, with false routes and dead-ends, potential traps waiting to be sprung. The balyons must somehow know the right path, possibly guided by the helsk itself; however, intruders could get lost before they knew such a thing was even possible. Only Gelthorn's keen tracking was keeping them on what, they hoped, was the safe route.

As it turned out, Gelthorn did have the right trail, although how safe the route was could be debated. It led them into a vast, carefully-constructed chamber. The room was so huge it must have been taking up space under several buildings, perhaps beneath their basements, to remain undetected. The space was certainly needed, given the room's occupant. Technically, occupants, Wimberly realized, noting the dozen or so balyons skulking about. It was forgivable that she'd missed them, given the behemoth that sat in the chamber's center. Unless another giant monster had coincidentally decided to invade, the party had successfully found the helsk.

Tremendous was the first word that leapt to mind, and it applied to scale rather than grandeur. The helsk was not the largest monster in existence—far from it—but it was so misshapen and sprawling that the creature seemed to stretch beyond its natural space. Towering over the balyons, with the upper parts of its body only a few feet from scraping the ceiling, the helsk was a splotchy purple mass with warped, unnatural faces spotted along its flesh. Thicker versions of the balyon legs kept it supported, while countless tentacles, sprouting from its surfaces in no discernible pattern, flicked through the air, almost as though they were tasting it.

One by one, the tentacles would reach down, carefully picking up a balyon and raising it to one of the disturbing faces. A new mouth appeared on the top of the balyon's head, which then spewed the food it had eaten into the helsk. When the process was done, the balyon was allowed to float back to the ground, at which point it scuttled away toward a nearby hall. No doubt, it was returning above ground to make another meal run for its boss.

Tactically speaking, there was good and bad in the situation. Although surrounded by balyons, all of whom would no doubt attack the instant their maker was in danger, the helsk itself didn't appear especially tough: no natural armor, no fangs or weapons, only sharp legs and tentacles that seemed too thin to have much strength. They were probably designed for lifting balyons, meaning they didn't need to be powerful to get the job done. The flip side was that since they had no chance of sneaking closer to the target, they would have to fight their way through the balyons before they could even have a chance at nearing the helsk. And thin though the tentacles were, there was still a ridiculous abundance of them. Weak or not, there were too many to ignore, and helsks wouldn't be problematic if they had no defenses of their own. It was going to fight back, and not knowing how put them at a disadvantage.

"Ugly son of a bitch, isn't he?" Chalara whispered. "Almost looks familiar though, like…" Chalara paused, searching her memory for the tenuous thread it had uncovered. Worlds away, a dice hit a table and rolled twice before finally landing with the number twenty face up. That tenuous thread became a solid rope, hooked to something deep in her past, and, with impossible ease, Chalara hauled the memory to the surface of her mind.

"Fuck me, I've seen these before." Her eyes had gone wide as information surged through her brain, ostensibly from a book she'd read during her training. "Not in person; the mage who taught me magic insisted we learn something about all aspects, including the planes. I'd forgotten the name, but there was a picture of this thing, and I could never wipe that sight from my mind. They're a type of monster called 'unnaturals' that hail from the Plane of Chaos. While not too tough physically, helsks have a lot of magical resistance. Also, those tentacles are more dangerous than they might look; they secrete a toxin that slowly numbs and paralyses. Helsks exist as walking tanks that make their own troops. The balyons protect them from physical danger, resistance weakens most direct magical damage, and forget about trying to target its mind or body. The kind of magic we use was never designed to deal with that sort of biology. The only exception I know about is magic tinged with order, spells from those especially dedicated to laws and maintaining peace. It's the opposite of chaos, so anything from the Plane of Chaos has an inherent weakness to it."

The rapid-fire facts had shot out of her mouth almost unbidden, like the knowledge existed to be shared. When it was done, Chalara took a second to compose herself before looking back at the others. "I hope you all can think of good shit to do with that, because to me, it sounds like we might be pretty fucked."

It felt like a lot to take in, but really, there were only a few key elements they needed to focus on. Wimberly was already looking over the battlefield, new information percolating in her mind as she reassessed the situation. It didn't sound like helsks had much in the way of physical protection, assuming one could get close enough. That wasn't such an easy proposition, sadly, since the balyons would swarm anyone who appeared. The endless tentacles made getting close, or even shooting arrows from a distance, a difficult proposition, too, since they surrounded the center mass like an undulating web. Magic might be able to pass through more easily, but as Chalara had just told them, it wouldn't work well against the helsk. The balyons, based on what they'd seen so far, lacked such protections. It made sense; the stronger a body the helsk needed to produce, the more effort it would take, and balyons were meant to be easily replaceable.

Nearly on cue, there was a wet, squishing sound as a gooey sack dropped from somewhere under the helsk, landing with a disturbing symphony on the stone. In seconds, a beak pierced the thin membrane as four fully grown balyons made their way out of the excretion.

"Unnatural seems a very fitting term for these beings," Timanuel noted. He was waiting with them, patient and ready as the more tactically inclined members of the team worked out a plan.

With a start, Wimberly realized that, as a paladin, especially one of the god Longinus, it was entirely possible that Timanuel could use magic touched by order. That was the first good break they'd had in a while, as it meant that he could at least potentially injure the helsk.

"Timanuel, forgive me, it's been a while: could you run through the spells you know so far?" Wimberly kept her voice low; they hadn't been spotted so far, but the more they talked, the likelier it became. This was going to be hard enough without being discovered before they were ready.

"There aren't many," he warned her. "I've got the paladin standards like Illumination, Healing, and Bless. Also, one from following Longinus, specifically: Blade of the Righteous. I can enchant my sword with the power of my god, creating a slight glow and substantially increased damage."

Wimberly held an array of curses in her mind rather than loudly spitting them out, albeit not without effort. If there was one spell in that list that might have helped them, it was Blade of the Righteous. Bless was purely divine, yet if Blade of the Righteous really channeled the actual power of Longinus, god of heroics and valor, then there was no way it wouldn't come with a tinge of order. But they couldn't send Timanuel into that swarm alone. He'd be torn to shreds before he ever got close, and if they went along, then they'd die, too.

Her eyes ran across the others, taking in every element and feature. There had to be something they could do, something in her arsenal, or theirs, that would let them pull out a victory. There was no other option. Timanuel was being patient only because he understood the need for strategy, but they all knew that he was going to fight this creature. It was tormenting innocent people in town; no paladin could walk away from this and hope to keep that title. She had to think of something.

Chalara was a powerful caster, but her magic would be wasted on anything other than the balyons. While Gelthorn had some magic, her arrows were her truest strength. She might be able to get some good shots in despite the tentacles, at least until the balyons rushed and overwhelmed her. Timanuel had already listed his spells; aside from that, he was a man with a sword and a shield—certainly useful, just limited in this situation. That left Wimberly herself, who had an abundance of gadgets and tools socked away, just nothing that might help bring down such a huge, well-defended creature.

Considering the limits they were dealing with, the parameters of the situation, Wimberly couldn't see any path to victory. And yet, something in her mind wriggled. This was a new kind of idea, one not born purely of analyzing the problem as presented. In her time traveling with these people, Wimberly had begun to realize that perhaps some rules weren't quite as immutable as she initially thought. There could be a way to win, if they could manage to shift things ever so slightly.

"Timanuel, that Blade of the Righteous spell, how many times can you cast it?" Wimberly asked. "And am I right in assuming that it's meant for swords?"

"Technically, I could use it on an axe or a dagger, any weapon that could be genuinely considered to have a blade." Timanuel paused for a brief second, eyes closing as he sensed the power still within him for the day. "If I pushed myself to the limit, I could at most cast it three times, but that would completely tap me out on magic. No healing, no blessing, nothing else."

That was a serious risk; Timanuel was the only one of them who could heal. They had potions, of course, but they could end up unconscious or bound, at which point the vials would do them little good. It might be worth it, though, if Wimberly could get the results she needed.

"One more question." Picking the right approach for this was key. Wimberly didn't just have to make a case to Timanuel; she needed to make it good enough for the god he served. "Longinus is a god of the people, right? Fight for the innocent, protect the weak, the standard that paladins aspire to?"

Timanuel beamed visibly as he nodded. "Without question. Longinus teaches that the highest calling of the powerful is to protect the weak."

"Then I need you to pray for some wiggle room in that Blade of the Righteous spell," Wimberly replied. "That helsk is hurting people, more than we can possibly know about. Innocent people, who want nothing more than to go about their days in peace. I think we can stop it, right here and now, although not without personal risk. I'll make that trade, and we both know everyone else here will, too, but only if I think there's a real chance of victory. So pray, Timanuel. Pray and ask Longinus if, just this once, in the name of the innocents who are counting on us, he's willing to be especially open about the idea of what constitutes a blade."

He didn't appear especially sure about this plan, but Timanuel did as he was told. Quietly, he kneeled and clasped his hands before him. Admittedly, the stance wasn't strictly necessary; Timanuel just liked to show his god the respect of praying on a bended knee, especially when asking for a favor.

To the surprise of everyone, it was a short process. Timanuel had barely hit the ground and shut his eyes before they popped back open, his torso swaying slightly in the process. "I'm not the most adept at interpreting the will of the gods, but that message is hard to misunderstand. We are on the side of right, and while rules cannot be broken, they can be interpreted in different ways. I think, so long as you aren't stretching the bounds too far, we've got permission to go outside the box."

With one last glance toward the helsk, Wimberly readied herself to dole out instructions. Once they started this, it would go much too fast. If they weren't prepared, they'd be dead before the battle even properly began.

"Then prepare whatever you need to cast. Things are about to get downright hectic."

35.

The priestess of Kalzidar stood beneath the starry sky, a soft shiver running down her spine as she gazed at the lovely darkness between the hideous flecks of light. Soon, her god would extinguish them, one by one. First the kingdoms, then the world, then out to the stars, once he grew more powerful from every living being praying only to him. It wouldn't be easy, for nothing worth doing was. Kalzidar was wise, and in his wisdom, he was patient. Conquering a world, killing the other gods, these were not acts that happened on a whim. Such accomplishments required forethought, planning, and careful execution. Although the priestess did not know what role she played in the entirety of what was to come, she knew her task was special.

There were many followers of Kalzidar working to make his dream a reality, but only she had been granted the assignment of something personal to her god. These foolish tools bowing to a god of servants had committed the ultimate offense, had weakened her god and delayed his ascension to the lord of all existence. For that, they would not merely die. For that, they would suffer.

Already, the heavenly bodies overhead were shifting. Soon, Kalzidar would be stronger. Not enough to conquer other gods, especially not so soon after losing a shard of his divinity, but he would have the necessary power to put his plan into action. The groundwork had started being laid mere days after these heretics wounded Kalzidar. The priestess was only the latest in the array of followers tasked with aiding in this goal. Kalzidar was many things, both great and terrible, but above all, he was a god who repaid those who struck against him with increased retribution.

And this group had quite the retribution coming, indeed. Soon. One more day of waiting, of preparing. One more sunset, and then she would march. One last day, and then they would know the wrath of Kalzidar.

*   *   *

It started with an arrow. One of the three "blades" Timanuel had managed to successfully enchant. Gelthorn fired the softly glowing projectile; there had never been any doubt or discussion on that front. The weapons they had were limited. Each one counted. None of them could approach her skill with a bow, or her cool head in battle. In spite of the dire stakes, her hand was steady as she took aim. There was no signal to wait for;

Gelthorn's attack would *be* the start of the battle. From there, everything flowed, which made the first shot vital.

Her breathing was measured as she stared at her target, making careful note of the tentacles as they waved and wriggled through the air. Save for the ones lifting balyons, the tentacles appeared to move automatically, an involuntary function, like a heartbeat. While that did mean that they never completely stopped, it also made their patterns predictable. That might not hold true once the helsk was under attack, but for now it presented a window of genuine opportunity. All Gelthorn had to do was hit; that didn't mean that hitting well wouldn't make their job easier.

A little longer as Gelthorn made certain she knew the patterns and zeroed in on one of the horrendous faces dotting the purple flesh. They might be no more vulnerable than any other part of its body, but it wouldn't hurt to try. If nothing else, they provided a more distinct target than a randomly selected patch of skin.

The sharp *twang* of Gelthorn's bow echoed through the chamber, drawing the attention of the nearest balyons. That was fine, expected even. Once the first blow was struck, the time for stealth came to an end. Every adventurer's eye was on the arrow as it soared on a direct course with the helsk. As it passed into the shifting web of tentacles, it went by undisturbed, proving that Gelthorn's assessment held true. Some tentacles did break pattern, moving toward the arrow, but they were too slow. More interestingly, the few that drew close suddenly stopped, as if scared away. Evidently, that weakness to order meant more than mere elevated damage.

Her arrow drilled into the forehead of the face, piercing what would have been the brain in an actual person. The face's mouth opened, contorted into a scream of pain. They'd been hoping for that, counting on it in fact. What they hadn't expected was all of the other faces to join its sudden acapella performance of suffering. The noise hit like a blow, making Gelthorn wish she hadn't been gifted with half-elf hearing. Sound drilled into her head, her mind, trying to make her very body turn against her. It wouldn't work: she was stronger than that. Through sheer force of will, she fought off the urge to shake and vomit. Not far off, Chalara was doing the same; Timanuel had put a hand on her shoulder for encouragement. He might lack spells, but the presence of a paladin always seemed to help fend off such attacks.

Unfortunately, Timanuel would have no such effect on the herd of balyons that were suddenly clacking loudly across the stone, racing toward them. Hurrying, they rushed into their new position, trading a place to hide for a defendable position. Nearby was a small alcove—probably used for storage at some point. It wasn't much: a few feet across and slightly higher than it was wide. Just enough for one person to stand in comfortably, or two, if neither person minded an occasional elbow in the ribs.

Gelthorn took her spot in the alcove, followed by Chalara and Timanuel. The paladin positioned himself in the very front, barely in the recession at all, pitting himself between the balyons and his friends. Chalara took a spot slightly to the side, giving Gelthorn more room to work in at the cost of leaving herself slightly more exposed. The core of this plan—their part of it, anyway—revolved around Gelthorn making the right shots at the right time. Timanuel and Chalara were there purely to keep her safe so she could take careful aim.

A surge of magic came from Gelthorn's side as Chalara laid down a blast of fire centered on a mass of charging balyons. She might not be able to fight like Timanuel, but Chalara could still make their enemies regret bunching in a clump.

Another blast lit up more balyons, and they finally took the hint to spread apart. Although this wouldn't actually reduce the number of enemies they had to face, it would—ideally—lower the number Timanuel had to deal with at any one time. If they started to swarm him, Chalara would remind them of the dangers of grouping up. She only had so much mana, however, which meant the use of big spells like that was limited. Chalara could only make them afraid of swarming until her mana ran out. They had to hope the lesson stuck before then.

The first balyon crashed against Timanuel's shield, only to be hurled away when the paladin pushed back. With no time to brace, the balyon went flying, its own buoyancy working against it. Another ran up on Timanuel's side, only to catch a blade in the face that sent it tumbling back into a nearby group of its kin, bowling them over in the process.

These creatures were designed to be resilient more than menacing. They didn't need to successfully kill their prey to feed the helsk, only get enough bites and survive the encounter. Against someone prepared, someone they couldn't swarm over with their advantage of numbers, they were ill-suited to be on the offensive. It was why the party had been willing to bet on this plan, once Wimberly explained the situation. With coordination and care, they could theoretically hold out, at least until Timanuel tired and the others ran out of magic or arrows.

Of course, none of that meant Gelthorn didn't have to fight against distraction as she saw bounding swaths of balyons moving toward their location. She put them from her mind as best she could. The other two would deal with the drones—Gelthorn's task was their monstrous creator. Another arrow was readied, and seconds later, Timanuel heard a whistle as it sailed past his ear on a direct course with the helsk.

The tentacles were faster this time, and Gelthorn's shot not quite so precise. It slammed into the wall of tentacles, snapping in half as the appendages crushed it. With the break, however, there was a flash of green light. Vines burst out, ensnaring the very tentacles that had stopped the arrow. Soon, it was a tangled mess, a knot of green vines and purple tentacles all bound together.

A small sigh of relief slipped from Gelthorn's lips, unnoticed in the boisterous noise of Chalara lighting up another cluster of balyons. No one had been sure whether or not her Vine Arrow spell would work on the tentacles; the whole thing had been a gamble. They weren't exactly counting on it, but it did make Gelthorn's job easier. With a section of the defensive tentacles tethered, there were now much larger windows of opportunity to utilize.

She wasted no time, firing mundane arrows into more of the faces. While none produced a sound quite as revolting as the first blow, thick blood still oozed from the wounds, and the helsk did let out groans of pain. The more damage Gelthorn could do, the better their chances that their big move would work.

Checking her quiver, Gelthorn noted that she was starting to run low. They'd been planning to resupply in this town, but getting hurled into a sudden battle with unknown monsters for hours hadn't left much time for shopping. That wasn't their only dwindling resource, either. Chalara was looking worse for the wear, cuts and bruises on her arms where a few balyon beaks poked through and a telltale sway in her stance that betrayed her mana was running low. Still, she was the picture of health compared to Timanuel.

Their paladin was panting, scratches and missing bits of flesh dotting nearly every exposed part of his body. He'd managed to drive back the horde at the expense of his own health, taking swipes and pecks from the balyons as he sent them flying. Despite being visibly tired, he caught another charge without missing a beat, stabbing a balyon through the head when it foolishly left itself open. Kill when possible, rebuff when not; that was the strategy they'd been given by Wimberly.

Across the chamber, in a direction only she was looking, Gelthorn caught a small flicker of movement. At last, Wimberly was nearing her proper position. Everything they'd done so far—the enchanted arrows, baiting the balyons, harassing the helsk—all of it had been for Wimberly's sake. When their gnome had produced a set of oddly-spiked boots and gloves, claiming that they would allow her to move along the walls similar to a spell's effects, it was hard to swallow. Then again, after she detailed the rest of her plan, the wall-climbing part seemed downright reasonable.

It was a crazy strategy; they'd accepted that from the start. The problem was, no sane strategy gave them a shot at victory, which meant crazy was the best they were going to get. While Gelthorn, Chalara, and Timanuel were holed up, drawing the attention of every monster in the room, Wimberly had snuck as close as possible to the behemoth in the center and started ascending the wall. Like most of the gadgeteer tools, Gelthorn didn't entirely understand how the creations were able to manage such feats, but she imagined that was likely how outsiders felt about magic. Understanding wasn't necessary, only trust, and they all trusted Wimberly with their lives.

She wasn't quite there yet, unfortunately, so Gelthorn shot another arrow into the helsk, striking it on the side opposite from Wimberly's approach. Timanuel's breathing was growing louder, his body running largely on pure determination by this point. A half-hearted blast of fire erupted some ways off, singeing a few balyons without managing to fling them more than a few feet.

"Fuck me. I'm tapped." Reaching into her robes, Chalara produced a dagger, stabbing it into the head of a balyon that had decided to only pay attention to Timanuel. "Out of magic, anyway. Still got my stabbing hand, so I'm not done yet."

"A little longer," Gelthorn told them, firing once more. This time, the arrow didn't make contact. It had been a tad too rushed and ended up swept aside by a defending tentacle. Only two more arrows left, and one of those couldn't be used until Wimberly was in position. Carefully, all too aware of the increasing numbers of balyons around them, Gelthorn readied her final mundane arrow.

Slowly, Wimberly was making her way up the wall, nearing the top of the ceiling. Those hooked gloves and boots with the strange mechanisms were proving their worth despite the shoddy appearance. That was comforting, especially given that their survival now rested on the functionality of another Wimberly gadget.

While she was scanning, Gelthorn noticed a balyon near the back that was breaking from the crowd. It wavered; one of its sides appeared to be facing Wimberly's direction. Without hesitation, Gelthorn fired her last regular arrow through one of the balyon's eyes, sending a deflated mass to the ground. Much as she might have liked to do one more attack on the helsk, she couldn't risk a balyon raising alarm. Not when they were this close.

Wimberly stopped soon after, flashing Gelthorn a signal that only her half-elven eyes could make out from such a distance. At last, they were ready to continue. Unfortunately, Gelthorn wasn't the only one to notice the gnome's new position. Their luck had seemingly run out: the helsk began making a new set of noises, drawing the attention of the balyons. Tentacles began to rise from its body, heading toward the intruder lodged on the ceiling. They would reach Wimberly easily, and the instant they did, this fight was as good as over.

No time to worry. No time for fear, or doubt, or uncertainty. No time to notice the way Timanuel was barely standing, or the blood running down Chalara's body, or the increasing amount of balyons swarming their position. The world fell away as her hand clutched the softly glowing arrow, light in her hand as she pulled both it and the bowstring back. A face. She had to hit a face, had to make the helsk hurt as much as possible. For an instant, all of existence was gone, leaving only Gelthorn, her bow, and her target.

It felt like everything happened the second she let go, time stumbling back into flow at an extra brisk pace to make up for how long she'd lingered in a moment. Her aim was true, the arrow drilling deeply into the center of another face. The howl came again, and Gelthorn barely bothered to fight it. Her attention was entirely on Wimberly. It was only now, with her task finished, that she registered what the gnome had done.

Wimberly was falling before the arrow had landed. She'd let go as soon she saw Gelthorn fire. Too trusting, that one; although, in this case, it paid off. Dropping through the air, Wimberly was ignored by the tentacles; she'd targeted the section knotted together with vines. Landing heavily atop the purple flesh, she dug her hooked boots and left hand in, leaving her right one free. Her impact came seconds after the arrow's, meaning that she was at the epicenter of the howl as the screaming faces opened.

The breath in Gelthorn's chest refused to leave as she watched, every part of her aware that if Wimberly lost control, then everything would have been in vain. It was a prudent fear, albeit a wasted one. Despite the auditory assault, Wimberly refused to yield. From her side, she produced an orb with a glow just like the enchanted arrows had borne. With a few flicks of her thumb, Wimberly activated the device and jammed it down the nearest open howling mouth she could reach.

Unlike with some of her previous devices, there was no explosion or visible effect when this one triggered. Of course, that might have been because it was hidden inside the body of the helsk. Learning how the balyons fed the helsk had actually been quite the useful revelation. The fact that they spat it into those faces meant the food went somewhere. The helsk had internal organs of some manner, so that meant it had parts it needed. Having Timanuel use the last enchantment on Wimberly's "blade grenade" gave them a way to seriously injure the helsk internally, the only way they might actually manage to kill it.

That wasn't to say there was no show at all, however. In place of the usual explosion effects, the helsk began to shake as purple goo-coated chunks of what might generously be described as food began to fire out from its various mouths. The tentacles whipped about wildly, no longer displaying any discernable pattern. Likewise, the balyons were losing their focus, all but those directly in front of Timanuel wobbling on their legs, halting the push forward.

Drawing her own blade, Gelthorn stabbed the nearest balyon she could reach over Timanuel's shoulder. With her now able to pitch in, they managed to cut down the few balyons still attacking. Gelthorn traded positions with Timanuel, guarding him and Chalara while they each downed a potion. The wailing from the helsk was getting worse. Some of its legs had already collapsed, yet it wasn't dead quite yet.

The moment Chalara and Timanuel were ready, they dashed forward, knocking aside the unfocused balyons. Racing at a sprint, revitalized by their potions, the trio reached the helsk in no time. Dodging the wild tentacles wasn't easy, but it was a far sight simpler than if the appendages had been targeting them. Together, they stabbed the helsk over and over, coating the ground in its viscous purple blood. There was no more strategy or tactics; it had taken all they had to reach this point. Either the helsk would recover and kill them all, or they would slay it first. There was no middle ground.

At long last, the helsk gave a shudder and collapsed to the ground, its body deflating like the dead balyons. Gelthorn didn't stop, though. She kept hacking, slicing away tentacles until she at last found a small pair of legs poking out from a nearby section of legs. Carefully, being sure not to touch the toxic defenses, she dragged Wimberly out. Aside from being paralyzed, their gnome didn't look much worse for the wear. Just to be safe, Gelthorn poured a potion down her friend's throat.

It didn't manage to free her completely, but by the end of the vial Wimberly was moving her head once more. "Please, please tell me we got it."

Chalara would have joked about failure, but that was not Gelthorn's way. "The helsk appears to have been slain. If this is a trick or a defensive measure, then it is a highly effective one."

"Seems doubtful. Nothing about these monsters is subtle." Wimberly paused, using visible effort to turn her eyes toward the balyons, who had all collapsed into a heap when the helsk died. "How about that? It actually worked. Honestly, I was not giving us great odds."

She looked away from the balyons and back toward her team. "Hey, Timanuel! When you pray to Longinus next, tell him I said thanks for playing along. We couldn't have done it without his help."

"My pleasure," Timanuel replied. "Although, you're welcome to send the prayer yourself. The gods listen to all, not just their paladins. Especially those who rush into danger to protect those that can't protect themselves."

"Pass. Mithingow is a jealous one." Wimberly tried to move her arm and found it sluggish, but responsive. Glancing over at the helsk, it seemed crazy to think that the four of them had managed to bring down something so huge. "And I'm pretty sure I just used up all the good luck I had allocated for the week. Or month. Or maybe year. Point is, I'm not going to push it."

Chalara wandered over, offering her wineskin to the group. "I'm with Wimberly. You have to enjoy the wins while you can. They don't last forever."

36.

When Timuscor had been referred to Notch's blacksmith, he hadn't been quite sure what to expect. Eric, having spent some time assisting the smith, assured Timuscor that she was cordial, but also admitted that they'd spoken little. The people of the town were nice, yet undeniably eccentric, as was often the case with those of such power. Shandor, somewhat conversely, as it turned out, was the quiet type. She was also eight feet tall, with thick muscles and a pronounced jaw with matching forehead. If not for a few faded memories of his prior incarnation—the time from whoever had come before him—Timuscor might not have recognized her for what she was: a half-ogre. Unlike half-orcs, such as Grumph, half-ogres were much rarer. Ogre-human interbreeding was difficult for a multitude of reasons, but a few half-ogre tribes had managed to spring up through the years.

They were renowned as warriors. Mixing the raw strength of an ogre with the tactical capacity of a human often created dangerous foes. Given that Shandor had made it to Notch, she must have been such a case; although whatever deadly arts she knew weren't exactly on display. If not for the location and the oversized furniture, Timuscor could have been visiting any blacksmith shop throughout the kingdoms.

"Good morning." Timuscor's greeting was met with a gentle grunt of acknowledgment from Shandor, who was sharpening a longsword that was as much a piece of art as it was a weapon. Trotting in at his side, Mr. Peppers stayed quiet. "I wanted to see if there was any progress on the order I placed yesterday. Obviously, I don't expect it all to be done, but given the threats on the horizon, I'll take as many pieces as I can get."

With care, Shandor set her current project down, then rose from her reinforced chair and walked over to her counter, where she cracked open her leather-bound ledger. A thick hand moved down the surprisingly well-written entries, settling on one of the most recent orders.

"You ordered boar armor, yes? With magic." Shandor tapped the entry heavily, eyes moving between it and Timuscor, then down to Mr. Peppers. "You seem strong enough. Is it necessary to drag your pet into battle?"

That was a fair question, one Timuscor had asked himself more than once. Lacking a better answer, he decided to respond with the same truth he'd ultimately settled upon. "I'm not entirely sure that Mr. Peppers *is* my pet. Maybe he's my friend. Maybe he's my partner. Maybe he's something else. All I know is that every time I'm in a fight, he gets in it with me. I could buy a pen or a cage, but that doesn't feel right. I'm not going to tell another creature what choices it can or can't make; that hits a little too close to what everyone in this town has lived through. But at the same time, I care about Mr. Peppers. So if he's following me into battle, the least I can do is give him the best protection I've got the gold to afford."

From his side, there came an audible snort from the boar's snout, though what it meant was lost on Timuscor. Shandor, on the other hand, looked between the two once more before nodding. "Good. I don't make armor for tools. Only for people and partners. You have truth in your eyes, and your partner has loyalty in his."

It was more words in one go than Timuscor had gotten in the entirety of placing his order, a process that mostly consisted of nods, sighs, and annoyed grunts. From behind the counter, Shandor produced a small wooden chest that appeared light, until she set it down and it produced a sonorous *thud*.

"Armor shifts in size, as requested. Also had one more enchantment added: the metal will be as strong as the bond between you. More you trust each other, the better defended he'll be."

That was beyond anything Timuscor could have asked for or envisioned. It wasn't just a boon—not purely. Shandor evidently meant what she said about not making armor for tools. If he didn't treat Mr. Peppers like a friend, or at least with respect, then the armor would weaken, potentially becoming worthless. A blessing or a curse, depending on the kind of partner Timuscor chose to be.

"Thank you very much. Anything that makes him safer, I am happy to pay for, and an enchantment like that might prove lifesaving in the battle ahead. I will not forget the kindness you have shown." Timuscor lowered his head in a respectful nod to Shandor.

When he looked up, he saw the first visible expression on Shandor's face: surprise. She hadn't expected that reaction, but unless Timuscor was getting the wrong message, she looked pleased by it. It faded after several seconds, just before Shandor reached out, holding her enormous hand open in front of Timuscor.

"Show me your sword."

Timuscor had already trusted this blacksmith with Mr. Peppers' safety; a blade was well below that in terms of importance, so he handed the weapon over readily. It wasn't as if anyone in Notch needed to take his weapon to kill him.

Shandor examined it closely, turning the longsword around in her hands. "A good sword. Strong. Simple. Sharp. Not for you. Durability was traded for speed in the design. Meant for attackers. Paladins defend above all else. Need a sword made to last."

Setting it on her counter, Shandor made no motion to return the weapon. "But I will do my best to sharpen and repair it before sunset. Can't offer to make you a new one. Shandor weapons are distinct, famous. Even after this long."

"I understand. Notch isn't part of the rest of the world, and that includes its crafts. Sending new weapons by a renowned smith out into the kingdoms at large would eventually tip someone off that you were still around." Timuscor was tempted to point out that, in theory, she could forge him one solely for use in the coming battle, but held his tongue. Shandor probably had ample duties one her plate before this evening, and that was assuming it was even possible to make one of her weapons in a day. While she'd gotten the armor done fast, it was obvious from the gentle enthusiasm and expertise in Shandor's voice that weapons were her true passion.

His response earned him a grunt that didn't seem as annoyed as some of the others. "Glad you understand. You still need a better sword. A sword for a paladin."

"Much as I appreciate the compliment, and can understand the confusion given my choice of weapons and armor, I'm actually not a paladin." The words pained Timuscor to speak, as they had every time they'd left his mouth. "It is my dream, but I've yet to find a god who would allow me into their service without also gaining my allegiance and devotion."

To his surprise, Shandor leaned forward, grabbing his chin in her dense fingers and tilting it upward so they were staring into each other's eyes. "Missed the doubt before. There it is. Strong. Deep. Holding you back."

With unexpected care, she released her grip on Timuscor. "Except for the doubt, you have a paladin's eyes."

"Does that mean something?" Timuscor was mentally stumbling, trying to keep up with all the sudden turns in the conversation.

"It means you are almost paladin, which is the same as not being close to paladin at all, in effect." Shandor shook her head as she picked up Timuscor's sword. "More paladins these days, but I liked the old way better.

Oaths and truth, the will of one who refuses to yield. More isn't always better. Come get the sword this afternoon, before dinner."

With that, she retreated to the rear of the shop, leaving Timuscor with Mr. Peppers' new armor and a sudden burst of unanswered questions.

* * *

The room was simple: stone walls, floor, and ceiling, only a single door to break up the monotony. That door was something, however. Made from a gleaming metal unlike anything Eric could place, with different minerals racing through it like veins of ore in a mine. Except these veins glowed with a shifting array of colors. Just touching the door had nearly bowled Eric over from the ambient power. Whatever intention Jolia had intended for this room, she clearly didn't want anyone getting in or out.

That worked well for their purposes. Fritz had specifically requested somewhere heavily fortified, so anyone who discovered them couldn't make an easy kill while also stealing the artifact—apparently, they would be virtually helpless while controlling the Bridge. How long she'd been working was anyone's guess. Eric had been led to the room by Kieran, only to discover Fritz covering the entire space in arcane signs and symbols, using a softly glowing chunk of purple chalk.

Every surface, ceiling included, had some degree of drawing on it. Lines and circles, plus shapes Eric didn't recognize and that hurt his brain to look at for too long, all of it naturally leading to a single area on the floor. In that space were two circles, directly across from one another, with a smaller circle between them. Blinking away the unnatural shapes, Eric focused on the circles, one of the few places in the room he could look at comfortably.

"For a trader, you sure do know a lot about magic rituals," Eric said.

"For a rogue, you sure do announce your presence when walking into a room," Fritz shot back. "You here to learn about me, or controlling the Bridge?"

Eric wasn't completely sure those subjects were as different as Fritz wanted him to think, but this was absolutely not the time to go down that particular rabbit hole. They had hours until an entity claiming to represent Kalzidar was supposedly going to overrun the town with an army of automatons. Dealing with that took clear precedence over his curiosity.

"The Bridge. Am I supposed to sit in one of those?" Eric pointed to the trio of circles, earning a nod from Fritz.

"Either of the big ones is fine. Bridge goes in the small one in the middle. I'm almost done, so we can start soon. Based on my conversations with Kieran, I think the first task everyone wants is to find out how true the line about an automaton army coming here is. If we can punch through the barrier blocking our communication, we can find out what the situation actually is. That work for you as a starter project?"

Breaking through a barrier didn't seem too tough, given what Eric could recall about holding the Bridge. Those memories were choppy and hard to string together, but he could never forget the daunting sense of power that came with touching this artifact. What it could do wasn't the question; the Bridge was capable of feats beyond their dreaming. They, as the wielders, were the ones who might be lacking. Seeing Fritz's handiwork throughout the room put Eric at ease, however. She knew what she was up to. Under her guidance, they could break through.

"After everything Notch has done for us, reestablishing their links to the outside is the very least we can offer. Tell me what to do, and I'll comply," Eric said.

"Well, for now, go sit in the circle out of my way and wait. I need a few more minutes to finish up before we get started." Fritz turned her attention back to drawing her odd patterns through the room.

As he waited, Eric forced himself to stare at the unnatural parts that hurt his head, pain be damned. One day, he might need this knowledge. A mere inkling of it could make the difference; adventuring had taught him that every tidbit and tool could mean survival. Even if it did eventually feel like someone was slowly pushing a dagger through his head, Eric continued.

Pain, he could bear. Losing one of his friends because he came up short, that would be too much. It had almost happened once. Eric wouldn't permit it to happen again.

* * *

While the adventurers prepared, each attending to their various tasks, Kieran stood before almost the entire remainder of the town. Only those who had work to do, such as Shandor and Simone, or the few like Agramor who never left their domains, were missing. The rest had gathered in the only location large enough to house all the citizens of Notch at once: The Hall Under the Hill.

It was massive. Three giant tables ran the length of the room up to the back of the hall, where a stage was present. On holidays, Notch would gather here, a room originally designed as a shelter in case of attack. In the beginning, when Notch was new, old habits and paranoias were hard to shake. Fallback areas and escape plans were established in case war ever made it past their safeguards. Being strong didn't turn them into idiots who were careless with their lives; the people of Notch had been on guard and safety-conscious enough to survive a lifetime of adventuring. Those traits came with them as they settled down, helping make Notch the hidden safe haven it had become.

Over time, necessity had shifted the use of this massive area. They added the tables and benches first; this spot predated Brock's tavern, so it had originally been used for meetings and needed places to sit. Then they had a festival here and wanted entertainment, so the stage was added. Then came a kitchen, then chairs with cushions, and so on. This hideaway had softened on the inside, but they never allowed a single element of its outer defenses to rot or break. Nice as comfort was, in Notch, survival always came first.

Kieran looked out from the stage on to dozens of faces he knew by name. These were his people. Part of his town. They'd put their trust in him, and now, because of choices he'd helped to make, their village was in danger. When it was over, he would take responsibility for that as best he could. Stepping down wasn't an option; no one else wanted to do his job. They'd been leaders, champions, great politicians, and had left it all behind to have a simpler life. The life Kieran was supposed to be protecting.

"From the beginning, I knew this day would come." Probably not the way Jolia or Brock would have started things, but Kieran needed to do things to his own satisfaction. Always had. "When one takes an endless view of things, which we all did when we began regularly eating from that tree, it becomes inevitable that we'd be discovered eventually. In many ways, we're fortunate this is how it's happening. Our enemy has no desire to spread our secret to the world, or to force us to vanish and find a new location. They merely want to kill us, to wipe us from the map. For most towns, that would be scarier, but Notch isn't most towns, now is it?"

That got a stir; some of the half-orcs near the back lifted their heads higher. In a city of people who'd reached incredible heights, pride was always a strong button to push, reminding them that they were not some measly peasants fearing an invasion of bandits. They were legends; any one of them could step onto a battlefield and change the momentum of a fight.

"I can't ask anyone here to fight," Kieran continued. "When you came to this town, I promised each and every one of you that a life of killing was in the past. Jolia, Simone, Brock, and I undertook the responsibility of protecting this place when we agreed to be the town council, calling on you for your respective talents only when sincerely needed. We intend to honor that. Whatever comes tonight, we'll try to drive it back. The adventurers who lured the evil here will do their best to help, weak though they are. But, as things stand, we don't know what we'll be facing. If they really have the Helm of Ignosa and an army of automatons, our force may not be enough. It's very possible that we'll lose."

Elsewhere, such words might have caused a commotion. Not here. Not in this town. Living life as an adventurer often meant victory or ultimate defeat, and one couldn't survive such a lifestyle without accepting that death was a very possible outcome. Legends died, too, and the citizens of Notch had each looked into the face of the reaper, even if they'd escaped the scythe. Kieran was right; he could lose. In any fight, he could lose. Which was why he fought smart enough to survive.

"If that happens, if we fall, then you'll have to make a choice: run or fight. I won't tell you which to choose in that scenario; you'll probably know for yourself based on how easily we were killed. Should you decide to run, however, it is imperative that you do so without using magic. With the power our enemy has shown, we can't trust any of the magic that involves connecting Notch to the outside world. Jolia tried to teleport a frog last night and ended up with a green and red mess on the floor. That's why we're meeting here instead of in a pocket dimension—even those doorways are currently suspect."

Unlike Kieran's prior announcement, this did summon a few whispers from the throats of the crowd. Most had dealt with some form of counter-magic before, but losing access to a tool so many depended on was never an ideal situation. Kieran let the murmurings continue for half a minute before moving on. This was a call that needed to be made in response to the attack; discussing it here was a waste of their limited time.

"I would like to ask some of the citizens here to volunteer for a task, if they're willing. With magic in question, we need a way to signal everyone regarding the fight. Ideally, you'll all scry the whole thing and be perfectly aware of the situation; however, we can take nothing for granted right now."

This incident was making Kieran keenly aware how much of their planning and defenses centered on magic, something he'd have to address, assuming they survived. Losing certainty in its effectiveness made magic virtually useless, and compromised countless defenses.

"Little about this situation is ideal, so it feels presumptuous to imagine that plan will be," Kieran added. "As a backup, I would like to have some citizens come witness the fight. You'll be on the fringes, and while there is some danger in that, it's far less than anything you've faced before. Our watchers will each be given horns. When the battle is done, one way or another, they can signal the rest of Notch. A single horn means victory. Two means that we've been bested, but the remaining enemies can be easily routed. Three means run, all hope is lost. They who make this call should be some with battle experience, ones you all would trust to make that judgment if you can't make it for yourself."

To Kieran's relief, several hands went up, including those of people he would absolutely trust to make such a decision. Beyond that, he could see the eyes of many a Notch citizen hardening. They'd come here to leave a life of violence and bloodshed behind, but none would have made it to this place if they were the type to run from a challenge. Whatever happened to him and the adventurers, Kieran had a feeling that Notch wouldn't fall. Even if no one was currently jumping up to join the fray, their pacifism wouldn't survive intruders coming for their homes and families.

There was enough power in this room to conquer a kingdom, and if Kalzidar's minions weren't careful, they'd bring every bit of it crashing down atop their god's head.

37.

"And that brings us to the gauntlet." Jolia held up the golden glove with red trim, showing it to Simone, who made an entry in the ledger at her feet.

Sorting through the magical items brought in by the raiders was a cumbersome task, one they'd been planning to handle bit by bit as time allowed. It wasn't as though the citizens needed these tools or the gold from selling them, so under normal circumstances, it would have been a side project until completion. The threat looming over them had changed things significantly. With only a few people planning to fight—at least until they knew what the threat was—making sure the few combatants they had were well-equipped became a top priority. It had called for a reevaluation of all the equipment from the first battle, scanning thoroughly to see if there was anything that might be of use.

"Let's see here." Jolia adjusted the pair of spectacles she'd donned, examining the gauntlet more thoroughly. Many of the items were warded powerfully enough to suggest that their prior owners hadn't wanted any random caster knowing their secrets. Fortunately, wards could be tricked or circumvented, presuming one had the mana and the skill. Jolia didn't expect this alone to work—most items required at least a spell or two before they'd give up their secrets—but this time, she was treated to a nice surprise. "Oh! I actually know this one already. Kieran identified it the day of the fight and I know the history, so we can skip getting past the wards. This is a Gauntlet of the Fire Warden. Some wizard from a few centuries ago was trying to channel the power of the entire Plane of Fire through a single tool. He never fully succeeded, although he did manage to produce some powerful gauntlets in the process."

Simone took the glove away after finishing her ledger entry. The moment her hand touched the golden metal, her eyes widened. "I still can't believe a mere raider was trying to wield something like *this*. No wonder he got warped into a fire elemental. You'd need to be nearing our skill level to handle this much fire magic."

"That's true for most of this stuff," Jolia agreed. "Much too powerful for anyone without considerable skill and control. Not to mention that some of the items would put so much of a strain on a normal person's mana supply that it would outright kill them. Same problem as most of our equipment."

The trouble with helping the adventurers get gear wasn't a lack of equipment—between pet projects and old keepsakes, Notch was littered with weapons and armor capable of giving even attacking dragons a second thought. Unfortunately, gear of that power usually demanded fuel and complexity, making it beyond that which weaker adventurers could handle. Most of the equipment in Notch could only be used by the powerful, those who had ascertained a certain level of capabilities. Good-hearted as the adventurers were, it didn't make them suddenly stronger. With time, the town could have forged new equipment for them all, but sunset drew closer with every passing moment.

Their rushed sorting through the raiders' gear had largely been a bust, though there were a few bright spots: a ring that helped protect the wearer, a necklace that sharpened the eyes and ears even in darkness, a pair of boots that heightened the owner's speed. They were tools that the adventurers would be able to use, even with their limited capabilities. Hopefully, they would find more as they inspected the goods with greater care.

Jolia reached into the wooden box where the "to sort" pile was being stored. She rummaged around before finally clasping a hilt firmly in her hand. "Looks like we're doing a sword next. Big one, too, larger than a normal longsword, although it must have some kind of enchantment on it to make it more wieldy. Otherwise, I wouldn't even be able to do this."

On cue, Jolia stopped gently tugging and hefted the blade out of the box with one mighty yank. It came free, briefly wavering overhead before slamming into the floor. Thankfully, they'd taken the scabbard off the owner's corpse, so it merely made a clatter rather than cutting a shortcut between Jolia's home's first and second story.

"Mind giving me a hand with this?" Jolia offered the hilt, still clutched in her hands, to Simone. They needed to examine it, and while she could manipulate the weapon using magic, the less they used during examinations, the better. More spells tended to cloud the environment, making their job harder.

Without paying attention, mind still clearly on the gauntlet, Simone strolled over and accepted the weapon. An instant later, there was another clatter as the sword crashed to the ground, accompanied by a hiss from Simone as she leapt back and held her hand close to her chest. For a moment, there was wild violence in her eyes, a small peek at the kind of attitude life had demanded from her to survive this long. It passed as she uncurled her fingers, revealing a dark burn in the same shape as the hilt across her palm.

"Again! The damn thing got me again!" It was hard to tell if Simone was madder at herself, the sword, or Jolia, but she was definitely miffed overall. "Kieran checked this one. Hints of divine magic, some complexity, that was about it. The idea was to give it to Thistle if we can change the size, Timuscor otherwise."

"Divine magic? Now that's curious." Jolia hopped off her stool, walking over to a large chest behind a shelf of ancient tomes and next to a bowl of bubbling green liquid, near the rear of the laboratory. She rummaged around for nearly a full minute before emerging with a stopped bottle filled with a dark purple substance. On her way back over, she paused and picked up a few pieces of parchment. That done, she got back atop her stool and set the bottle down on the edge of the table. "The salve is for your burn."

"I'm undead. Healing is one of the many benefits," Simone reminded her.

"Yes, but you heal slowly from divine injury, and you're a grump the entire time. Use the damn salve while I find our entry for this sword."

Although she wore a haughty expression while doing so, Simone took the salve and rubbed it onto her burned palm. There was a slight tingling as a soft purple glow moved across the charred flesh, leaving behind perfectly unmarred skin in its place. "When did you make this?"

"I was tooling around with some reagents a few years ago and discovered it by accident. Thought it might come in handy, but the undead of Notch are smart enough to avoid divine magic, so it hasn't been needed yet." Jolia's hand moved briskly through the document, finally stopping at an entry on the second page. "Here we go. Looks like this sword was wielded by a raider against Gabrielle. Kieran's notes are here too. Let's see what the barbarian remembered about it. Sharp, sturdy, but no mention of special powers, especially not divine ones." Leaning a little closer, Jolia double-checked one section. "Except that there was a resonance effect when the blade hit her axe. Gabrielle certainly didn't know that, but from what I'm reading, the conclusion is inevitable."

"A resonance with Gabrielle's axe?" Simone looked at the sword once more, inadvertently taking a step back. "You're sure about that? For a resonance to happen, the weapons both need to be of near-equal power, with diametrically opposed magical elements."

"It's a divine-powered sword—the burn on your hand proves that. And since Gabrielle's axe made her a demi-lich, it feels safe to say there's a strong amount of what some might call unholy magic in there," Jolia rebutted.

On reflex, Simone bristled at the words "unholy magic" the instant they struck her ears. "Necromantic magic isn't unholy or evil. True, it does harm the living the same way that divine magic heals them, but that doesn't mean it can't have constructive purposes. Divine power just has a better image than mine: it's the magic of life. Death is a part of that too, however, and the magic of death is equally as important in the balance of things."

"Just trying to make the point of why they were probably opposed." Jolia muttered a short incantation, and the sword rose off the ground. Much as she was trying to avoid extraneous spells, there was no helping it this time. Simone couldn't touch the thing without hurting herself, and Jolia was a gnome; the simplest solution was to use magic and hope it was worth the risk.

The sheath slid off the sword with a motion of Jolia's hands, permitting her to draw close and examine the actual blade. She put on her enchanted spectacles, then cast a few more identification spells seconds later. A wrinkle of frustration formed on her forehead as she began casting more and more, slipping past the wards and enchantments piled atop one another.

For a lesser caster, even some archmages, the task would have been impossible. But years of relaxation and drinking hadn't yet stolen away the brilliance and determination that had once earned Jolia the title of Royal Mage, the most powerful caster in all of her kingdom, tasked with defending the capital and the king in the event of invasion. That life might be behind her now, but the lessons it taught weren't. Among them was the knowledge that any lock could be picked, no matter how difficult, if one was willing to put in the time and effort.

Finally, Jolia stepped away from the sword. Sweat dripped down her forehead, and Simone was watching with a concerned expression. "How long was I at it?"

"Almost half an hour. A little longer, and I was going to make a run to the tavern for some ale to lure you out." Simone looked relieved, despite her flippant reply.

"Might still have you do that. Mithingow knows I could use a drink after this one. That thing is *strong*, which makes me wonder just how powerful Gabrielle's axe is." A hint of curiosity, more than suspicion, flicked through Jolia's eyes as she looked at Simone. "If it's on par with that blade, then it's no ordinary enchanted weapon."

Simone nodded. "Hers is a unique piece. Under different circumstances, I'd have offered to buy it for later study. Sadly, that's not viable given her condition and attachment. Makes me even more curious to know about this one, especially since a raider had no trouble using it."

Snickering slipped from Jolia's lips. "The raider swung a sword around; that's not the same thing as saying he used it. It took me a while to crack through all the protections and see this find for what it is. We're looking at a Divine Blade, Simone. Been a long while since I've even heard of one of these turning up."

There had been an abundance of possible explanations for the weapon, and the longer Jolia took to unravel the mystery, the more Simone had entertained this as an explanation. Even with that preparation, she still didn't entirely believe it at first. "You're sure?"

With a wave of her hand, Jolia made the sword slowly rotate, showing off all its angles. "Fits the bill, doesn't it? In most hands, it seems like a normal, well-made sword. Even a bit of visible enchantment to make it more tempting to new wielders. But when wielded properly by a paladin, it becomes an instrument of holy fury, unlocking the true power hidden away inside."

"If you're right, then you know what that means." Simone gestured to the spinning sword, unable to keep a slightly sour look from her face when looking at it. "That thing *can't* stay here. Divine Blades are meant to be lost and found, over and over, until they discover a new paladin to wield them. If it stays here, it's going to draw in more outsiders, regardless of the precautions we take. Not even Notch can stand against the direct will of the gods, and they're the ones who made the rules for Divine Blades."

"I'm aware," Jolia assured her. "But for all the magic this one has, shape-changing isn't among them. Trying to add another enchantment to this would be unlikely to succeed at best, catastrophic at worst. With time to study and work, I could make it happen, just not on the fly. Regardless, Thistle isn't going to be capable of wielding this."

"Then he wasn't meant to," Simone shot back. "That's how these work. Maybe it's for the best. Fully activated, there's a chance this thing could overwhelm someone of his level, just like our own advanced equipment."

Jolia's reply didn't come quickly. She paused the conversation to look over the floating sword once more. "Possibly, but this isn't some mindless enchantment that sucks down mana. It's meant to be a tool that grows with the wielder, so I have to imagine there are controls in place. Perhaps you're right, though. Guess that means we'll go with giving it to Timuscor. It's still a fine blade, and in the hands of a knight it will be a useful weapon, even if its true potential lays dormant. Assuming they survive, that also gets it out of Notch."

With no time to try altering the size and the knowledge that it would only cause trouble if it remained, Simone couldn't see a better option. It was something of a waste, handing over such a powerful tool to one who couldn't fully utilize it, but it wasn't as though knights didn't need sturdy swords. In Timuscor's hands, it would move through the world until it found a true wielder.

"I suppose that's our best option," Simone agreed. "Now, sheath that thing and put it aside already. We've got a lot to get through before this afternoon."

Jolia did as requested, sliding the sword back into its scabbard and moving it over to the small pile of identified items they'd be giving to the adventurers. Minimal as it was, it would have to be enough if war came to Notch. Hopefully, that wouldn't happen, but Jolia had lived for a long time as an adventurer.

She knew the taste of the air before a storm, the heaviness of the wind, the looming shadow of death, although whose had yet to be determined. Every instinct she had told her this day would end in bloodshed. Not for the first time in her life, Jolia deeply hoped to be wrong, all while knowing, deep down, that she wasn't.

38.

"I really, truly, from the bottom of my heart, despise dealing with gods." Fritz was panting as she leaned back, brushing sweat from her forehead and pointed ears. "We can break for a while. Probably need to, and at this point, it seems undeniable that we require a new strategy."

Eric blinked slowly, pulling himself back to the real world. Working with the Bridge in this new way had been almost intoxicating. It was so easy to get lost in the drifting place between worlds that working with the Bridge opened up. Especially this time, using Fritz's ritual. Unlike when he'd just grabbed the Bridge, this didn't come with a crushing pressure in his mind, threatening to overwhelm his very sanity. Conversely, the technique also lacked the sudden rush of understanding that came from a bare-handed grip. It meant they had to go slower to make things happen, be more deliberate; but it also allowed them to retain a greater sense of control.

"Did we not break the barrier?"

"Yes, and no." Fritz held a dangerous gleam in her eye as she stared at the still softly glowing artifact between them. "The good news is that we've confirmed the enemy definitely has a piece of the Bridge. I know what it feels like when two pieces are set against each other, and that's what just happened. Using the full power of this piece against theirs, we can punch through the Bridge-based communication barrier they've got around this place. Unfortunately, it looks like Kalzidar also erected a divine barrier fulfilling the same function, and since we have to use our piece of the Bridge to counteract theirs, there's not enough power to punch through both."

Eric understood. Powerful as the Bridge was, sheer force didn't help when it was pitted against itself. Two pieces could cancel one another out; however, that would make them functionally useless for anything else. Kalzidar was taking zero chances.

"Can one god really stop all the others from reaching their followers in here?" Eric asked. "They should be as strong as he is."

Fritz gave a shake of her head, sending a few drops of perspiration winging through the air. "Not all gods are of equal power, and Kalzidar is an old one. Don't ever underestimate him. You are right, however, in that one god couldn't block communication between all the others and their followers. That's probably why he's worked to keep you penned in— blocking off a specific area is a much more manageable task. Plus, don't forget that based on what you all discovered in those scrolls, Kalzidar's power is temporarily increased."

"Kieran told you about that?" Eric asked.

"Kieran told me everything, because he wants me to succeed. And the more I know, the better the chances of that happening." Fritz's fingers tapped against her knees in a seemingly random order as she continued staring at the Bridge. "This wasn't a total bust, at least. We confirmed they have a piece of the Bridge. We discovered that us not contacting the outside world is a high priority for Kalzidar. And we know where all of their piece's energy is being devoted, because it took the full power of this piece to counter it. Do you realize what that means?"

Initially, Eric almost said no, but he held his tongue to properly consider the situation. At a glance, all of the news they'd uncovered seemed bad. Their enemy had an artifact as powerful as their own, plus the support of a god who was even stronger than normal. Communication with the outside world was cut off… or was it? Something tickled in Eric's mind, a thought worth considering, but not relevant to the question at hand. What was the upside to all that they'd seen? Most of what Eric took from the lecture was that they were doubly cut off from the world, both by the Bridge and by divine magic.

As the thought flickered through his head, it clicked. Eric saw the same vulnerability that Fritz had. "It means that if they're spending all their energy to block us from reaching the outside world, then they don't have any left to block our piece of the Bridge from doing anything else. We're stuck in here, but we've got free rein to do as we please in preparation."

"Precisely." There may have been a touch of impressed surprise in Fritz's tone, or perhaps Eric was deluding himself. "With this, we can reshape the land, lay traps and surprises, offer you the most advantageous battle you could hope for."

"Given what's supposed to be coming, we're going to need it." Eric could still feel the tingle in his mind, a momentarily dismissed thought that refused to be ignored. Now that the Bridge question was answered, Eric decided to voice his concern. "I also realized something. I don't actually think Kalzidar is trying to keep the outside world away from us. I think he's trying to keep us away from the outside world."

Fritz raised an eyebrow and motioned for him to continue.

"This threat has been around for a while now, as has the blockade. Ever since we arrived, Thistle hasn't been able to talk with Grumble. Yet despite all those precautions, you were able to stroll right in. I know you're more than what you seem—we all do, at this point—but you just said you couldn't punch through a god's barrier, so I'm guessing you're not quite on Kalzidar's level. If he really wanted us cut off, with no information getting in or out, then shouldn't he have at least *tried* to stop you?"

Silence fell as Fritz gave his words sincere consideration. There were explanations she could potentially offer, but all of them required more speculating than was strictly wise when seeking an existing truth. "You're right. Maybe he wanted me here because I helped you all the last time we met and that ended in him losing a chunk of his divinity, but that still means he wants me dead more than he cares about me bringing news from the outside world. For all he knew, I could have talked with people from Lumal the day before and brought you word about the automaton army, only he's still doubling down on keeping us locked up."

"He's more worried about us getting information out of here than he is about information coming in," Eric surmised. "But why? What do we know that would be useful out there?"

"Save yourself the time. Don't bother going down the rabbit hole. There are too many possibilities. Could be he's bluffing somewhere else and threatening to crush them with the automaton army while actually marching it here. Maybe there's a coalition hunting his forces that would gather here if they knew. Hell, maybe he hasn't even stolen the helm yet and doesn't want us to tip off Lumal by checking in. That's just off the top of my head. Besides which, even if you could puzzle it out, do you have any new ideas for reaching the outside world?"

"No," Eric admitted. "If the Bridge can't do it, then I'm not sure what would."

Carefully, Fritz reached over and tapped the artifact once, causing a soft glow to reappear within its depths. "It's annoying, but a good lesson for you to learn early on. The Bridge when whole is supposedly all-powerful, capable of changing the very nature of the world. But pieces of it are just that: pieces. They can't do everything, and if your enemy has one, then the advantage becomes functionally neutralized. Never forget that these are tools, not a substitute for power and skill of your own."

Eric nodded as he settled back into position, resting his hands on the circle like Fritz had taught him during their first attempt. Instantly, he felt the connection return, their stone room fading as he slipped into the alluring light of the Bridge.

The last words he heard before being completely swept up were from Fritz, identically positioned with Eric, palms pressed carefully into the chalk. "Of course, a tool is most useful when wielded by someone who understands it, so let's make sure to give you a thorough education while we've got the opportunity."

* * *

After what felt like the worst possible twist of luck, things were looking up. None of the party would have chosen to teleport into the chaos of yesterday, but in the glow of a new day, there *were* benefits to the ill-omened start. For one thing, their killing of the helsk had vaulted them to the status of local heroes, word spreading like wildfire as the balyons all dropped dead and other warriors rushed to find the cause. They'd emerged from the cavern, a few chopped-off helsk faces held as proof of their deed for Lumal, only to find a crowd nearby. The moment they were spotted, a cheer went up.

From there, it had been a blur. Healing magic was cast on them right away—too much, honestly—and they were all but dragged through town to the acting head of the city. Thank yous were given, promises made, and then they were in a tavern, being bought drinks by every person who could stuff into the building.

The town was going to have a lot of hardship moving forward. Countless people were dead, buildings needed fixing, and they were going to have to find out who had helped get that helsk underground in the first place. But no one who lived in these monster-infested lands survived for long without learning to savor their victories, and that was precisely what they all did.

When the next morning came, they found a priest waiting to cure their hangovers, and were then led out to four horses that had been loaded with supplies, food, and modest bags of coin. The head of the town was there, too, thanking them again, apologizing that he couldn't offer more no matter how they waved him off. It was a relief when they were finally atop their horses and riding away from town. In some ways, the gratitude was harder to deal with than the helsk and balyons had been.

On the upside, with no need to hunt down a helsk and the unexpected acquisition of strong horses, they would easily make Lumal before night. Gelthorn double-checked the map as they rode, glancing up from it every few seconds, just to be safe. The plains were dangerous; with nowhere to hide if an enemy spotted them, their only options were to flee or fight. The sooner they knew someone else was approaching, the easier that choice would be to make. And with Gelthorn's eyes, they should have a fair bit of warning, assuming she kept her guard up.

"So what's the deal when we get there, anyway?" Chalara called from just behind Gelthorn. They weren't riding hard—being alert and on track were more important—so conversation was possible with a little effort. "We burn all this stuff?"

"We conduct an entrance ceremony," Timanuel corrected, riding slightly closer. He had, of course, been the one to take careful notes when they first learned how to enter Lumal. "There's some kind of site near the entrance. We offer up our potion and trophies, the fire burns them down to their essence, and that creates the doorway we need to enter Lumal."

Wimberly sped up a tad so she could join in. "If it's this hard to get in, should we have loaded up on more feathers and helsk faces? Would make a return trip much easier."

"No need." Folding the map, Gelthorn gave most of her attention to the horizon and the unknown dangers that might lurk just beyond it. "Once inside, they will provide us with a rune to return, assuming we don't anger or insult them. I once knew a merchant who had such a rune; he could step through any doorway and vanish to Lumal, then return with new wares and items. It only worked once per week, however."

That got everyone's attention. It was rare that Gelthorn talked about anything in her past. All they knew of their companion was that she was a forest warrior, a half-elf, and unerringly loyal. The rest were minor details—interesting, to be sure, but not essential. No one pressed the issue for more. Gelthorn would speak about her past when she was ready. And if that day never came, then so be it. The future was far more important.

"That's pretty handy," Chalara said. "Much easier than all this shit."

"Yes, but the runes can be removed for any reason the officials of Lumal demand, if it's even granted in the first place, so we must all be polite and deferential." Gelthorn's glance at Chalara wasn't especially subtle, but neither was it meant to be.

For her part, Chalara never missed a step. "I get it; once we're in, I go into Diplomatic-Chalara mode. That's where I pretend I can't speak and just stay silent the whole time. I've tried being nicer, but I'm not great at that, so this is what I settled on."

"Can we replace you with the diplomatic version all the time?" Wimberly asked.

"Sure. Just remember that most of my best spells require verbal components," Chalara shot back.

Wimberly rubbed her chin as though in deep thought. "Honestly, it might be worth the trade."

"Not until we're actually in Lumal, it isn't." Timanuel rode up closer to Gelthorn, helping her survey what lay ahead. "These lands are known for being plagued by monsters and raiders, so we all need to be ready and at our best. But only for a few more hours. As much of a pain as it is to get into Lumal, the silver lining is that it's virtually impossible for monsters to enter. Once we're there, we can take a day to fully rest and check out the city."

"Until then, keep your eyes moving," Gelthorn added. "Got a few more hours ahead of us, and that assumes we don't get slowed by another fight."

Silence soon settled over them once more as they pressed on, riding for Lumal, hoping that, just until the end of the day, their luck would hold out. After the night they'd had, the gods at least owed them that much.

39.

Grumph sat in the warm grass, basking in the afternoon sun. To many, it would seem like he was merely relaxing, but a seasoned mage would have guessed that Grumph was meditating, seeking to improve his control over mana in the few remaining hours before battle. As was often the case, the "expert" would have been wrong. The half-orc wizard was, in fact, merely relaxing in the afternoon sun.

Fighting would come soon. Blood, death, loss, pain, fear, all swirled together in the concoction they referred to as a battle. A few hours spent frantically trying to better grasp a skill it took years to master wouldn't make any difference in what lay ahead. Taking time to properly center himself, however, to find a place of calm and peace within the storm, now that might actually make a difference. A cool head was always better when it came to making life and death decisions on the fly.

"Knew I'd find you here, old friend." Thistle hunkered down next to Grumph. Once, it would have taken him a few minutes to lower his warped bones to the ground, but the blessings of a paladin had strengthened his body. Such a simple thing, getting up and down, yet so many took it for granted in a way that Thistle never would. Even so, in the old days, Thistle had also had his wife, Madroria, to help him with such tasks... and Grumph knew that given the choice, the gnome would have traded every spell and skill his title conferred if it meant another day with his deceased love.

"Have to prepare." In truth, "prepare" might be a generous term. They were facing a battle with an enemy of unknown strength—one controlling a potentially unkillable army—and they had been cut off from the guidance of the gods. Grumph was doing the best he could with what he had, something that had been true more or less for his entire life.

"Aye. Prepare for the marching army of automatons, who are supposedly going to try and raze a town filled with former adventurers of legendary power." Thistle let out a sigh and carefully rubbed his temples. "I know I'm getting on in years, but this might well be the first time I've truly felt *old*. Days now, I've been puzzling this over, and no matter what angle I come from, I can't see Kalzidar's move. I'm losing my touch, it seems."

Grumph snorted loudly. "Or you're just not as wily as a god."

"Dearly, truly, I wish that were an option," Thistle replied. "Unfortunately, I can't afford to be a step behind anyone, not even a god. My mind is all I've ever had to offer. There are better fighters, truer paladins, more dependable friends, but when it comes to plans and scheming, I have a genuine shot to come out on top."

With some effort, Grumph repressed a shiver. None of the others had known Thistle before Maplebark. They'd never seen the wild-eyed gnome who would go to any lengths to win, to survive, cost be damned. Madroria had tempered him, and settling down into a life of peace hadn't hurt either. He preferred this version of Thistle to his younger, more hot-blooded counterpart. While it was true that Thistle may have lost some of his edge in the process, this version rarely ever scared Grumph. The old Thistle often had.

"We've come far," Grumph said. "Further than I hoped for."

It was true. When first setting out, Grumph had merely prayed that they would live long enough to get the mad king's attention off of Maplebark. Not only had they escaped the lands of Solium, they'd even gotten through an entire second kingdom intact. It was an amazing feat, especially considering their humble origins. If this was where the journey took them, Grumph could find peace with that. He wished he could save the others, though. They were younger. They still had potential full lives ahead of them. Grumph and Thistle had journeyed together and seen much. Should they fall, it wasn't quite the same tragedy.

Noticing that Thistle was still silent, Grumph decided to nudge him along. The gnome had a bad habit of getting too caught up in his own head when he grew fixated on a problem. "Tell me your best guesses."

"The first is the most obvious, but does still have to be considered: the automaton was sending an honest message, and in a few hours, we'll be overrun by more of them. Least likely, of course, since Kalzidar doesn't seem the type to give us actual fair warning. But that's where we hit the problem. If it's not true, then why go to so much trouble to pen us in like this? That only makes sense if Kalzidar wants us away from a different fight, yet I cannot, for the life of me, think of a situation where a god would fear our party. Even destroying the heart was simply us completing the last step in a process that started centuries before we got involved. I don't have other guesses, because they're all too far-fetched. Until I can figure out what it is that Kalzidar wants, and how we're involved, I can't piece together his plan."

"Then what makes us unique?" Grumph probed. Thistle rarely needed actual help when pondering; he just did it better with a friend to keep him on the path of productive thought.

Thistle took his time with the question, giving it proper consideration. "Gabrielle's condition is rare, but not unique, and given that we only just learned about it, I can't imagine that to be what is driving all of this. Eric has the ability to use the Bridge; however, Fritz just told us that folks like him aren't impossible to find, so this would be a lot of work just to kidnap or kill him. While Timuscor is a good man and a fine warrior, at the end of the day, he's a normal knight, putting all this echo business aside. Again, hardly common, but not unique. You, old friend, may well be the rarest among us all. A half-orc wizard is far from a common sight, yet I can't seem to figure out why that would make you a target. Although you're learning and improving fast, there are stronger mages out there. Which only leaves me. As the one who actually destroyed his piece of divinity, revenge makes sense, but there are countless other ways for a god to have me killed."

To his surprise, Grumph realized that Thistle *had* in fact missed something. Whether it was stress or his focus on the well-being of the others, he'd slipped over a rather key detail. "You didn't destroy Kalzidar's divinity. The sunlight did."

A long stretch of silence ran between them, broken by a string of curses spat from Thistle's mouth before he moved on to more acceptable words. "You're right. And Grumble was the one who let that sunlight break through. Grumble was the one whose paladin betrayed Kalzidar in the first place. Grumble is the one Kalzidar would want revenge on, and if his power is truly heightened, then this is a perfect opportunity." Looking down at the magical armor protecting his body, Thistle ran his hand across the cool metal.

"Grumble only has a single paladin. One sole emissary to serve his will, a paladin who has now been caged and cut off from his god. I wouldn't expect that to matter, but based on our situation, I have to presume it does." Standing from the grass, Thistle brushed aside a few blades. "Grumble being the target is the first theory I've hit on that at least makes some sort of sense, even if there are a lot of unknown factors to account for. I'm not sure how that knowledge will help, but I do feel more on solid ground with some idea to start from. Your help, as always, is indispensable, old friend."

Grumph merely responded with a nod as Thistle strode away, off to dig into some lead or thought that was buzzing around his brain. That was the way he readied himself, just as Grumph rested in the sun. Both of them could taste the blood on the wind; something was coming.

And once it arrived, it would find them waiting and ready, with weapons drawn.

*   *   *

When the alert came, Russell almost didn't catch it. He was getting the house ready for their next session, when the party would finally reach Lumal. After yesterday's surprise city-wide fight, he hadn't been sure they'd make it. Only careful strategy, exceptional cunning, and several amazing rolls had delivered them from the den of the helsk. Now, at last, they were nearing Lumal, and Russell could hardly wait to see what came next. That section of the module was sealed, as were several others, meant to be opened only when the party arrived. Russell had never been the type to peek ahead, and that was before he knew there was magic wrapped up in all of this. He wouldn't dare break that seal before it was time; there was quite literally no telling what the consequences might be.

As he was putting sodas in the fridge, his phone beeped. It happened just as he was finishing up with a pack of cans, fortunate timing that allowed him to notice the noise. Initially, Russell thought he'd check it later, but he couldn't risk it being one of the players with a question. This would probably be a long session, and starting off by dealing with issues that could have been solved beforehand would only drag things out.

Yanking the phone from his pocket, Russell saw that it wasn't a text he'd gotten, it was an email. Clicking on the icon revealed a message from an address he nearly didn't recognize. In his defense, he'd only seen it once before, when he sent the first missive reaching out. The message read:

"Hi there, Russell! That was quite an interesting email you sent, talking about artifacts that reach between worlds. Love the imagination. I'm not sure how you got my address, but we're always looking for creative types at Broken Bridge Publishing. I'll attach a link at the bottom to a temp agency we use. Drop them a line so you can be in the system, and we'll see what openings there are. Thanks so much for the interest.
P.S. If you're interested in a more direct job, try speaking to Calsius in Venmoore."

Russell nearly dropped the phone as he read that first sentence. He hadn't signed the last email, and he'd used a dummy account with no personal information tied to it, so how in the living hell did she know his name? Aside from that, the reply was almost aggressively normal, treating him like he'd been trying to pitch an idea for a job. Anyone he showed it to would get exactly that impression, which was no doubt the point. Except for that last line about Venmoore... it didn't really fit with the rest of the email, and the name tickled at his memory.

Digging through some of the older modules, Russell pulled up a map of the kingdoms. Sure enough, past the western border of Alcatham and Urthos, in the northern part of the Thatchshire kingdom, there was a city named Venmoore. Was she fucking with him? Making a joke out of his supposed delusions?

No. That's what it would read like to almost anyone else, but Russell knew that the magic was real. He'd fought against it for too long. Now that he'd finally accepted his new reality, he wouldn't be tricked into believing otherwise. Assuming that Mitch had told the truth—and if he was lying, Mitch would have made himself look better—then the woman on the other side of this conversation knew what was going on as well. Probably more than Russell.

When looked at from that perspective, the final line made more sense. She was telling him to prove it. If he really was capable of interacting with a being from that world, then this was a path forward. If not, then she'd just dismissed someone fishing for information. The only people who could move past this point were ones capable of interacting with the other world—the people who had the modules.

Sitting down at the breakfast table near the back door, Russell looked over the email several more times before putting his phone away. He would tell the others after they got to Lumal, after tonight's game. They'd worked too hard to get here. They deserved to see the payoff, and if he told them about the message, the party might reorient to Thatchshire right away. Russell was a GM first, an investigator second.

With that done, he turned his attention back to getting things ready. The others would get here soon, and Cheri was bound to wake from her nap eventually. Everything needed to be ready. He put the email, the questions, and everything else out of his mind. It had taken a lot of work for them to reach Lumal, and as GM, it was on him to properly present their payoff. Truth be told, he was probably more excited than the rest of them to break open the module's seal.

There was no telling what kind of magic and wonders the city of Lumal might hold.

40.

The tavern looked surprisingly busy, despite the relatively few people inside it. That appearance was all the more impressive given that the building was meant to hold far more than the paltry ten people, and one boar, currently present. The rest of the town was absent, the background faces that Gabrielle had grown accustomed to seeing on occasion having vanished, leaving only those who were preparing to fight. Notch's contribution included Brock, Simone, Julian, Jolia, and Kieran, who was pacing about. Gabrielle's party was present, as well; Thistle and Grumph were whispering in the back, Eric had a sleepy stare she hoped he planned to lose soon, and Timuscor, with a newly armored Mr. Peppers, was at a table near the bar. As for Gabrielle, she was lounging in a chair, watching the whole thing. There was tension in the air, a tingle across her skin. Although it had been beyond her in Maplebark, Gabrielle had begun to grasp what people meant when they said they could feel a battle approaching.

"Everyone, I think we're ready to get started," Kieran announced. Gabrielle noticed he was resting a hand on the hilt of his sword now, yet one more small sign of the approaching danger. "Let's start by having Jolia and Simone hand out any of the recovered raider gear they think will be useful. Hopefully, Fritz will be here by the time that's done, so we can go over the traps she and Eric laid."

Gabrielle was tempted to ask where exactly Fritz had gone, but she tossed the idea aside with a lazy smile. Fritz was a whirlwind; she went where she wanted, and good luck to any who tried to keep up. It was one of the things Gabrielle liked most about the elf trader.

"Okay, you lot, time for the goodies." Jolia pulled a seemingly small bag from her side, dipping a hand in to pluck items out. "For the most part, you can divvy these up as needed. One or two do have limits on who can use them, though. Speaking of: we've got a Ring of Shielding." From the bag she produced a golden band with a line of white material woven through it. "It helps protect the wearer from damage, but since we took it from a dead man, I wouldn't rely on it more than dodging and common sense. Unfortunately, the enchantment is based on divine magic, so Gabrielle won't be able to wear it. Don't fret, the amount isn't too strong. You can touch it without issue, or be near someone wearing it, but if you tried to use it you'd feel like you came down with a sudden illness."

"Got it. No ring for me. My mother's greatest fear has finally come to life." Gabrielle meant it as a joke, and it did get a few chuckles from her friends, but to her surprise, she felt an echo of pain in her heart. Overbearing as they could both be at times, she missed her parents. Sometimes, when the others slept and the stars were high overhead, Gabrielle would wonder how they were doing. They probably thought her dead after she vanished, and that was for the best. They wouldn't possibly recognize the woman she'd become. Nevertheless, it might have been nice to give them the chance.

Jolia set the ring on the counter then went back into the bag, pulling out a black, knotted cord that ended in a small silver pendant. "Next up is a necklace that sharpens the senses, allowing you to even see in the dark. No limits on that one." The necklace joined the ring, and Jolia went back to rummaging. Her next pull from the bag was substantially larger than the prior two. "After that, a pair of boots that increase the wearer's speed. Again, no limits on those."

To Gabrielle's surprise, Jolia paused before reaching in again, muttering a short spell under her breath. The gnome's hand dug deep into the bag, emerging with the hilt of a sword. As it was drawn, Gabrielle's eyes widened. She *knew* that blade. It had been Elnif's, the one that had caused both their weapons to shake when they clashed. True, it hadn't shown any magic beyond that and being exceptionally sharp, but something in her gut told her there was more. Still, if it was strong, better it be in their hands than their enemy's.

"Here's our other limited option find," Jolia explained, somehow holding the blade with a single arm as she set it on the counter. "Good sword, strong and durable, but again with a tinge of divine magic, so a no-go for Gabrielle—not that any of us imagine she'd trade out her axe. If you can bless it and find someone to shrink it, then it would be a fine fit for Thistle. As is, I'm fairly certain only Timuscor can use it."

"But Shandor went to the trouble of sharpening my blade," Timuscor protested.

Jolia shrugged. "Then keep this one as a backup. Shit happens, weapons get lost or stolen; never hurts to have a spare." Her words were true, not that it mattered. Somebody was taking this sword out of Notch, be it as backup or cargo.

Timuscor clearly didn't have a counterargument for that, so he merely leaned back in his chair and nodded. With the sword finally deposited, Jolia reached into the bag once more, coming out with a leather cuff that had been dyed white—or perhaps crafted from some kind of white flesh, now that Gabrielle looked a little closer.

"Funnily enough, this one actually doesn't function on divine magic, despite what it does. It's a bracelet made from the hide of a mana-beast. Their kind are rarely seen on our plane, and they're brought down even less frequently. They come in a variety of hues and abilities; this one's flesh was well-suited to healing magic. Wear this, and any healing spell will have an increased effect."

All eyes went to Thistle. He was the only one among them who could even use healing magic, so it seemed a natural fit. The paladin had stopped talking to Grumph and was paying close attention as the items were laid out. Considering the information he had, Thistle tapped his fist on the table three times before turning to face the others.

"Based on what we know, it seems the best uses for this gear are to give Timuscor the sword and myself the bracelet. Gabrielle can't use the ring, and Eric already has a pair of speed-enchanted boots, so it makes the most sense to give our barbarian some added mobility. That leaves the sharpened senses necklace and the ring that shields. My inclination is to have Grumph use the ring while Eric takes the necklace, but a case could be made for going the other way. Any objections to this allocation of items?"

Everyone shook their head, save for Eric, who forced his eyes fully open and piped up. "Necklace works for me. I've got good armor, but a rogue is only as useful as the dangers they can spot. Plus, Grumph can use all the extra protection he can get, since he's stuck with robes."

"Agreed," Grumph rumbled.

Jolia headed back to the bar as Kieran stepped forward. She was, for a change, sticking to water. Evidently, the threat was serious enough to demand a clear head, at least for the night. Just as Kieran opened his mouth to speak, the tavern door slammed open and Fritz came bursting through.

"Who needs energy? Because I've got potions hot from the cauldron, ready to be guzzled down. Eric, you first. We might have overdone it with the Bridge today; you look like re-cooked hell." From the softly clinking pouch in her hand, Fritz produced a vial with light red liquid inside. She handed it over to Eric, who glared down suspiciously.

"You expect me to drink a strange potion you're handing me?" Eric asked.

"Look at that, someone has gotten better at being a rogue since our last adventure." The grin on Fritz's face didn't dim; her self-assurance was locked firmly in place. "But no need to worry. These are potions to recover from fatigue and temporarily remove the need for rest. Using them for more than three days in a row will cause you to pass out, or occasionally die; however, for one night, there's no real risk. Guards of the wealthy use these to stay vigilant."

He was still staring at it, uncertain, but eventually, Eric tipped the potion back into his mouth. If she wanted them dead, there were much less obvious ways to make it happen. No sooner had he lowered the vial than Eric shivered. As the shiver ended, he stood up straighter, bloodshot eyes clearing in seconds. All of the weariness had been wiped away, leaving Eric looking as if he'd just finished a sound night's rest.

"That is *dangerous*. If not for the warning, I could see how adventurers might try to replace sleep with these." Eric gingerly set the empty vial down on the table, visibly surprised by how alert he'd become.

Fritz snapped it up and tossed it back into the bag, then pulled out several full vials. She moved as she spoke, handing out the containers. "Everyone here who isn't a legendary former adventurer or undead, drink up. If this fight drags out, we could go late into the night, and these will make sure none of you gets drowsy."

Following Eric's lead, Grumph, Timuscor, and Thistle swigged down the contents of the vials Fritz gave them. The effect was less pronounced than it had been on Eric, but after everyone shivered, they did seem more alert. Getting sleepy while fighting through the night was a risk Gabrielle hadn't considered, though she should have. There was so much more to a battle than merely swinging a blade, and just when Gabrielle felt like she was getting a handle on things, she realized there were yet more elements to account for. How long until she felt truly competent, the way everyone in Notch did? Despite knowing that she was a pebble comparing herself to a mountain, it was impossible not to. One day, she *could* be like them. That was the glory of being an adventurer: her path was whatever she made of it.

Of course, that was only true for as long as she kept surviving, so Gabrielle leaned in to pay close attention as the conversation turned to Fritz and Eric's traps. Notch was a fine town, but she wasn't ready to meet the end of her journey quite yet.

*　　*　　*

Many ignorant fools in the world thought that when one followed Kalzidar, they were required to sacrifice their name. Names were lost, that part was true, but sacrifice implied that the worshipper gained nothing as compensation, a fact that was obviously untrue. Kalzidar's followers were not those who gave willingly. He was served by those who sought power, information, wealth, or any other means to fill the burning ambitions within their hearts. They would never have given away something so precious as their names just to worship a god; there were plenty of other gods who would hear their prayers for free.

No, the loss of a name was no sacrifice. It was a trade. The first display of his power. Other gods offered boons and blessings, promises of favor for those who served them well. Kalzidar dealt in no such uncertainties. He expected results from his followers, and in turn, he provided results when they succeeded. To serve Kalzidar well was to be always gaining, growing, becoming more than what a person could ever have been on their own. The name was a demonstration he used on newcomers.

Their names were not lost, not truly. Kalzidar took the terms, simple words in concept, but words that had been so thoroughly soaked in the essence of themselves that the two were inseparable. He burned everything superfluous away, cooking it down to a single skill or talent that defined who they had been, before he warped that feature into something of true power. They who served Kalzidar lost their names, but in return, they gained a new magic born of their own past.

Stories raged, even among Kalzidar's own followers. No one was sure what dark magics were out there. The power to create swords of pure mana, to shatter stone with a whistle, to turn paper figurines into monsters, to pass unseen through any crowd or ward—these and a dozen more hints of what might be floated around at any time. There were even whispers of a former priest of Longinus who'd gained the power to summon devils, although that one seemed too far-fetched to believe with only rumor. Rumor, however, was all she had. To serve Kalzidar was to live in secret, even from one another.

Once, in another life, the priestess had been a woman who loved nature. She'd had a name then, a family. It was a simple life, working the farm during the day, spending her evenings in the nearby forests and fields. Looking back, it all seemed so serene and unreal, like she couldn't believe it had happened to her. In a way, it hadn't. That version of her had been mortally wounded the day she came home to find her farm and home in ashes. In the days that followed, she would learn that adventurers were seen near her home, speaking with her parents and siblings. They had apparently wanted something—food, shelter, gold for no work, adventurers always had an endless list of wants they expected fulfilled. Whatever it was they sought, her family had either lacked it or denied them. So the adventurers had burned everything they had, including their bodies.

It was impossible to know how long she'd been broken by her grief, only surviving in the glow of the endless fury she felt for those beasts who'd taken her whole life away. Those days were lost, a swirl of pain and numbness that persisted until she was at the altar. She could still remember that moment, feeling Kalzidar's presence for the first time. There was no comfort in it, and that was refreshing. She didn't want comfort, didn't want to be told that the gods would see to things and it would be okay in the end. Kalzidar knew that from the beginning. He never tried to offer her warmth or hollow promises. What he offered her was the truth.

The world was cruel. Life may end in a moment. The only ones who could survive, who could protect what they cared for, were the powerful. Kalzidar didn't present some religion where one might work their way into his grace through ill-defined acts of goodness. He showed a map to power, pure and simple. Those who served well were rewarded; those who failed were cast aside. The world was cruel, and so were Kalzidar's means. Unlike the world, however, he lived up to his end of the bargain. When he struck a deal, it was honored. The priestess had done several smaller tasks already and felt her magic grow as consequence. If she pulled this off, the reward would be incredible.

In the forest, shapes began to move, lumbering forth. What had once been a sincere love of nature so deep it was rooted in her very name had been altered, warped, and improved. The shape her magic took was something of a surprise, but it shouldn't have been. By that point, there was nothing in her more connected to who she was than her grief.

The sun hung low. Time was drawing near. She checked her bag carefully, making sure she had everything she needed for what was still to come. Not every magic item they had taken was for those incompetent raiders to find. Several were held back specifically for tonight. They might not all be needed—planning for contingencies meant getting gear for specific problems—but one item had to be ready before she started her march.

From within the bag, the priestess produced a long staff made of a stone dark as midnight. At the top, it splintered into several claw-like appendages, as though the staff were reaching out to grab something. She stepped closer to the spot on the ground where Kalzidar's treasure lay slightly pulsing amidst the runes she'd painstakingly drawn.

In truth, this ritual and the magic in it were a mystery to her. Only Kalzidar's divine, precise guidance had allowed her to create this site properly. Once she removed the treasure, the barrier around Notch would vanish. All that would keep them barred was Kalzidar's power—much of which would be needed elsewhere tonight. That was why she'd been instructed to wait until the last moment, when the adventurers would be busy preparing for her arrival rather than trying to break through the communication barriers.

Slowly, inch by inch, she moved the staff closer to the glowing artifact sitting atop the grass. When the first of its claw-like arms was near enough to touch the target, her staff suddenly sprang, seizing the chunk of glowing crystal and clutching it tightly as every arm wrapped around it. Moments later, new runes lit up along the shaft of the weapon, quickly reaching her hand. It took all she had not to drop the staff right then and there. There was so much power contained within, the staff seemed like it would break from trying to control it. As she held on, the priestess realized something, though. The staff wasn't trying to contain or control the power: it was merely aiming it. This new tool lacked the versatility of an unfiltered connection with the treasure, but made up for the trade with simple usability. By wielding the staff, she could increase the effect of any spell or item she used, assuming she didn't completely overload her target by mistake.

Unbidden, her eyes darted to the shapes in the trees before she shook loose the idea. They were too important. She couldn't afford to risk destroying them, especially not before she was ready. There were a few test items she'd experiment on in the brief time before she needed to move. Only one item would likely need this boost to work. For the rest, it would simply make things more interesting.

An entire town of former adventurers against one priestess of Kalzidar and the treasure he'd entrusted to her. Victory might seem impossible to an outsider, but there were many kinds of victory here. Not all required slaying every enemy. Although, if the night did end with her razing their entire village, the priestess would consider that an unexpected bonus.

After what they'd done to her family, she never tired of making adventurers suffer.

41.

    The site of the entrance ritual was easy to identify. Finding it, however, turned out to be an unexpected challenge. In a sea of open space, Gelthorn didn't anticipate much difficulty in locating a simple stone altar, yet despite following the map precisely, she saw no sign of it until they were, quite literally, nearly on top of the site. It turned out that whoever made this place had used a slight incline before a miniature crater to hide the location from riders unless they knew what they were looking for. Between the tall grass and the carefully constructed landscape, spotting this place without knowing it was there took exceptional vision and attention to detail.

    Once discovered, the site itself was unimpressive: a stone arch, set in front of a stone bowl and built in the center of the crater, surrounded by three stone altars arranged in a triangle around it. Gelthorn and Chalara examined the altars carefully, searching for any concealed sign or rune that might hint at which trophy went where. Ultimately, they discovered nothing, which proved sensible after some consideration. There were several different options for what they could have hunted, so assigning specific items to specific altars would only make the whole endeavor needlessly more complicated. Nevertheless, they had to be thorough. After everything it had taken to get these components, the idea of starting over was untenable; more likely, they'd just move on to a new adventure.

    Carefully, they unpacked their hard-won prizes: the feather of a golden roc, the eye of a lyranx, and a face from a slain helsk. Each so seemingly small, when held in a hand. It would be impossible for anyone else to feel the weight of the effort, fear, and blood that had gone into acquiring each one. But the spell would know. It wasn't just about the items; it was about the power it took to earn them. Some components, like material for their potions, could be purchased. Others, like the helsk face, could only be earned. When dealing with magic, details mattered.

    First came the potion, poured into the stone bowl. As it landed, the archway began to glow. Next came the golden roc feather, which dissolved within seconds of touching the potion. An instant later, one of the three altars glowed the same hue as the archway. The other altars lit up as they added the eyes and face, respectively.

    "Now, we wait," Chalara informed them. "When the magic finishes, the door will be ready. Going to take a while, based on what I've heard. And on that topic, our portal only stays open for a few minutes, so we need to be ready to move as soon as we can. Much as I love a silly risk, getting here was tough, and I'm not in the mood for a do-over."

All of her party took note of the fact that even she was being serious and readied themselves appropriately. There might be more than they knew about, one last test to pass before getting through, and they wouldn't be caught unprepared. They'd fought hard to gain entry to Lumal; they wouldn't lose their chance now. Not without putting up the best fight they could.

With weapons ready and nerves tense, the party drew closer, kept their eyes on the door, and waited.

*　　*　　*

They knew their enemy was coming. Agramor had sent word the moment someone entered her forest. None of the adventurers had met the druid as of yet, but no one in Notch doubted her report once it was received, so she was evidently the trustworthy type. If Agramor had sent more information than just the fact that someone was approaching, it would have been appreciated; although, since concealing magic was in play, they could hardly blame her. Evidently, a dark sphere moving through the woods was all she could glean. No sights or sounds, not even smells, were drifting through that barrier. The one thing Agramor seemed certain of was that there was no way it was big enough to hide an army. In theory, that should have been comforting, but in practice, it meant they had no idea where their enemy's forces were or how they'd arrive, assuming they were real.

Once they gave up on that assumption, then there truly was no way to guess at what was coming. Even with an inkling of what he suspected was going on, Thistle hadn't been able to fully unravel the point of all this. So much effort, just to keep them here. It didn't make sense, which could only mean that he was missing something. Until he knew more, Thistle's nerves refused to settle down; he was anxious to have an enemy he could see, confront, and ideally dispatch before their true sinister intentions were laid bare.

"I see the dome. They just emerged from the woods and are heading this way." Eric's necklace was already proving its worth, as the rest of the party squinted to try to make out a dark blob off in the distance.

It took a full ten minutes for the dome to properly come into view, and another fifteen before it had drawn close enough to merit concern. Weapons were out, but not raised, as their wielders waited patiently to see where this was going. Just as the dome was nearing the town square, Kieran stepped forward. His own blade was still in its sheath. Given the speed with which they'd seen Kieran move, the time it would take to draw was probably negligible, unlikely to make any difference unless he had an opponent who was equally as quick.

"Fun an entrance as that is, it's also as far as you go like that. I don't want to tarnish this town with blood, and since you don't have an automaton army with you, I'm sincerely hoping you've come to talk. If you don't show yourself, however, I'll have to assume the worst. And naturally, after that point, I'll have to *do* my worst. Let's not go down that road. Not unless it is unavoidable."

At first, it seemed like the dark dome must be blocking sound from getting in as well. Kieran's speech was met with neither reply or reaction, like it hadn't been heard at all. Nearly a minute later, just as he was inching forward, a woman stepped out from inside the sphere. She wore simple, gray traveling clothes, and would have slipped past them in any street or village without drawing a second glance.

That was, until one looked her in the eyes. There was something in there, a rage that had grown stronger with time, warping and twisting until it was all that remained of whoever she'd once been. Her hatred had bored her out from the inside, devouring or casting off everything else, until there was no more person at all. Just a puppet held aloft by strings of anger.

"In his infinite wisdom and mercy, my god sends me with a message of compassion." She may as well have spat the words, for all the sincerity they held. Still, they listened. If there was a chance to end this peacefully, it was worth taking. On the other hand, if she was trying to distract them, then it still paid to keep an eye on her, even as they scanned for other potential threats.

"Kalzidar has decided that waging war on the town of Notch is not in anyone's best interest. You would lose your lives and homes, while he would acquire new enemies of considerable power. While you are less than a horse's shit on my god's shoe compared to his might, it is undeniable that you could make trouble for the mortal worshippers who serve his glory. Kalzidar has no quarrel with Notch. He only seeks fair retribution for what these blasphemers stole from him. To that end, I have come with an offer."

Moving slowly, she produced a small item from a pocket at her side. Most of the adventurers looked at it with uncertainty, save for Thistle and

Grumph. They, along with a few others from Notch, recognized the magical item, even if it had been a long time since either had laid eyes on one.

"I'm sure seasoned warriors such as yourselves know a Stone of Challenge when you see one, but for the sake of the uneducated thieves, I will explain," the priestess continued. "These are magical devices popular in the wealthier kingdoms, used when people wish for a battle to go uninterrupted. Traditionally used for duels, they will conjure a barrier around those fighting, preventing others from interrupting. It will also block spells, enchantments, and other kinds of magic from outside the sphere. Now, obviously, this simple charm couldn't hope to stop the powers of someone from Notch, but if they do give you aid, then the fractures will show in the barrier. It is not a tool to stop all outside cheating, merely to make it visible when such actions occur."

The speech was flat and clearly rehearsed. Even as she visibly tried to keep herself neutral during the explanation, her gaze kept flashing when it fell upon them. No matter what reasonable-sounding words Kalzidar had told her to say, there was no hiding the hatred that coursed through her.

Lowering the cube to her side, the priestess forced her eyes back to Kieran, not without some effort. "The great and powerful Kalzidar has decided to permit your town to remain hidden away and untouched. In return, he asks only that you allow me to fight these adventurers uninterrupted. Win or lose, we leave this town as is. Unless you intervene, of course. At that point, you are no longer neutral parties, and Kalzidar will have no choice but to send his army across this land and leave only dirt in its wake."

"You say you want to have a match, yet I can't help noticing you're still keeping that dome up. Got a few tricks hiding in there?" Jolia was squinting slightly, doing all she could to pierce the veil without openly casting a spell. Until they really understood the situation, changing its dynamic could be dangerous.

For her part, the priestess was unbothered by the accusation. "I brought allies, of course. Four of them, in fact. Five on one isn't a fair fight, is it? As for the bubble, are you in the habit of openly giving out all your tools and magics before a duel? Perhaps you'll next talk to the rogue of the group and tell him not to sneak around a battlefield. The element of surprise is a standard part of combat; don't pretend I'm somehow duplicitous for using it."

She had a point, not that it mattered. The whole situation was entirely too reasonable for Thistle's liking. This was how someone sensible might handle a grudge, not a god with Kalzidar's reputation. He was renowned for his vengeance; the brutality of it soaked his legends. Marching into town, demanding a duel—none of that was his style. But their options were limited at the moment. They either played along, or didn't.

Odd as the situation was, Thistle's instinct was to go with it. The magical barrier wouldn't be able to stop anyone from Notch, so if the priestess pulled something, they could easily jump in. There would, of course, be repercussions, but if they didn't indulge her plan then that would be their situation anyway. Doing things her way, at least for a while, offered them an opportunity to finish this peacefully. That was an option worth hanging on to for as long as they could.

"Us versus you, and no matter how it plays out, you leave this town in peace. That's the deal, right?" Thistle stepped forward, earning a look of disgust from the priestess. As the one who actually held Kalzidar's divinity as it was destroyed, she must have hated him most of all. Nevertheless, she swallowed her feelings and gave him a curt nod.

"As Kalzidar has ordered, so will I obey. That is the offer he instructed me to make, so it is the one I will uphold."

Pretty words, not that they could be trusted. Although swearing to follow her god's orders seemed like it meant they could trust her, Kalzidar was a fan of trickery, and had no compunction about his followers using it. There was nothing they could believe in her words. Only what she did would show them the truth. Better to get every piece of information possible before starting a town-wide battle.

"Then we will honor the request as well. So long as the duel is a fair one, we do not wish to drag Notch into our feud with Kalzidar." Thistle glanced at the people of Notch, making sure that they would follow his lead. He needn't have worried. The seasoned citizens could all see where he was leading things. As for his team, they were already at his side. They either saw the same angles he did, or trusted their paladin enough to follow him. For the time being, Thistle didn't care which.

Once more, the priestess nodded. "Then let us move slightly away from town, and we can begin. As you had time to prepare traps, I'm sure you won't object to me choosing the location."

That part took Thistle by surprise, but he didn't fight her on it. She had a point, and given the approach she was using, it was hard to deny her.

So long as she acted in the spirit of fairness, the priestess had the right to demand the same in return. That was one of the drawbacks of being a paladin—even when he knew better, Thistle had to give his enemies the chance to be decent. Once she betrayed them, however, all bets would be off.

Together, everyone walked to an empty patch of grass not too far from the town. The entire trip was tense; every adventurer, current and former, waited for something to spring out and surprise them. Their only warning that the trip was over came when the dome suddenly halted, the priestess stopping right along with it.

She faced everyone—first the people of Notch, then the adventurers. "Since I took off my own weapons and armor to face you peacefully, I trust there is no objection to permitting me a moment to prepare? Seeing as all my enemies already have their own equipment at the ready."

Another request that seemed reasonable, yet still set Thistle's teeth on edge. The longer this drew on, the more he wondered if it was a mistake to let the priestess dictate so many seemingly minor terms. True, they could add the people of Notch to the fight at any time, yet some part of this still wasn't sitting right in Thistle's gut. They'd missed something, he knew they had, and until Thistle figured it out, he was fighting half-blind, unsure of which actions he could take without inadvertently playing into her hands.

"Of course. We wouldn't attack someone who was defenseless, not before the duel has even started," Thistle assured her.

"Those who wish to fight should get within fifty feet of my dome. The rest of Notch, please stay farther out. I will activate the stone and give you fair warning before the bout begins. If I fail to do so, the people of Notch may attack me freely without fear of Kalzidar's reprisal, for I will have disobeyed his orders." With that, the priestess walked back into the dome.

Much as he didn't trust her, Thistle nonetheless motioned for the others to spread out around the dome. If they were going to play along, they'd go all the way with it. Bunching up was too dangerous; it would make an easy target for one spell, so they needed to position themselves carefully. Thistle took the south of the dome, right where the priestess had entered. Timuscor and Grumph were both on the western side, defaulting to a duo to cover one another's weak points. Eric was opposite Thistle, on the northern side of the dome, while Gabrielle was at the eastern point. As for Mr. Peppers, he was, as always, only a few feet from Timuscor, tusks at the ready.

"On the count of three, I will activate the cube and drop the dome. At that point, the duel will have commenced. The winners leave, the losers die here." A brief pause while everyone shifted and adjusted their weapon grips. "One... Two... Three!"

The barrier snapped into place, but something was off. Thistle had seen Stones of Challenge used before, and the surge of magic brought on by their activation was never this powerful. Whether it was the lessons of Notch or pure experience, Thistle could feel the mana surging through the air, reinforcing the magical wall between his party and the outside world. This was much, much stronger than anything he'd experienced in the past. How in the world was she doing this?

That was the moment Thistle could finally focus through the rush of mana and give his attention to the area that had previously been concealed by a dome of shadow. To her credit, the priestess hadn't lied. There were only four other beings around her, all of them dark green. Thistle might have paid them more attention, were his gaze not stolen by the priestess.

She was surrounded by branches and thorns, a woodland castle forming around her. Aside from a few more trinkets, she looked much the same, save for the staff in her hand. It was horrendous, twisted and gnarled, like living rot. Yet worse by far was what lay at the top of the staff—a glowing chunk of crystal that Thistle often saw in his dreams and nightmares.

The Bridge. She'd brought her piece of the Bridge onto the battlefield with her.

And based on the way her Stone of Challenge was pulsing with the same unnatural light, she hadn't brought it along just for show.

42.

Shocking as the sight of someone swinging around a piece of the Bridge was, Timuscor didn't have time to indulge in staring. No sooner had the dome vanished than the opponent nearest to him and Grumph began to move. It was humanoid, in the sense that it had two arms, two legs, a torso, and a head. For a creature made of branches, thorns, and grass, the shape was impressively well-sculpted. Timuscor almost thought he saw a face in the leaves coating its head, just before the plant warrior slammed both its arms down onto Timuscor's shield.

The blow was incredible, driving him back and nearly to his knees. If the shield he used wasn't enchanted, there was a real possibility it could have broken from that single hit. These monsters were strong, and worse, relentless; Timuscor realized that his opponent wasn't letting up. It moved in closer, ready to pummel Timuscor while he was off balance.

That endeavor failed when a blast of fire slammed into its face, courtesy of Grumph. Much as Timuscor might have liked to see it go up in flames, the monster slapped at its head and, seconds later, the fire was out. Worse, Timuscor noticed that the seared portions were slowly reforming, ash replaced with new growth.

"These are not some animated topiaries to be trifled with," the priestess called out. Her reasonable façade was gone now, naked madness plain on her face as she cackled with joy. The snaps and shudders of her growing fortress tried to drown her out, but the woman would not be denied. "My allies are born of the power Kalzidar gave me. His dark magic flows through them, and no simple spell will burn them away."

Hardly ideal, but not insurmountable either. If the dark magic of an evil god was what protected these things, then the power of a good one should negate it. Even if he couldn't talk to him, Thistle was still a servant of Grumble, and as such, he had the power to temporarily bless weapons. It would drain his mana; however, given the circumstances, there wasn't likely to be a better use for his magic, anyway.

Chancing a look across the battlefield, Timuscor saw Thistle dive out of the way of another, smaller plant person, coming up near him and Grumph a moment later. Moving quickly, Timuscor threw himself between the large foliage monster and the others, giving Thistle enough time to cast. Once Grumph's weapon was enchanted, they could hopefully trade off. Timuscor would be more effective once his sword was blessed as well, assuming he ever managed to get in a single attack.

"Thank you, paladin, for being so wonderfully predictable." Just as Thistle finished the hurried mutterings under his breath, Timuscor could hear another sound follow on its heels. A snap, like a lock being set, and a rush of mana. Slamming his shield into the plant monster, Timuscor drove it a few steps back and checked to see what had happened.

Thistle and Grumph were looking at Grumph's staff, momentarily confused. In the priestess's free hand, there now rested a small box with runes atop it, a bright glow coming from beneath the lid. It made no sense to Timuscor, but Thistle's eyes narrowed as he saw the box. "A spell sealer. You waited for me to bless something so you could lock it away."

"Did you think you were the only one who could plan and scheme before a fight?" The priestess moved as if to tuck the box away in her pocket, but it was impossible to be sure with the sizable fortifications blocking her from view. "These don't last long, and they can't snare every spell, so they've never become too popular. However, I've found that spell sealers do have the occasional use."

She was enjoying this. Enjoying tormenting them. Enjoying watching their attacks bounce off her allies, or strike without leaving significant marks. This woman would tear them all limb from limb, laughing while she did it. Rage tried to rise within Timuscor's breast, but he shoved the feeling away. Anger was well and good in the right situations, but this was not one of them. He needed a clear head to make calm, split-second decisions. As the others scrambled, it was on Timuscor to give all he had protecting them.

"The priestess has sealed my spell of blessing." Thistle raised his voice, making sure the others could hear him. "I can't add blessings to any of our weapons for some time, likely until the end of the battle."

To an outsider, it might have seemed like Thistle was warning the others that the fight had taken a bad turn, and there was some truth to that. Timuscor knew enough to listen for the choice of words, though, and he noticed that Thistle had only cautioned that no new weapons could be blessed, a firm reminder that they already had a couple in play.

On cue, Eric darted forward, slashing at the legs of a more slender, faster plant monster harassing Gabrielle. While her own weapon, fearsome though it was, cut only small sections away, his had a far more pronounced effect. The moment his short sword—the blade inherited from his paladin father, who had laid a permanent blessing upon it—struck, a flash of white-blue light tore across the living flora's skin. Smoke rose from the wound, and when it cleared, there was a sizable chunk of roasted greens across the creature's leg.

Not needing a verbal hint, Gabrielle fell into position behind him. There was a chance her axe's special abilities could have similar effects, slicing through the magic that gave these tree people form and movement. Unfortunately, that move came with risks, and it was a surprise they'd only get to play once. There was some chance, meager as it was, that Kalzidar didn't know precisely what her axe could do. None of *them* had even known until arriving here in Notch, so it was definitely possible. If so, then his priestess wouldn't be aware either. There was no way a woman who'd come so prepared had already sprung every trap in her arsenal. Better to hang on to their surprise card until it became essential. For now, she could defend Eric while he carved up the plants.

Nearby, Thistle was doing much the same. With Timuscor and Grumph blocking for him, the gnome tossed his first two daggers into the larger monster's torso, creating flashes of light and sizable holes wherever he struck. Spells could be locked, but the primary weapons of a paladin were so frequently exposed to divine magic that they always had a blessing. Sadly, Timuscor realized that the wounds were healing, albeit at a much slower rate than the ones inflicted by normal weapons. That was okay; they could still win this by doing enough damage to destroy their opponents. Assuming they got a chance, of course.

It hadn't escaped Timuscor's notice that there were still two unutilized plant people—a near matching set a full foot shorter than the slender counterparts. They were in positions equidistant from the priestess, who was glaring angrily at Thistle and Eric. Her fortress had slowed its growth, but the work was largely done. She'd become sealed away within layers upon layers of enchanted thorns and branches, leaving only enough space to see the battlefield and potentially contribute. If that was not her intention, she likely wouldn't have bothered to leave any such vulnerabilities. One allowed holes in a fortress wall to fire arrows through, not to enjoy the view.

Also curious was the fact that Mr. Peppers was hanging back, not far from Thistle. The boar usually charged right into battle on Timuscor's heels. It was unlikely he'd suddenly turned coward, which left Timuscor to assume that Mr. Peppers thought that was where he needed to be. The idea might seem ludicrous for a simple boar, but he'd long ago accepted that his partner was no mere beast. More than that, Timuscor realized he trusted Mr. Peppers' judgment, to an extent. The instincts of a wily animal were often better developed than those of men. His presence at Thistle's side meant that there was still more danger to come.

"I knew the paladin's blades would stink of his god's tainted divinity, but I didn't expect there to be another." Radiating hatred boiled in her eyes, yet there was also a sincere joy in her smile as she produced another item, a glowing orb that fell from one of the holes in her fortress and rolled slowly across the grass. "Good. You'll make him quite happy. This one has been starved for weeks. I imagine he's quite ravenous by now."

A surprisingly soft tinkle reached Timuscor's ears, the only warning he'd receive that the glass orb had cracked. He would have paid more attention to the process, but attacks from their plant monster demanded his shield and attention. Despite the holes Thistle was putting in it, the damn thing refused to slow down. By the time Timuscor had a chance to look back, a thin veneer of white smoke was fading, leaving something he'd never seen before shuddering to its feet.

The creature was horrific, mottled black-and-silver skin stretched across a long, wiry frame that would reach at least seven feet when standing upright. Its hands and feet were disproportionately large, ending in sharp claws on every toe and finger. The face, or lack thereof, was the worst of it. No hair, no eyes, no ears, only more taut skin, a row of slits that could be a nose, and the mouth: wide, slobbering, with teeth that resembled obsidian stones. The being looked more like a monstrous life-support system for a mouth than an actual creature.

Behind him, Timuscor heard Thistle suck in a short gasp before letting it out as a single strained word: "Ravisher."

"I'm impressed. You know your denizens of the Chaos Plane." She was grinning from ear to ear, completely lost in the thrill of her latest murderous surprise. "You wouldn't believe how many helsks we had to let through before a pack of these finally crossed over. After that, it was just a matter of giving it the right appetite."

The ravisher whipped its head around, the slits above its mouth expanding and contracting. Timuscor shifted his footing. Thistle had just landed a blow on the plant monster, so it had momentarily retreated. If the ravisher came for his group, it would create the risk of them fighting on two fronts. Timuscor would intercept it, allowing Thistle and Grumph to finish off the plant while he bought them time. If it went after the other two, Gabrielle could do the same for Eric.

After a few seconds, the slits stopped widening so frequently. That was the only warning they had before the ravisher leapt forward, careening directly toward Timuscor, Grumph, and Thistle. Reacting as he'd planned, Timuscor pivoted, setting himself firmly between the ravisher and his friends. It didn't slow down, perhaps couldn't, given its breakneck speed and considerable size. Rather than absorb the pounce on his shield, Timuscor took advantage of its cumbersome heft and slid to the side, letting the attack strike empty ground.

Not one to waste an opportunity, Timuscor brought his freshly sharpened sword down onto the ravisher's back, intending to cut through its spine, if it had one. To his shock, the blade bounced right off, sparking as though he'd struck an anvil. As it turned out, the ravisher also was not one to waste an opportunity.

Moving unnaturally fast, it jerked forward, its huge mouth widening even larger. It was too close and too quick for Timuscor to dodge; there was barely even time to think. Acting purely on instinct, he angled his sword as best he could. The maneuver worked, in that the ravisher's open mouth came down directly on Timuscor's blade. Rather than carving through the back of its skull as he'd hoped, the weapon was suddenly stopped cold. Not by the back of the ravisher's head, either. No, it was the monster's teeth that halted the attack.

It had bitten down on Timuscor's sword. For a fleeting second, he thought it was a defensive move. That idea lasted only until the harsh shattering noise reached his ears. He was wrong. The ravisher hadn't bitten down on his weapon; the creature had bitten *through* it. It gulped, once, then opened its mouth again. He could see the teeth marks at the edge of the blade, more than half his sword now gone, vanished into the beast's belly, or wherever it digested steel. Moving fast, Timuscor leapt clear, pulling what remained of his sword back, too.

"Timuscor, throw away that sword," Thistle yelled, hurling his daggers into the plant monster Grumph was holding off as fast as they would return. "Ravishers can eat anything, and they grow immune to it as a consequence. I once saw some living in a volcano, swimming through it like a lake, living off lava. She's given that one a taste for metal. That's why your attack didn't work. And once it starts a meal, it won't stop until it finishes."

"So astute, just as I was warned." The priestess was taunting them, her duo of guards still close to her side. Already, the pet ravisher was moving once more, thick tongue drooling on the grass as its head followed the movements of Timuscor's blade. "But will you figure out the true danger in time, wise gnome?"

Timuscor paid her as little mind as he could afford. Whatever game of jibes and strategy they were playing was beyond him. He was trained as a knight, and combat was the only time he felt he genuinely added to the party. That was how he earned his keep, how he showed his friends how grateful he was to be a member of the group. Without hesitation, he reared back and hurled the sword across the battlefield. It landed heavily in the grass, only a few feet away from the priestess's protective shell.

"Fetch," Timuscor muttered, more in hope than command. Mercifully, Thistle was right. The ravisher instantly bounded after the blade to finish it off. "Maybe try some of *her* metal while you're at it."

"Silly man, haven't you noticed? I wield no metal, and neither do my plants." The priestess's eyes flashed joyfully as she watched the knight's weapon vanish into the ravisher's mouth. "Soon, none of you will either. After that, well, since all your blessed weapons are metal, I imagine my lovely plants will have a much easier time tearing you apart. And oh my, what a surprise your souls will find on the other side."

Her eyes narrowed, and the cascading hatred grew more focused, more dangerous. "You still don't understand the real punishment you're facing, paladin. If you did, you would bash your skull against the barrier trying to break through. Don't worry, though. You'll find out quite soon."

43.

From the instant Fritz saw the woman wielding the staff, she'd put it together. Even before Jolia inspected the barrier, only to find it was far, *far* stronger than what the item should have conjured, Fritz had expected as much. Wielding a piece of the Bridge was no easy feat. Eric had only managed as much as he had thanks to a touch of talent and dire straits that helped him focus. Producing sustainable, useful effects on the fly would take someone years of practice to manage, especially in a combat setting. Building a tool, on the other hand, was far more achievable. It worked on the same premise as the ritual Fritz had used, but she refused to trade precision for convenience. Used as a tool, the effects the Bridge would be able to produce were limited. Amplifying other items would be one of the simpler tasks to give it, and could be useful in virtually any situation, especially with preparation.

Knowing the trick was the easy part; the harder conundrum was deciding what she should do. As things stood, the priestess hadn't technically broken the agreement. All she'd done was increase the power of the magical barrier, reinforcing the divide they'd already agreed to. The purpose was clear; she didn't want the Notch citizens to have a choice in helping, but that *was* in the spirit of the challenge. The priestess had yet to break her word. She'd laid out a challenge and was seeing it through. Granted, so far, she had the upper hand; however, that was part of agreeing to a battle. There was a chance her friends might simply lose just because they weren't as strong. Whether Fritz should do something about that or not, she was still deciding.

"I don't get it. Why go to all the trouble of threatening Notch, risking us fighting too, only to cut us all out at the end?" Simone shook her head as she watched the ravisher finish off Timuscor's sword. "I'm sure it's some sort of complicated trickery, but this type of strategy has never been my preference."

Kieran nodded. "The risk was minimal for someone with cunning. It's no secret that we like to avoid bloodshed when we can these days. The odds of Notch actually picking a fight were staggeringly low, and by pretending to include us in the attack, there was a strong chance those five would underprepare. Most adventurers, when surrounded by people of our skill level, would assume that we could handle whatever threat was presented. That group's questioning and paranoia of the situation worked out to their benefit. They always assumed they'd have to fight, and prepared for it appropriately."

They had been preparing, Fritz wouldn't argue that point, but how effective it might be was still up for debate. Theoretically, Fritz could use their piece of the Bridge to work against the priestess, undoing whatever augmentations she commanded that staff to cast. Was that really the best use of her energy, though? Truth be told, this was a grudge match against a representative for a god who had a legitimate vendetta against the party. Kalzidar wouldn't give up just because his priestess failed. He'd come again and again, until the fight was no longer worth it. If those five wanted to walk this path, then they had to be capable of doing so under their own power. Otherwise, she'd be risking Kalzidar's wrath only to have the party die in a few weeks, anyway. Fritz couldn't afford Kalzidar's—or any other god's—attention to be placed too closely on her. She'd given up so much to gain anonymity; losing it would make her goals thousands of times more difficult.

"Until she does something that actually breaks the rules, we should stick to the agreement," Fritz said at last. "Besides, with her piece of the Bridge occupied, cracking through Kalzidar's communication barrier just got a lot more manageable. Let's help them by figuring out what exactly is going on. That might turn out to be exactly what they need."

"And if it isn't?" Brock asked.

Fritz gave a somber shrug. "It's Kalzidar, so figuring out his goals is bound to help someone stop them, even if it isn't pertinent to this particular group."

"She's right. We have a window for information. We should use it," Kieran said. "But the Bridge is back in the safe room. By the time you arrive, it might be too late."

Fritz met his eyes, and Kieran's world briefly spun. Whether it was the proximity of another Bridge piece or merely his survival instinct kicking in, the mask of Fritz slipped for him, for a moment only, reminding Kieran just who it was he was talking to. "Of course, you've made preparations for such a situation, haven't you?"

"Added a teleportation altar outside the room before we left." Rummaging around in one of her pockets, she produced a small rock with a glowing rune on top. "Kept the keystone on hand, just in case. I'll get to work. Kieran, run over and meet me there. You're probably the only one fast enough for it to matter. Everyone else, keep an eye on the fight. If she breaks a rule, you decide what to do about it. Also, don't be shocked if a bird or a mound of dirt starts talking. I'm going to relay messages as easily as I can in the moment, which probably means using the Bridge rather than a spell."

Giving a quick wave, Fritz vanished in a flash of the same green light that was glowing from the stone. An instant later, Kieran took off at a dead sprint, moving at speeds that were difficult for even the citizens of Notch to track.

"You ever worry that we're all going to end up serving that woman one day?" Jolia asked.

"I don't worry about the courses of storms, the desires of gods, or the schemes of mages. They're things I cannot affect, so it's a waste of focus," Brock replied. "Besides, if she wanted to rule, she would still do so."

Jolia refused her gaze's attempts to waver from the battle back to where Fritz had vanished. "Maybe. Or maybe she just wants to rule *everything*, and this is how she's going about it."

*   *   *

The sky was growing dark as they waited. Gelthorn scanned the area every few minutes to be sure no one was sneaking up on their position. Even knowing that the ceremony would take some time, the wait was taking a toll on them. They were right here, after working so hard to get this far, but now was the time when things usually went wrong. A band of thieves, or some hidden monster, would probably charge in, pitting them in a life or death battle just as the window to enter Lumal opened, forcing them to fight for both success and survival. Yet, as minute after minute passed, no such threat emerged.

Meanwhile, the swirling magic of the archway was growing more substantial by the moment. Smoke and color twisted in its depths, giving the occasional flash of something beyond. It was never much—the shadow of some looming building, a burst of unexpected light from a new source—but the more intense it grew, the harder it was to look away from. Even Gelthorn had trouble keeping her head on a swivel.

Then, without ado or warning, it changed. The colors vanished, leaving only a thick smoke in the door. A gust of wind blew some of it out, sending it across the ground, where it quickly vanished. The party looked at each other as understanding set in: that wind hadn't come from around them. It was ready. The doorway was complete.

"Kind of thought it would be a grander view than a bunch of smoke," Chalara mumbled as she lifted her bag. "I suppose they like to play it private to the very end. It better be impressive and memorable when we get there."

"Shouldn't be much longer." Gelthorn took a test sniff of the air, noticing new smells coming through the opening. There was sound, too, but it was muffled. Magical doorways might not be the best eavesdropping tools. The smells, though… there was familiarity there. Oddly, the most notable smell was soot and fire, an oddity that lasted only until she took a closer look at the smoke around them. It wasn't pure, or magical. Just dark and heavy, the perfect sort for obscuring what lay beyond a doorway. More pageantry, from a town that clearly survived on the stuff, given what entering had demanded.

Together, they linked hands and ran through the newly formed door, entering Lumal at long last. When the smoke finally cleared from their eyes, they were treated to their first look at the City of Secrets, the Sealed Civilization, the Center of Knowledge since time immemorial. Chalara had been right about what to expect: the sight they encountered was both impressive on a scale of horror and something none of them were ever going to forget.

*   *   *

Sliding back into the room where they'd left the ritual—and the Bridge—ready to go, Fritz wasted no time in making a connection. She could still feel the lingering effects of their earlier work; all the traps she and Eric had laid across potential battlefields had been nothing more than effort wasted on a distraction. Taking a breath, Fritz put her annoyance aside. That was to be expected when dealing with a cunning enemy. Part of the priestess's tactics had been spreading their focus too wide, so they'd waste time on fruitless endeavors. It was why Kalzidar had gone to such great lengths to keep them cut off from news of the outside world.

The bigger problem was that Fritz knew there was more at work here than what she'd seen thus far. Kalzidar was a petty, vengeful god, but he wasn't a complete idiot. This was a *lot* of trouble to go through just to kill a few adventurers who could easily be picked off along their travels. Why do it like this? Why so much scheming and set-up? She didn't know, not yet, but that was about to change.

Using the power of the Bridge to punch through Kalzidar's barrier was an almost minor effort. Though it was hard to be sure without breaking the ritual, Fritz strongly suspected he'd dialed back how much power he was investing in the communication blockade. Other items on his agenda probably took higher priority, now that the attack on Notch had commenced.

With the Bridge maintaining a hole in the barrier, it should now be possible for Fritz or the others to use magical messages. That took time, however, so the trader decided to do some quick reconnaissance while she and her artifact were already connected. In the back of her head, a slight throb formed, the precursor of far worse pain to come. She'd used the Bridge a lot today; calling on it even more was taxing her mind. That was a minor concern. Fritz had pushed herself vastly further than today would need, and there was plenty more she could do before the pain moved from annoyance to actual danger.

Extending her senses, she used the ritual to look beyond her current location, moving miles away in the span of a thought. The Bridge couldn't be used to locate individual objects or people the way spells could, but if the user knew where they were going, it could show them virtually any location. It was an ability most useful to those who had traveled far and wide across the kingdoms, which was part of why Fritz spent her time doing precisely that.

It took only seconds for her head to fill with visions of Lumal, a city with which she was intimately familiar. In both her current and former positions, it served as a wonderful source of knowledge and resources. The earliest parts of her journey had been spent ransacking the libraries of Lumal, hunting for any clues or tidbits she could find. Part of her—a sentimental piece weathered down throughout the years—still held a nostalgic fondness for those endless stacks of books. Perhaps that was why she let out a small tear as the vision came into view.

By the time Kieran opened the door behind her, having made the run in barely over a minute and a half, Fritz was already back on her feet and ready for him. Her lone tear was gone; a dangerous glint now shone in her eyes. The moment Kieran saw that expression, he knew there was more at play than they'd realized. "What's the report?"

"The report is that, while I still don't know exactly what's going on, I now understand why Kalzidar was so keen on keeping this place blocked off," Fritz told him. "It wasn't for the adventurers. Well, not just for them, at any rate. He was trying to keep all of Notch sealed away, because, as hidden as you might be, there are a few in Lumal who know about your secret village. People who would have called on you for help in a time of serious distress."

"Lumal is the most well-defended place in all the continent's kingdoms." Kieran had been there himself, and the defenses were of a caliber that even he considered adequate.

"It used to be, but not anymore." Fritz paused, the images of what she'd seen still flickering through her head.

"Lumal is burning. It may well be already lost."

44.

She was toying with them—that could hardly have been more obvious. Two of her four humanoid plants, which Thistle had begun to think of as plantoids, were still doing nothing more than standing in front of her like personal bodyguards. Sending even one more into the fray would put his people on the defensive; they were already working hard to deal with the two mindless, attacking plantoids she'd spurred into action. Even with a few blessed weapons, his party could be overpowered by the strength of her forces. Yet the priestess refused to give the order. Instead, she'd pulled out a ravisher with a hunger for metal and turned it loose.

Why play a new card when she already had what could well be a winning hand? Thistle's eyes roved while the ravisher gobbled up the remains of Timuscor's sword. As soon as that thing moved again, he wouldn't be able to risk looking away, so Thistle worked hard to absorb every detail he could. The attacking plantoids had backed off for a moment, both of them recovering from the divine wounds left by his and Eric's respective weapons. Thistle paused, reconsidering that fact. Neither had been so wounded that it was risking death, so why not keep pressing the attack on the chance of killing an adventurer? If these were summoned warriors, their deaths meant nothing, especially when traded for killing a target.

The priestess was cackling. The ravisher was almost done with its snack, there were two unmoving plantoids right in front of the miniature flora-fortress, and two plantoids readying themselves to attack. His own people looked relatively fine, save for Timuscor, who appeared slightly distraught by the sudden loss of his sword. Despite the fact that they still had a numbers advantage—at least until she got the other twin plantoids involved—they were fighting on the defensive. That had been acceptable when they were still trying to draw out her plan, but the battle had been on her terms for too long. If they wanted to take control, they needed to start sweeping some of her pawns off the board.

"Grumph and I will deal with the ravisher." Using an overhand toss, Thistle lobbed one of his daggers through the air, where Timuscor snatched it easily. "Everyone else, kill the plants however you can. Sorry it's not a sword, Timuscor, but that's one of our only blessed weapons at the moment. Make it count."

Timuscor asked for no more than that. With his shield raised, he raced toward the heaviest plantoid, the one Thistle had been peppering with dagger strikes. They met in a sonorous *clang*. Leafy appendages stopped the charge cold, the plantoid's superior strength winning out. Timuscor wasn't merely a burly bruiser, however. He was trained as a knight, and that meant competency with all manner of weapons. Using the distraction of his shield, Timuscor leaned around and with his free hand jammed the dagger into his enemy's side several times. Tough as the creatures were, their lack of armor meant that they were incredibly vulnerable to strikes from blessed weapons. The plantoid couldn't just slam through an enemy like Timuscor; it was going to have to out-fight him.

Across the battlefield, Gabrielle and Eric stepped up their aggression as well. Gabrielle still hadn't activated her anger or her axe, but she was plenty strong enough on her own to distract and block against the swifter plantoid while Eric slipped in to deliver strikes wherever he could. Even with blessed weapons, unfortunately, their opponents were shockingly hardy. Whatever magic flowed through them was incredible, perhaps even augmented.

Thistle had nearly forgotten that tonight, Kalzidar's power was greater than normal. The priestess mentioned that these creatures came from his magic, so it stood to reason that they'd be enhanced as well. That thought alone nearly knocked his mind from its train of thought. If this one priestess was seeing a substantial increase in power, how much damage were the rest of Kalzidar's people wreaking tonight? Thistle tossed the idea aside before he could dwell on it. He didn't know how strong these plantoids were meant to be. Perhaps they weren't augmented at all. If that were true, though, then it meant their enemy was all the more powerful. None of the options Thistle had to consider were especially good ones.

Worse, his time had officially run out. The ravisher gulped down the last of Timuscor's sword, the slits on its head beginning to expand and contract once more. It was sniffing; Thistle already knew that much. He had to make sure the scent it caught was in his direction. Otherwise, it would pounce on an existing fight. With a quick motion, Thistle whipped a spare dagger—one lacking the inherent blessing of a paladin's main weapon—into the ground between him and the ravisher. Movement caught its attention, as did the scent of freshly unsheathed metal. In a bound, it had crossed the gap, scooping the dagger up with its long tongue and crushing it between those obsidian teeth. Thistle's spare dagger wasn't of the same quality as Timuscor's sword, so it was gone in seconds, ground into quickly swallowed splinters.

Thankfully, he'd already drawn its attention, and before the ravisher had a chance to sniff again, Thistle was in front of it. With a free hand, he clanged heavily on his armor, making sure it heard the sound. "That was a mere morsel. If you want a true meal, come and give me a bite."

As a mindless creature ruled by hunger, the ravisher needed no more convincing. One bound took it on top of Thistle. It pinned the gnome easily as those massive jaws opened wide, bringing the dark teeth down on Thistle's breastplate. Unlike the sword and dagger, it didn't easily chomp right through. In fact, its teeth were grinding against the armor, unable to make so much as a scratch.

Inheriting the armor of Grumble's first paladin had been a deeply spiritual, emotional moment for Thistle, but since then, he'd mostly enjoyed the protection on a practical level. Despite having taken a direct strike from a dragon, he hadn't actually been sure that it would stand up to the continued gnawing of a ravisher, so this was a welcome discovery. It was still possible the creature could make headway with enough time, which was why Grumph had already moved into position.

They had come a long way from Maplebark, and in their journeys most had upgraded parts of their equipment. There were still a few items from their first trip that had endured, though. Thistle's magical belt and sheaths, Gabrielle's armor, Eric's inherited short sword, and of course, the demon-bone sword that Grumph had warped in his mage trial. He had eventually incorporated the sword into the tip of his staff, which meant he technically wielded a spear. On top of being forged from the bones of a particularly nasty type of demon, the weapon bore a slight lightning enchantment, and, most importantly of all, had not one ounce of metal within.

Lining up his blow, keenly aware that the next one wouldn't be so easy, Grumph took advantage of Thistle's distraction and slammed the demon-bone blade through the ravisher's back. It burst out the front with a spray of black ichor. The wizard had hoped he would kill it outright by hitting the heart, or at least cripple it by clipping the spine. Strangely, he felt neither as his thrust finished. It was like the ravisher was all shell and muscle, with nothing else to hit.

It did feel pain, though. A horrendous screech reached Grumph's ears as the ravisher wrenched back its head and howled. Turning at what should have been an impossible angle—if this being possessed bones—it swiped at Grumph. The attack was crude and jerky. Electricity surging from the weapon was enough to weaken, not incapacitate, but the blow still managed to shove Grumph back a full foot. These things were powerful. Had it been intent on eating them instead of their weapons, they might already be in bloody heaps.

The ravisher reared back for another attack, seeking to strike Grumph while he was still off balance. Before it had a chance, the sound of scraping metal rang out as Thistle sliced at it with his other blessed dagger, the only one he could reach under the ravisher's near crushing weight. Annoyed as the monster was by the augmented staff rammed through its chest, its hunger still evidently topped everything in priority. In a blur, it slapped Thistle's hand down, knocking the dagger from his grip. Before he had a chance to think, let alone try to recover the weapon, it was gone into the ravisher's mouth.

This one did demand a little more chewing, so Grumph grabbed hold of his staff and jerked it upward, trying to cut from the chest to the neck. Whatever the biology of this thing might be, Grumph felt reasonably certain it would stop eating things if he cut the head from the body. It wasn't a solution that worked every time, but the number of creatures that could keep fighting after decapitation was limited.

He managed to widen the wound by a few inches; however, the ravisher wasn't without survival instincts. It spun around, ripping the weapon from Grumph's grip before slamming both its arms into the half-orc's torso. The blow sent him flying back toward one edge of the barrier, where he landed heavily. Almost as an afterthought, the beast reached around and yanked the staff from its back. Giving the weapon a test sniff, it cast the staff away without another thought. The ravisher then leaned back down to Thistle, licking his armor with that swollen tongue. Moments later its head was back in the air, sniffing.

"We didn't just feed that one metal, you know. We went out of our way to feed it every piece of blessed metal equipment we could find. While it *will* eat any metal, it has an undeniable preference for the kind you're counting on."

She'd barely finished speaking before the ravisher was off Thistle and lumbering toward Eric and Gabrielle with stilted, jerky movements. At least the staff-stabbing had left electrical damage, though how long the effects would last was anyone's guess. Thistle looked from the priestess to the ravisher, and then to the pair of twin plantoids still standing silently in front of her.

It made sense now. This wasn't a battle. It was torture. That was why she hadn't unloaded all her tools at once and crushed them. She wanted them to keep fighting, keep hoping, coming up with new ways to win that the priestess could blow apart. They knew Kalzidar was a vengeful god, but they'd forgotten that he was renowned for his cruelty as well. Simply killing the party wasn't enough; he wanted them to suffer first. When the killing did finally start, Thistle had a hunch that he wouldn't be the first to go. They would start with the others, slaying his friends one by one as he, their paladin, failed to protect them.

He had to figure something out, and soon. Thistle held no particular fear of death; as a paladin, he knew what awaited him on the other side. Still, as much as he looked forward to seeing his wife once more, it wasn't worth the lives of his friends to hurry the reunion along. Thistle might be okay with dying, but he would be damned if he let Kalzidar take the others along with him.

*   *   *

It was clear they were losing, even before the ravisher had taken out one of their three remaining blessed weapons. Gabrielle could count, too, and it hadn't escaped her attention that half of the priestess's flora forces were relegated to guard duty. Grumph getting hurled through the air was enough motion to draw her attention, which turned out to be a good thing, since not long afterward, the ravisher whipped around, making a run for Eric.

Holding off the surprisingly graceful attacks of their first enemy was taxing enough; the creature of leaves and branches was adept at slipping aside every time Eric came in for a strike, turning devastating blows into glancing ones. Eric still had the soft glow of the gem on his sword's hilt, meaning he could deliver a single, devastating attack before it needed a day to recharge. That wasn't a strike they could waste on a potential blow: it had to be a sure hit. Unfortunately, as Gabrielle watched the ravisher shudder and bound toward them, she found herself wondering if perhaps they shouldn't have been a little more daring. If they could have downed the plant first, they wouldn't be in nearly so dire a position.

No, that was silly. Gabrielle checked the field once more, making sure the twin plants were still rooted in place. Killing one enemy would likely just mean they got another rotated in. Better to hold on to their limited abilities for when they could count the most. Of course, she did still need to deal with their immediate problem. The ravisher couldn't be allowed to reach Eric. Not only was his sword an heirloom, it was now the best blessed weapon the party had. Losing it would both wound and weaken them.

The trouble was, Gabrielle's axe, magical though it had proven to be, was made of metal. She wasn't so sure it would be easy to bite through, but in this case metal was a weakness, a weakness that would definitely make injuring the beast more difficult. There was a chance she could use her axe's abilities to negate the ravisher's protections; however, she'd never attempted to use it in such a manner. Not to mention, she hadn't actually tried to use the axe's negation powers since her change. It had always seemed like a needless risk to take, something better reserved for optimal conditions.

Had she been trained as a knight, taught the proper uses of weaponry and battle, Gabrielle might have faltered in that moment. Thankfully, her education was that of a barbarian. Her time with goblins had shown her the way smaller, weaker creatures fought. They had no rules or dignity; the only thing they cared about was survival—of the clan first, then of themselves. Hers had been an unintended education in the methods of improvisation, tactics, and listening to one's instincts.

With a toss, Gabrielle flipped her weapon through the air, catching it after a single half-rotation. Her grip was roughly a foot above the head of the axe, the remainder of the shaft sticking up like she held a staff. In her human form, the weight would have been too great to wield in any manageable way. Fortunately, she was no longer fully human. And there was a reason some people gave themselves willingly over to undeath: the perks were nothing to sneeze at, and enhanced strength was only one of them.

This had all happened in a matter of seconds, too slow if the ravisher had been moving at normal speeds, but just fast enough thanks to its jerky lumbering. Whipping the shaft of the axe around, Gabrielle cracked it across the head, sending the monster sprawling back. It landed heavily, shaking itself and slowly trying to rise back up. Although the attack had been a surprise and her next strike wouldn't be so easy, Gabrielle felt a rush of elation. It had worked. She had a way to fight this monster. With luck, she could smash its head in, and they could focus on the plants.

Gabrielle's attention was locked on the ravisher, a move that was understandable, but ultimately unwise. To her credit, she could hardly have known that the first act of the plant twins would be to move together in a coordinated attack. She felt something sharp—several somethings sharp, actually—try to jam its way through her back. Most of the sharp objects were stopped by her demon-hide armor; however, one branch managed to find a gap, stabbing deep into her midsection. Even while already turning to defend herself, it was too late to stop the other plant twin's attack—a slam that was rapidly nearing her head. Jerking around so as not to take the attack in the face and risk her vision, Gabrielle felt a blow that should have torn her neck from her shoulders land on her skull.

While her body held, the attack flipped her from her feet, causing the world to spin until she came down hard on the ground. She was facing up, looking at a surprisingly starless night sky. It might have been pretty, if not for the pain in her gut and the ringing in her ears. Evidently, the priestess took the protection of her pet ravisher seriously, if she'd decided to finally let her guards join the fight.

Just as that thought went through Gabrielle's head, a pair of figures appeared in her vision, blocking out the empty night. The twins weren't done with her. Already, wickedly sharp branches were emerging from their hands. No, they hadn't come to stop her from neutralizing the ravisher. It seemed the priestess had finally decided to start killing, and Gabrielle was her first target.

45.

Clouds of ash billowed up from below, swirling in with the smoke and drawing coughs from everyone as they struggled to make their way off the arrival platform. It was hard to tell under the current circumstances, but from what little they could make out, this appeared to be some sort of receiving area for those first arriving in Lumal, set slightly apart from the nearby buildings. There were lush seats, as well as signs directing people to all of the wonderful destinations Lumal had to offer. Of course, most of that was on fire, though a few remaining pieces were enough to give context to the observant.

"Again? Fucking two bad teleports in a row? I think this module is getting a little repetitive," Chalara complained between coughs.

"Or maybe it was giving us a hint that we shouldn't always assume we'll end up somewhere peaceful," Wimberly countered. "A hint that we ignored, even after last night. We still didn't walk through that doorway expecting a battle."

Gelthorn quietly drew an arrow as sounds from nearby reached her ears. "No, we didn't, but we're certainly ready for one now."

Timanuel took the cue and moved into position in front of Chalara and Wimberly. Gelthorn was too mobile during a battle, he couldn't effectively tank for her, so he focused on protecting the ones who needed a shield. "Ready."

After prepping her bow, Gelthorn crept forward, down what would have probably been a lovely marble hallway under other circumstances. As things stood, the nicest feature of the hallway was that it was made from stone and therefore had yet to catch fire. Her own steps were near silent, but there was no muting the sound of a fully armored paladin walking over marble. Deciding that stealth was out, Gelthorn realized that their only shot at surprise was to get there quickly. Making a motion for the others to follow her, she darted ahead, moving as fast as she dared.

Getting too far ahead was dangerous; however, she was also the only one who might have a chance to analyze the sounds and make a call before an enemy noticed her. If escape was possible, they might have to consider it. That would go out the window should they see people in trouble—such was the cost of traveling with a paladin—but otherwise, she could probably convince Timanuel that it was more honorable to wait, learn, and strike well than to throw his life away in a brawl.

Hurrying around a corner, Gelthorn skidded to a stop, unsure of how to process what she saw. A pair of huge men in golden armor held the arms of something that was shaped like a human, yet was clearly not. The fact that the creature was made from metal was the first giveaway, as was the fact that a third guard was slamming an enormous greatsword down on the creature's neck, over and over, the cut barely expanding with each blow. As the third guard kept cutting, the metal man continued to struggle, and from the way it swung its huge captors around, Gelthorn knew the damn thing had to be strong.

There was no chance to consult the strategists—that metal warrior looked as though it could break free at any moment. Making a snap decision, Gelthorn barked out orders as the others caught up to her. "Help them hold the arms as best you can, and if anyone knows a way to damage that thing, do it."

Racing forward, she grabbed hold of the right arm, where the guard was more visibly struggling to keep control. Now that she was this close, Gelthorn could see the metal man had no legs, wounds that looked suspiciously like acid burns lingering where his thighs ended. Even with two limbs down, the monster was this strong? How deadly were the fully capable ones?

Her guard gave Gelthorn an uncertain look as she grabbed hold, but he was smart enough to accept help when it was needed. Seconds later, Chalara was at her side, taking hold with what little strength her sorceress's body could provide. "I know about these things; most mages do. They're called automatons, built by some crazy asshole a long time ago. The fuckers are basically immune to magic. Hence why all casters know to avoid them."

On the other side, Timanuel was helping to pin the left arm, while the guard with a greatsword continued slamming his blade into the automaton. Progress was being made, just not quickly enough. From the corner of her eye, Gelthorn noticed that Wimberly had wandered over to the front, a healthy distance from the swinging guard, and was looking the automaton over carefully. Given her size and proportional strength, it was questionable whether or not she could have even reached an arm to hold, so perhaps she'd found a better use for her skills.

Even with the adventurers' help, it was a struggle to keep the automaton contained. Finally, after several more minutes of hacking, the guard managed to cleave through, sending the head tumbling to the ground. In a surprisingly speedy movement, the same guard yanked a dark bag out from a pouch on his belt and slipped the head inside. Almost instantly, the struggling came to a stop.

"Is it dead?" Timanuel asked, releasing his grip and flexing his hands.

"No. They don't die, because they were never alive in the first place." The guard who'd done the slicing held up his bag, jiggling it gently. "But if you cut off the heads, they lose access to their senses. Can't attack unless they can identify a target. Have to either blind the heads or get them far away from the rest; there's some relay potential between head and body otherwise."

Wimberly, who had slipped closer to examine the automaton, let out a sharp gasp as she suddenly took several steps back. "That's... the seal of Ignosa. But it's so new, how is that possible? Ignosa's Unfeeling Army marched millennia ago. His story is taught to all gadgeteers, a warning of what happens when ambition outstrips morality."

The head guard—in that he both seemed to be the one in charge and was also holding an automaton's head—looked her and the others over more carefully. "His army was deemed too powerful to destroy, and too dangerous to leave in the world, so it was brought to Lumal for safekeeping. Given the direction you're coming from and the lack of attunement runes on your person, I presume you just arrived here. What are your names?"

It didn't escape Gelthorn's notice that, as the guard spoke, his lackeys moved in closer around them. "Isn't it traditional to introduce yourself first?"

"Hoit Mercruft, lieutenant of the Lumal Guard." His tone was polite, but no one missed the fact that he'd adjusted his grip on the greatsword. "Now, I'm going to have to insist on your names. We know there are servants of Kalzidar at work in our city, and we cannot afford to take risks for propriety."

The half-elf's eyes widened at that revelation. No wonder they were being sticklers about names. With a shallow bow, never letting her eyes leave the blade, Gelthorn introduced herself. "I am called Gelthorn, warrior of the forest."

"Chalara," the sorceress added, keeping her class to herself.

"I'm known as Wimberly, and if possible, I'd like to take a closer look at this." Their gnome was practically crawling into the open hole on the automaton's neck as she strained to see its inner workings. "I bet there are techniques and builds in here that haven't been seen for centuries."

The guard, Hoit, paid her little mind as his eyes turned to Timanuel. "Some knowledge is lost for good reason, but given our circumstances, that may be permissible. First, one of you still needs introduction."

When Timanuel bowed, he did so deeply, putting his eyes to the ground and exposing the back of his neck. It was a gesture that showed the utmost trust and respect, and a risky one to perform before a person they didn't know who held a sword the size of this one. "I am Timanuel, paladin of Longinus, and if you are in need, then I shall give all I can to help."

At his words, the expressions on every guards' faces relaxed. "You should have gone first," Hoit told him. "No paladin would travel with priests of Kalzidar, and Longinus would never permit you to mingle with that rabble without bringing it to your attention."

"How do you know he's telling the truth?" Chalara asked. That earned her a few dirty looks from the party, which she easily shrugged off. "What? He's taking us at our word while the city is burning. I'm curious about why."

"Normally, I would greatly enjoy detailing for you the various wards and enchantments throughout Lumal, including the ones used by its guards. As things stand, you'll just have to trust me that we would know if you lied." Hoit sheathed his blade, tucking the head bag onto his belt. "Travelers, I thank you for your aid, and apologize for my brusqueness. Were it possible, I would send you back through whatever portal you used to enter; however, by now, it will have closed. Our exit portals are under attack, some have already fallen, but last I checked, not all of them were down. I will do my best to guide you toward one, though I can make no promises toward your safety or the ability to leave."

"We can help fight," Timanuel volunteered. That response earned a harsh chuckle and a sad shake of the head from Hoit.

"Forgive me, paladin, I know your heart is in the right place, yet this fight is not for you. A noble spirit would perhaps buy you one extra second of life before you were torn easily apart."

Hoit paused to look them over once more, then nodded to his guards. "Drag the body along while we move. Let the gadgeteer see what she can see. At this point, any potential help is welcomed. While they prepare, I will do my best to fill you in on the situation. Be forewarned, there are many answers I do not yet have. We are reacting as best we can to the threat; not all information has yet been circulated."

With a shared looked between everyone except Wimberly, who was still trying to dive into the automaton, Timanuel signaled his understanding. "We know how hectic these things can get."

Ignoring the shared look, Hoit began to explain. "The Vault of Sealed Magics was breached moments after sunset. We do not yet know how, but according to the few reports we've received, four priests of Kalzidar managed to infiltrate Lumal. Their power is incredible, and it seems they were purposefully selected for the task. I can't imagine how they knew their way around so many wards and defenses, but the results prove they somehow managed. It is not yet fully known how much they managed to take; all we have confirmed to be missing so far is the Helm of Ignosa and one of the last remaining Chronoglasses. Even that we only know because of the army of automatons wrecking the city and the temporal distortion beyond our borders."

"Hang on. The sun just went down a little while ago. You're telling me someone did all of this in, what, an hour?" Timanuel thought back to the flames and destruction he'd seen, gulping as he wondered what a force like that could do to cities without huge armies of guards in obviously enchanted armor.

Chalara tapped him on the shoulder. "They mentioned a Chronoglass. Those are legendary artifacts made by an archmage who hated wasting all his time on paperwork. Higher-level magic can do things like slow or stop time for an individual, but that limits interaction with the world, so he decided to see if there was a way to do it on a larger scale. The Chronoglass was that solution; it can shift the flow of time for an entire geographic area, meaning he turned it on in his office and could spend ten hours working, whereas only an hour would pass outside the walls."

The look of shock on Timanuel's face was so apparent, even Hoit took note and decided to step in. "She is correct, but such a distortion is impossible when the entire city is encompassed in its field. While time is moving faster for us than it is in the outside world, to know to what extent would require a skilled caster to determine."

"The army, I can see, but why mess with the flow of…" Chalara trailed off, understanding kicking in. "Because it means help will take that much longer to arrive. Even if the displacement is only two-to-one, that means an hour of destruction here is an thirty minutes out there, doubling the time it will take for any reinforcements to arrive."

"Again, you are correct, but currently that is not our concern," Hoit told her. "My last orders were clear: as it stands, we cannot hold against the army of Ignosa. Specialists have been dispatched to deal with Kalzidar's servants and recover the helm that controls these metal monstrosities. Until they succeed, the Lumal guard will assist in the evacuation of all citizens and travelers alike."

Hoit bowed to them, using the same vulnerable style that Timanuel had. "I am sorry for the timing of your trip. If it survives, I hope you will one day return to Lumal. Today, we must focus on trying to get you out of here. My men and I will do all we can to aid in your escape, but be warned, we are not strong enough to deal with these threats. Should one come for us, we will try to hold it back while you flee. Do not hesitate; do not try to lend us aid. Paladin, as the legal authority in this city, consider that a lawful order. Longinus teaches you to obey such missives, and as a combatant, I trust that he understands that there is no point in more dying here than necessary for a distraction. Your task is to escort these three, and any others you find, to the evacuation point. Do not deviate from it."

Harsh as the words seemed, Timanuel knew what Hoit was doing. Paladins couldn't run from those in need without good reason, but by boxing him in with a task and the law, Hoit had effectively made it impossible for him to stay if they were attacked. He'd ensured the adventurers would have one more potential distraction to rely on, even if the guards were already dead.

"Your orders are heard," Timanuel replied. He was careful to acknowledge them without agreeing to anything. That decision would be made in the moment, based on what was right. Hoit had given him a choice, and Timanuel intended to make the most of it.

"Good. Then ready yourselves to move swiftly." Hoit motioned to the other guards, who hefted the automaton body with Wimberly still on top, digging through every piece she could grab. "And remember, these are not enemies you defeat. They are the ones you pray dearly to escape from, and nothing more."

Chalara couldn't help but ask, though the answer was evident in Lumal's state. "Isn't there someone here who can fight these things?"

"Several, all of whom are doing so, but people do not call these automatons Ignosa's Unfeeling *Army* without reason. There are too many to stop, so instead, our most powerful fighters are protecting key points, such as the exit portals." He stopped, looking down a new hallway, toward the unknown. "Supposedly, there is also an emergency force the Head of the Guard can call upon, but given that the Chronoglass is in play, I doubt that we can depend on them."

Hoit drew his greatsword once more, taking it carefully in his grip as they began to move. "I'm afraid that, tonight, Lumal is on its own."

46.

Between the already closing wound in her torso and the ache in her skull, Gabrielle was reasonably sure that if she weren't already one of the undead, those attacks would have turned her into the real dead. As the figures overhead closed in, Gabrielle felt a familiar sensation rising in her chest. It wasn't fear, she realized with a sharp sliver of surprise. At some point, Gabrielle had found peace with the truth that she might die on this journey, and while she was hardly eager to meet that end, it didn't terrify her the way it had before adventuring. No, what was rising in Gabrielle didn't want her to run. It wanted to fight, swing, maul, and eviscerate. Fury was burning inside her, begging to be let out.

It was the same as that night in the goblin camp, watching her green friends being cut down by demons. She wasn't angry that they'd hit her. No, Gabrielle was fuming because she finally grasped the truth of the fight: they were being played with. Now that the game was done, this priestess was going to pick them off, one at a time, until it was over.

Well, fuck *that*.

Gabrielle's grip on her axe tightened. She'd been holding back all this time out of fear, uncertain of what her new condition truly meant, of what wielding her axe properly might tear from her. But that minor concern was nothing in comparison to all of her friends being slowly murdered by plants. Perhaps using the axe's true power would unmake her. Maybe it would kill the plants. It might not even activate anymore. The outcome was irrelevant, at least in regards to her decision. Any chance they had, they would need to take. It was the only hope of survival the party had. Time to quit being afraid and uncertain. Time to start remembering that her role was that of a barbarian.

It was time to get angry.

The rush of mana flowed in, Gabrielle could feel it acutely now, swelling her already heightened muscles, narrowing her focus down to the enemies who were reaching to finish her off. Prone, with two enemies right above her, was not the best position to start a fight from. Thankfully, an ice spell slammed into one of the twin plants, momentarily drawing their attention.

With a glance, Gabrielle could see that Grumph was back on his feet, shaken, but not yet downed. That ring they'd tossed on him had probably helped keep his sternum from being crushed by the attack. Alive or not, the half-orc was visibly weakened, so Gabrielle didn't wait to see if the twins would switch their targets. This was *her* godsdamned fight, and she wanted to hack the twins apart herself.

Using more strength and grace than her living body would have been capable of—at this point in her training, anyway—Gabrielle flipped backwards and leapt to her feet, axe still in hand and at the ready. That got the twins' attention once more, not that they would have needed to wait long for a more obvious interruption. Gabrielle slammed her axe's head into the torso of the one on the right, yanking it back to reveal that she'd managed to cut impressively deep into its thick body, though the wound was healing, just as the mundane attacks had.

That was expected; she just had to check. Last time she'd used her anger, there had been side effects. Now, she knew what her axe could do on its baseline. It was time to see if it could still chop magic. Mentally reaching out, she connected to the weapon and activated it. Before, when she used this power, it would injure her with every strike, trading her own health for the power to conquer the arcane. With what she was now, a single blow might suck the spark of life from her animated corpse. Fully aware that was possible, she'd have to make this strike count for all it was worth.

Rearing back, the axe already brimming with power, Gabrielle slammed the weapon down right into the left twin's chest, cleaving into the spot where a heart would be.

The world slowed, all sound and movement grinding to a halt. Even she was frozen, locked in position, her axe in the midst of burying itself into the left twin's body. Her mind cleared, the fog of fury momentarily lifting, yet not dissipating. This was new. Normally, when she drew on the axe's power, all she heard was the voice—dark and foreboding, from somewhere deep within the axe. It had always been unsettling, yet she'd never seen anything quite like this before.

—**You are unfit to wield.**—

Wow. In comparison, this opening made the previous demands for blood and life seem positively civil. Gabrielle formed the words firmly in her mind, just as she would if she were still capable of moving her mouth. "Sorry, asshole, did you want me do more drills or something?"

—**You have no life to offer. You draw from my power to sustain what little remains in your altered body. The price must be paid.**—

Okay, that part made some sense, she had to admit. It was common knowledge that magic *always* came with a price, be it a simple cost of mana or something more severe, like the wounds she had endured. Trying to circumvent that simple fact was often how true abominations were made. Still, it didn't mean they were dead in the water quite yet.

"Why does it have to be my life? I've been killing things with this axe just fine to keep myself going. What if I fed you the blood of others?"

—To wield that power demands a sacrifice. The pain of others is no true sacrifice.—

"No... but in a way, that is my life, my blood, now." Gabrielle was realizing the loophole even as she spoke, building the road while the carriage careened down it. "I need that power to live. So using it for this *is* me making a sacrifice. I'm putting myself at greater risk in order to wield that power, and I'm still spending life to do it. The life of others, and of myself. If anything, I'm paying double."

Bargaining with a magical item was not necessarily the smartest, sanest method to undertake, but Gabrielle needed this. Even with her undead strength and anger, she could only dent these monsters. Cutting through the magic that sustained them was possibly her only chance to turn the tide of this battle. This had to work; the others were counting on her.

It was impossible to know how long she waited for a response; with time frozen from her perspective, there was no way to measure the passing of moments. When the voice did return, Gabrielle could have sworn there was something new—a very small drop of humor, perhaps even fondness, in the tone.

—You seek to distort the rules to serve your own ends. My master would have approved. The bargain is accepted. Take care that you use the power carefully. Should you exhaust the supply of stolen life, your body will fall as well, and even I do not know whether it will rise again.—

Before she had a chance to consider what that meant, time was back in motion. Her axe bit deep into the torso of the plant monster, going farther than her attack on the right twin had with comparable ease. As it cut, the axe destroyed everything nearby, turning the leaves and branches to dust. It didn't burn at them, the way divine magic could; her weapon simply unmade the creature as it moved.

The attack went completely through the plant monster, which fell limply to the ground as the enchantment giving it motion was sundered. In a single blow, Gabrielle had reduced the enemy force, the first of her party to land a kill. The move was so unexpected that the entire battlefield, save for the ravisher and Eric, paused in shock. It was a good thing, because the wave of exhaustion that hit Gabrielle a second later would have left her deeply vulnerable.

Powerful though the blow had been, using it had considerably drained the pent-up life energy inside the axe. One more like that, and she would be down, potentially for good. Worse, since the plants had no blood to give, she'd recovered nothing from the kill. Wait: that wasn't entirely true, she realized. There was a new energy flowing into her, being sucked inside along with the mana that sustained her fury. Not life, but not as far off as she might have expected. It felt like mana, only slightly altered.

With a start, Gabrielle realized that she had absorbed a small portion of the magic that had been sustaining the spell. What use that had, if any, was a complete mystery. For at the moment, she was happy enough to discover that it wasn't directly harmful.

The unholy shriek that pierced the battlefield wasn't magical, but it unnerved all who heard it just the same. Standing in her flora fortress, the priestess looked as though she was about to rip her way out. Tears ran down her face as she stared at the pile of dust that had once been one of her minions. It was a substantially more intense reaction than Gabrielle had expected to see from a follower of Kalzidar, especially when it was one of their disposable minions that had been felled.

"Coran… you killed Coran." Fingers shaking, the priestess gripped the outer edge of her fortress with her free hand, streams of blood pouring over the thorns puncturing her flesh. This woman wasn't just cruel or unstable, she was completely mad. What tragedies had brought her to this point was anyone's guess, but the pain in her eyes and the shape of these creatures, sized as though they were a family, offered a not so subtle hint. "What's Luran going to do without her twin? You weren't supposed to be able to hurt any of them."

"Battles are full of surprises," Gabrielle shot back. Her guard was raised, ready for an attack from the remaining plant twin, apparently named Luran. Deep down, she cursed the wave of exhaustion that had momentarily weakened her. If she hadn't needed to recover, she could have struck while the priestess was surprised. Not only would putting her down probably end the fight, but currently, Kalzidar's follower was the only enemy within reach who could fuel her axe. If Gabrielle wanted another magic-cutting strike, she would have to pay for it with the priestess's blood.

"That they are." The priestess's eyes were locked on Gabrielle's axe, no doubt trying to figure out if she could replicate the attack, although the mere fact that the barbarian hadn't already done so with an enemy nearby weakened her ability to bluff. She hoped the one-hit kill would at least make the priestess hesitant. Unfortunately, despite the tears and the blood still freely flowing, a smile cut its way across the priestess's face. Her bloody hand raised from the thorns, dipping into her robes to produce another magical item: a brooch with dark metal in the center. "The great Kalzidar warned me that you might hide some of your tricks, but in his wisdom, he prepared for such eventual—"

Neither woman noticed the dagger until it hit, knocking the object out of the priestess's hand and sending it skittering across the ground, outside of her fortress. Both looked to the side, where they found Thistle grinning, another blade already in his hand. "Terrifying as Gabrielle can be, I suggest you not forget there are others in this fight."

Panic hit the priestess's eyes, and that was all Gabrielle needed to see. If their enemy wanted that item, then Gabrielle would make damned sure she didn't get it. Sprinting across the battlefield, her speed amplified by her new enchanted boots, Gabrielle was on direct course for the object.

Unfortunately, she wasn't the only one. A foot slammed down on the item, covering it in leaves and branches as it wound deeper into the body of the quick, dangerous plant monster. Now that she was looking for it, there were hints that this abomination was modeled on someone who'd once been female. A mother, perhaps? With Eric trying to keep away from the ravisher, this one had been free to reorient. The priestess, it turned out, wasn't the only one losing track of her opponents in the chaos of battle.

This was at least a fairly straightforward problem. Gabrielle just had to hack the monster up before it could get that brooch back to the priestess. Whatever effect the item had, there was no way it would be good for her party. All in all, their situation wasn't much better than it had been before, but at least she now felt like they were finally *in* the fight. Gabrielle had embraced every tool in her arsenal and was giving all that she could. Now, she just had to hope her friends could come up with tricks of their own.

Until then, she had pruning to do.

47.

The time-warping made things more complicated. From what Fritz could tell with the Bridge, the distortion kept shifting. Trying to hold a temporal bubble over an entire city was going to produce unstable results. Still, even when Lumal was closest to their own time stream, wasting a minute here was ninety seconds there. It was a bold move on Kalzidar's part, a way to make the most of his power spike. Despite the Chronoglass being in effect, his minions would still have their amplified abilities for as long as the constellations held. The item wasn't strong enough to slow down the stars, obviously; those under its power were simply spending more time in the same night. Later, when exiting the area, everyone's bodies would feel a tremendous strain. It was one of the many reasons why Chronoglasses had been sealed or destroyed—too many people overused them, and the cumulative tax was more than they could survive.

From Fritz's perspective, it was a matter of time and effort measured against results. Saving Lumal was a lost cause, but that wasn't as dire as it sounded. This wasn't the first time someone had decided they wanted the city's treasures, and confident as they were in their security, there were also contingencies in place. Most of the Vault of Sealed Magics would have been locked down by now, shifting their rooms to different planes where they would be unreachable without specific spells and passcodes. Important assets such as the library were already enchanted to teleport their most valuable contents to a safe house if an attack was triggered. Fritz actually knew where those were going, because she'd been part of the enchanting, back in her old job.

Saving the city would simply mean preserving buildings. Much would be lost, but few things were truly irreplaceable. Lives, on the other hand, were another matter. Plenty of people without the right spells were stuck in that hellhole, trapped in a fight they wanted zero part of. There were too many places to leave for all the exits to have been destroyed, but Fritz had been able to note a few that were already down. Fighting Ignosa's metal warriors was too big a task to take on as things stood; however, protecting the exits was a far more manageable goal. The leaders of Lumal were legendarily cloistered—even in her old position, Fritz had never been able to get everything she wanted out of them. Helping to save their citizens was a serious debt, though, the kind for which she could think of several uses.

Sadly, even at her best, Fritz couldn't have stood against an army of automatons. But she did know people who could.

That was part of why Kalzidar had kept all of Notch locked down. When Lumal was in serious trouble, they would call for help, and there was a chance that some of the former adventurers here might not be able to resist people being so close and in need. In a plan that had proven to be complex and well-considered, such a glaring mistake stood out even more. The effort had been wasted; no one in Notch wanted to rejoin the larger world, even for a battle. This was their sanctuary, a place apart from everything they'd left behind. Had Kalzidar let them be, they would have left any trouble in Lumal to the current adventurers, just as they had with past incidents.

But he hadn't let them be. Kalzidar had driven his prey here, forcing the townsfolk to spend time with them. He'd gone even further, had purposefully cut off all outside communication, even between gods and their followers. Kalzidar had poked the bear, while at the same time delivering reminders that the lives outside these walls belonged to real people, whose deaths mattered. He'd given her an opportunity. Whether or not she could capitalize on it was another question.

Reaching down, Fritz scooped up Eric's piece of the Bridge. Much as she wanted to take it with her, it would be much too risky. Here, it had dozens of warriors who could stand against dragons acting as its guards. Taking it to Lumal would be the equivalent of handing it over to her enemy, and now that she knew that Kalzidar wasn't above using the Bridge, she had to be careful to not let any more pieces slip into his clutches.

It was one of the few balances in their world that the gods couldn't directly wield the Bridge. Their powers refused to interact with it in any way. Fritz had a theory that it was because the gods were entirely of their world, beyond the reach of the interlopers, so they were unable to use an item that straddled more than one realm. That was only a theory. And besides, the gods could still use the Bridge through their followers, assuming they were willing to trust one with such power. Since Kalzidar had sent one he was clearly willing to sacrifice, then there were doubtlessly more in his employ.

Fritz was already using the piece to limit the temporal drift between the two points, so punching through and opening a doorway wouldn't be much harder. Once they were through, she wouldn't be able to sustain the temporal anchor anymore. There would be no one else who could arrive with backup in time. Whoever she brought through was all she that would have.

Hand still clutching her piece of the Bridge, Fritz channeled more of its power across the landscape she was exceedingly familiar with, having spent all day laying the now-useless traps. She stepped out of the warded room, allowing her awareness to spread across the town. Not far from the square, the priestess was still fighting the party, largely concealed from view by the glowing dome. The rest of Notch was watching, attention held by one more distraction meant to keep them from acting.

With a small exertion of effort, Fritz directed the Bridge's power, forcing a pathway between the two points. Before her, a ripple appeared, widening until she was no longer looking into a hallway, but rather at the grassy area where the adventurers fought a priestess of Kalzidar.

A sharp whistle escaped her puckered lips, grabbing the attention of Brock, Jolia, and Simone. They all turned, but only Brock was surprised to find a portal waiting for them. He looked from the dome to the hole in space, apparently deciding Fritz was more worthy of his current attention. "Something happen?"

"Kalzidar *does* have the Helm of Ignosa. Only, he's not using it here—not yet, anyway. He's currently laying waste to Lumal. If we want to stop him, then we need to act quickly, and I really can't emphasize that enough."

There was a long look on Jolia's face before she started to turn back toward the dome. "Lumal has sufficient defenses."

"Lumal has already fallen," Fritz corrected, drawing a touch of surprise to Jolia's face, albeit a fleeting one. "Right now, it's a question of how many will escape, how much damage is done, and whether or not the helm is recovered. Those first two might not concern you, but given how close Lumal is to Notch, I hope you can see why the third one should. Kalzidar promised to march that automaton army through your home. One has to imagine that stopping the army now, in the chaos, will be a far sight easier than stopping them when they rip through your forest."

"That assumes the guards of Lumal aren't capable of recovering the item on their own." Despite the doubt in his words, Brock was already making slight adjustments to his posture, mentally readying for combat. He knew where this was headed, even if he wanted to take the long way 'round. "We might be exposing our existence for nothing."

Fritz shrugged. "If you're that worried about getting spotted and recognized, then stay. I'm just telling you what's happening and offering a path. It's your town; risk the safety of it if you want."

To their surprise, it was Jolia who started forward, grumbling under her breath. "Simone, Lumal has quite a few wards against the undead, so you'd be weakened and needlessly vulnerable. Stay here, watch the fight finish, and make sure that, no matter how it goes, Kalzidar's woman is gone when it ends. The rest of town is watching, so if she does produce a surprise, you'll have backup. Brock and I can handle this."

"Kieran is coming, as well," Fritz told them. "He saw to the heart of the problem as soon as I brought him up to speed. Said he needed to get something first. I imagine he'll be back any second, quick as that man can move."

The look shared by Jolia, Brock, and Simone was impossible to miss. That news worried them for some reason. Perhaps she should have asked more questions about what, exactly, Kieran had gone to fetch. Too late now. And even if it weren't, this was probably fine. Anything that made his friends concerned was probably going to be a vestige of his former life, and Fritz was perfectly fine with having the old Kieran with her on the battlefield.

"Three of us," Brock said, doing the math.

"Should we recruit more?" Fritz asked.

Brock laughed quietly as he shook his head. "No one else would go. We're the town guard solely because we're the only ones with any tolerance for battle left. Besides, for this kind of work, three is plenty. Defending an entire town is one thing, but this is just pursuing a target and smashing everything in our way. Killing is always easier than protecting."

"Then let's focus on doing it quickly." Fritz glanced back to the stone hallway where her portal led. Kieran hopefully wouldn't be much longer. If he wasn't there in the next few minutes, she'd have no choice but to leave without him. Even with the Bridge, she couldn't entirely negate the time difference, meaning that every moment he lingered came with a heavier cost in Lumal.

There was a little time left, though. So long as he hurried.

* * *

The blade was long and sleek. Even to the trained eye, it appeared a simple silver sword, just a tad longer and thinner than the normal sort. One would need magical skill nearly on par with Jolia's to see past the veiling enchantments to the magic sealed within. A sword could be many things in the hands of a wielder: weapon, tool, threat, defense, a myriad of options as the situation demanded. But not *this* sword. It had only ever had one purpose, a task at which it excelled without peer. This was a blade made for killing. No more, no less.

Gently, Kieran slid it back into the black sheath, attaching it to his hip. He hoped he wouldn't need to draw it, that he could lend aid with his usual weapons—simple swords with basic enchantments for durability and sharpness. He'd enjoyed his time in Notch, getting to be more than just a killer. If Kieran gave over to the battle, he wasn't sure who would come back. When his old personality had vanished, leaving him as an echo, it was a chance for a new start. A new life; a new Kieran. A man without rivers of blood running through his past.

But even if the part of him that had wanted those killing skills was gone, the talents remained. Kieran was made for slaughter; everything about him had been honed to that purpose. There was no way of knowing how he would react when the fog of battle and the lust for blood overtook his mind. Kieran could only pray he'd have the sense of mind to use the black-sheathed sword on himself, should the need arise.

Refusing to fight wasn't an option. Kalzidar held his grudges, and Notch had stood against him. Now that they knew he had taken control of an automaton army, it was only a matter of when they would come for Notch. Not if. Evacuation was certainly viable, but Kieran's stomach twisted at the idea. This was their home. They'd built it on the fringes of the world and had worked hard to stay out of everyone's way, and yet, the gods had still come knocking. No, if they ran now, they'd be running forever. If Notch wanted to be left in peace, then they had to show the world what happened to anyone who came courting war.

Kieran would destroy Kalzidar's plans, tonight, while the god thought himself most powerful, partly to protect Notch's lands, but mostly to protect the city's reputation. They needed to send a clear message to anyone who dared turn his village into a plaything.

When tonight was over, neither Kalzidar nor any other god would dare to use Notch as a pawn or threaten its safety. Kieran was personally going to see to that, no matter which swords he had to draw.

48.

Gabrielle was fighting the faster plantoid, Timuscor was trying to distract and withstand the assault of the bigger one while Mr. Peppers stabbed at its feet, Eric was dodging the ravisher, and the other twin plantoid was running up on Gabrielle's flank, no doubt to back up its leafy brethren. Thistle and Grumph had both been momentarily forgotten in the skirmish, right up until Thistle's dagger smacked a brooch from the priestess's hand. That had given them a rare moment of opportunity, a chance to consider the situation before they made their next moves.

With only two blessed weapons remaining on the field, they couldn't afford to let either one be eaten. Timuscor had Thistle's other dagger, and Eric's sword was being kept away from the ravisher's mouth purposefully as the rogue leapt about. Whatever trick Gabrielle had pulled with her axe didn't seem to be repeatable, at least not right away, so they couldn't count on help from that. The most logical option was to reinforce Eric and Timuscor, preserving their blessed weapons so the tools could be used to finish the fight. But that would leave Gabrielle to deal with two very dangerous threats. Strong as she was, they'd cut her down eventually.

"Grumph, help Eric! I've got Gabrielle." Since the half-orc's staff was likely to be the only weapon they had that could hurt the ravisher, he had to join the fight against it. As for Thistle, truthfully, he'd have sent any other member of the party to Gabrielle's side in this situation before himself, but he was the only one who wasn't already fighting.

The trouble was, he needed a weapon that could make a difference. With his spell sealed and a blessed blade down, all of his other daggers were mundane, save for their returning enchantment. Just as Thistle was reaching for one, a familiar shape landed in front of him. It was one of his primary daggers, the last survivor of the set. With a quick look up, he met Timuscor's eyes just as the knight slammed his shield into the plantoid.

"Take it! I can't get a deep enough hit on this one, anyway. Better it be put to good use. We'll hold out, so help Gabrielle." With those words, Timuscor took another slam to the shield, driving him back nearly a full foot even braced by both arms. Thistle wished he could refuse the gift, but he needed it. While Timuscor could hold out thanks to his strength and training, paladin powers were the only real advantage Thistle had in times like these. Yes, he was good at scheming and forethought, but once the real fight started, even the best laid plans quickly went awry. Right now, all he had was his armor, one blessed dagger, and a body amplified by divine magic. It seemed like it should be so much, yet as Thistle neared the green twin running up on Gabrielle, he feared it wouldn't be anywhere near enough.

Slashing, Thistle landed a blow on the creature's leg, sending it stumbling, interrupting the attack it had planned to launch at Gabrielle. Not letting up, Thistle stabbed it twice more before leaping back to dodge a counter. "Come on, you lazy plantoid. You'll need to do better than that to get me; one of the benefits of being a small target."

"Is that what these damn things are called?" Gabrielle's voice was raised as she blocked and slashed at her limber enemy. "I've never heard of a plantoid before."

"Just naming as I go. Keeps things easier." Thistle hopped in to stab again, but underestimated the enemy's speed. With a flurry of movement, it bashed Thistle's breastplate, hurling him back through the air. The gnome came down on his feet, mostly unharmed thanks to the incredible armor, but the plantoid was already back on its branches. Though the blow he'd struck was slowing it slightly, Thistle could already see it recovering.

He dearly hoped these monsters were so strong solely because of Kalzidar's extra power; otherwise, the evil god's servants were more dangerous than Thistle had realized. It seemed unlikely that they'd be *this* resistant to divine magic under normal circumstances, so it was probably the boost, not that this notion made things any easier on Thistle in the moment.

An unexpected upside to the attack was that he'd managed to ensnare the plantoid's attention, meaning that Gabrielle wasn't flanked just yet. That wouldn't last if he couldn't prove himself to be a credible threat, however. Thistle whirled the dagger in his hand as he and the plantoid circled one another, each trying to decide what the optimal strategy was. For Thistle, it was really a matter of figuring out which tactics would make him seem like an attention-worthy danger without getting batted around the battlefield. On top of everything else, that plantoid strength was nothing to joke about.

As he moved, Thistle narrowed his mind, focusing only on his surroundings. He could hear Grumph land a painful blow on the ravisher, see Gabrielle losing ground in his side vision, and… something else. Thistle realized that he could feel his body pulling in mana with unexpected clarity. Whether it was the adrenaline of battle or the rush of focus was hard to say, but Thistle was finally able to truly see what the instructors had been trying to teach them. To his surprise, he could also feel a tingle of mana running through the dagger in his hand. That made sense: a paladin's primary weapons became blessed by virtue of being constantly exposed to concentrated divine energy, so the mana in the blade should feel similar to his own.

A wicked grin appeared at the edges of his mouth. Finally, Thistle had an idea. Technically, he'd be stealing this move from Grumble, but followers were supposed to take inspiration from their gods. Redirecting his mental energies, Thistle took hold of the mana flow, guiding it with his will. The task was coming easily, naturally—a little too much so, in fact. He had a feeling that Grumble might be helping with this, and Thistle had no objection to the aid. After everything Kalzidar had done to stack the fight in his favor, a little heavenly intuition was the least they were owed.

The mana moved, flowing into its new destination. As it did, Thistle noticed his body growing slower, more sluggish. The easiest mana to manipulate was that filling his body, which made it the only viable source in these circumstances. His paladin strength was going to be diminished until the process was over, a necessary trade-off of using the magic for another task. Unfortunately, it was just about at that moment the plantoid recovered enough to attack, leaping forward with arms raised to crush the gnome in a single blow.

Rolling to the side as best he could, Thistle barely avoided the strike. Worse, he was only getting slower. If he wanted to survive long enough to see the plan play out, it was time to start moving.

* * *

The ravisher was hurt, but not down. That alone would have been bad enough, yet their luck failed them even further as it swiveled around to sniff in Grumph's direction. Initially, it had only cared about Eric, making Grumph's task of sneaking up and stabbing it in the leg exceedingly simple. After cutting through its chest with little effect, Grumph had decided to go for crippling blows rather than killing ones. He would switch tactics again once they figured out where the damn thing's weak spots were; until then, their best option was to slow the ravisher down.

An unfortunate jerk to the left turned a strike meant to take off an entire leg into a wound that was deep, but not insurmountable. Black teeth loomed before Grumph as the ravisher snapped its mouth open and closed, nose-slits stretched wide as it decided whether it cared more about the prey that could hurt it, or the prey that held a tasty morsel. Were he a tad more confident, Grumph might have fired off a spell while the creature was undecided. But his mana was far from infinite, and seeing the way the priestess had countered every tactic they had so far made him hesitant to waste a spell until it was absolutely necessary. Thus far, she hadn't stopped him from casting, but he also hadn't gone for anything too potent.

Instead, Grumph swung his staff near the ravisher's head, eliciting a jerk backward and a snarl. The goal was simple: get its attention away from Eric and his sword, freeing the rogue up to go help the others. Grumph wasn't as quick as Eric, and even with the new ring, his armor wasn't superior, so the wizard was under no illusions about how this would go. He'd be in a fight of attrition, trying not to falter before the others could finish the battle. Thistle wouldn't have approved; he loathed sacrificial maneuvers, even when they were needed.

Stabbing at the head, Grumph kept the ravisher a few steps back and out of biting range. Behind it, Eric looked uncertain. His eyes glanced over toward Timuscor, then Gabrielle and Thistle. Both needed help. He just had to decide who to aid first. The obvious choice was Timuscor, who had a single opponent. Freeing him up would make the second fight easier, since they'd finally have a numbers advantage. As Eric's eyes moved, he seemed to reach the same conclusion, starting over to Timuscor. Then, damn him, the rogue looked back over to Grumph, who was rapidly retreating under the ravisher's assault.

Grumph couldn't pay full attention to Eric—he did have his own fight to deal with—so it was with no small amount of shock that he noticed the man's graceful movements creeping up behind the ravisher. Shaking his head, Grumph tried to urge him away. Even with a blessed sword, that blade was still metal, and the ravisher had shown complete immunity to such weapons thus far. In the pommel of the short sword, a gem glowed—the enchanted item that gave Eric a single powerful strike once per day. Though that might help, Grumph couldn't imagine it would make a significant difference. He locked eyes with Eric and was surprised by the intensity staring back at him.

This wasn't some idiotic attack doomed to fail; Eric had a plan. What that might be, Grumph couldn't imagine, which meant he had a choice to make. Trust his teammate and play along, or try something on his own. Even if he hadn't already seen Eric prove his judgment several times over, Grumph had no other ideas. Any plan was better than his, which consisted of trying to bleed out slowly. Stepping back, Grumph continued to harry the ravisher, keeping its attention on him with a few careful slices. There was no way it couldn't smell Eric's sword in the area, but evidently, the leg attack had been enough to make the ravisher care about safety over hunger. It wasn't afraid of a nearby metal weapon, and with good reason, so the attacks stayed centered on Grumph.

He had no clue what Eric was waiting for, so when the strike finally came, it was as much a shock to Grumph as it was to the ravisher. The gnashing monster had tried to swipe at Grumph, claws just barely sliding off a thin magical barrier, when the effort sent it tilting forward, slightly off balance. That was all Eric needed as he leapt into action. His sword's blade glowed with the same light as the gem, and Grumph hoped against hope that it would be enough to pierce the ravisher's flesh.

As it turned out, that was a needless concern. Eric didn't hit the ravisher's skin. He wasn't even aiming for it. Instead, he thrust directly through the hole in its upper torso, twisting the blade as it passed so that the hilt positioned correctly. The weapon slammed down, striking the ground, the power of the strike digging deep through the stone and dirt, going all the way in and taking the ravisher with it.

It happened in a flash, yet when Grumph got a look at the finished product, he instantly understood. Eric hadn't been trying to kill the ravisher. He'd merely pinned it down. The sword was jammed through its own unbreakable flesh, staking it to the ground. Not wasting a moment, Eric leapt forward, using his entire body to take hold of a single arm.

"Hurry! It can reach its back, and it's too damn strong to hold down for long."

Of course, the ravisher would be able to get out of this. Pinning it was only step one. They'd finally managed to stop the thing, though, and Grumph had a weapon that could do real damage. Whispering a few words, Grumph quickly cast as he hurried over to the struggling ravisher. As he moved, his muscles began to swell, the magic of the spell already taking effect. He tended to use the invigoration spell, which heightened the strength and endurance of the recipient, on their melee fighters most of the time. Today was an exception, because he lacked the time to hack and slash at these limbs. They didn't know how long the ravisher would stay down, so every blow needed to count.

Rearing back, Grumph put everything he had into the swing. There was a spark as the demon-bone blade hit the ravisher's skin, causing it to twitch and tense, and the weapon cut true, cleaving the arm off in a single hit. Ravishers were dangerous, deadly creatures, but if one could overcome their defenses, then they actually weren't that hardy. Had this one not been immune to metal, they could have cut it apart in minutes.

The wound enflamed the ravisher's struggles. It tried to reach around and grab the sword with its free hand, moving at angles impossible for a normal creature. Did this thing even have *any* internal structures? Grumph would have checked the arm he'd just severed, if Eric hadn't already been on top of the other, doing all he could to keep it away from the sword. This time, Grumph didn't need a cue. He hacked away at the limb immediately. Unfortunately, it was a harder task, since this arm was thrashing about, and he had to avoid Eric as well.

It took four hits to finally cut the appendage off; the ravisher struggled to the very end. While Eric turned to the legs, Grumph cast his attention to the head. If he decapitated the ravisher, that might be enough to kill it, but it would also open an easy path for removing the sword. Thanks to Grumph's earlier attack, there was enough of a gap near the neck that once its head was off, it could easily slip out. The chances of it surviving were infinitesimal, yet Grumph still turned away. After seeing everything else this otherworldly being had been able to shrug off, there was no sense in taking chances. The ravisher would be just as dead if he decapitated it after he took its legs as it would be before, and on the chance that they were wrong, then at least the hungry monster would still be left unable to attack.

Grumph got the left leg off without much issue; however, the right kicked and squirmed despite Eric's best efforts. Just as Grumph was lining up his shot, a huge blast of energy burst through the air, knocking him sideways. When the wizard finally managed to haul himself up and look at the source, he really wished he hadn't.

There were some sights a life would be simply better without.

49.

The dagger was almost ready. It was nearing the point of disintegrating from the amount of mana contained within. Thistle kept careful watch on it, even as he scrambled away from his enemy, the sole remaining twin plantoid—the one the priestess had called Luran. Darting around the battlefield, Thistle managed to catch view of Eric's spectacular strike that drove the ravisher to the ground. It was a heartening sight, especially as Gabrielle and Timuscor fought just to maintain a stalemate. For his part, Thistle likely would have been stopped long ago if not for his armor. Every blow Luran landed sent him hurtling around, leaving the gnome scraped and bruised, but not crushed. It took all he had to focus on dodging while keeping up the flow of mana into the dagger.

Finally, Thistle reached the end of the process. Whether his weapon was ready or simply at capacity was impossible to say; his likely-divine intuition didn't stretch to actual knowledge. Rather than hurl the weapon right away, he waited and dodged for a bit longer, letting the strength return to his limbs. A potent dagger was no use if he lacked the power to make an accurate throw. Much as Thistle would have liked to use it on the priestess, she was too well guarded. The fortress made her highly difficult to hit, even when she was showing herself. There were also bound to be defenses Thistle couldn't see. If they wanted to bring her down, the first step was taking out her minions. With more of his group free, Thistle could employ new tactics, forcing her out of her thorny defenses.

That meant his dagger was destined for a plantoid. One was on him, one on Gabrielle, and one on Timuscor. Breaking through all that foliage was going to take muscle, meaning that, in terms of pure strength, Gabrielle was the best choice. All the better if she could manage that axe trick once more. Ideally, it would give them a chance to reclaim the priestess's brooch, and keeping anything she wanted away from her hands was simple common sense.

Thistle waited until Luran's next attack, then sped up, his legs moving faster as the gifts of a paladin returned. Buying himself enough space to aim, Thistle eyed Gabrielle's plantoid carefully, waiting until it had reared back for a slam on her, and let the dagger fly. Its course was true. It flipped through the air and buried itself in the graceful plantoid's chest. Thistle held his breath, waiting to see if there was enough divine magic in the dagger to do real damage.

That same breath was expelled in shock as an explosion of light tore through the air, sending Gabrielle flying back with a scream. In an instant, Thistle's heart dropped. He hadn't expected the effect to be anywhere near that big, so large that it would hit Gabrielle too. Worse, Gabrielle was also weak to divine magic, meaning the blast would do serious damage wherever it hit. Thistle raced over to her fallen body, taking note of the burns across her face and hands. Healing her with his magic was impossible; it would only do more harm. But Thistle had planned for such a possibility, even if he wasn't particularly enthusiastic about the method he'd come up with.

Moving fast, his ears still filled with ringing from the recent explosion, Thistle pressed the back of his hand against the axe, cutting into his flesh. Pain came quick and steady, but he endured, even as his body started to feel weaker. Thistle cast a spell of healing on himself, and the feeling faded without vanishing. After a few seconds, Gabrielle stirred, though she was still severely wounded.

It had all happened in less than a minute, which shouldn't have been much. But as Thistle looked over to the priestess, he realized just how long a minute could be, and why the free plantoid hadn't hit him while he was healing Gabrielle. Luran had been busy, it seemed, shifting through the debris of the other plantoid. Aside from burning flecks of shattered dagger, it had found the brooch concealed in its brethren's body—the brooch that now glowed brightly in the priestess's hand.

Already, the change was happening. The winding thorns and branches that formed her defenses wormed their way into her, fusing with her flesh. To Thistle's horror, Luran soon began to do the same. The ground rumbled as vines and roots appeared, dragging the remains of the fallen plantoids—as well as the one still fighting Timuscor—over to her. With a start, Thistle noticed a thrashing figure and realized she was drawing in the ravisher as well, or what remained of it. Evidently, Eric and Grumph had managed to take most of its limbs. Glancing back, Thistle saw both of them slowly rising up; the blast must have caught them totally off guard. Their eyes widened as they saw the priestess, body riddled with wriggling plant life. Eric put a hand on his sword. Evidently, the vines had just pulled the ravisher off, rather than dislodging the blade, leaving Thistle to watch as Eric struggled and failed to pull his weapon free from the ground.

That was an extremely unlucky break, given that Eric's sword was the last blessed weapon on the battlefield. Thistle now realized that by packing his dagger to the point of near-destruction with divine mana, he'd created a bomb, not an empowered attack like he'd unintentionally used against the demons so long ago. Such was the trouble with testing a new skill on the battlefield; even with intuition, some lessons came down to trial and error.

Before them, the priestess was growing, the new mass adding to her previously average frame. Already, she'd reached nine feet tall, and was still increasing. Thick armor made of thorns and dark bark coated the majority of her skin, with sections on her arm and chest covered in the same leafy grass as the plantoids. The few parts of her skin that still showed had turned mottled, similar to the ravisher's flesh, though not entirely the same. Her head grew and warped as a crown of sharp branches burst out like a tangle of horns, blocking easy attacks on her eyes and face. When she opened her mouth, they could see a long tongue covered in vines, surrounded by teeth stained gray, rather than the onyx of the ravisher.

She was absorbing them, that was obvious, but as he observed the shift in coloration, Thistle hoped she wasn't getting her minions' strengths in their entirety. If the woman had just become metal-proof, the fight was as good as over; Grumph's staff would never break through all that armor, let alone get near her flesh. None of them could, Thistle realized. The dark magic was reinforcing everything, meaning they needed their blessed weapons to break through—the blessed weapons they only had one of, one currently jammed in the ground at that.

In a surprising twist of fortune, Thistle turned back to find Grumph taking grip of the stuck weapon. Between the half-orc's natural strength and the way his muscles were bulging with magical aid, yanking the weapon free should have been a simple effort. Their good luck was not long-lived, however. No sooner had Grumph reached down for the sword than a set of vines wrapped around his arms.

They came from the priestess's left hand; the leafy material of a plantoid had shifted into a ranged weapon. With a tug, she yanked the wizard from his feet and whipped him through the air, bringing him down on the nearby ground with a *crunch* that left Thistle cold. It was too much. Not even someone as tough as Grumph could have survived it. Thoughts of survival were replaced with images of vengeance as he started to turn toward their giant enemy.

A slight stirring caught Thistle's attention, though. Grumph wasn't dead quite yet. That ring had saved him from some damage, and the spell's boost must have given him enough endurance to survive. How long that would hold true was anyone's guess.

With Gabrielle stable, Thistle was off like a shot, racing toward his oldest friend with healing at his fingertips. Unfortunately, he was hardly inconspicuous. The vines around Grumph released, surging toward Thistle instead. A flash of silver appeared from nowhere, creating a sudden wall between Thistle and the vines. It was Timuscor, shield ever at the ready, Mr. Peppers following only a few steps behind. He caught the vines on his shield and, without a plantoid attacking endlessly, was finally able to unsheathe the blade he'd been given as a backup. Swinging it around, he managed to strike the vines, driving them back. There was a slight smoking from where they'd touched the blade, but not the full flash of fire they saw from the blessed weapons hitting. The sword *did* have a hint of divine magic—just nothing potent enough to count as a true blessing.

It was enough to drive the vines off for a moment. Thistle slid to the ground at Grumph's side, healing fast to stabilize the wizard. Grumph's heart rate slowed, and his breathing grew normal as the worst of his injuries faded, but he was still in bad shape. That wasn't likely to change soon, either. Hurting himself to heal Gabrielle had consumed a healthy amount of Thistle's power, and reviving Grumph was no small chore. He had enough left to keep someone alive; bringing them back to full health was more than he'd be able to manage. Unless Gabrielle's healing patched her up in time, it looked as though they were going to be facing the chimera-priestess without their wizard, barbarian, or blessed weapons. That left them with only a disarmed rogue, a near-spent paladin, and a knight wielding an unfamiliar sword. Not the odds Thistle would have chosen for a fight, especially when they were trapped without any method of escape.

"Get them up as best you can," Timuscor said, stepping closer to the priestess. "I'll hold her off."

"Timuscor, you know you shouldn't—"

"I'm not throwing my life away, Thistle." Timuscor kept walking, shield and sword at the ready. "I finally got it, watching you fight today. A paladin's job isn't to die for his party. It's to protect them with every breath *in* his body. Sometimes, that will cost everything, but that should never be willingly accepted. I have to keep living to keep fighting, to keep protecting you all. *That's* the cost of being a paladin: not a death, but a life spent in service to those in need. I'm fighting to buy you time, not to sacrifice myself. So move quickly."

His speech ended as he drew near the priestess. A volley of vines fired off from her left arm, driven away by a swing from Timuscor's new blade. He leapt back from another shot to the right, swiping at them while keeping his shield raised. For a moment, he seemed to have found her rhythm. Thistle felt his spirits rise as he hurriedly poured more healing magic into Grumph—enough to get him capable of casting. As a wizard, Grumph didn't need to be on his feet to help the battle.

The stalemate lasted for nearly a full minute, longer than Thistle would have expected. The turn came when Timuscor tried to dodge another attack of vines, only to discover his legs stuck in place. Eyes wide, both of the adventurers traced the bindings along the ground to the priestess's legs, which were coated in the green plantoid substance. She'd drawn his attention with her arm vines while sneaking up on him using the ones on her legs.

Timuscor tried to raise his shield; however, this time, the priestess didn't attack with vines. She drove one heavy, bark-armored fist into his shield, sending Timuscor tumbling through the air until he landed with a crash of metal. Already, Mr. Peppers was sprinting over to him, a sign that told Thistle all he needed to know about the knight's health.

There was a good chance Timuscor was either dead or dying. And with the priestess in the way, there was no way Thistle would be able to heal him. Especially since there was no longer anyone around to draw her attention.

50.

Stealth had never been this particular group's strongpoint. Between Timanuel's armor, Chalara's volume, and Wimberly's gadgets, they tended to prefer hitting fast and hard to sneaking around. That didn't mean they were incapable of the tactic, however, when occasion demanded. It only meant they weren't especially good at it.

Fear was a powerful motivator, though, and as they crept from hallway to hallway, following the lead of the guards, each adventurer took care to step as quietly as possible. Thankfully, even the heavy armor of Timanuel and the guards was partially muffled by the chaos outside. Between the fires, people screaming, and various noises they couldn't place, there was plenty of background noise to conceal their movements.

That was a much-needed lucky break, as they nearly encountered two patrols of automatons passing through the halls. Each group had three roving metal killers, all walking in perfect unison. No one needed to state the obvious: if they were found, they were dead. It had taken three guards to hack down a lone automaton that had already lost its legs. Against three at full strength? They probably wouldn't even last long enough to buy the others time to escape. Thankfully, care and stillness allowed them to remain undetected as the patrols wandered past.

Chalara noticed that they didn't seem to be looking for anyone; they weren't turning over vases to expose hiding spots or setting up ambushes. They were just walking, strolling around to look for anyone still breathing. That did make some sense, she supposed. Controlling this many troops couldn't be easy on a single person, even a skillful caster. The most efficient strategy would be to give the bulk of the group simple instructions, then directly manage only when essential. If she was right, it meant they would encounter more patrols on the way, but it also increased their odds of getting past without being noticed.

When the last trio was gone and her party started moving once more, Chalara explained her theory in the quietest voice she had. Wimberly looked up from the automaton corpse to nod in agreement. That was something. An intellectual advantage might not have been their preference, but in light of the automatons' incredible physical gifts, it was the most they were going it get.

They continued on, going as quietly as possible, until Hoit checked around a corner and held up a hand, instructing them to halt. Looking back, he put up a single finger, then pointed to the corner he'd just checked. The message was clear: one automaton in the hall.

Chalara didn't know hand signals very well, so she held out her left palm, flat, and with her right hand, pretended to be a pair of legs walking across a flat surface. She cocked her neck and raised both eyebrows, doing her very best to imply the existence of a question mark.

Hoit seemed to understand, which made it even more disappointing when he shook his head. Mimicking her motions, he made a flat plane and a pair of legs, too, only his stood stock-still. Shit. That meant this one was planted: a sentry, rather than a patrol.

This time, Chalara's finger-legs walked a more purposeful path around the edge of her hand, intentionally avoiding the center. It was a rudimentary way of asking if they could go around, but it got the point across. Sadly, she was met with another shake of Hoit's head, though this time, he didn't bother with more finger gestures. There were probably several good reasons why they couldn't use another route, just not the kind they could talk about at the moment.

Which left them with a lone automaton, standing guard in a hall they needed to cross. Even with the overwhelming numbers advantage, the fight would be a tough one, not to mention loud. Fighting one automaton was a maybe; with luck and the right moves, it was possible they'd win, albeit not without casualties. But if even one other joined the fray, that would be it.

Chewing on her lip, Chalara ran through their options. Fighting should be a last resort, especially with such terrible odds. They needed to move the thing, which required a distraction. Could any of them escape, once they drew its attention? Unless the guards were hiding magical resources, probably not. Then again, if the automatons were set to go after *any* life they found, there might be another way.

It wasn't magic Chalara had gotten to practice with much—their fights tended to be quick and dirty—but after that fight with the lyranx, her sorceress powers had grown, enough that she'd gained the power to cast new spells. One, in particular, had called out to her; it was a power she'd been waiting some while to achieve. Muttering the verbal parts as softly as she was able, to the point where Chalara worried it wouldn't work, she wove her new spell into existence.

On the ground nearby, a soft light appeared, growing quickly and then fading to reveal a dark cat that stood several feet tall at the shoulder. It looked at them all with hungry eyes. Had this been a different situation, there would have been a very verbal reaction to seeing Chalara conjure a panther, albeit a small one. Creating more powerful creatures demanded more mana, and knowing what this one's purpose was, Chalara had elected to save the energy.

She guided it silently; the thread of mana connecting it to her was also a conduit for her will. Everyone moved back, into the nearest alcove and out of sight, while Chalara sent the panther forward at a casual gait. It loped in front of the door, not bothering to pause, and kept going. Around the corner, they could hear movement already—thunderous clanks from the stone hallway. Immediately, Chalara ordered her panther to run, commanding it to go as far away as their connection would allow. Without delay, the deadly feline picked up speed, not quite getting out of sight before the automaton came tearing out of the hallway and saw it race around a corner. The mechanical sentry gave no signs of slowing, turning with unnerving precision and racing off after the panther.

Seeing it chasing down her summon, Chalara mentally gave the cat permission to unmake itself when caught. The creature was shaped from mana rather than truly alive, but that didn't mean it needed to suffer needlessly. Her experience in the dragon's cave had left Chalara, and the woman who controlled her, with many questions about the fundamental nature of what was and wasn't real. Better to err on the side of compassion, just in case.

As soon as the automaton vanished, they moved, hurrying through the previously guarded hallway. It wasn't an especially long stretch, but when they emerged, they were on a completely new side of the city. Grand, sweeping balconies stretched out before them, showing off a view that would have been dazzling if it weren't engulfed in flames. Chalara realized that the hall must have been connecting entirely different buildings, perhaps even city sections. No wonder going around wasn't an option.

With a rush, Chalara noticed something else. Below their balcony, some distance off, was a golden platform that rose from the ground. On it, magic was flowing as doorways of flickering light gleamed. Automatons were trying to attack both the platform and its foundations, but were being repelled by a veritable sea of golden armor. More of Lumal's guards, then. Perhaps *most* of Lumal's guards? By grit and sheer numbers, they were holding back the automaton attackers as people made their escape. How long they would last was another question.

Hoit pointed out the platform, in case anyone had missed it. "That's our goal. The guards need help, and you can use the portal to escape. Move fast, but stay quiet. We cannot risk discovery just because we caught sight of our goal. Those numbers don't help us until we're there." He kept his voice low, yet the authority in his tone never wavered. The man clearly took his position, and the duty it entailed, seriously. While that wasn't Chalara's style, she could respect it nevertheless.

As they crept along, Timanuel sidled up next to her, also speaking in whispers. "That's the first summoning spell I've ever seen you cast."

"It's the first summoning spell I ever wanted to," Chalara replied. "The lower-level ones are mostly for fodder. I held out until I got something a little more... appropriate."

"How is a panther appropriate?" Timanuel kept his voice low, but wasn't entirely able to shake the incredulity from his tone.

The response he got was a gleeful smile that told him he'd just given Chalara precisely the setup she had wanted. "Everyone knows witches have black cats. I just gave the old image an upgrade."

* * *

Leaving the Bridge behind not only meant that Fritz couldn't slow the time displacement anymore; and technically, she couldn't leave without it. Of course, a mage of Jolia's talents would be able to create a portal for them if needed, and Fritz did have some last-ditch options of her own, but it was still a vulnerability, one she minimized by staying out of sight as soon as the other three split up, each racing off to lend their aid wherever it was needed most.

Even after all these years, their adventuring instincts hadn't dulled. No sooner had Brock, Jolia, and Kieran arrived in this chaotic hellscape than they began analyzing the damage and discerning where both their targets and the exit platforms were most likely to be. They'd only paused long enough for Jolia to layer an enchantment on top of Brock and Kieran before finally adding it to herself. Originally, Fritz had been annoyed by the gnome's idea, but once Jolia had relented and cast it only after they'd arrived, minimizing the time lost, was Fritz able to see the use in the technique. Though the enchanted illusions wouldn't fool everyone, they would at least offer an excuse of reasonable doubt. With what the town of Lumal was going to owe these three when the fighting ended, she had little doubt the figureheads would back whatever explanation the adventurers of Notch decided to offer.

None of that was Fritz's concern. When the other three ran off, she'd rummaged around in her bag until she produced a glowing bracelet. This trinket had limited appeal, since it served one dedicated purpose: it allowed a person to hide from magical vision sources. Most people used them when they were afraid of being scryed, combined them with other magic for true invisibility, or when they needed to sneak into a place where the guards had enchanted vision. However, since the magic did nothing to stop normal vision, the demand for such tools was limited, keeping them cheap enough that Fritz could afford to stock the items for when she *did* have a customer with a pressing need.

Slipping it on, Fritz casually strolled through the halls of Lumal, ignoring every automaton she passed and being ignored in return. People seemed to forget that even though they were resistant to spells, automatons had still been built *using* magic. With no eyeballs or nerve endings, the only vision they could possibly have was magical in nature, meaning that Fritz occupied a giant blind spot in their perception as she slowly made her way through town.

Never was a stop or a misturn made; she knew precisely where she was, and where she wanted to be. In many ways, Fritz considered that to be her greatest strength. All these adventurers out there, wandering around with only a generic thought of what they were aiming for. "Do good" or "Find gold" or something else seemingly simplistic, yet with no actual goal in sight. She was not among them. Fritz knew what she wanted, and she had for a *very* long time. For centuries, it had seemed like a hopeless struggle; however, in the last few years, something had changed. More pieces were popping up; ones she'd never heard of before were entering play. At long last, she had momentum, and she wasn't inclined to let it fade.

Fritz arrived at a pair of gleaming golden gates. They were smashed into pieces, scattered across the road like a corpse left as warning. A damn shame, too. These gates had been a marvel of magical crafting. They could discern a visitor's intent, desires, and whether or not they were trying to smuggle anything dangerous. The nature of some of the items in the Vault of Sealed Magics made these doors necessary to permit entrance, meaning that they couldn't be simply locked away. One such example was the fact that many of their items were tied deeply to the gods, and were therefore the destination of pilgrimages. Complicating matters further, without that continual faith from a god's followers, such items' power could fade. There were similar issues with various items of different sources, as well. In the end, Lumal had been forced to allow visitors into the Vault of Sealed Magics, albeit only after they had passed through the gates and another few dozen safeguards. This wasn't the first time someone with wicked intent had found a way in, but it was by far the most successful theft in Lumal's history.

Tempting as it was to assume the robbers had broken the gates to gain entrance, Fritz had a hunch that the automatons had done the actual smashing. Wrecking these gates would take a while for most people, giving the guards plenty of time to react. If the thieves had that manner of power, the army might not have been necessary.

As she made her way up the road—a single path with now-vacant guard stations perched on either side—Fritz noticed that a dozen automatons were waiting at the end, standing in formation, no doubt to stop anyone who might desire to gain entry. Moving silently, lest she draw unwanted attention, Fritz crept through. Years of skulking around dangerous places had left her surprisingly adept at staying unnoticed. Just when she was nearly past, Fritz noticed that one automaton on the end looked different. When she examined it more carefully, the issue became obvious.

This automaton, the one at the left edge of the formation, was destroyed. Someone had put a dozen puncture holes in its torso, along with several more along the arms and legs, as well as cutting off its head, though it remained propped up on the neck. The automaton had been killed before any of the others, could notice, let alone react.

Fritz resisted the urge to make any sort of satisfied noise. It was heartening to see that even the great Kieran had slipped up after so many years. He must have been spotted; otherwise, he wouldn't have wasted the time to wreck the automaton before it could raise the alarm. She'd rib him about it later, when the day was won. Mid-battle aspersions didn't seem appropriate.

If nothing else, at least she wasn't the only one breaking into the Vault of Sealed Magics. Kieran probably assumed it was where the person with the helm had holed up, taking the town's best-defended position. Fritz wasn't planning on stealing the helm back; that was what the warriors of Notch were for. She would, of course, help out in whatever ways she could, but Lumal could hardly expect her to contribute without *some* manner of weapon. And was it her fault if the best equipment was tucked away inside the vault? True, by now, the whole place was locked down, the rooms sealed away in other planes. Then again, that was only a problem if one wasn't intimately familiar with the sealing mechanisms, though said person would also need extensive knowledge on planar gates and a general idea of where the rooms had been shifted to.

Rummaging through her bag quietly, Fritz dug for the tools she would need. With luck, she could find what she was after and slip out before anyone noticed. If fortune was really on her side, she might even run into Kieran along the way. She couldn't remember the last time she'd seen him truly in action, and there was no telling if she ever would again. There were some sights that only happened once or twice in a lifetime, even with elven longevity.

51.

The fog surrounding him was familiar, a fact that shamed Timuscor to his core. After a speech about understanding the value of his life, he'd gone and gotten crushed, probably to death, or most of the way there if he was in *this* place once more.

You did fall, but such was not your purpose. You fought to live, to save, to protect. You have done well, Timuscor.

"Enough to ask for help?" Timuscor still had no idea what this voice was, or where it came from. But it was something unknown, unaccounted for by the priestess. If he could get even the smallest amount of aid, it might be enough to make a difference. With him down, his friends would be even more exposed. All the more reason why a paladin needed to live. Except, of course, that Timuscor was not a paladin.

To aid you now would be to unmake your achievements at the verge of victory. This can only be done by you. I have offered nothing, save for a few prompts to keep working, a modicum of encouragement. All that you have done, you have done on your own. You found the truth of paladins, Timuscor. Now find the truth of yourself.

With no other options, Timuscor closed his eyes—an odd sensation, since he was presumably already unconscious. He was drifting, without the fog. When he focused, he could feel his body, battered and bruised, yet still breathing. As Timuscor's attention lingered on his breath, he felt something more than air being pulled inside his body. Mana. Even now, he was struggling to fight, to act, to do more than die on the ground. Something was different, though. The mana had changed, or rather, the *type* of mana he was drawing in had changed. This was new. Different. This was... divine?

As if the act of noticing had broken some barrier, the flow of direct divine mana increased dramatically, pouring through Timuscor and slowly healing his shattered body. Timuscor was not a quick thinker, nor a fast study. His talents had always been of the physical variety. He was a man more suited to a punch than a discussion. That did not mean he was incapable of learning, of understanding something previously beyond him. Although he moved at his own pace, Timuscor never wavered or halted, and at long last, his journey had reached the summit.

Timuscor finally understood.

* * *

Thistle was still reeling from the shock of seeing Timuscor casually downed when the priestess lumbered forward, her enormous chimera body taking proportionally enormous steps. His mind flew, calculating, reexamining the situation, searching for any advantage they could turn in their favor. A few long shots sprang to mind—try to use Gabrielle's axe himself, or attempt to free Eric's sword—but they were delays at best, and he knew it.

"Grumble, I know I am not always the most devoted or subservient of paladins, and I probably ask for more attention than is due. Even so, if it is within your power to grant a miracle, you would find me eternally grateful." Thistle stood, drawing two of his returning daggers. They weren't blessed, but a paladin fought to the end. Any scrape he could leave, any scratch, any chance at victory, he would take.

"No Grumble. No other gods. Only Kalzidar." The priestess grinned, showing off her warped mouth once more.

The smile was short-lived, however. Her attention suddenly darted across the battlefield. Thistle's was only seconds behind, as the sudden wave of divine mana was impossible to ignore. He half-expected to see Grumble himself arriving on the scene, finally doing some of his own dirty work. What met Thistle's gaze was, somehow, even more shocking than if he'd guessed right.

Timuscor was standing again, leaning on his re-sheathed sword, divine power flowing off him in waves. With every step, his gait improved as more injuries vanished. At his side, Mr. Peppers was keeping pace, caught up in the torrent of mana bursting out of the knight. Was it a spell? Some kind of item effect they'd missed? Maybe the sword had hidden healing properties, and Gabrielle had simply killed the first owner too fast for them to kick in.

More noise caught Thistle's ears, and he turned just in time to see the priestess taking a step back. Intentional movement or not, she was scared, and with good reason. This was an insane amount of mana to be gathering in one place, more than Thistle had seen for a very long time.

Timuscor noticed the movement, too, angling his approach so the priestess was forced away from any of the others. Moving steadily, Timuscor positioned himself directly between Thistle and Grumph, with Eric and a still-wounded Gabrielle making their way over to join them.

"Sorry it took me so long to grasp." There was something different about Timuscor, Thistle realized. While always resolute and loyal, their knight also carried an air of uncertainty about him, an enduring symptom of his unexpectedly gained freedom. For the moment, that uncertainty had vanished. In its place, Thistle found an almost terrifying level of dedication.

"My mistake was looking in the past." As he spoke, Timuscor adjusted his shield and armor, doing the best he could with the sections that had been dented. "It was never about who I was, or where I came from. And it wasn't about the gods, either. They make it easier, more accessible, but the power has never been solely theirs to grant."

Reaching down, he pet Mr. Peppers, who looked like he was glowing with power. The divine energy around Timuscor wasn't dissipating at all—if anything, it was getting stronger. Reaching back, Timuscor once again drew the spare blade from its sheath. There was a flicker of something in its steel, a curiosity Thistle would no doubt have investigated further if not for his friend's sudden transformation into a magical tornado.

"Timuscor, what in the heavens is happening?"

He didn't receive a direct answer. Instead, Timuscor started forward once more, sword pointed directly at the priestess. "Yield to me, now. Renounce Kalzidar while you still draw breath. Break his grip upon your soul while it is still possible, or be cut down."

From anyone else, the priestess might have laughed, but there was nothing funny about the amount of divine mana flowing around Timuscor. Still, she was smart, and had probably noticed the same issue as Thistle: the mana was unfocused. It made a dangerous aura around Timuscor, but fell vastly short of what such magic could accomplish when directed. This had turned into a harder fight for the priestess, not an impossible one.

There was no masking the deep, aching hatred in her eyes as she glared down at Timuscor. "You think to turn me from my course? That a weak adventurer is going to defeat Kalzidar's chosen? No, I do not believe so. I refuse your offer, knight. Strike me down if you have the power." The priestess was calling his bluff.

To Thistle's surprise, Timuscor nodded. "You are right that I am weak, compared to the powerful warriors of the world. But I have the strength to stand here, to face you. That's all the calling ever was, really. We put so much ceremony and divine law on it, yet at the end of the day, it is simply the will to stand between the innocent and the wicked. And anyone can choose to make that stand. My failing was in seeing the calling as something to die for, rather than a cause that must drive one to keep living. One cannot make an oath without both conviction *and* understanding."

For the first time, Thistle suspected what was actually going on, and his eyes grew enormous. If his guess was right, if this was real, then Timuscor was about to do something supposedly impossible outside of ancient myths. At Timuscor's words, the power increased even more, radiating off the young man who stood in the heart of the storm.

"Perhaps you will be proven right in your assessment of the fight, as well. You are certainly powerful; I can admit that my failure is possible. Just know that you are wrong on one account without question. I no longer serve any kingdom, and therefore, cannot rightly be called a knight."

Timuscor lifted his backup blade higher, the metal flashing once more. "I pledge my sword to the innocent in need. I shall serve the kind, and the weak, and all who seek to live in peace. For so long as I live, I will strive to protect, to save, to endure." The light was burning now, a white fire in the center of the field. Thistle could barely even stare into it anymore, yet he forced himself to continue. Given what he expected to come next, there needed to be a witness.

Deep in the light's center, a figure remained barely visible—Timuscor standing unbothered by the ridiculous amount of magic around him. Raising his head, his eyes met the priestess's, absolute certainty reflected in their depths.

"My name is Timuscor, and I *am* a paladin."

For the second time that day, an explosion of power tore across the enclosed battlefield.

*   *   *

Standing outside the dome, Simone had taken a few dozen steps back as the tremendous amount of divine magic grew steadily stronger. Despite the obfuscation meant to hide the fight from her eyes, Simone was more than experienced enough to enchant her sight and pierce the veil. At first, she'd feared it was a spell cast solely so she could witness the adventurers' deaths, but as soon as Timuscor rose, Simone realized she was seeing far more than that.

As a woman who specialized in working with the undead, divine magic was something she knew nearly as much about as her own subject. It was a worthless mage who didn't learn all they could about their weaknesses.

She knew about gods, and priests, and paladins, but Simone had more knowledge than what they were now. Simone knew their histories, their myths, even the tales of their origins.

There had always been legends about paladins. Many faiths held that they were, and always had been, servants of the gods. But others taught truth over dogma, insisting that the first paladins were not given their power by the gods at all. Rather, they were mortals who found a way to tap into the divine aspect living within the mana that flowed through all things, who could draw on it without needing to filter the mana first, direct from the source. It seemed like such a little thing, and yet, what it represented was incredible.

Almost every person in the world could pull in mana in its raw form, then slowly draw out the aspects they needed. It was part of why paladins and priests were not able to heal indefinitely. Even if they were constantly absorbing small amounts of mana, they needed time to filter it down to the divine aspect. The power to draw a specific type directly from the mana stream would require a level of synchronicity that boggled the mind. Someone would have to be so completely, so thoroughly merged with the essence of such magic that they could pull upon it like the power was their own.

No wonder the gods had taken over passing out the role of paladin. Not only would the natural paladins be few and far between, the kind of strength they wielded was beholden to no master. Creating their own paladins, giving them the ability to slowly draw out divine magic, ensured that they would have a force of loyal holy warriors who could be replaced as troops were lost. And over time, in what had certainly been an unexpected bonus, the first path to paladinhood had been lost. The few who might have made it on their own instead pledged themselves to the gods, because that was the only route they knew.

Personally, Simone had always considered herself a skeptic. She of course believed in demonstrable things, such as gods and spells, forces that were provable. The idea that anyone could manage to forge a connection between themselves and a specific aspect of magic had always seemed ridiculously farfetched. She'd dismissed it as a favorite theory of those who simply hated paladins. However, Simone was also willing to admit when she'd been wrong. The study of magic demanded such humility, if one wanted to reach its highest levels. And given what she was watching happen now, Simone backed up a touch more as she swallowed the seemingly ridiculous truth.

When Timuscor raised his hand and began to speak, Simone wove a shield in front of herself, just to be safe. There could be no doubt about it now. She could see more than just the torrent of magic surrounding the former knight; her eyes showed her the strands of mana weaving through his body, joining to the bright nova of light that was in his soul. Even before the oath was done—simple words meant merely as a vessel to express the conviction within—she knew. When the explosion washed over the battlefield, burning away the obfuscation from the dome, Simone was prepared. She waited eagerly, unable to suppress her inherent curiosity. Regardless of the fact that it came from divine magic, this was a moment worth witnessing.

For the first time in unknown centuries, a free paladin was being born.

52.

As soon as he could see, Eric's first concern was Gabrielle. Given a blast of divine magic like that and her already weakened state, he was afraid he'd open his eyes to find nothing but ash. To his shock, she was unharmed by the explosion; her only wounds were the slowly-healing ones she'd taken in the battle. And yet, Eric felt his own body moving more easily. Not every wound was fully healed, but he was no longer bleeding from the slashing blows the ravisher had managed to land during their fight. Nearby, he could see Thistle and Grumph both looking over, the same expression of concern on their faces.

"I'm okay," Gabrielle announced when she caught sight of their expressions. "Somehow, it passed me over."

"Of course, it passed you over. Undead or alive, you're a good person. This power is meant to fight the wicked. I would never permit it to harm an innocent." Timuscor's voice was still strong, echoing forth as the light around him faded. When it was gone, what stood before them was a man who looked much the same as he always had—same blond hair and dented armor, same wide shoulders and tall frame, even the same stance as he gauged his enemy. What had changed was something in his face. It was as if the determination he'd risen with had crystallized in him, fundamentally replacing his previous core of uncertainty.

Thistle, on the other hand, looked like he'd just tried to swallow a ghost. "You mean to say that you purposefully excluded Gabrielle from that effect on our area? Without any spell training or preparation, that would require a level of control on a near-instinctual level, like you were commanding a muscle."

"A fine analogy. That's exactly how I would describe the sensation," Timuscor agreed, his attention still locked on the priestess. She had fared much worse in the explosion and was covering her face with a pair of now singed and smoking arms, clearly on the defensive.

With the storm of divine magic finally subsided, the priestess lifted her head from her arms, reassessing the battlefield. A snort from her malformed lips sent leaves spreading everywhere as she rose to her feet once more. At a towering fifteen feet high, she was still a terrifying opponent to face down—with her ravisher-like skin and thorny wooden armor she looked more monster than person. Compared to her, Timuscor looked like little more than a child holding a needle. A needle that was softly glowing, Eric realized. When did that borrowed blade start to light up?

"All that for a minor area attack? You disappoint me, knight." With a contemptuous wave, the priestess fired vines from both her hands. It was clear she planned on overwhelming Timuscor, so he couldn't block.

Dodging to the side, Timuscor avoided the attack from her right arm, but allowed the left's vines to wrap around his shield and hand. Before she could pull them tight, he swept his blade across the leafy tendrils, slicing them through like simple strands of grass. At the touch of his sword, the vines burst into flame. This was not a mere quick flash, like when the blessed weapons hit. Blue-white flames leapt along the grassy surface, climbing up the vines toward their source. Much as the adventurers would have loved to see the priestess torched, she released the vines to the ground before the flames could reach her hand. Interestingly, Eric noted that the normal grass didn't catch fire.

"Your sword..." The priestess glared down at Timuscor, taking note of the new glow on his blade at last.

For the first time since he'd gotten up, Timuscor looked momentarily confused. "As I hoped, the rush of divine power was enough to bless my weapon, although I didn't expect it to work quite *this* well." There was more than light coming off that blade, Eric noted as he focused his vision. There were runes as well, deeply layered magic. Timuscor might have blessed the blade, but unless he'd attained the power of a god, there was no way he'd added all those enchantments that were now flickering into action.

"You have no idea what that is. You cannot wield such a weapon! Those only come to life in the hands of a... worthy... *paladin.*" The priestess's eyes narrowed. "It seems you spoke true, former knight. I don't know how you've done this, but I know my master will reward me greatly for the death of a paladin."

She leapt forward, abandoning the use of vines and instead leaning on the enormous reach of her arms. Swinging low, her first fist barely missed Timuscor as he ducked to the side. He raced in, trying to get closer, but with a single step back, the priestess reclaimed the space she'd given up while forcing him to dive out of the way. He slashed at her arms, leaving flaming scars in the bark, but this didn't catch fire and spread like the vines had. It was still impressive enough that even an off-handed slash easily parted the organic armor, leaving exposed sections of the priestess's forearm in view.

Despite finally being able to hit her, Timuscor was at a disadvantage, thanks to her size and reach. If she landed one of those direct blows, he'd be hurt, and there had to be a limit on miraculous recoveries in a day. More than once felt like pushing their luck. He needed their help.

Aiding Gabrielle, Eric helped her over to where Thistle and Grumph were lying. "What can we do?"

"Enough mana for one more invigoration." Grumph was looking rough; the wave of divine magic and Thistle's healing spells were all that had gotten him strong enough to talk.

"I may be able to serve as a minor distraction," Thistle added. "But it will be hard to turn her eyes to anyone but Timuscor."

Eric was having the same thoughts. How were they going to help? She'd beaten them fairly handily already, and that was before she'd consolidated her minions into one powerful threat. Then again, that strategy had drawbacks, too. Instead of many targets, they now had only a single enemy to deal with. Separating them at the start of the fight was a smart technique; the party leaned on their teamwork and trust to overcome individual weaknesses. Now, with a potent distraction, they had a chance to make something happen.

Looking over the situation, an idea popped into Eric's head. It was more than a little crazy, and could very well cost him his life. That normally might have given him a brief pause, but after watching Timuscor rise to fight from the brink of death, Eric felt a burning determination in his chest. Although he'd heard legends that some paladins could inspire their allies, Eric had never been able to imagine what that effect might be like. As it turned out, he rather enjoyed it. His fears weren't gone—fears were too essential to one's survival to lose entirely—yet they were shadows of their former selves. Eric could see clearly, his mind unclouded by worry or terror, and he knew what he had to do.

"Grumph, cast the invigoration on me," Eric said. "I've got a plan."

"Does it have anything to do with the giant shape running toward us?" Gabrielle pointed over her shoulder, where a mighty mound of metal was gleaming in the moonlight. Eric paused to wonder when the dark haze of the dome had vanished, but his attention was quickly captured by the creature's surprisingly graceful movements.

"Shockingly, no, it does not." Eric held his arm out for Grumph to cast on; they didn't have much time to lose. "But I am extremely curious to see where that goes."

*   *   *

    Timuscor could hear the others talking, though he was too far off to make out what they were saying, especially as he dove under another massive fist digging into the ground. His armor, normally a saving grace against enemies, was hindering his movements, making it harder to dodge. Even as strength beyond his own surged through his limbs, those same appendages were locked away in the suit of metal. He needed mobility, but the priestess would hardly agree to a pause so he could strip some bits of armor away. Fortunately, Timuscor knew he wasn't alone. He hadn't understood why Mr. Peppers had run off during the explosion, not until he heard the charge approaching. Of course, at his new size, the boar would need more room for a running start.

    To his surprise, Timuscor realized he didn't even need to look away. He could feel Mr. Peppers' movements, even from a distance. The same divine glow that now permeated Timuscor was radiating from his partner, only it didn't feel new. This had always been Mr. Peppers; he'd been ready since the first day. Timuscor was the one who'd needed to catch up, and now that he had, the boar's true power was finally on display.

    As dangerous as Timuscor's blade was, the thundering sound of an enormous, armor-covered boar rushing toward her was enough to draw some of the priestess's attention away from the weapon. Her arm rose, aiming those damned vines, but Timuscor rushed the other side, taking advantage of the distraction. With two threats closing in, the priestess chose to stop the paladin rather than the big pig.

    That turned out to be a poor decision. Mr. Peppers' now-enormous tusks tore a slice through the back of her left leg, leaving a flash of blue-white flames smoldering briefly in the wound. Her scream was equal parts pain and frustration as she turned her eyes toward the large, escaping form. "How? How did you bless a mere animal already?"

    "I didn't. Mr. Peppers needs no blessings, for he shares all of mine." Timuscor held out a hand as the huge boar passed him, taking hold of a grip in the armor and swinging onto the massive metal back. May the heavens bless Shandor. That smith had realized this might happen and built the armor to accommodate a rider. "He's my partner, you see. For what is a paladin without his trusty mount?"

Timuscor swept the battlefield as Mr. Peppers ran, his faithful companion easily destroying the issue of mobility. Thistle was up, daggers in hand. Gabrielle and Grumph were recovering slowly; neither would likely be able to jump in again soon. Eric was running, but not toward the priestess. It looked almost as if he was fleeing the battle. Then Timuscor looked a touch ahead of Eric, and understanding set in. He turned back to Thistle, who simply nodded.

In a way, it was the simplest plan there was, a classic that dated back to the earliest days of their legends and myths: the paladin held the enemy's attention while the rogue snuck around. Timuscor liked that; there was something to be said for the classics. Especially in perilous situations. With one touch, he turned Mr. Peppers, sending his mount back toward the priestess.

As a knight, Timuscor had received ample training in both riding and fighting on horseback. Riding a giant boar was a different experience, yet it all felt strangely familiar. Perhaps it was part of being a paladin, or the simple fact that he was connected to the creature he rode, but Timuscor was completely comfortable after less than a minute on Mr. Peppers' back. A fortunate break, because they were going to have to work together if they wanted to survive.

The moment they drew near, a fresh wave of vines shot out, arcing for Mr. Peppers' legs. He made no attempt to dodge, permitting the vines to wrap around his legs as fast as they could, and tearing them apart with every heavy step. The moment the vines hit Mr. Peppers' skin, they wilted, their magic faltering, leaving them as little more than true weeds—the sort easily uprooted. At least they'd be able to get close without much issue, not that things would be easier once they were within fist-swinging range.

Her first attack came down hard, sending a spray of dirt across Mr. Peppers' side as he jerked left, avoiding the blow. That order hadn't come from Timuscor, nor did the next one, which led to Mr. Peppers suddenly speeding up to avoid a glancing strike. Mr. Peppers wasn't just running; he was the one in charge of their route and defense, freeing Timuscor up to focus on fighting. The paladin did precisely that, and when the next fist swung down, he was ready.

Mr. Peppers banked hard to the right, avoiding the descending arm, but Timuscor leaned left with his sword raised, raking the blade across the priestess's arm. While he couldn't slash deeply at that angle, the howl of pain from the priestess proved how effective even a minor wound was. His blade caused her serious pain, even when only cutting her armor. What would happen if he could finally manage to pierce her flesh? With any luck, something bad for her and good for them, though Timuscor was a long way off from landing such a blow. He was harassing her, keeping her attention on him so she wouldn't think to go after the others. If she tried, they both knew he'd capitalize and she'd regret it.

Unfortunately, that left them in something of a stalemate. She had trouble hitting him atop Mr. Peppers, and Timuscor couldn't get near enough to do any real damage without her retreating. Something would have to give, or it would come down to a battle of skills.

Behind the priestess, Timuscor caught sight of a slinking figure. He urged Mr. Peppers to charge once more. If there was any chance of this working, he needed the priestess to be completely focused on him. One stray glance, and this day would take a very bloody, tragic turn.

Spurring his boar on faster, Timuscor lifted the glowing blade high, making sure the priestess knew that he was coming to do harm. As she lowered her stance to face him, the figure behind her made a quick hop and left Timuscor's line of sight. There was no reaction from the priestess, meaning Timuscor had succeeded in distracting her. Now, he had to make sure her attention never wandered.

After all, it would be a poor showing if, on his first outing as a paladin, he couldn't even serve as a proper distraction for a climbing rogue.

53.

Was there any way to be prepared for scaling a giant enemy who would crush you to bits upon discovery? If so, Eric had to imagine that he was as close as one could possibly come. His body still tingled with the augmentation Grumph had given him—enough strength to pull his short sword from the ground at last. The magical boots had brought him here swiftly, and his color-camouflaging armor helped him make the approach unseen. Grumph had even lent Eric the magical ring, offering him some chance of survival if he was caught. So many things were in his favor, yet Eric felt woefully out of his depth as he leapt onto the back of the priestess's dense leg armor.

She showed no reaction when he landed on her, her attention fully on Timuscor. That was the first hurdle cleared: either she couldn't feel things on this armor, or sensation was subdued enough to not notice a human slowing her down. How strong was she that she didn't even notice his weight? More determined than ever not to find out firsthand, Eric started to climb, making his way higher up her body.

At fifteen feet, it wasn't an especially tall height to scale; however, the going was difficult. On top of having to stay unnoticed and silent, Eric had to carefully avoid the scores of thorns poking out from the bark-like armor itself. No doubt, the protection was meant to stave off precisely this kind of assault. Too bad for the priestess, Eric had been trained by one of the most merciless, and talented, rogues he'd ever heard of. Elora's teaching methods were brutal, yet, as Eric swung up from the leg to the lower back, avoiding piercing his flesh, it was hard not to feel a swell of gratitude for her.

He was forced to momentarily halt his climb, as Timuscor came into range and slashed at the priestess while she did her best to hit him right back. If she'd punched him down instead of over the first time, Timuscor would certainly have been crushed, and Eric suspected she was dearly regretting that mistake. Of course, it meant she'd be less likely to make it again, which added to the precariousness of Eric's situation.

When Timuscor rode past, swinging wide in a circle, Eric began to move once more. It wouldn't be long before the next engagement; Timuscor was purposefully keeping her off balance and defensive. The priestess moved too much in battle, so Eric had to make the most of these windows. He got halfway up her back before Timuscor returned, forcing him to hang on while his target darted to and fro, trying to strike without being hit in return.

Another pause, and Eric made it to just below the priestess's shoulders. Almost there; one more climb would get him home. Unfortunately, Timuscor's charge forced the priestess to literally jump backward, lifting and then slamming Eric roughly down against her back. He winced as a few thorns pressed tight against his chest, not quite puncturing his armor. Mentally thanking Grumph for the loan of his ring, which had almost certainly made the difference, Eric groaned inwardly. Despite his control and lack of sound, the jig was already up.

"What?" The priestess started to turn toward him. Of course. When he'd come down hard on her back, she must have felt the impact. With no chance to think, he had to make a choice in the moment. There was enough time to drop and run; he was limber and could dodge a few attacks if needed. That was on the ground, though. Up here, he was an easy target. Sadly, Eric also knew that if he took that route, she'd be wary for more climbers. This trick either worked now, or not at all.

Using his augmented strength for all it was worth, Eric hurled himself upward, onto the priestess's shoulder. Thorns punched into his left palm as he took the first grip he could find. Stealth was no longer a priority, nor was safety. Everything that wasn't speed lost all relevance. Using his free, uninjured hand, Eric whipped out his short sword. Nearby, he noticed Timuscor drawing close with another charge. Good. She would need to split her attention, and that meant one of them would have a chance to land a blow.

Her left hand reached across her chest, on a direct path to knock Eric from her shoulders, while her right came plummeting down toward Timuscor and Mr. Peppers. Neither strike was as accurate as it should have been, the split attention showing itself. Timuscor easily dodged his blow while leaving a wound on her armor, and Eric narrowly got out of the way, throwing himself onto the priestess's head. More thorns tore into his left hand as he took careful hold of an armored section on her brow.

"A pest. A useless pest who would sting me with a metal weapon my skin will repel. You are infuriatingly stubborn prey. Accept Kalzidar's judgment!"

"Going to have to politely decline that offer." Eric swung up while he spoke, building momentum as he saw both her hands coming to snap him in half. "Also, in your next life, I would urge you to learn one simple fact about humanoid bodies. There's a reason the ravishers lack sight. Eyes don't have skin."

Coming back down from the swing, Eric used all of his momentum and augmented strength to stab his short sword directly into her enormous right eyeball.

*   *   *

If Timuscor thought his own attacks drew shrieks of pain, it was nothing on the horrendous howl that split the battlefield when Eric struck. Her hands were already on course to claw the rogue, who was still drawing small flashes of light as he attacked, making sure the damage was done. The instant she caught Eric, he'd be dead, which meant that Timuscor couldn't allow her to succeed. Thankfully, Eric had had the good sense to wait until Timuscor was already charging and nearly upon her.

For the first time in the fight, Timuscor and Mr. Peppers were able to get close to the priestess without having to dodge her attacks. Using the freedom, Timuscor rose high on his mount's back, leaning in and slashing at the priestess's leg as he passed. Unlike previous strikes, this one was able to bite deep, past the armor, and into her supposedly protected flesh. Several runes along the blade flashed as Timuscor made contact, leaving a trail of blue-white fire burning on the outer side of her left leg.

Evidently, the flames must have *hurt*. This time, it wasn't her armor or her vines that were aflame; it was the priestess herself. Those clutching hands suddenly changed direction, all thought of her eye momentarily dispelled by the need to put out the flames on her leg before they could spread.

Practically speaking, it was the right call; Timuscor couldn't fault her for it. If that fire spread, she could be roasted before there was time to act. But every action in battle came with a cost—doing one task meant that there were others left unattended to. In this case, saving her own life left a rogue with a blessed weapon free to do as he pleased for the next few seconds.

Such a mistake wasn't lost on Eric, who immediately took hold of a chunk of armor along her nose and flipped around so that he was now looking at her left eye. For the priestess, Eric must have filled up her entire field of sight. It was the last image to be burned into her vision before the steel struck.

Timuscor heard the screech before he saw the flashes. He was getting close again, ready to provide Eric with a distraction, but the rogue leapt clear of the priestess and rolled along the grass before coming to a stop. Eric rose quickly, giving Timuscor a thumbs-up. It was done; the priestess had been blinded. As a rogue, he couldn't hope to help with the magical armor that still protected her and the ravisher-fortified skin. So instead, he'd made Timuscor's task easier.

The flames on the priestess's legs had gone out after she smothered them, so her hands were free to grope aimlessly along the ground. With her vision gone, she knew Timuscor would be coming, just not from where. For a moment, he hesitated. Was this right? Was there honor in slaying a weakened opponent? His vision turned to the still-wounded bodies of Grumph and Gabrielle, where Thistle tended to them. This woman served evil; she had tried to murder several of his friends without remorse and would kill many more if given the chance. The paladin's resolve set. He'd sworn to stand against evil, and that meant seeing things through to the end.

Although there was clearly no hiding the sound of a giant boar making a charge, merely knowing the direction he was coming from wasn't enough. Mr. Peppers had been capable of dodging when she'd made targeted attacks; he easily slipped around as she smashed the ground in futile fury now. Timuscor lined up his own slice carefully, starting a new fire as he carved deep into her right calf.

Shrieking, the priestess stumbled as she tried to smother the flames, her weakened leg buckling under the weight, bringing her to a knee. This was what Timuscor had been waiting for. Rather than ride Mr. Peppers out wide for momentum, Timuscor circled him right back around. Over the sound of her own fury and pain, the slower boar managed to slip in close. Timuscor got as high as he could, sword at the ready.

Mr. Peppers ran directly into her left leg, causing her to sway unsteadily. Timuscor, however, had a different target. Using her lowered position and his height atop the boar, he drove his sword deep into her abdomen—through the armor, through the skin, and into her organs. True, between the armor and the size difference, his weapon couldn't reach very far, but the blow landed clean just the same. When Timuscor pulled his blade out, it wasn't fire that met his eyes. Rather, a burning light shone from the wound, growing steadily in intensity.

On instinct, Timuscor urged Mr. Peppers back, guiding the boar away as fast as they could get. It proved to be a wise decision, as soon a wave of dark bile escaped the priestess's mouth, washing over and killing the grass at her feet. Her armor began to fall away in jagged, rotten chunks, and her grassy sections withered before their eyes.

The priestess was shrinking as the light grew brighter, her power rolling off in waves. From somewhere in her foliage, the staff holding a piece of the Bridge clattered to the ground. Had she been able to see it, they might have worried, but as things stood, the priestess barely seemed to be holding on. Her hands were over the wound in her stomach, trying to smother a fire that wasn't there. Timuscor understood. The fire was inside her now, burning away the dark magic infusing her body. It occurred to Timuscor that, were she able to hit him with a similar weapon of evil, he might very well endure the same process.

Moving steadily, Timuscor dismounted from Mr. Peppers and walked back toward the priestess. He noted that the others followed and made no move to stop them. If she still had a trick left, it was better they all see it so they could fight back. Standing over her, Timuscor looked down at the woman. She was dying, and fast. Soon, she would be beyond saving.

"It's not too late. You still live. You still have the freedom of choice. That wound will kill you; I don't think any of us could save you, even if it was right to do so. But your soul will live on. Do not allow Kalzidar to claim it. Renounce him, here and now, with sincerity in your heart. He is a cruel god to dwell with, even more so to those who have failed him."

Despite being blinded and bleeding, the priestess managed a laugh. This was no chuckling at the gallows, either; there was sincere joy in her. "Failed him? Oh my, you may be a paladin now, but you have much to learn about the ways of gods. I have not failed my master at all. He ordered me to contain you all here, to fight you; he even gave me the freedom to kill all but Thistle. However, such was never my true task. I am a messenger, and in losing this fight, my message only becomes all the more important. Where is Thistle, enemy of Kalzidar? Have him come close so he can see the truth in my words."

Without hesitation, Thistle approached. "I'm here. I presume this has something to do with why I wasn't permitted to be killed?"

"Indeed it does." The priestess faltered, letting out a hack of a cough. "Damn it. I wish I could savor this moment, but time draws short. I'll content myself with savoring your pain instead. Kalzidar doesn't want you dead; that's too easy a punishment for a paladin. He wants you to suffer. There were many reasons to break into the Vault of Sealed Magics, not just to take the Helm of Ignosa. In that place are many wonders and items to do seemingly impossible things... things like enter the Hall of Souls and pull one from its afterlife."

The realization hit Thistle harder than one of her giant punches ever could. He'd been wrong. Kalzidar wasn't going after Grumble at all. No, the god of dark magic was targeting Thistle, but not by coming after him directly.

"That's right. Kalzidar took her while you were busy fighting with me. I'm so close to passing, I can feel my master's delight. He says to follow the crows, paladin, and eventually, perhaps, you will find her." She looked over at him, empty sockets gazing directly at Thistle. "Tell me, before I join her, any words for your beloved wife, Madroria?"

Thistle's hand was on his dagger, raising the weapon overhead, but it was pointless. The priestess slumped to the ground as the light in her guts faded out. She was dead. Timuscor's attack had done its job.

Which left Thistle no other outlet for his rage and pain than to scream, stabbing his dagger pointlessly to the ground. No one interrupted him; they were still reeling from the news themselves.

Finally, after a few minutes, Thistle managed to calm himself. When he rose, however, something had changed.

There was coldness in his eyes, an expression that almost none of them had seen before. Without meaning to, Grumph shuddered. Unlike the others, he did know that look. And he understood what side of Thistle Kalzidar had just set loose.

54.

The platform was finally in sight. Unfortunately, in the time it took them to reach it, the situation had grown substantially more dire. A new wave of automatons was pressed against the guards, and several more inhuman adversaries now blocked the pathway to the platform itself. From where Wimberly and the others were standing, there was a long, glass-like bridge running to the golden-trimmed area where portals flickered into and out of existence as escaping people ran through them. Given that the bridge material was supporting several guards and automatons, the latter of whom were smashing against it, all while getting only small cracks, it seemed a safe bet that this was not mundane glass, if it was in fact glass at all.

But strong as the material was, the automatons *were* causing cracks. Small as they might be, every repeat blow added to them. With enough time and attackers, they would bring this bridge down just as they would break the platform itself. There was no stopping the automaton army; the most any of them could hope for was to escape while there was still time.

Timanuel and Hoit led the charge. It was their only option, and everyone knew it. Fighting was out, and there were too many automatons to distract. All they could do was run forward and pray that they'd survive. They were nearly to the first set of automatons when a figure landed hard on the bridge in front of them, causing the group to hurriedly skid to a halt. At a glance, there was something about this man that spoke deep into their souls and told them to be wary.

It wasn't just the rippling muscles, or the glow of untold enchantments racing across his skin, or the way shadows kept his face unnaturally obscured. It was in the way he moved, in the calm that rolled off him even as he stared down the impossible odds. Was this one of Lumal's elite? Wimberly glanced over to Hoit and the guards, all of whom were looking extremely confused. Not one of theirs, then. So, just another adventurer?

"If you've got a heartbeat, and you want to keep it that way, stay behind me. Been some while since I fought seriously, and the augmentation spells my wizard cast only make me more dangerous. I can't promise you won't get caught in the splash."

No one had time to ask what "the splash" was before the hulking man before them became a blur, too fast to properly track. His fist smashed into the nearest automaton, shattering the arm it managed to raise in the nick of time. The second blow was on the heels of the first, less than a second behind, and this one connected with the automaton's metal head. Chunks of scrap tore through the air, debris from the automaton turned into a makeshift projectile by the sheer force of the blow.

Wimberly's breath caught within her chest at the sight of such strength. At least that explained what "the splash" meant. Against a normal enemy, it would have been incredibly impressive. Against an automaton that had taken three fully trained and well-equipped guards to subdue, it was outright miraculous. Who in the hells had this kind of power, and why didn't she know them?

As the thoughts hit, a blue smoke wafted down onto the battlefield. Turning her head up, Wimberly caught sight of a fellow gnome floating above, sending the smoke spiraling towards them. When it touched her, Wimberly's eyes grew unfocused for a brief instant, before returning to normal. Except, as she looked at their savior, Wimberly noticed that he remained out of focus. Wait, had it even been a he? She couldn't quite picture the warrior anymore, just an overwhelming image of muscles and power.

The gnome was casting a memory spell. Had it been viable, Wimberly would have yelled at the woman, demanding an explanation. She was too high up, unfortunately; Wimberly would catch the attention of automatons long before the wizard took notice. Moving fast, Wimberly yanked out her sketchbook and began to draw. Usually, this was where she put down design ideas for new gadgets, but at that moment, her only goal was to capture the memory before it faded completely. Wimberly didn't try to bring up the face in her mind; the more she tried, the further away it slipped. She just drew, trusting her hands and instincts to remember what her brain refused to. There was a chance that this had no point—the man was a stranger to her even before the memory spell—but someone didn't want Wimberly to remember this. That alone was plenty enough reason for her to consider it worth hanging on to.

It took Wimberly under a minute to finish her sketch, which was enough time for their savior to clear every automaton off the bridge. He ran toward the platform proper now, viciously hurling or shattering each enemy he encountered. Their way forward was clear, so the party pushed ahead, not wasting this opportunity.

It didn't escape Wimberly's notice that the platform was beginning to sway, however. The automatons below had done too much damage—two of the four support pillars were compromised. As fast as the unmemorable warrior was, there was no way he'd be capable of making it down there in time. Were they hoping to evacuate everyone before the platform fell? It was an ambitious plan, to say the least, but given the chaos Lumal was in, that might be the only option they could manage.

Sounds like an earthquake, a deep rumbling, were Wimberly's first clue that she had miscalculated. With the memory fog engaged, it appeared the wizard had turned her attention to actually aiding the people in need. Four sets of huge arms, made of dirt and stone, burst out of the ground, followed by four heads and bodies. A quartet of gigantic earth elementals rose, two taking the place of the damaged pillars, two working to sweep away the attacking automatons. Although the metal saboteurs didn't seem damaged by the elementals, the sheer size difference between them made it simple for the earthen behemoths to send automatons flying.

Wimberly's eyes went back to the other gnome with a new level of respect. Those elementals *had* to be ancient, for them to be so large. Summoning even one took a mage of exceptional skill. To summon four at once, this woman must have been among the top casters in the entire world. Wimberly wasn't even surprised to notice that her eyes went unfocused when she looked at the wizard. These two didn't want to be remembered, and with the kind of power they were throwing around, Wimberly could think of ample reasons why.

All of that was interesting, but also secondary compared to their race for the portals. Getting through, making it out of this place where they were little more useful than mere farmers or peasants, was their primary goal. This short time of feeling helpless had given Wimberly a new appreciation for what non-adventurers must feel like in a world of monsters that could kill them with a single blow. Already, the gears inside her head were turning, contemplating new types of gadgets that anyone could use. Wimberly shoved such notions aside. They were good, useful thoughts for down the line, but today, her focus was on living through the next hour.

An unmistakable din of colliding metal rose from behind them, and Wimberly already knew what she'd find as she turned. A new battalion of automatons had arrived at the head of the bridge, at least a dozen strong. Worse, the huge warrior was already on the platform, meaning that the party itself was blocking him from getting over to help. That was assuming he'd even noticed the new trouble brewing; the man was a blur as he sent one enemy after another flying off the platform's edge, but there were *so* many. He wouldn't be done in time to help, even if that was his desire.

"Run!" Timanuel gave the order, not that they had any other real option. On this bridge, with no room to maneuver, they'd be ripped through in seconds. At least on the platform, they would have a chance to get out of the way. The party and guards sprinted as one, dashing across the cracking, glass-like bridge with all they had.

Most of them made it. They could be forgiven, in the heat of all that was happening, for failing to remember that one of their members was smaller—and proportionally slower—than the rest. As soon as he made it to the platform, Timanuel stepped aside, clearing a path while preparing to hold off any automatons on their heels, and looked back, if only for a few seconds. It was only then that he saw Wimberly, their eyes meeting as she raced with all she had, still substantially behind the others. He tried to move toward her; however, the rest of the party rushing past barred his route.

When the shadow fell across Wimberly's path, she knew what it was immediately. No other creature would be casting such a broad, unnatural shape in the light of Lumal's burning buildings. She turned, not because she wanted to fight, nor imagined there would be some surprise waiting. Wimberly merely decided, in that moment, that if she was going to die, then she would face her end head-on. What awaited her was precisely what she'd expected—an automaton raising its fist. She readied for the end, even as her brain scrambled to find some weakness to exploit. Then, the fist moved.

For a flicker of a moment, Wimberly thought the blow was so strong she'd died without even feeling it. But the attack never actually hit her. She could still see the fist, frozen, roughly a foot from her face. Peering around it carefully, Wimberly noted that the other automatons behind her would-be killer were frozen as well. In fact, as her eyes scanned the area, she couldn't see so much as a single trace of moving metal.

What had been Lumal's greatest threat was now a collection of statues dotting its landscape, all perfectly frozen, some midway through a step or attack. A few fell over; however, the majority were balanced enough to stay standing. With slow, terrified steps, Wimberly backed away from the automaton, half-expecting it to fly back into action. There was no movement as her pace picked up and eventually turned into a run. She joined the others on the platform, and still there was nothing. Not from the nearby automatons, nor any of the ones they could see throughout the city.

All of Ignosa's Unfeeling Army had gone still as the grave.

*   *   *

Slipping out of a room that connected to another plane, carefully closing her bag, Fritz noticed a fleck of blood on the floor that hadn't been there earlier. Using her long, elven ears to give a proper listen, she realized there were sounds coming from farther along the tunnel. It didn't seem to be fighting, which meant the battle had probably already finished. Turning, Fritz made her way up the hall, easily avoiding a few traps and countermeasures meant to slow or kill thieves when the Vault was locked down.

It only took a few minutes before she found what she'd expected. This room might have been a lounge or a study, one of the spots designated for visitors to peruse tomes they weren't permitted to remove. Whatever furniture had been here was largely in splinters, save only for a single chair. In it sat Kieran, holding the head of an unremarkable man with dark hair upon which perched a metal crown. Scorch marks ran up and down the walls, and a half-dozen automatons were scattered about in various states of disrepair. The image it painted was of a hard battle, but Fritz knew better. At best, the priest would have let loose one torrent of magic before Kieran reached him. This whole scene had probably manifested within the span of seconds. Long fights were the realm of knights and paladins, not assassins.

"I see you did the job." Fritz was careful to keep her tone neutral. It had been a long time since Kieran dressed in black; he unnerved even her in such a state. There were few things that still scared Fritz, but the people of Notch were ones she didn't dare take lightly. Especially those who watched over it. Everyone else had put the killing behind them, but Notch's guardians were willing to soak their hands in blood if the need arose, if only to make sure the rest didn't have to.

"I'd hoped to simply take the crown. He either invoked a spell to bind it to his head, or the crown can create such an effect on its own. Whatever the case, it wasn't coming off. So I found another way, as I always have." The head in his hands was dripping, yet not so much as a spot stuck to Kieran's outfit. Having it enchanted against blood was one of the most practical purchases he'd ever made, a fact that sometimes still kept the man up at night. "Hopefully, it was just me. If Jolia saw someone and failed to save them, she'll be down the bottle for a month, and last time Brock had to kill again, he locked himself away for weeks to work on the tavern."

Fritz didn't have comfort to offer on that front, so she stuck with the truth. "I didn't see anything besides automatons here. Odds are good that's all they've had to deal with."

"There are at least three other priests out there, though I imagine most of them have escaped by now. That's how they managed to get so much from the Vault before it was sealed off. All of them struck simultaneously, stealing their targets at the same time. Once the safeguards kicked in, they already had everything they wanted. The Chronoglass is over in the corner; it had to stay here to work. They escaped with two other items, one of which concerns us on a personal level, and the other that should worry us for practical reasons."

"Your priest managed to talk that much before he died?" Fritz asked.

In response, Kieran produced a sheet of parchment from a pocket on his shirt and held it out. Stepping around the debris, Fritz made her way over and took it from his hand, giving it a thorough perusal. "Huh. He knew he was going to die here, so he made a taunting monologue in letter form. That is… dedication?" As her eyes kept going, the pieces clicked together. "Well now, this makes more sense. Stealing the soul of Thistle's wife out of the heavens, that is diabolical. Even for Kalzidar, it can't have been worth all of this, though."

"Keep reading," Kieran encouraged. "It wasn't just about vengeance."

When Fritz reached the end of the letter, her fingers inadvertently tightened. "Are you fucking kidding me? They got one of the three Stones of Severing? Those are supposed to be stored in completely isolated pocket planes, accessible only to the owners. Do you have *any* idea of what those three can do when united?"

"They can create a permanent rift between the planes, allowing beings of hell, chaos, and shadow to come through, along with any other type of planar resident," Kieran replied. "With all three, Kalzidar could unleash a wave of death in any location he chose. He could turn this entire world into the playground of monsters."

Kieran didn't know the half of it. Those stones were capable of opening countless permanent rifts. In the wrong hands, the world wouldn't just be the playground of monsters: it would be theirs in every measure and sense. They would overrun the cities, slaughter adventurers and normal citizens alike. Knowing Kalzidar, he would make bargains to ensure his faithful were spared, if only so they could keep feeding him their devotion, even as he purged every other god's followers. A world ruled by monsters, overseen by Kalzidar—that was what those stones could create. And if he succeeded, it would be Fritz's fault.

Folding the paper carefully, she handed it back to Kieran. "The good news is he doesn't have them all. I would know if he did. My guess is that he went after this one first, because as soon as word got out that someone was hunting them, Lumal's protection would have grown even tighter. The bad news is, I can't stay for long once we get back. I need to warn one of the owners, and then start putting in protections to make sure Kalzidar doesn't get any others."

"I appreciate that you're taking this seriously, but I'm surprised to hear you getting involved," Kieran admitted. "Generally, you stick to the merchant and messenger role. It's rare that you roll up your sleeves and participate anymore."

"Would hardly fit my new role if I did." Fritz sighed, annoyed at herself that she'd need to do even this much. There was no getting around it, sadly. "These stones are an exception. I have to make sure they don't fall into the wrong hands. I'm responsible if they do."

From his chair, Kieran watched her face. Against most people, Fritz's expression said only what she wanted it to. A master assassin was an expert in body language, however, and he saw more than she wanted. "Once, you told me about an experiment that failed horribly, an attempt to create your own version of the Bridge, rather than hunt down all the pieces. You told me you considered it your greatest mistake, but you never told me what it was."

"And I wish I wasn't giving it away now. Unfortunately, that seems to be where we are." There was no getting past it, so Fritz opted to tell the truth. If nothing else, it might convince Kieran to lend some help. On this task, she would accept any aid she could get.

"Yes, Kieran. I'm the one who created the Stones of Severing. Which is why I know how important it is that we keep them from Kalzidar."

55.

No storm this time; no howling wind screaming in Thistle's ear. No tavern, either. He was in a temple of Grumble, one that looked quite similar to Ulkin's in Alcatham. Thistle had barely made it off the battlefield before he was overwhelmed with exhaustion. While it was possible that the events of the fight and the revelation at its end had overtaxed him, Thistle suspected this was more divine in origin than physical. It had been quite a while since he'd been able to speak with Grumble, and gods were not renowned for their patience.

The moment Thistle had found a chair and shut his eyes, he was in the temple. It was a tad brusque, but given the situation, Thistle appreciated the lack of theatrics. At the front of the temple, sitting in front of the altar, sat the mundane-looking kobold who was anything but. While hardly haughty, Grumble did tend to carry himself with the aura of confidence that belonged to gods, beings of incredible power beyond the scope of mortals. Today, that aura was substantially dimmed, and there was a sincere look of sadness on his scaly face. Wordlessly, Thistle made his way over, slowly pulling himself up next to his god and taking a seat.

"I've gone over it in my head a dozen times already, just in the walk from outside to the tavern. As angry as I am, and please do not mistake my calm for a lack of fury, I cannot in good conscience hold you accountable for what happened. Kalzidar outplayed us both. He sealed me away, kept our eyes from the real target, and went so far as to use a piece of the Bridge to cut off the communication between us. Even if you knew everything that happened in there, what can I expect you to have done? I'm the one you would task with tackling such a problem; with me sealed away, you had only priests and followers to turn to, none of which could stand against the kind of power I saw today."

It was not an easy thing, to forgive when the pain was so fresh. But Thistle was more than just his emotions; he was capable of seeing moves ahead. There was a chance he was being too easy on Grumble, letting the god off the hook lightly; however, in the long term, it was essential. Thistle couldn't expect to mount a rescue campaign against a god without one in his own corner. Preserving this relationship was more important, and if he did so in a way that left Grumble feeling in his debt, all the better. Should Thistle need a touch of help down the line, it would be nice to have some leverage. Besides, the simple truth was that Thistle didn't really blame Grumble.

Thistle blamed himself.

"Kind words. Exactly the sort of forgiveness and decency I would hope to see from my paladin. Yet we both know that I am not without fault. I brought you to this life, Thistle. If I'd left your group alone, you'd certainly be dead, but compared to what you face now, perhaps that wouldn't be so bad. I am sorry for the situation you've found yourself in. Were it in my power, I would steal Madroria's soul back this moment. Sadly, she dwells in Kalzidar's domain now, and not even we gods can pluck souls at our leisure. To remove one takes exceptional power and access to specialized tools. I can no more remove her than I could steal the soul of any of his own faithful."

"Aye, that's about what I'd suspected." Thistle didn't know everything about the gods, but he assumed that Kalzidar wouldn't have gone to such trouble if it were that easy to shuffle souls around. "Which means that, if I want her back, I have to play his game."

The kobold twisted, looking Thistle over carefully. "Play his game? You haven't realized the danger you're in yet, have you?"

"I'm sure Kalzidar intends to kill me, but I don't plan on letting him until Madroria is rescued. I'm an adventurer. I'm always at risk. One more person after my death doesn't change things."

To his surprise, Thistle felt a scaly claw fall on his shoulder. The moment it landed, a feeling of peace and security trickled through his mind. Grumble was comforting him? Like most things gods did, it was more effective than the mortal version.

A heavy breath was Thistle's first clue that the kobold had more bad news to share. Thankfully, Grumble didn't leave him in suspense long enough to figure out what it was. "Thistle, you are at risk in a way you never have been before. Do you remember your condition for becoming my paladin? The *one* thing you asked for in return for service?"

"To be reunited with my wife." It hadn't been an accident; the fact that faithful paladins who served their gods well were raised into higher heavens after passing was part of the selling point for those who joined. A chance to stand in their god's glory—in a position of reverence, no less—was appealing enough for many to lay down their lives to obtain. Thistle had needed to ensure that he and Madroria ended up together, even if his position would warrant something different.

The hand squeezed, bringing in a fresh wave of comfort. "My exact words were: 'I will ensure your spirit is reunited with your wife's.' I know that, Thistle, because I gave you my word. A god *always* knows their promises. We are bound by them. This time, that phrase feels especially appropriate." Grumble took a moment, gathering himself. It was the first time Thistle had ever seen the god, any god, do such a thing, and it unnerved him more than Thistle would have expected.

"Thistle, Kalzidar has done more than take your wife. He has stolen your own afterlife, as well. By my own promise, I must see you reunited with Madroria when you die. If that should happen now, as things stand, then the only way that I could do such a thing would be to release all claim on your soul and turn it over to Kalzidar. In his realm, torturous as it would be, you'd have your reunion."

The last pieces fell into place as understanding fully set in. It was a realization he'd have come to on his own, with a little time to think. Perhaps that was why Grumble had called him so quickly; he wanted to be there as Thistle came to terms with the true situation. "So, Kalzidar not only has Madroria, but if I fall before we save her, I'll be lost as well. It pains me to say it, but that bastard played us well."

"Loss is part of my religion," Grumble told him. "Minions, as a rule, rarely taste victory. More often, they are trod upon or kicked around. The luckiest ones get ignored. But I do not teach defeat, Thistle. We fail, we learn, we try, we fail again, yet we persist. To be a minion is to live without hubris. You must learn every failing you have and take ownership of them, if you wish to keep another from exploiting such weaknesses first. Yes, we lost this day, but we did not lose everything. Kalzidar's intent was to leave you truly alone, to kill off your friends so you had no aid to call upon as you rescued Madroria. And the tactics Kalzidar used came with costs of their own. Attacking Lumal stirred up more gods than just me. As for stealing a soul, that is no small crime."

"No, it is *not*."

The voice came from the front of the temple, a soft noise alerting Thistle to another figure arriving in the same spot he had. The person was of his and Grumble's size—gnomish, and female, with a familiar insignia stitched across her robes. With a glance, Thistle knew her. How could he not? Even if she had never been his god, in his lowlier days, Thistle's chief job had been cleaning and caring for one of her major temples.

Thistle stepped down, then inclined his back as best he was able to with a warped spine, managing a serviceable bow. "A welcome to you, Mithingow, god of the gnomes."

"You're never that quick with the bows to me," Grumble complained.

"Your dogma is less formal than hers. Besides, I am not inclined to be rude when courting allies." Thistle looked up from the ground with no shame at his words. This was a meeting of people angry at Kalzidar; he needed the formation of a coalition. Whether Grumble realized it or not, Thistle was on more than a rescue mission. God, mortal, it didn't matter. Kalzidar had crossed a line. Once Madroria was safe, Thistle planned to take Kalzidar's head, a warning to all the gods of what would happen to those who stole the dead. He hadn't figured out quite how he'd do it yet, but there was plenty of time for that. Right now, he needed allies more than schemes.

Mithingow nodded, looking Thistle over with a critical eye. "You know my ways well. I, however, am not familiar with you, paladin of Grumble, nor did I know your wife. Countless souls dwell in my realm, and I meet relatively few. But that does not matter in a situation such as this. Madroria was a dutiful follower and servant, who earned her place through a lifetime of devotion. What Kalzidar has done is about more than just one soul. It threatens the entire system by which we reward our faithful. Hear me well on this, paladin. Were Madroria my dearest friend and companion, I could not be more incensed by her abduction. Kalzidar has made an enemy today."

"More than one." Grumble rose from his seat as well, taking a stance next to the god of the gnomes. "Many gods had followers and temples in Lumal. An attack like that is a blow to their egos, and while it's not quite the same as the personal slight dealt to Mithingow, you will find many sympathetic to our cause. With preparation, we can gather a force capable of recovering Madroria."

The words were heartening, yet Thistle remained unmoved. This was all nice to consider, good ideas to think about, but the fact remained that with every passing minute, Madroria was in that monster's grip. A plan, a campaign, who could guess how many obstacles there would be to clear before he'd get the merest chance of seeing Madroria, leaving her to who knew what fate in the time between.

"Useful as I hope that will be, my patience for such tactics is lacking." Thistle noted that both gods were surprised by his response. They hadn't expected him to talk back, not at a time like this. "I had hoped that, as this was a divine issue, it could be quickly resolved by the gods. Seeing as that is not the case, I'm going to pursue a faster means of recovery."

Though Mithingow said nothing, Grumble shook his head. "Thistle, I know what you're thinking. If a piece of the Bridge was capable of stealing a soul, Kalzidar would have used that technique instead of going to such trouble. Those artifacts have never reacted well when dealing with divine realms or magic; it's the reason so few have used them to challenge the gods. I'm sorry, but you can't use one as a shortcut."

No, Grumble was probably right. Thistle couldn't use *one* piece of the Bridge and hope for such a miracle. But it wasn't like there was only a single piece of it out there. In fact, with the priestess's death, her chunk of glowing crystal had fallen into their possession. Before, even that might not have inspired Thistle with much hope. Seeing Eric lose his mind when holding two pieces together had made it clear there was a limit. After Fritz teaching him how to control it with rituals, though... no, he almost certainly wasn't there yet. Fritz was, but her help would come with a high cost—one Thistle would gladly pay, assuming he was able. Still, there was no reason to put all his potions in one bag. If the gods wanted to help, he would play along with their plans as well. More plans in motion meant more room to maneuver if one went awry.

Mithingow, perhaps misreading his eyes, perhaps subtly aiding his plans, spoke up. "While I certainly understand your concern over Madroria's well-being and the corresponding need for expediency, you need not worry quite yet. Kalzidar has stolen her, but she is not without some protection. As a devoted soul connected to my divine realm, she is still tinged with my power. I will do all I am able to extend and prolong that protection. It won't last forever, but Kalzidar is not able to do her any true harm yet."

"I see. Then I apologize for my brusqueness," Thistle told them. "What would you have us do next?"

Reaching over, Mithingow tapped Thistle lightly on the forehead, sending a ripple of light across his skin. "Follow those directions to a temple of mine just inside the eastern border of Thatchshire. There are implements there that we'll need, tools and magics purposefully sealed away. Not every object of power was hidden in Lumal; many are tucked away across the kingdoms. When you arrive, help shall be waiting. From them, further instructions will follow."

While Thistle did nod to signify his understanding, his eyes went to Grumble for confirmation. Mithingow was indeed a god, but she wasn't *his* god, and it was a foolish paladin indeed who forgot where his orders came from. Thankfully, there was no dissent as Grumble met his silent question with a toothy kobold smile, one that Thistle found less troubling the more he saw it.

"Very well. I shall spread the word among the others, and we'll ready ourselves to head out right away." Thistle hesitated, unsure of whether or not to broach the topic of Timuscor. What he'd done certainly seemed worthy of the gods' attention, yet neither had mentioned it thus far. Was this, too, a test? Maybe, but still, the gods were in his debt right now. If there was a time for them to talk about the emergence of a new paladin, this seemed the opportune moment. "And Timuscor?"

The scaly claw hit his mouth as soon as the words were out. "Fear not, he will recover. Do not waste words on such things now; our time is short, and we must focus on the important matters."

Thistle's mind raced, quickly puzzling out his god's strange actions. Nothing he'd said was a lie—Timuscor had been injured, so his recovery was real, and Grumble was right about there being more pressing issues. However, the way he'd shushed Thistle was odd, perhaps not to other gods, but certainly to those who knew how Grumble treated his followers. That, combined with the offhanded dismissal, painted a clear picture: this was not something to discuss with another god around.

Much as Thistle might have liked more answers, he could see the wisdom in Grumble's prudence. What Timuscor had done was supposedly impossible, possibly blasphemous in some religions, so making it immediately public could come with serious risks... risks they didn't need right now, especially when trying to build an alliance with other divine beings.

"In fact, Thistle, I'm afraid your time grows short. I have work of my own to do. We will speak again when I am able. Until then, follow Mithingow's directions to the temple. And take no unwarranted risks, my paladin. I don't need to tell you that your death currently comes with eternal repercussions." One orange claw tapped Thistle in the chest, popping his astral form like a soap bubble and sending him back to the world of the waking.

With him gone, the surroundings faded. There was no longer any need for a setting. Mithingow looked at the spot where Thistle had been for several moments before turning to Grumble. "He's more dangerous than he lets on."

"When I met him, the bloodlust was faded," Grumble replied. "Life outside of adventuring had warmed him. I won't say that I'm happy to see that kind of ruthlessness rekindled, but I'm not sad about it either. To be a minion means to be weak and to live in fear. Perhaps it's fitting that their paladin be more deadly than most."

"And you still think he's the right one?" Mithingow asked.

Grumble merely shrugged. "He's the first in a very long time. Whether he's right or not is up to him to prove. That is the beauty of mortals—with every choice, they define their own destiny."

56.

"Sweet sorcery. I was expecting epic quests and fun loot, not a mad sprint for the exit." Cheri set her dice aside and poured herself a fresh glass of wine. "On the other hand, nobody got possessed and none of our shit started to glow, so I'd call this a success, especially since we didn't lose any characters. Plus, Hoit gave us teleportation stones to return once Lumal is open to visitors again, so we can give this place another try."

The rest of the table's players were stretching and relaxing as well. With their successful escape, the session was officially coming to an end. There was still more side tasks they could do; however, the Lumal section of the module was finished.

"It was the timing that killed you all," Russell explained. "Taking the isolated routes instead of dealing with non-player characters pushed your arrival back. When we unsealed the section, I did some reading. Except for the helsk fight, this whole thing runs on a timetable. If you'd gotten there sooner, you could have done stuff in Lumal. I bet there was even a way to prevent the attack. By the time you made it, you were too late." Although he didn't bring it up out of politeness, the module revealed there actually had been a way to theoretically win: the whole army could be stopped by killing a single enemy, just like the helsk fight had taught them. Of course, that information worked better when the party arrived with enough time to use it.

"I liked it," Tim said. "Even though we didn't get to do what we expected, showing up mid-battle made the world feel more lived in. Like they weren't just waiting for our characters to show up. There was other stuff happening around us."

A few of them twitched slightly at his words, all too aware that Tim might be more correct than he'd intended. But Cheri was right; even with the surprises, it was a normal game session. After playing through almost an entire module without incident, their games had become gradually less tense. Russell hoped he wasn't about to undo all of that, but he really didn't have much choice. They deserved to know the truth. What came next was in their hands. Russell was the GM, and only the players decided what a character would do, which direction they would go. If the party didn't want to pursue this lead, then he'd have to let it pass.

From behind his screen, Russell pulled out four folded pieces of paper and began to hand them out. "One last thing before we break. I recently received this email. Now that the session is over, I felt it only right that you read it, too. The copies are identical; just take one and pass it down."

His players unfolded their pages, cheer giving way to concern as they noticed the expression on Russell's face. Together, they began to read.

*   *   *

In spite of their victory, it was a dour mood that had settled over those gathered at the tavern. Neither Brock nor Jolia were talking much. Fritz sat in the corner with Kieran, whispering fervently. Simone was having an in-depth discussion with Timuscor and Gabrielle, leaving Eric and Grumph to sit quietly with Thistle, who kept staring off into space for long stretches at a time. Only Mr. Peppers, once more returned to his normal size, was cheerful, sitting around munching on some scraps Brock had put out.

They'd won, technically. Lumal still stood. All of the adventurers were alive. The Helm of Ignosa was recovered, and no automaton army had marched on Notch. It should have felt like a good day. But the price was too high. Deep down, they knew they hadn't truly come out on top of the exchange. The tolls they'd taken on Kalzidar were ones he'd planned for, pawns he was willing to sacrifice. Removing them weakened him, but not any more than he'd expected. While Kalzidar hadn't gotten everything he wanted today, he'd gotten enough.

Sitting at the bar, Jolia licked her lips as Brock set a fresh glass down in front of her. Her hands gripped the mug and lifted. For a moment, she happened to catch sight of the rest of the room in the metal reflection, giving her pause. She turned the bronze mug, made durable to survive the usual roughhousing of a tavern, taking in the worry and uncertainty on each of the younger adventurers' faces. She'd worn that same expression many times before. Adventuring wasn't always about winning the day. Sometimes, it was about slinking away, licking one's wounds and trying to find the strength to go back out there. In the young days, it was easy. No loss or deed lingered in an adventurer's mind.

For the ones who changed, the echoes, it was a different matter. Every pain weighed on their shoulders, and some carried the guilt of each kill in the backs of their minds. Jolia silenced those ghosts in her own way, but that didn't mean she wanted to see others start carrying specters of their own. Not before they had to.

"That's about enough moping, I think." Jolia spun in her stool, away from the mug, to face the rest of the tavern. "We took some lumps on this one. I won't deny that. Thistle's wife has been stolen, Kalzidar has one-third of an item that could destroy the entire world, and the bastion of Lumal was half-razed to the ground. It would be easy to look at this day and feel nothing but loss, which you would all be damn fools for doing."

Jolia hopped down, summoning her staff with a gesture and leaning on it as she began to move through the tavern. "From what Simone told us about the fight, it sounds like you made serious progress during the battle. Gabrielle, you discovered enough power to destroy the enchantment of a deadly creature with a single swing. Thistle, you learned to direct your mana in the heat of the moment; do you know how long it takes most paladins to master that skill? Grumph and Eric, without you two helping to control the battlefield, the day would have been lost. And Timuscor…"

At his name, the man turned in his seat, beaming at her. To her, he looked much the same. Whatever confidence he'd wielded in battle had faded once the blades were sheathed. Still, there was something different in those eyes. Before, Timuscor had always looked as though he had an unspoken question on the tip of his tongue. He wandered through his own life as if he'd find an answer to his existence around any corner. The questions were gone now. In their place was simple, yet stalwart, resolution.

"Timuscor, you did something that most would consider impossible. Something not even one of us has ever seen. You bound your soul, your very essence, to the aspect of divine magic that lives in all mana. You became a paladin of your own accord, with no god to aid you—the first free paladin in untold centuries, if not millennia. That is astounding."

"Also dangerous," Fritz added. All attention swung in her direction, an experience she was plainly familiar with. "Do you know one of the other popular names for what he is? Some call them *true* paladins, implying that the ones made by the gods are lesser. How do you imagine some of the more devoted sects will respond to the idea of that kind of paladin?"

Of all the things to feel at such a statement, Timuscor looked a touch embarrassed by the term. "I meant no offense. I merely wished to serve the greater good without owing allegiance to a god's agenda. I certainly wouldn't use such a term to describe myself."

"Doesn't matter. If they know what you are, they'll see you as a threat. Especially if they see you light up that sword." Fritz nodded to the blade set before Timuscor on the table, housed in a sheath. He had offered to return the borrowed weapon upon arriving, but so far, no one had taken him up on it.

"Aye, the sword is something special, too," Jolia agreed, forcefully trying to keep things on a more positive note. "But you needn't worry about it activating willy-nilly. A Divine Blade isn't some cheap sword that burns or sparks. Those are rare weapons indeed, forged with magic long ago lost to modern mages. In an ordinary warrior's possession, it is nothing more than an especially sharp blade. In the hands of a worthy paladin, it becomes keener and more dangerous, even slightly amplifying a paladin's abilities. When wielded by a worthy paladin against a proper foe, a being of great danger and evil, the weapon takes on its true form. Blazing with light, it tremendously aids the paladin, as well as becomes a weapon that can cut any armor and wound any evil creature. That latter situation is fairly specific though, so unless someone as skilled as me is inspecting it, they won't know what you have."

Timuscor took the words in heavily, looking down at the sword. "Knowing what this is, I cannot in good conscience accept such a gift. It is too powerful to entrust to one as new as me. Please, find a more worthy paladin to carry such a blessing."

The snort came from across the room, where Kieran was finally hauling himself up. "Doesn't work that way. At a certain point, magical items develop preferences. Not a full personality, not everytime, but they'll have quirks, especially weapons. That sword glowed for you, Timuscor. It recognized you as worthy. It chose you. As a swordsman myself, I would say that to ignore the blade's will would be disrespectful." He made his way over, leaning down and looking closely at the sheath.

"Besides, who do you think we would give this to? Paladins don't come here, not ones that can still fight, and I shouldn't need to tell *you* why. We could store it, certainly, though what good it would do, I can't fathom. These weapons are meant to be in the world, to be in use. If you meet another paladin who you feel can wield the sword better, and the weapon will accept them, then it is yours to pass on. Until then, you are the paladin meant to hold this blade. It is a noble obligation, one not to be cast aside without consideration."

"That said, we might want to throw an enchantment or two on the sheath before you leave, just to help keep a low profile," Jolia added. She was annoyed at how the conversation had gotten away from her, but at least they were discussing practical issues. Talking, planning, that beat silent moping any day. "Although, you're welcome to stay and rest for a bit more, if needed."

"No. Thank you very much, for all of your kindness and hospitality through this unusual situation, but no." It was the first time Thistle had spoken in some while—since recounting his dream from his brief nap, in fact. There was still distance in his gaze; however, at least some of his attention was now in the room with them. "Time is of the essence. The longer we take, the greater the danger my wife is in. I've been given a task, a direction to follow. Until I take that step, I can't plan any further ahead, so I hope you'll all understand my eagerness."

A solemn cloud spread back out over the tavern, the reminder of Madroria's situation pulling almost everyone down. The sole holdout was Gabrielle, who suddenly stood from the table, marched up to the bar, and had Brock begin filling mugs of various sizes. One by one, she passed them out, until every person in the room was holding a drink. Only once that was done did she raise hers.

"This was a bad day. Let's not sugarcoat that. We won, in that we survived and grew stronger, but Kalzidar definitely walked away with more of the victory than we did. What he did—to Lumal, to Madroria—all of it is unforgiveable. So let's not forgive him. Let's do what Kalzidar did when we—yeah, *this* party—destroyed a piece of his divinity. Let's learn from our failures and come back even stronger. This was a bad day, but it's nearly over. Tomorrow is a new one. Tomorrow, we start the journey to reclaim Madroria, and make Kalzidar regret he ever laid a finger on her to begin with."

The room didn't break into spontaneous applause, and the mood wasn't suddenly cleansed of sadness. Everyone did drink, though, lifting their mugs and celebrating the toast. Gabrielle had managed to get everyone looking forward, for now, and that was the first step in getting them moving.

Thistle appreciated her efforts, overt as they could often be. For him, however, the toast wasn't required. His mind was already looking ahead, well past what he'd told any of the others. As the room filled with sounds of toasting and sipping, as well as scattered conversation, he looked across to Fritz, meeting her eyes and nodding to the door. With no more than that, Thistle made his way out, looking to anyone watching like he was doing nothing more than getting some air.

It took nearly ten minutes before Fritz arrived. Thistle didn't know what it would take to extricate herself; he'd just been sure she would do it.

She appeared from the tavern looking much the same as usual. Same worn, well-made traveling clothes, same arrangement of bags and pouches slung across her body, same easygoing manner that put people off guard. Placing her had taken Thistle quite a while, long after they'd parted ways in Briarwillow. Funnily, it was her parting demeanor that provided the final clue. While she'd meant to scare him off, Fritz had accidentally shown him the kind of authority she was used to wielding.

Once she was outside, he began to walk, and she followed. They made their way out of the town square, up the road, to a nice path of purple and white flowers. There was nothing special about the plants, save simply for the fact that they were positioned in a place where it would be hard for others to overhear. The people of Notch might still be capable of spying, but Thistle wasn't trying to hide this from them.

"Let's start with what I know. As I'm going to ask a favor, that feels like the gracious opening move." Thistle's voice was gentle in the night. Not lowered, but not raised either. He was working to sound as casual as possible. There was a chance Fritz might kill him before this was done, so he wanted to offer as few reasons for her to do so as possible. Unfortunately, his next words were the likeliest ones to see him slain. "The prime portion is this: I know who you are. Or rather, who you were, before."

The elf's eyes narrowed, examining his carefully, with a far more intense expression than she would ever let the others see. "If you're expecting me to confirm some theory of yours by bursting out in agreement, you need to think more of me."

"Not at all. I was simply waiting to see if I'd get a chance to continue or not." Slowly, Thistle bowed as best as he was able. He couldn't quite manage the formal version of showing vulnerability, but as he looked back up, Fritz was looking slightly less fearsome.

She nodded to him, cautiously. "Tell me what you think you know, and what you want. We'll go from there."

"I haven't filled in all the details yet," Thistle admitted. "What I have figured out is that you seem to have woven a spell beyond anything I've ever seen or heard of. You rewrote the minds and history of the entire kingdom, of several kingdoms, to remove yourself from it. Except, I can remember you. When I take a sincere look at myself, at what makes me unique, the answer for why becomes obvious. The Bridge. You used the Bridge to create your spell; it explains how you could have managed something so incredible. We already know that being around pieces when they're active causes unusual effects. I've been around the Bridge plenty while the others used it—enough to weaken your spell, I'd imagine."

There was no change to Fritz's expression as Thistle spoke. She took in every word with sincere consideration. If she was going to stab him or hug him, Thistle couldn't guess, which was clearly the point. All he could do was speak the truth and hope it worked. If not, he'd have to come up with a new plan, something far more dangerous.

Finally, Fritz spoke. "An interesting theory, though it fails to account for a simple question: if I was someone of note, why is it that only you remember me? The others have been around the Bridge just as much, if not more. Past that, even if it were true, what would you hope to gain by talking about this with me?"

"Help." Slowly, all too aware of how easy it would be to fall, Thistle lowered himself to his knees. Fritz's impassive expression widened for a flicker of a second; even she was shocked to see a paladin beg. "Grumble and Mithingow mean well, but Kalzidar's cunning is substantial. This was not a haphazard move. He is putting things in motion, and what we saw was a mere first step. I'm afraid that if I follow blindly, we will lose. Were it my own life, that would be acceptable, but I will not risk the others, and certainly not Madroria. We need more. We need to attack from angles Kalzidar won't predict. We need the power of the Bridge, and a master to wield it. Because, if you can do one impossible thing, like make a world forget you, then maybe you can do another. Perhaps you can help me topple a god."

"An interesting proposal." Fritz might have denied her talents more readily, were Thistle not supplicating so. He had cast aside his pride to ask for her help. She could at least answer him honestly. "Whatever I might have been before, I am a trader now, Thistle. You're asking for something significant, so I assume you have something to trade."

Still kneeling, Thistle gave a quick nod. "We now have two pieces of the Bridge. Aid us, and they are yours, as are any others we claim in our efforts to save Madroria. I would promise you the one we've hidden as well, but only Eric knows its location, and I cannot make an oath for another to keep."

Only because Thistle was looking away did Fritz permit the spark of interest in her eyes. She cleared it quickly; giving away one's desires in a negotiation was tantamount to failure. "And what makes you think I have need of more pieces? If I cast such a spell as you've implied, then I must already have at least one."

"More than that, I suspect. However, you don't want *some* of the pieces, do you? The others don't recognize you because they didn't know who you were in the first place. I was more traveled than them, than even Grumph. I saw some of the Mage Guild's celebrations, the ceremonies where even their highest members were present. I cannot imagine that anything less than a completed artifact would satisfy an archmage, especially when she's given up her seat at the Table of Mages to search for the pieces."

Killing him would have been easy. Some of the people of Notch would see through whatever excuse she used—a lingering evil plant bursting out of the flowers, perhaps—but few were likely to care. Adventurers died constantly; it was part of their lifestyle. Fritz stayed her hand, however. In just the time she'd known them, this party had run into or uncovered four pieces of the Bridge. She'd been actively hunting shards of it for so long, and not even she had ever managed to find so many in such a short time. Whether it was fate or happenstance, these adventurers had momentum. While Fritz didn't relish the idea of having someone out there who knew her secret, Thistle hadn't tried to exploit it. He'd made her a deal—a very fair one, at that—rather than trying to push his leverage. On top of it all, Fritz rather liked this group. They did interesting things, and she was nothing if not a fan of new experiences.

"Very well, Thistle. Rise to your feet. I will not make you any promises yet, but I will listen to all you have planned. If it pleases me, I'll help. If not, you will tell no one of this meeting or what you know. Does that present an issue?"

"None. I am grateful for even the opportunity to explain myself." It didn't take long for Thistle to return to his feet. There was fire in him now, an urgency he'd been clamping down in front of the others. Every minute standing still was torture, yet he endured it out of necessity. Planning and forethought were his strengths, his best chance at overcoming Kalzidar. Next time they clashed, Thistle had no intention of being the one caught by surprise. God or mortal, it made no difference. Kalzidar had stolen the soul of someone Thistle loved.

Even in a paladin's heart, there was no mercy for that kind of sin.

Epilogue

The morning sun rose over a peaceful settlement, dotted with farms and cottages of styles from a dozen different lands and kingdoms. If one looked close, they could see figures walking the lines of their properties: folks in simple wear, without finery or blazing magical items to show off wealth. All that marked this town as unusual, from a glance, was the fact that everyone seemed especially young and healthy. There might have been a few other indicators—a scar here, a quick motion to the side there—that betrayed the truth, but few would ever draw near enough to notice them. Notch was a quiet, isolated hamlet, and the last several days of excitement had been more than enough for the residents.

Perhaps that was why there was little fanfare as the adventurers saddled their horses in the town square. Thistle hadn't been kidding about not wasting time; they weren't even taking a day to rest. Physically, they were all healed—the town priest had seen to most of them. A few summons had helped Gabrielle fuel her axe, which in turn removed her own wounds. The weapon was still a burden, and her condition a curse, but merely knowing how it worked made the whole endeavor more manageable. The detour would have been worth it for that alone, if not for the terrible cost Kalzidar had added.

While the adventurers readied themselves, Notch's town council sat in Brock's tavern. Kieran, Jolia, Simone, and Brock were all gathered around a table, with Fritz sitting slightly off to the side. All four of the non-elves were staring Fritz down, waiting for her to laugh, or say that she was joking, for her to do *something* to make her prior words untrue. After nearly a full minute, it was clear that no such reprieve was coming.

"You're serious about this. I know you've always been fascinated by that artifact, and that you've been hunting pieces to experiment on, but that is nothing compared to what you're proposing. Even if you can gather all the pieces, and know that there are others collecting them you'll have to steal from, no one is sure what happens when they're joined. Not the gods, not the adventurers, no one. How do you know you aren't building a magical device that will destroy the entire plane?" Kieran kept his voice calm. He'd known Fritz long enough to realize she responded better to reason over emotion.

"That one seems pretty unlikely," Fritz countered. "The mere fact that we're finding pieces at all means the artifact had to be shattered, and since none of them react destructively around the other chunks, someone else probably did the shattering. You are right, though. It's a mystery, and if there's one thing I know about this world, it's that no mystery stays unsolved forever. I've brought you all up to speed on the situation; you know more pieces have been appearing lately. Maybe it's coincidence, maybe it's fate, probably something in between. Either way, I see an opportunity, and I want to seize it... unless you'd rather see someone else beat us to a potentially all-powerful artifact."

In truth, Kieran wasn't sure Fritz *would* be his first choice for such responsibility. She wasn't malicious; however, she did have a tendency to cast off things that held her back, especially when in pursuit of some new item or magic. She'd even left her role at the Mage Guild when it became too cumbersome, though she did install a proper replacement first. As a trader, she was fair and upfront, and as a friend, she'd been reliable. Fritz was far from perfect, but if Kieran had to back someone who was capable of succeeding and whom he trusted to not be outright evil, then she was in the top five. The others, unfortunately, would have no interest in such an endeavor, so Kieran was left with little choice.

"We don't fight anymore." Kieran held up a hand, cutting off Fritz's objection. "Last night was a very rare, special occasion. There was a potential threat to our town that we were cutting off early, and in the process, we only destroyed automatons. My blade alone tasted blood, and I assure you, it was enough to quell the appetite for a long time. I cannot speak for the others, but if you call upon me for help, understand that this is a condition I do not intend to violate. No blood. If the situation cannot be solved without killing, then I am not the resource for the job."

"Nor am I," Jolia agreed. Next to her, Brock and Simone were silently nodding their agreement. The message was clear: while they might be willing to help her, violence was off the table.

Fritz was only mildly discouraged. Having a shock force of unstoppable warriors would have made things substantially easier, but she'd known from the start that wouldn't happen. Even getting them this receptive was a victory in and of itself. She imagined the presence of the other adventurers had helped with that. They were a walking reminder that, much as Notch might like to pretend otherwise, the town wasn't truly disconnected from the world at large.

"What about for a Stone of Severing? Are you willing to kill if I find one of those?"

The words hung in the air, drifting slowly down like a fallen feather. Finally, Kieran laid a hand on the hilt of his blade. "I swore to defend this town, and if the world goes, we go. So yes, Fritz, I will draw my sword for you if, and only if, the fate of the world is at risk. Otherwise, I will refer you to someone else if fighting is what you require. Who that is will depend on exactly what threats you are facing."

The grin on Fritz's face made Kieran wince. She'd just gotten something she wanted out of him and wasn't shy about showing it. "That will be plenty. Thank you, Kieran. Together, with our pooled might and wisdom, I think we might very well have a chance at succeeding."

There was danger in her eyes as they flitted about the room, taking in every nuance and detail in that unnerving way of hers. "I can hardly wait to see what a completed Bridge is capable of doing."

*   *   *

The pages were piled in the middle of the table, tossed there as each player finished reading the email and fully understood its significance. Wordlessly, Cheri went to the kitchen, returning with a sizable glass of water. She took a deep sip, then turned away from the others and sprayed it through the air in mock surprise. "There, does that more or less encapsulate what we're all feeling?"

"I didn't expect... of course, there would be... it's just..." Bert smacked himself once in the side of the head, gently, and the rambling died off. "Sorry, I can get stuck on things too easily. Need a little jarring to break up the spiral. I guess what floored me is realizing that it's not just us, is it? We speculated before, but this is as close to proof as we'll get."

"No, it isn't." Alexis was forcing her tone louder, closer to Gelthorn's. "The closest to proof we'll get is in Thatchshire, where actual evidence is waiting for us."

Bert swiveled in his chair to face her. "Are we sure? And if so, how will that even work? This is still a module, one that other people are seeing. Let's say we get the next one, and find this dude in Venmoore—what happens then? Is there going to be a whole letter to us printed in that module? Because the other options get really scary the longer you consider them. Maybe the character will pop out, or yank us in, or connect us to the dice, or any number of unknowns that we can't calculate for. I get it—that's the nature of magic—I'm just advocating that we not stroll into this with the assumption that it's safe."

"Save your worry. I've known from the moment Russell got possessed that none of this was safe." Cheri winked at him before taking a normal sip of her water, poorly disguising the worry in her face. "That's part of what makes it fun."

Steadily, almost unconsciously, attention turned to Tim, who'd been silent thus far. Despite his relative inexperience with gaming, the young man played his character to a fault, doing all he could to embody the ideals of what a paladin should be. What they would decide to do was still in contention; however, if they wanted to know what the right thing to do was, Tim was their default guide.

"Together, after what happened in the dragon's lair, we decided to keep going. To chase the magic. This makes it feel real in a way I hadn't expected, but it doesn't fundamentally change what we're doing," Tim said. "Either we give up on it all now, or we go to Venmoore. There's no point in chasing if we aren't going to follow leads. I'll support whatever choice the group makes, just make sure you're ready to see it through."

Russell coughed into his hand, a quick and dirty way to steal attention back at the game table. "It bears mentioning that we don't even have the next module yet. Until we do, you won't be able to head to Thatchshire, anyway, so there's no need to make your minds up right now. I showed you that email because I don't want to keep secrets from you all, not because we're making a choice today."

His words swept much of the tension from the air, a collective holding of breath let out by the players. Only Bert still looked worried, although it was hard to tell if he was truly concerned or simply deep in thought. "I disagree. Let's not just wait for our next step to present itself. We should decide and start making preparations. There are bound to be side quests we can do, items we can hunt, things to prepare ourselves for the next adventure. Better to pick a path and start down it now, so we'll be ready when the next one arrives."

Given his words, it was fairly obvious which way Bert was leaning, and he didn't find objections from the others. Alexis gave a thumbs-up, while Tim stuck to nodding. Cheri was the only one to respond verbally. "I'm down for that. Some of these fights were tough, and seeing how outmatched we were in Lumal left a bad taste in my mouth. Let's pick up another level, and maybe some new tricks in the time we've got."

"Should we hunt for them in the real world while we're waiting?" Several sets of surprised eyes focused on Tim, who immediately turned flush. "I mean, the email came from a person on our side of the game, right? If we can find them, talk to them in person, maybe we can get them to tell us more."

"Maybe," Russell said, though there was little conviction in his tone. "To an extent, we'll be hunting them. We have to keep on Broken Bridge's trail if we want the next module anyway, and I've got a hunch that finding a real lead on them might lead us to our email buddy. Given how out of reach they stay, though, the game is probably our best bet. At least we have a name and a location in there."

Deep down, Russell hoped he wasn't the Pied Piper leading his friends off to their deaths. By nature of his role, there was little he could do. As GM, he set the scene, built the stage, but the players wrote the script. Their actions, their choices, determined where the story went. He couldn't tell them which path was the right one. He could only do his best to prepare them for whatever lay ahead.

* * *

Grumble sat on his throne. It wasn't especially grand, not unless he was entertaining visitors. Most of the time, it was a simple chair with an extravagant number of cushions the kobold could nest in. Comfort had always been his greatest decadence, a stark contrast to his mortal years spent shivering on a stone floor. There was nothing comfortable about the seat today, however. The full weight of his responsibilities as a god sat heavy on Grumble's shoulders as he contemplated the dilemma before him.

Somehow, Timuscor had done something incredible. He'd become attuned to divine magic in a way mortals weren't supposed to be capable of. Even in Grumble's mortal days, the free paladin was nothing more than myth and whisper. As a god, Grumble should see the newly-born paladin as a threat to the established system. After all, if mortals relearned that they could serve the calling without owing allegiance to a god, would so many still choose to kneel? Of course, that ignored the fact that, even in myth, free paladins were incredibly rare, and the simple truth that no other had been born in untold ages meant it must be a hard power to attain.

A scaly claw ran down Grumble's snout as he realized his mistake. He didn't *know* of any other free paladins that had been born since the ancient times, but that didn't mean there hadn't been any. Casting his attention to Thistle and his friends, Grumble could see each of them easily, save for Timuscor. The same divine magic that fueled his new gifts also concealed the paladin, making him difficult to see. If the boar was still with him, it was completely hidden—as a creature purely made of magic, the protection was more effective on it.

At first, this new development had puzzled Grumble, until he gave it more thought. Divine concealment was a necessary power for any that filled such a role. Paladins who served no god fought only for the greater good. Sooner or later, that was bound to run them across the path of an evil or ambitious god. Being able to move undetected by a god's magic would make such paladins a far more dangerous threat. Grumble didn't love that there were now factors in play he had little control over, but he could certainly see the value in a divine warrior that was nearly invisible to the gods. True, he didn't have Timuscor's loyalty, but Thistle did. Where the gnome led, Timuscor would follow.

For now, Grumble resolved to keep the incident to himself. While it might have gained him some small favor with the other gods to report a free paladin, Grumble was a fan of the underdogs. He had to be, as god of the minions. Seeing someone throw off the shackles of a system, seize power for himself, bow to no master—it was the kind of spirit Grumble could admire. The others would be mad when they found out, and Grumble was prepared for that. Let them be angry, if they wanted.

If things went to plan, then by the time they found out, it would be too late to matter anyway.

*　　*　　*

Eric was briefly surprised to see Timuscor saddling his normal horse, before he realized that riding a giant armored boar around was going to attract more suspicion than any of them needed. Their trek would be a long one—west across the plains of Urthos until they made it to the emerald meadows that signified the beginning of Thatchshire's kingdom. Even from there, they had quite a way to ride. Thistle's directions were taking them just past the borders, near a city called Venmoore.

Jolia had offered to open a portal for them, but Thistle had declined. Evidently, there were preparations to lay, so even if they arrived early, there would be nothing to do. Despite the fact that he hadn't said it, Eric suspected

Thistle's other reason for wanting to ride there was training. On the road, there would be dangers and threats, but also the opportunity to hone their skills. Especially for Gabrielle and Timuscor, who were still learning about their new abilities, that practice could prove vital. They'd barely survived that last fight—only a genuine miracle had gotten them through. If the others were feeling anything like Eric, then they wanted to be stronger before the next one.

It was strange. When they'd left Maplebark, Eric's chief concern had been living long enough to get attention off their town. Once that goal was accomplished, it became about surviving in general. Even his training with Elora had been about figuring out how to be good enough at his job that he could help the party keep living. Kalzidar had changed that. Taking Madroria, sending the priestess against them—it was clear he wouldn't stop. Eric didn't want to just keep surviving anymore. He wanted to become strong enough to fight back, to not live in fear of what some god or king would decide to do with his life. In a way, he suspected the journey of every adventurer involved such a realization at some point.

From the tavern, Fritz emerged, making a beeline directly for Eric. "There's my guy. Where did you leave the piece?"

"Back in the ritual room." Eric had been tasked with retrieving the priestess's piece of the Bridge, as he was the only member of the party who could safely touch them. Honestly, he wasn't convinced that leaving it for Fritz was the best idea, but Thistle had made the point that none of them could safely use two pieces, not even Eric. Better to put it in secure hands, especially since they were set on angering a god. No sense in making Kalzidar stronger if they fell. "I couldn't get the staff to let go. Guessing that's something you can handle?"

Fritz patted her bag. "I'm sure I can find something in here that'll be up to the task. Got your own piece stored safely, I trust?"

It was Eric's turn to pat something—in this case, his backpack. "Safe as anything in this world can be, I suppose. If luck is with us, the morning's peace should at least hold until we get out of the forest and back onto the plains."

"Oh, I wouldn't worry about that, if I were you. Agramor apparently agreed to escort you all out. After everything that's happened, I don't think they're taking chances."

"I've heard that name a few times, but never met the person," Eric admitted.

Taking his arm, she spun them around until they faced the tree line further down the road. "She's a druid, prefers to stay close to nature. Never was great with people, even less so now. Trust me, you won't be able to miss her when she wants to be seen."

Sure enough, even from this distance, Eric could make out a huge shape deep within the trees. He wasn't entirely sure what it was; only that it had fur, horns, and a tremendous size. Something that big had been lurking in the forest all along? Or was that Agramor herself, using a druid's famous talent for shapeshifting? Either way, it was a presence bound to make the horses feel skittish and the adventurers feel safe. It would be strange, getting back on the road, but Eric was ready for it. Nice as some rest had been, being around such powerful, dangerous people left him constantly on edge, even if they were friendly.

"I suppose we don't have to worry about losing her in the brush," Eric chuckled. "Do you ever get used to this place?"

"I certainly hope not. What's the point of going on if spots like Notch become mundane?" Fritz shivered; whether it was theatrical or genuine, Eric couldn't tell. "Traders and adventurers have that much in common; we're always on the move. Hopefully, it won't be long until our paths cross again. It's not every day I meet someone who can handle wielding a piece of the Bridge. Even rarer that said someone is a looker."

Eric blushed. It wasn't the first time Fritz had teasingly flirted with him, but even with the time apart, he still hadn't figured out how to react. The elf merely grinned and kept going, as if she hadn't noticed his embarrassment.

"This time, I know it won't be long. I've got some business up near Thatchshire, as well, though I'm taking my own route. Keep those eyes peeled and at the ready when you're crossing the plains. As the most alert one in the bunch, I'm counting on you not to let something so precious fall into the hands of mere bandits."

The blush faded as Eric's mind turned to serious matters. He looked Fritz right in the eyes, making sure she saw the depth of his resolve. "Now that I know who's after us, I doubt I'll take so much as an unnecessary blink."

Fritz's own eyes sparkled as she considered the words. "I'll say this much: if nothing else, you certainly sound more like a rogue these days."

*   *   *

A flash, and then darkness. That was all she remembered. One moment she was at peace, and the next, suddenly the world was tumbling, chaotic, mad. It was like she was alive again.

Finally, the world was becoming clear, the stones of her prison cell snapping into focus. There was a glow lighting up the dreary interior. Looking down, Madroria realized that the glow came from her. A lovely bluish light that radiated out of the core of her ethereal form.

"Mithingow's shine." As a priestess in her living days, Madroria knew the light well. Even now, in some unknown pit, her god's protection gleamed in the darkness. Rising to her feet, she surveyed her surroundings. No doors. No windows. Only stone, dark like it had been formed from soot, at every turn.

Food and drink were no concern; she was still quite dead and therefore lacked such physical needs. The larger issue was what her presence here meant. How had she been pulled from Mithingow's realm, and for what purpose? Based on the decor and the waves of twisted magic trying to press past her protective glow, she hadn't been captured by a friendly god. A move against Mithingow, perhaps? But why take a lone priestess? Unless whoever had stolen her had taken more. Were there other cells like this one, stuffed with the gnome god's faithful?

Sitting down again, Madroria ignored the spells attempting to weave torture upon her. If someone expected minor magic like that to be a challenge, they had substantially misjudged the skills of their prisoner.

"Interesting." He was there with no warning, stepping out of shadows formed by her own light. Features cloaked by a tightly pulled hood, dark clothes, he could have been anyone passing by in any town. The voice was simple as well, flat and unremarkable, the kind meant to be forgotten. "I didn't expect her power to persist even here, in my realm. When one undertakes something new, they must be prepared for surprises, I suppose. Stealing a soul will undoubtedly provide me with all manner of fascinating discoveries."

For a devoted servant of the divine, there was no need to wonder who had appeared in the room. "Kalzidar. So, you have taken umbrage with Mithingow. Stealing those who have given all they have for her is a cruel, calculated blow, I grant you, but her fury at such a slight will shatter mountains."

The hood leaned in, peering at Madroria more carefully. "You address me by name, to my very face. I see now where the paladin learned his bravery. Yet you lack his perception. You've over-assumed. I did not steal Mithingow's *followers*; I took just one. The dead wife of Grumble's paladin, who has earned my wrath—which, I assure you, will not stop with something as simple as mountains."

It took Madroria several seconds to process all of that. She'd had only a single husband in her life, so the lone candidate Kalzidar could be talking about was Thistle. The paladin part seemed like it must be a mistake, but he'd said a paladin of Grumble. If there were any god Thistle would serve, it would be the god of the minions. So, since she'd been dead, he had not only become a paladin, but managed to deeply anger a wicked god.

Were Thistle here, she'd have kissed him with pride.

"And now you're holding me as a ransom, or, more likely, as bait for a trap." Remaining seated, Madroria crossed her legs and closed her eyes. Kalzidar wasn't the only one who needed to learn about this new situation. Madroria had never been a ghost, nor trapped under the power of another god before. She'd have to determine what she was still capable of before she could start working on her escape.

"Perhaps you're more perceptive than it seemed," Kalzidar said. "Enjoy your peaceful stay, while it lasts. Soon, I'll find a way to break that protection, and when I do, we can get things started properly. I do need to ensure your husband has adequate motivation, after all."

"I cower in thought of the day." There was nothing fearful about Madroria's tone, however. She hadn't even bothered to open her eyes. When only silence was the response, she peeked out and noted that the room appeared empty. Whether it was or not would be impossible to say—in the realm of an evil god, she could trust nothing but herself. Every sight, every sound, came at Kalzidar's discretion. Only the light of Mithingow and her own mind were real in here. The rest, she would have to treat as illusion. It was the only path forward.

Calming herself was surprisingly easy without a pulse or breath to bother with. Centering her mind, Madroria looked deep within herself, to her connection to Mithingow. Focusing on that above all else, Madroria began to pray.

* * *

Together, the party rode out of the forest, leaving the giant form of Agramor watching from the trees. After so long being stuck in there, the ride out of Notch was surprisingly uneventful. A goodbye with the town council had been short, but sincere. Neither group had chosen to end up in the situation they had, yet they'd come out the other side with respect for one another.

In another life, Timuscor could see settling down in a place like Notch. When his body wore down, who wouldn't be tempted by trees that granted youth and a city virtually unassailable by monsters? Retirement didn't come for paladins, though—not the leaving for a new, quiet home sort, anyway. A paladin's retirement was the permanent kind, and it was a milestone Timuscor planned to put off for as long as possible.

To his surprise, Thistle made his way over, settling into a pace at Timuscor's side. "Forgive me for taking so long to ask this—my mind has been quite occupied—but how are you feeling? Any unexpected effects or sensations? Any fears or concerns?"

"Thistle, after what Kalzidar did, you owe me no apologies for being distracted," Timuscor assured him. "I do feel different, though. Not a bad kind of different. Physically improved, of course—an expected boon of becoming a paladin—yet it's more than that. I feel steadier. Surer. Like I've planted myself on solid ground for the first time in a long while. Does that make sense?"

"Aye, it makes too much sense, if anything. You've been adrift, knowing what you wanted, but unsure of how to obtain it. Now, you're no longer plagued by such doubt. You're a paladin, which makes the next step obvious: go forth and do good. It's the same step we reach every time a battle is won and a day is saved."

Thistle glanced upward, then back near the tree line, before continuing. "We're all proud of you, Timuscor, proud of what you did. But you know that we can't talk publicly about it, right? When other gods learn what you are, they won't all be happy, and we can't handle more enemies with what we're already facing. From this point on, it must be a secret."

The words rang true; Timuscor could understand where Thistle was coming from. They already had one god pitted against them. More would make their efforts even more laughably impossible than they already were. All the same, Timuscor knew the answer he had to give.

"I will not lie, Thistle. If I am asked what role I fill, I shall say with pride that I am a paladin. If they ask me whom I serve, I will announce to all nearby that I serve the innocent in need above all else, even the gods. But if I am not asked, then I see no need to volunteer such facts. I've always been naturally quiet, and I don't expect that to change, save for the times when it must."

Reaching over, Timuscor set a steadying hand on Thistle's saddle. "Please know I say this with respect, but perhaps, when going against a god of darkness, it is prudent not to give over any more aspects of ourselves to his domain. Living in truth, in the light, is something few can do. As paladins, we should strive to be among those few, don't you think?"

There was a long pause before Thistle replied, in which he gave the words sincere evaluation. "I think that you and I are different kinds of paladins, Timuscor, and I don't just mean the way we got our abilities. You have good, strong instincts. Follow them. Trust yourself. Trust whatever intuition or dedication brought you to this point."

Thistle lowered his voice slightly, ensuring that the others wouldn't overhear by mistake. "And if, in the course of this journey, you and I should disagree on what the right path forward is, trust yourself. Stand your ground. Do not give in to me just because I am older, or have worn the mantle longer. I fear this situation may compromise my judgment, take me to places not suited for a paladin. Put faith in your instincts, Timuscor, because soon, you may need to be the righteous voice who keeps us from taking a dark turn. I am sorry to ask such a heavy task of you so soon, but you wanted to be a paladin. That is part of what it means to wear the title."

"Then I'll do all I can to live up to your expectations. Do not give up on yourself so readily, however. I would never have reached this point without a worthwhile paladin to learn from," Timuscor replied.

Thistle gave him a weak smile, one of the first he'd shown since yesterday's fight, before riding up closer to the front, near Eric. As he reached the rogue, Thistle drew near to him, voice once more kept low. "You noticed them, right?"

"Of course. Several were waiting when we left the woods. Think they'll trail us across the plains?"

"Or different ones will take their place," Thistle surmised. "For now, do nothing. We'll figure out how to deal with our escorts eventually. Until then, we ignore them. It's best not to let tormentors know whether or not they're getting under your skin."

The party rode on, losing sight of the small stretch of forest that led to a hidden town inhabited by former adventurers. They turned their horses to the west, away from the sun, toward a new kingdom that they could only hope would have what they needed. And as they rode, six crows flew overhead, watching and leading, guiding them in the same direction they were heading. Whether Kalzidar knew where they were going or simply enjoyed playing games was anyone's guess.

For Thistle, it made no difference. A line had been crossed, a gauntlet thrown down. This ended when one of them was dead, and not a moment before. He wasn't even sure it was possible for a mortal to kill a god through normal means, which was why Thistle had purposefully avoided conventional methods. Kalzidar had his divinity, and Thistle's party had the Bridge. They could do things that weren't meant to be done, could break the unspoken rules—in the time since fleeing Maplebark, his party had done so several times, usually by accident. It was time to start acting, to break the rules with intent.

One way or another, Thistle planned to save Madroria.

Even if he had to tear down the very existence of the gods to do it.

About the Author

Drew Hayes is an author from Texas who has now found time and gumption to publish several books. He graduated from Texas Tech with a B.A. in English, because evidently he's not familiar with what the term "employable" means. Drew has been called one of the most profound, prolific, and talented authors of his generation, but a table full of drunks will say almost anything when offered a round of free shots. Drew feels kind of like a D-bag writing about himself in the third person like this. He does appreciate that you're still reading, though.

Drew would like to sit down and have a beer with you. Or a cocktail. He's not here to judge your preferences. Drew is terrible at being serious, and has no real idea what a snippet biography is meant to convey anyway. Drew thinks you are awesome just the way you are. That part, he meant. You can reach Drew with questions or movie offers at NovelistDrew@gmail.com Drew is off to go high-five random people, because who doesn't love a good high-five? No one, that's who.

Read or purchase more of his work at his site: DrewHayesNovels.com

Printed in Great Britain
by Amazon